PRAISE FOR THE LAST TRUE VAMPIRE

"Full of sexy vampires, strong women, and excitement."
—*Fresh Fiction*

"The chemistry is electric . . . Kate Baxter has done her job and masterfully." —*San Francisco Book Reviews*

"A jackpot read for vampire lovers who like sizzle . . . brimming with heat!" —*Romance Junkies*

"Mikhail and Claire's love story [has] that combination of romance, steam, and suspense."
—*Book-a-holics Anonymous*

"If you like the Black Dagger Brotherhood . . . pick up *The Last True Vampire*, you won't be disappointed."
—*Parajunkee Reviews*

"Kate Baxter has done a remarkable job of building this paranormal world." —*Scandalous Book Reviews*

ALSO BY KATE BAXTER

The Last True Vampire

THE WARRIOR VAMPIRE

KATE BAXTER

St. Martin's Paperbacks

This is a work of fiction. All of the characters, organizations, and events portrayed in this novel are either products of the author's imagination or are used fictitiously.

THE WARRIOR VAMPIRE

Copyright © 2015 by Kate Baxter.
Excerpt from *The Dark Vampire* copyright © 2016 by Kate Baxter.

For information address St. Martin's Press, 175 Fifth Avenue, New York, NY 10010.

ISBN: 978-1-250-05378-7

Printed in the United States of America

St. Martin's Paperbacks edition / December 2015

St. Martin's Paperbacks are published by St. Martin's Press, 175 Fifth Avenue, New York, NY 10010.

10 9 8 7 6 5 4 3 2 1

For my mom who instilled in me
both a love of reading and fantasy.

ACKNOWLEDGMENTS

Tons of love to my family, who continue to put up with me while I eat, sleep, drink, and breathe words. Thanks to my agent of awesomeness, Natanya Wheeler, and everyone at NYLA, and to my a-ma-zing editor, Monique Patterson, who has made my writing so much better in the past year that it's almost unrecognizable. Thanks also to Alexandra Sehulster and the awesome cover designers, copy editors, proofreaders, marketers, and publicity people at St. Martin's Press. You guys are the best! A shout-out to my friend and awesome beta reader, Chelsea Mueller, and to the Writer Chicks for being there when I need you. As always, any mistakes are my own, and to anyone I might have missed, you know who you are and what you mean to me.

CHAPTER
1

The creature that had once been a woman was standing out in the rain for shit's sake. Her face, tipped up toward the heavens—blasphemy. Monsters didn't have the right to look to the sky when they prayed. Yet there she stood, palms facing upward, eyes closed, while water and unspent magic collected in her palms.

Naya waited in the shadows, tucked beneath an umbrella as she watched the creature. Her fingers twitched, wrapped tight around the dagger's hilt. The sound of magic swirled in the air around her. A sound only she could hear, a melody sung to her soul. Only this tune was off. Too flat, and then, sharp. It offended her inner ear, the pitch not quite right. The hilt of the ancient dagger grew warm in Naya's hand, the blade hungry for the evil that had taken root and spread like a cancer in the body that had once been human. Tonight's retrieval had to be done by the book. Dark magic poisoned the woman's body and soul. Either willingly or by force, foreign magic had consumed the woman's body, the wrongness of the music's tune proof enough, and it was Naya's job to recover what lived inside of her before the magic burned through the body of its human host and went out in search of new prey.

Consume the magic. Contain the power and extinguish the demon it's created. The words rang true, even as Naya's stomach twisted in on itself. A streak of lightning cleaved the sky followed by a peal of thunder. The woman didn't even flinch—she was already in the grip of something too powerful for even a force of nature to interrupt—her features contorted and losing any sign of her former humanity.

A host, once infected with malicious magic, became a mapinguari. A demon whose singular thought was the creation of chaos. Naya watched as the magic manifested in the woman's upturned hands. Her long fingers became tipped with vicious claws and her legs bent at an odd angle, more avian than human now. Energy flowed from her palms, dripping to the black pavement like fluorescent paint in a room of black lights. The sound of it twined around Naya's soul, myriad wind chimes dancing in an unnatural rhythm to form a cacophony of sound rather than a beautiful melody. It was now or never. No longer human, the mapinguari wouldn't waste any time in cutting a path of death and destruction. Naya had an obligation to her people. To the innocent humans who lived in Crescent City. And to her own magic that abhorred the dark energy.

A disturbance tickled the air, like a wave of heat after a cool morning. The mapinguari turned to face her, teeth bared as a snarl worked its way up the demon's throat. Naya took a deep breath, steeled herself for what had to be done, and struck.

"Naya." Santiago Molina nodded his head in acknowledgment as she walked through the door of his shop. He eyed the brilliant gold box in her hand before meeting her face. "Another job well done, I assume?"

Another job. Sure. For the past week, the small town of Crescent City, California, had been swarming with mapinguari. *Well done?* She supposed she was good at her job. But did she like it? That was the million-dollar question. "Here." She shoved the gilded box into his waiting hands. "She was already starting to transition by the time I'd found her. Completely mindless. She couldn't contain the magic, either. It was leaching from her pores. I managed to neutralize the situation before she killed anyone, though."

Santi eyed the box, turned it over in his hands. Naya knew he would never think to open it, but no matter how many times they did this, he fidgeted like an Oxy addict in a pharmacy. Not many could control the magic once it had been repossessed. But it just so happened Naya was one of the lucky ones. One of many job perks she'd grown tired of dealing with.

"Paul's been asking around about you." She knew it would only be a matter of time. Still, the noose of implied servitude tightened at her throat. Naya tried not to immerse herself too deep in culture. Separating the real world from familial and tribal obligations was something she struggled with. She did her job, turned over to Santi at the end of every hunt the gold boxes that held the repossessed magic, which he turned over to the elders. Maybe there was a warehouse full of them somewhere, like a repo lot for stolen magic. The elders were simply the keepers of what she'd repossessed. None of them could handle it. That was Naya's job. And after her part was played, her only interest was in dragging her tired butt back to her house.

Naya cocked her head to the side and held out her hand.

Santi slapped a stack of bills in her palm and she turned, the bell ringing in protest as she swung the glass door wide.

"Keeping your distance isn't going to solve any of your problems," Santi said before she could get both feet out the door. "Pissing them off is just biting yourself in the ass."

She nodded, just so he'd know she'd heard, and let the door shut him out behind her.

Naya's Subaru Outback wagon looked like a soccer mom's ride. In Naya's line of work she needed a practical vehicle, and the Outback carried a lot of shit. She slid in behind the wheel and let her head loll back against the headrest. Fatigue tugged at her eyelids, but she didn't dare close her eyes. Every time she did, she relived the bloody moment when she'd stabbed the dagger into the woman's chest, piercing her heart. It didn't matter that she'd been more monster than human at that point. It never got easier, no matter how many times Naya had to remind herself that she was serving the greater good.

Her breath came in quick little pants as Naya gripped the wheel. Stars sparkled at the periphery of her vision and her heart beat a violent rhythm in her chest. Anxiety coursed through her; she fought against the sensation of suffocation—of helpless imprisonment—that threatened to lay her low. Thanks to the Subie's soundproof interior, no one heard the release of pent-up emotion and magical energy that burst from her lips in a scream. She hadn't even known the woman's name. But Naya had done what she'd had to do. Magic—malicious magic—corrupted those not born to control it. Magic in the wrong hands created monsters, and Naya's very existence demanded that she be responsible for damage control.

That woman had come by her power through unnatural means, whereas Naya had come by hers through birthright. Bruja. Shaman. Witch. Sorceress. Whatever her title, it was half a dozen of one or six of the other. The indigenous tribes of South America took their spirituality and magic very seriously, and her ancestors had crawled right out of the goddamned rain forest.

Naya's tribe, the Bororo, had taken on the responsibility of policing the magic in this world centuries ago. More specifically, they policed those who stole and misused magic in this world. If you didn't come by your gifts naturally, it was considered a crime against the natural order. A perversion. A break in the sacred circle. And once possessed by magic, those unworthy of wielding it became nothing more than mindless monsters hell-bent on death and destruction. Demons. The vile mapinguari of legend. Naya was an enforcer. Her job was to find the creature and play judge, jury, and executioner. It's not a job she would've wished on her worst enemy. The tribe paid her expenses, but aside from that, she didn't get many benefits. No insurance, retirement, 401(k). As for unemployment . . . The only way to get let go from her job was to be paired off in an arranged mating or die in the line of service. Personally, she'd rather die, and a *bruja* wasn't exactly easy to kill.

The woman's death tonight had been an unfortunate necessity. She'd already been too far gone to save and the magic she'd stolen had to be retrieved. She'd been human before she'd come by the magic, but once it had merged with her essence she had become something dangerous. Other. A rabid beast that had to be put down. Naya suppressed a shudder as she recalled the empty expression on the woman's distorted face, her irises nothing more than solid white orbs in her skull, and the snarl that tore from her lips before Naya drove the dagger into her chest. The woman was no innocent. Only through vile acts of darkness could true magic be stolen. And no matter how many times Naya had done this, she still could not reconcile her soul to the violent lengths people would go to possess true, terrifying power.

With a quick turn of the key the Subie purred into life and she pulled out onto the rain-drenched street. The entire city block was actually a small village and no one was the wiser. Her tribe's entire culture centered on the village circle. Time flowed in its circumference: the past, present, and future. And right now she wanted the hell out of it.

Panic pounded in her chest as Naya sped through a yellow light. She was always twitchy as shit after a repo, but tonight she felt like crawling out of her skin. A metallic tang burned her mouth, scorched with the evidence of what she'd done to that woman. That *creature*. Naya had had no choice but to kill the demon, she reminded herself, and what she'd done was no different from any repossession she'd performed in the last eight or so decades. So why did it suddenly feel so shameful?

The familiar tune of "Black Magic Woman" played from the cell phone mounted on her dash. His was one of only a few special ringtones programmed into her contacts. But only because she needed a good thirty seconds warning before she answered any of his calls.

"Where have you been lately, Naya?" Paul's voice scolded, despite his calm, level tone. He hadn't gone by "Paulo" for many years. Naya guessed he thought the Americanization of his name helped him blend in. She didn't have the stones to tell him he wasn't fooling anyone. "For weeks no one has seen you, and Joaquin says you haven't been at your apartment. You know you're supposed to stay close to the circle when you're not patrolling."

"I work all night. It stands to reason that I might not

open my door during the day because I'm sleeping. Wouldn't you agree?" She tried to keep her own voice as calm as his. "I haven't been hiding from anyone. Just busy." His silence was as good as a string of curses shouted in her ear. "It isn't necessary for me to check in all the time," she continued, wondering why she kept the conversation rolling. "Besides, you know I always get the job done. Santi has the box."

Over the dead air she heard the sound of a low growl, a jaguar, and she suppressed a shudder. Apparently Paul didn't appreciate her *pop and drop* system. "It shows lack of faith that you separate yourself from your people," he said in a strained voice. "Do you forget that you have vowed to serve not only the tribe, but our pod?"

How could she forget? The bastard reminded her daily. "I never forget a vow," she said as she hung a sharp left. She pulled the phone off the cradle and turned off the speaker function, putting the receiver to her ear. "I do what you ask, damned efficiently I might add. So don't ever call in to question my loyalty."

"Others would disagree." Gods, she hated it when he got all high-and-mighty. "You are bound to serve the elders until the time of your pairing. You should be happy to interact with the members of this pod. Attend tribal functions."

Fuck you. I'd like to see you try and make me go.

"I'll make you go if I have to."

Son of a bitch, she hated when he did that. Just as she opened her mouth to give her thoughts a voice, he ended the call. But not before she heard that warning growl one more time.

Naya drove out of downtown Crescent City ready to put as much distance between her and tribal business as possible. Every member of their pod lived on the same square city block of property, including her. Well, sort of. A few months ago, she'd decided that she'd be damned if she lived every day of her life near Paul and his antiquated bullshit, and rented a house ten or so miles out of town. That way, when she needed space—like tonight—she had a secret haven in which to lay low. Only Santi and her cousin Luz knew about the house and that's the way it was going to stay. Naya could trust them to keep her secrets.

With the switch on the back of her steering wheel she searched for an appropriate radio station. She found one that echoed her mood, all deep bass drops and screaming techno beats. Against the backdrop of night, blue and red lights flashed, reflecting off the wet street. A group of greasy-looking guys sat on the sidewalk, handcuffed, their heads hanging and water dripping from their lank hair into the gutters at their feet.

Criminals, more than likely.

And they deserved whatever those cops dished out.

Didn't they?

The voice of reason scratched at the back of her brain, *Yes. They did.*

Naya brought her hand up and rubbed her sternum, wondering at the sudden twinge in her chest. Probably nothing more than a little residual mojo left over from the repo. The pain increased from mild annoyance to sharp, pounding, *fuck me* pain. And then, the music began to play.

Not the radio. But the music only she could hear. The siren song that was the essence of magic in use. Only a *bruja* could hear it. And it wasn't an acquired skill. All of the women in her family had heard the sounds of magic since their birth. As fate may have it, she was one of only two living females in her family line. Which was why Paul had such a bug up his butt about her skipping tribal functions. In fact, she had a sneaking suspicion he was antsy to get her good and mated. And breeding a new generation of "ears" for their pod.

Lilting notes tugged at her chest, high, tinkling, and delicate followed by deep, hollow echoes. Whoever was using was close. And packing. Definitely not an amateur like the woman Naya had killed earlier in the night. This user had street cred and enough power to make not only Naya's chest ache but her ears ring also. She lost focus of everything around her, the magic enveloping her senses until only the ringing cadence of its presence remained. Her vision blurred, the wet pavement becoming nothing more than a smear across her eyes. *Shit.* Those cops weren't too far back; they'd notice if she swerved all over the rain-drenched road.

She eased her foot down on the brake, slowing to a cautious but not suspicious speed. Nostrils flared, she dragged in lungfuls of breath and expelled them slowly through parted lips. In through the nose, out through the mouth. She focused on the act of breathing in a futile attempt to curb the sensory deprivation caused by the magic's song. Tears sprang to her eyes at the beauty of the tune. So perfect and pure, only to dive into a raucous, offensive noise that made her brain pound in her skull. *What in the hell is going on?*

By small degrees her vision cleared and the road came back into focus. Two repos in one night—almost unheard of—especially so close to each other. She'd popped the first mapinguari in a back alley not far from here. Maybe two or three miles.

Alarms sounded in her brain, caution flags flying high. The possibility for disaster imminent. But the power seeking her out was too great to ignore. No way could she turn her back. Not because she had any great sense of responsibility. But because if she ignored it, an innocent

might be hurt. And no matter how divided her loyalty to
her pod had been lately, she couldn't allow another demon
to be born of malicious magic tonight.

As soon as she was sure the cops couldn't see her, Naya
flipped the car around in the middle of the four-lane road.
Right in front of a *no U-turn* sign. *Heh.* She retraced her
route for a block and when her vision began to blur again
she knew she was close. Pulling into an empty parking
lot, she killed the engine and gripped the steering wheel
while she took a few more deep breaths and centered her
own energy. No use going out half-cocked. Trouble was,
no matter how she focused, the meditation didn't bring her
an ounce of calm. She slipped out of the car, stumbling
in the parking lot as she felt her way to the hatchback. As
she pulled the latch, the door silently glided up and another wave of crippling sound caused her muscles to lock
up. If she didn't get to the abuser soon, the magic could
level the entire block. Unchecked power had a way of
backfiring in the wrong hands. Or causing a shit-ton of
chaos in the right ones. Either way, it was a lose-lose
situation.

She shook off the paralyzing effects of the magic's influence and dug through the case she kept stashed in the
cargo area. No way could she have hauled all of her gear
in a little coupe. The case was more like a shallow trunk,
with drawers and removable trays. At the very bottom of
her arsenal, Naya found the ammo she'd been looking for.
Though she wasn't opposed to using real bullets when the
situation called for it, the SIG had been modified to shoot
rubber slugs. Great for stoppage. She didn't shoot to kill,
especially if she didn't have a clean shot. That's what the
dagger was for.

The blade pre-dated history. Glowing citrine bright and
ever sharp, it disappeared into an obsidian handle wrapped
in old, oiled leather. Like an extension of her arm, the dag-

ger was precisely balanced as if forged specifically for her height, weight, body construction. And when she held it in her hand, Naya felt a surge of power that nearly knocked her off her feet. It was a killing weapon, a ceremonial tool, and the only thing that could extract the magic from the heart of the thief. Magic was a fickle bitch, and if you didn't follow every rule to the letter, well, you might as well kiss your ass good-bye.

She tucked the SIG into her waistband and held the dagger with a death grip. The target wasn't far off. She sensed a wave of power from the far side of the parking lot toward the rear of the abandoned retail space. A row of floodlights had burned out, no doubt from the surge of magical energy. Perfect for a sneak attack. Not so great for the thief.

Water pooled in the uneven asphalt and soaked through her Nikes and the hems of her jeans. But she didn't have time to worry about her soggy socks or the fact that she'd left her umbrella in the car. The notes drifting from the source of power pulled at her heart, no longer corrupt but almost pure. Why? *How?* She could think of nothing else, the melody urging her forward like a trail of bread crumbs. Looked like she wasn't going to dodge the elders tonight. They'd see her at the banishing after all, perhaps with one more gold box to add to their collection.

Rainfall masked Naya's approach in this asphalt and metal jungle. Her prey had no idea a hunter lurked in the shadows. Just the way she liked it. A surprise attack was so much more efficient than a mad rush. If the thief had already surrendered his humanity for magic, there was no question in her mind as to what had to be done. This would be a quick kill. A clean kill.

Disable. Disarm. Her instincts flared as she crept closer to the source of power. A steady beat, trilling, then deep, sang in the well of her soul, awakening her own seat of power that coursed through her veins like quicksilver. She'd never heard anything so . . . right. How could the music be so corrupt one minute and speak so strongly to her soul the next? Pulse racing, heart pounding, her body kept pace with the sound of the magic that increased in volume and tempo until it threatened to crash over her in a crescendo of raw energy.

Her prey was in sight.

As he leaned against a lamppost, his tawny hair fell gently across his brow, dripping with a steady stream of water. He was huge, with cords of bulky muscle that flexed with each shuddering breath he took. He ripped at his shirt, tearing the fabric from his body, and a feral growl echoed above the rush of rain. He kept his head bowed low over his upturned hands as shallow breaths caused his powerful shoulders to heave.

She had no idea why, but magic always pooled in the hands of the experienced and inexperienced alike. Amethyst light leached from his pores like sweat, dripping thick and sludgy before pooling at his feet. His fingers curled and Naya could tell from the set of his jaw that his teeth were clenched tight. This wasn't the typical theft-gone-wrong she was used to seeing. The magic's tune was now in perfect pitch, the purest melody she'd ever heard. But despite that, this guy was in serious trouble. Scared shitless or at the very least hurting like a sonofabitch.

Crouching low, she continued toward him. Her eyes watered from the power leaching out of him. She'd never felt anything like it in all her life. And she'd been around the block a few times. Her heart pounded in her chest and emotion swelled like a rising tide: anticipation, excitement, and . . . *tenderness*. A moan escaped his lips and he fell to his knees, dropping his hands onto the wet asphalt. The glow of magic spread out around him in a perfect circle like he was bleeding the stuff, and he threw back his head while he panted like a wounded animal.

Holy shit. What in the hell was she looking at here? Before she could answer that question the mystery guy hopped up from the ground like his ass was on fire. And made a beeline straight for her. May the goddess forgive her . . . she stood there like an idiot and just watched him advance.

Time seemed to slow and she saw the whole damned thing as though she were nothing more than a spectator. Water splashed out from beneath his feet, his head tucked down as he ran. He hit her in a football tackle, shoulder to her stomach, arms wrapped tight around her waist. It barely registered when he spun, cradling her against his chest as he took the brunt of the fall. Shit, she was dazed out already by the power the guy was throwing off. Forget keeping her balance. Her eyes opened slowly after impact, her lids dragging across her eyeballs, which felt as though they were floating around in her skull. She met his gaze nose to nose, his bright green eyes boring into her with an intensity that stole her breath.

"Protect. You. Naya," he gasped before losing consciousness right on top of her.

CHAPTER
2

Fuuuuuck. Hangovers were a bitch.

But the way he felt wasn't the result of going out and getting shit faced the night before. No, this was something else entirely. His lids dragged across his eyes, the room swimming in and out of focus. Where was he? The last thing he remembered . . .

Shit. What in the hell *was* the last thing he remembered?

As he shook off the dregs of what had to have been the most hard-core bender of his fucking life, he pulled his shoulders forward and met with resistance. Panic surged within him as he realized that his wrists were bound, his arms stretched high above his head and secured to a sturdy metal headboard. The flesh at his wrists, encircled with silver cuffs, was burned, and raw. He was so godsdamned weak that lifting his head from the pillow took more effort than he had to give. *Son of a bitch*. Nothing like waking up in the middle of your worst nightmare.

The low thrum of his pulse rushed in his ears and his vision darkened at the periphery as he was overcome with an emptiness that pressed his spine right down into the fucking mattress. Endless and dark, the sensation sucked at the center of his chest like an open wound. And on its heels, a burning thirst scorched the back of his throat. Fuck, he was going to pass out again. A haze clouded his brain, and for a moment nothing mattered more than abating the thirst and want that consumed him, causing his body to tremble.

Focusing his breath, he managed to slow his pulse and quell his panic, if only slightly. He needed a calm head if he was going to get himself free. His head bobbled on his neck as he lifted it to look down at his feet—*yup*, awesome—secured to the footboard with gods-damned chains and cuffs. Several more deep breaths helped to calm the panic that once again stirred his pulse to a frantic rhythm. The loss of control in this situation, the thirst that consumed him, the inability to move or free himself made him feel like bursting right out of his skin. *Deep breaths. This is nothing. You're fine. Don't jump to conclusions. Chill the fuck out.*

He let his head drop back to the pillow—damned thing felt like it weighed a thousand pounds—and closed his eyes in hopes that it would stop the room from spinning. Whatever had happened, it must have been one hell of a night. The deep breathing helped as much as focusing his thoughts. Already his pulse began to slow, and the urge to mindlessly thrash against his bonds abated.

First things first, try to get his head in order. Then he'd worry about the chains. Unpleasant memories washed through his thoughts, pulling him back into the past like a riptide dragging him out to sea. *Leave the past in the past. You're not in that place; you burned it to the ground.* No, he wasn't in that damned room, bound, beaten, and held prisoner by those who sought only to exploit him. But he was still chained, still a prisoner, only in an unfamiliar

place. The pounding behind his eyes wasn't helping him
to focus. At. All. His brain felt like someone had spun
it around a blender set to "liquefy." *Stay in the present.
Worry about now.* Details of the previous night seemed
to float just out of his grasp, like a word at the tip of
his tongue.

Okay, buddy, get your shit together.

Name? *Ronan Daly.*

Age? Well, the age on his ID stated his was thirty-
three. In reality, he was much, much older. Centuries
older. But that he knew this fact about himself was a good
sign. He hadn't completely lost his mind.

*Focus on the present. Don't think about the manacles
on your wrists.* Location? *Crescent City, California.* He'd
come to the city from Los Angeles. *On business? No.* His
reason for being here was personal. Fog settled on his
brain, the fire in his throat choking him. His secondary
fangs punched down from his gums and Ronan could
think of no time that he'd ever felt so desperately starved
for blood.

What was he here for? *Who?*

Ronan shook his head as if he could rattle the information loose. A face loomed in his memory, one with
flawless dark skin, deep brown eyes, and a fierceness that
made him mad with want. Was she the reason he'd left
L.A.? Or the reason he was going out of his fucking
mind tied to this bed? Hell if he knew.

Okay, moving on . . . Whereabouts? Ronan slowly
lifted his head and took in his surroundings once more. A
bedroom, too lived-in to be a rented room but not lived-in
enough to be a permanent residence. The furniture—
including the bed he was chained to—looked custom-
tailored to whoever lived here. Nothing hanging on the
walls, though. No personal photos on the dressers or end
tables, but no generic aesthetically pleasing art, either.

The entire space was pretty drab, actually. Sort of utilitarian, and didn't give him a clue as to where he was. Whereabouts: *undetermined.*

Situation? He tugged the chains securing him to the headboard and winced at the searing heat of silver against his skin. *Probably hostile.*

All right, so Crescent City. When did he get here? He could remember driving into the small town under the cover of night, but that was it. Everything between then and now was a dark haze in his memory.

The doorknob turned and Ronan made his body go completely slack. He closed his eyes and focused his breathing so it would be deep and even. The hinges creaked as the door edged open and the near-silent whisper of footfalls on carpet made his stomach coil into a tight knot. He let his senses do recon on the situation as his captor advanced. The footfalls were too light for anyone of substantial size and sounded more like tennis shoes or bare feet than the heavy thud of a combat boot, which didn't rule out Sortiari involvement, though he'd yet to see a slayer pad around in bare feet. If Ronan could manage to free himself, he had no doubt he could at least physically overpower his captor. He'd take what he could get at this point. It might be the only factor to swing in his favor.

Ronan took a deep breath and held it for a brief moment. The scent that filled his lungs reminded him of the forest after a heavy rain. Clean. Naturally sweet. It stirred his body into awareness, and remaining still became much more of a problem than it had previously been. Gods, that delicious scent. It drove him out of his fucking mind. He wanted to bury his face in it. Roll around on it. He wanted to *drink* it. Thirst punched at his gut, scoured his throat, and Ronan swallowed against the sensation. How long had it been since he'd fed? His heart still beat, his lungs still functioned, so it couldn't have been too long ago. But the scent invading his nostrils now made his entire body ache with bloodlust.

The urge to crack his lid and steal a peek was over-whelming. An impulse built inside of him, one that, once unleashed, could do some serious damage. And hell yeah, did he want to do some damage. But he'd spent years squashing that impulse, trained too well to act rashly. To fight blindly. He refused to lose control. It didn't matter if his situation was dire and his existence might very well be in danger. And so he swallowed down that impulse that was as much a part of him as his own limbs—and waited.

Something cracked in front of his nose a split second before the noxious odor hit him. Too bad he was already conscious, because that smell made him wish he were passed the fuck out. He jerked his head away from the smell and let it loll to one side as if he were just barely coming to. The sound of a heavy sigh gave him another clue to his captor's identity: too light and airy to be male. *Situation? Too soon to tell, but maybe not altogether hostile.*

A dazed moan escaped Ronan's parted lips. His act-ing skills were killer. The soft staccato of a toe tapping on the carpet broke the silence, followed by the sound of liquid being poured into a container—great, now he had to take a piss—as his kidnapper took a long swig of some-thing. The suspense was killing him, and so he cracked one eye, just in time to see a sheet of water splash down on him. He gasped at the icy chill, choking as it splashed up his nose. Yeah, *so* not the wake-up call he wanted.

"Good. You're awake." As if she couldn't stand to waste any of the water, the female standing over him shook the empty glass, sending a few stray drops onto his face. She seemed a little pissed.

Ghosts of sensation whooshed through Ronan, filling

his chest—his entire body—near to bursting. Emotion, strong and hot, choked the air from his lungs and the emptiness that had consumed him vanished in the presence of this female who stood above him, her dark eyes flashing with indignant fire.

His back bowed off the bed and Ronan's teeth clamped down as his secondary fangs punched down from his gums. The thirst that burned in his throat raged. An inferno burning too hot to quench. Desire took him in its grasp, his cock hardening as his need for this female's body warred with his lust for her blood. *Holy. Fucking. Shit.*

This unknown female had *tethered* him.

Situation? *Proceed with extreme caution.*

How could this have happened? Though still hazy, Ronan knew that this female was the one from his memory of the previous night. She had returned his soul to him, made him whole in an instant. Whether or not she knew it, this female was *his*. Ronan cocked his head to the side, all thoughts of being bound and held against his will forgotten. Maybe the chains were left over from a wild night with a little light bondage? Doubtful, considering his aversion to being bound. Damn, he wished he could remember. It would take one hell of a woman to convince him to allow himself to be tied up. Then again, would he not do anything for his true mate? He let his gaze roam slowly from her knees up the curve of her slender thighs and well-rounded hips and paused at the swell of her breasts. Her V-neck tee provided the perfect amount of cleavage and he let his eyes linger for a bit before he met her eyes. They reminded him of onyx, almost black, and sparkling despite the meager light. Her skin was deep brown and flawless. Warm. Her mouth . . . Jesus Christ, her mouth was gorgeous. Full—her bottom lip only slightly fuller—and set in what he assumed was a perpetual pout.

Had he kissed that mouth last night? Taken that delicious-looking bottom lip between his teeth? His want of her only intensified with the thought. Had he sunk his fangs into her throat while he fucked her?

Situation? *Maybe not as dire as I'd thought.*

"How do you know my name, vampire?"

Whoever she was, his mate was damned sexy when she tried to appear tough. Interesting question, though. She seemed unfazed by the fact that he was a vampire. This female was no dhampir, though. Nor was she human. Beneath her spring-rain scent, Ronan caught the tang of magic clinging to her skin. It sparked on his tongue like champagne. She was his. The knowledge of it was embedded in his very DNA. But as far as her name . . . he had no fucking clue. "I'm guessing we didn't have a wild, drunken one-nighter, then?" he drawled.

He couldn't help a triumphant smile as his words seemed to infuriate her even more. If he'd thought she was alluring when she was perturbed, she was fucking irresistible when enraged.

"Look, why don't we start by unchaining me, yeah? I'm a lot more cooperative when I'm not tied to a bed and dripping wet." He quirked a brow at her dubious expression. "You might want to at least try the polite approach first. Flies, honey, and all that. I *am* chained to your bed after all. Before I jump to any"—his gaze drifted to her cleavage one more time—"conclusions about what happened last night, maybe you should fill me in first."

"Not a chance," she said flatly. "You, answer *me*."

"Considering I'm the hostage here, and the events of last night have, ah, slipped my mind, I think maybe you ought to go first and tell me what I'm doing here."

She pulled a dagger from a sheath at her back and touched the point to his left pec, over his heart. The strange blade glowed like a damned canary diamond and practically screamed with energy. A warm tingle radiated from the tip of the blade as powerful magic flowed over his skin. The dagger was hungry for a kill. He didn't know how, but somehow he could feel it.

She put pressure on the dagger, as if readying herself to drive the blade home. A thrill rushed through Ronan's veins that he'd be at her mercy and the scent of her blood blinded him with need. "How 'bout you tell me how you know my name and why you're in town—*now*—or I'll run this blade through your heart?"

Situation? *Definitely hostile.*

The song was unlike anything Naya had ever heard before. There was nothing corrupt about it, the notes pitch perfect and the harmony so beautiful it threatened to bring tears to her eyes. A power resided in the notes, something so intense that it commanded her attention and at the same time made her want to retreat in fear of that power. This was the song she'd heard calling to her last night, the melody that robbed her of her senses and stole her breath.

Naya's hand shook, the dagger becoming unsteady in her grasp. She'd known the first time she'd heard it last night that the music was too pure for the magic to be stolen goods. After she'd managed to get the bulk of his weight off of her, Naya had been prepared to extinguish the magic and call it a night. But his full lips had parted on a breath, revealing the porcelain points of his dual fangs. Vampires were supposed to be extinct. But there he was, his head resting on her legs, as real and tangible as she was. Curiosity had gotten the better of her. The magic's song too pure for her to simply end his life. So she'd dragged him to her safe house and secured him with silver cuffs and chains. If the vampire hadn't stolen the magic, then how in the hell had he come by it? And why couldn't she shake the feeling that somehow she was meant to find this amazing specimen now at her mercy.

Naya shook herself from her stupor and willed her gaze from the hills and valleys of sculpted muscle beneath the dagger's point. "Did you not hear me? I said, answer me or I'll drive this dagger through your heart."

His calm demeanor scared her more than any shouts or threats might have. The vampire's brow creased in concentration as if he were trying to hold back a wall of water from a broken dam with nothing but the power of his mind. The way he looked at her was unnerving. Such deep intensity.

"I think a lot clearer when sharp objects aren't being jabbed into my skin."

Her eyes darted to his and she was momentarily taken aback by the beauty of them. As vibrant and green as the rain forest. His brows were tawny slashes, made slightly sinister by the look of concentration on his face, and he had the longest lashes she'd ever seen on any male. Plenty of women—including her—would gladly give up a limb to have eyelashes like those. She'd save a fortune in mascara. His cheekbones were sharp and his nose a fine, straight line. His jaw was equally strong, shadowed with stubble. Gods, but he was magnificent.

He cocked his head to the side and studied her with those gorgeous green eyes. "I'm going to assume that your silence means you're considering my request?"

She eased up on the dagger, pulling it away from his chest. The sound of the magic's song quieted and, after a moment, grew silent. Naya took a steadying breath as her own body calmed, no longer responding to the magic's call. All right, so the guy had been a little wound up. She guessed anyone would have been in his situation. "I'm not going to free you," she said as she took a couple of much-needed steps back. "But I still expect you to answer my questions."

"Magnanimous, aren't you?"

A lazy, tantalizing smile stretched across his mouth. So wicked. Naya's lower abdomen tightened and her fingernails bit into her palms. The vampire was built for sin, every inch of him tight and bulky with corded muscle. A killer, that much was apparent, and she couldn't help but wonder if his appetite for violence would rival his appetites for other . . . things. Naya swallowed, forced the lust rising up through her chest back to the soles of her feet. This male was dangerous. He could kill her before she even had a chance to defend herself. No matter how good he looked stretched out and bound to her bed, she couldn't forget that he was an unknown variable. And Naya couldn't afford unknowns.

The vampire sighed in resignation and tried to stretch his arms, wincing with discomfort. Raw, angry burns marred his skin where the silver made contact, but it couldn't be helped. The silver would weaken him and Naya needed an equalizer until she decided whether or not to alert the elders to the vampire's presence. "For starters, I don't know your name, so I'm not going to be able to help you on that one. I've never seen you before today."

Bullshit. After he'd sacked her like a quarterback, he'd said her name. And that he needed to protect her. A surge of emotion rose up in Naya's chest. Tenderness toward this male that she couldn't afford to feel. Protect her from what? Why? Who was he to her? And what did he know that she didn't? This was *her* town. Anything supernatural went down and Naya knew about it. The only reason he was here now was because he'd passed out afterward. "You're lying. You said my name last night."

The vampire let out a measured breath and Naya had a feeling that if his hands were free he would have raked his

fingers through the tangle of his tawny hair. "I don't remember a gods-damned thing about last night," he said. "I
may be wrong, but I think we've been over this. I'm kind
of drawing a blank here."

Amnesia? Sure, like she'd believe that pathetic excuse.
"This isn't a soap opera, buddy. The my-memory-is-gone
excuse is a little tired, don't you think?"

His mouth turned up in a half smile and Naya's stomach did a little flip. Damn, he was sexy. The way she'd
bound him showcased his muscled arms and chest in just
the right way. His shirtless state was a bonus as far as
she was concerned. His loss was her gain. She gave her
head a shake and tore her gaze from his body. *Gods, Naya.
Focus!*

"I never said my memory was completely gone. I just
don't remember anything that's happened since I got to
town." He let out a chuff of breath. "Hell, I don't even
know why I'm in this town. Maybe you could help fill in
those blanks, starting with why I'm chained to your bed?"
The question carried a decidedly sexual edge. Apparently
he wasn't too nervous to nix the cocky attitude.

"You're chained to my bed because I was feeling charitable last night and decided not to kill you on sight. I
tracked you to an abandoned parking lot just past downtown. Unchecked magic was leaching from you. Before I
could get the drop on you, you tackled me to the ground,
said my name, and that you needed to protect me." She
added, low, "And passed out. How's that for filling in the
blanks?"

The mischievous glimmer in his emerald eyes dulled
and was replaced with a calculating light reminding Naya
that, good looks or not, this male was an unknown variable she couldn't risk letting loose in the town. His arms
pulled against the bindings, more of a knee-jerk reaction

than anything, rattling the chains behind him. "Protect you from what?"

His tone vibrated through her, the rough edge coaxing a shiver to her skin. "I have no idea," she replied. "And since your memory has so conveniently failed you, I guess neither one of us will know anytime soon."

He studied her with that same inscrutable gaze, as though he were peering right into her soul. His expression softened and the tension in his shoulders relaxed a fraction or two. "Sounds like we didn't have a proper introduction. Aren't you even curious to know *my* name? Or are you more of a cut-to-the-chase sort of female?"

His patronizing tone did little for her mounting temper. Naya didn't care what his name was. If he was a threat, she'd have to put him down. Knowing his name wouldn't make that any easier. "I don't need or want your name. All I *want* to know is how you knew who I was, why you think I need protecting, and how you came by the magic, so I can decide what to do with you."

"Aside from my good looks, I'm not sure what magic you're referring to." Gods, this male was insufferable! Arrogant, even at a disadvantage. Naya choked up on the hilt of her dagger and centered her energy, lest her own magic echo her emotions and become uncontrollable.

"How do you know about vampires, female? And what are you that you could so readily identify me?" That half smirk returned to his mouth, drawing her eyes away from his. His voice dropped to a smooth, mellow purr that made the tiny hairs on the back of Naya's neck stand on end. She felt that tug in her stomach again, a rush of excitement that had nothing to do with danger. Well, maybe it had a little bit to do with the danger. *Sexy bastard*.

He thought he could control the situation. Manipulate her with his cocksure attitude and charming smile. Wasn't going to happen. Naya strolled to the window and let her fingers slide down the length of the blinds, enjoying the way his eyes narrowed and his brow pinched at the zip of sound. "You have fangs. I could sense the otherness in you, beneath the magic you've stolen. Silver doesn't seem to agree with you, though it glints in your eyes often enough. Of course, we could always put my theory to the test. Let a little afternoon sun in and see what happens."

His smile faded and he opened his mouth to speak. Before he could get the words out, her cell rang, interrupting him. *Damn it.* Whoever it was had *stellar* timing. She made her way back to the bed and leveled the dagger at his chest. "Make a peep and I'll gut you," she warned, careful this time not to let the blade make contact with his body. She checked the caller ID and rolled her eyes before answering, "What's up, Luz?"

"Paul told me to call and tell you to get your ass over to his place. I could be wrong, but I think he wants to see you." Her cousin's tone was much too light and playful to make Naya anything but livid. As her apprentice Luz was sort of a personal assistant as well, but she had a wild streak that drove Naya crazy. Probably why Luz always went out of her way to be a sarcastic pain in the butt.

"Tell him I'll be over in a couple of hours." She didn't have time for Paul's bullshit right now. She eyed the male chained to her bed, that amused half smile playing on his lips. "Better make that three."

"Uh-uh. Not gonna happen. Noway, nohow. Sorry, Cuz." How many more ways could Luz get her point across before Naya throttled her? Naya suspected her cousin was pressing her luck just to find out. "Paul said if you're not here in fifteen minutes he's sending Joaquin to pick you up."

Shit. The last thing she needed was to have Paul's son out looking for her. Joaquin would head straight for her apartment and there'd be trouble if he didn't find her there. He'd go out to look for her and wouldn't stop until he found her. Naya couldn't leave now, though. Not when she had this unknown element—very male, very muscular, *very gorgeous* unknown element—strapped to her bed like a sacrificial offering to some sex goddess. Joaquin didn't know about her house away from the tribal block and Naya wanted it kept that way. Especially since if Joaquin got a glimpse of the male chained to her bed, he'd go ballistic. If she wanted to keep her secrets protected, she had no choice but to leave. "Fine. I'll be there in a few minutes."

"See ya then, *chica*," Luz chirped before she hung up.

Great. Now what in the hell was Naya supposed to do? She eyeballed her captive one more time, deciding that the best course of action at this point would be to keep him nice and unconscious until she got back. She sheathed the dagger and went to the dresser at the far side of the room. From the top drawer she retrieved several jars and bottles with the herbs and supplies she'd need. She tossed a pinch here and a dash there into a mortar and ground them with a pestle until the ingredients were a fine powder. Then she sent some of her own power into the mixture, focusing her energy and drawing on her magic. The sweet tinkling of chimes echoed in her mind as the delicate threads, like spiderwebs, pulled with a slight tug as the magic resisted leaving her body. She coaxed it further and the tendrils drifted from her fingertips and into the stone bowl.

"I wish I could be more helpful, but honestly, just because I *supposedly* knew your name last night it isn't exactly just cause for chaining me to your bed. I'm not judging or anything; maybe you're just into some kinky shit." The vampire's tone was a little too playful considering the circumstances. A pleasant tingle drizzled from the top of Naya's head to the soles of her feet as she felt his eyes on her. She ignored his comments and continued with her work. "And since we're on the topic of kinky shit, you don't need to slip me a roofie, you know. I've never had to be coaxed to cooperate by a beautiful female before."

Despite his playful tone, she sensed his suspicion. It made the air heavy and thick with tension. Power awakened in him with his anxiety, the sharp twanging tones of the now-off-tune music only she could hear. No time to waste, she'd be cutting it close as it was. Once she'd infused the mixture with her magic, Naya scooped a pinch of the powder into her palm. She swiveled her head, took stock of her captive's muscular form, and added a second pinch of the powder to the first. Better to give him a little more than he needed than worry about not giving him enough. She clenched the mixture in her fist and brought her hand to her side. Sauntering to the bed with a casual gait, she paused near the headboard.

"Whatever you're about to do," the vampire warned darkly, "I'd reconsider."

Naya worried her bottom lip as she took in the hard line of his jaw, eyes narrowed and brow furrowed. Going against her better judgment, she asked, "What's your name, vampire?"

That sparkle returned to his eyes. "Ronan."

"I never reconsider my actions, Ronan." Naya brought her fist up to her mouth and opened her hand. Ronan scowled, his eyes flashing silver as he fought against his bonds, the sound of his magic lowering from a soft soprano to a deep, urgent bass. She took a deep breath and blew the powder into his face. The music died, his thrashing ceased, and he lost consciousness.

"Have a nice nap, Ronan," she said as she turned to leave. "Sweet dreams."

CHAPTER
3

Naya circled the block until she found a parking space in front of the building the tribal elders conducted business in. She got out of the car and leaned against the hood, eyeing the front door. It might as well have been a portal into another land. The structure was one of a dozen old buildings in the area that had been rezoned and converted into office space. On either side were apartment buildings. Each unit housed members of Naya's pod. Her own apartment was just down the block in another building. An apartment she rarely frequented lately.

It wasn't any big secret why her pod had taken up residence in California. For centuries they'd followed the *caminos de la magia*, invisible highways that covered the globe. Only it was magic that traveled these roads, a trail of bread crumbs called simply El Sendero that the Bororo followed in their eternal quest to protect magic and prevent it from slipping into the wrong hands. From the thousands who made up their tribe they'd divided into smaller pods that consisted of a few to several hundred Bororo and spanned the globe. Naya's pod had been in Crescent

City for almost a decade now. She had no idea how many generations it had taken before they'd wound up here. Naya's mother and grandmother had been born in what was now Brazil. Naya could only claim a century of years and all of them had been spent in the States.

Her tribe's history was well documented, though Naya had never been afforded the opportunity to sit down and study it. The sheets of old parchment and ancient animal skins that pre-dated her known history were locked away in a safe somewhere. The elders believed that knowledge belonged only to the worthy. And those not proven had no choice but to accept the mandates of their rulers. Which basically meant if you weren't a tribal elder—or didn't sport a pair of balls—you didn't know shit. Her grandmother had told her stories, though, and she knew that after the Conquistadors had ravaged South America the tribe had traveled north from the rain forests of Brazil and then later through Central America and Mexico before they wound up in the United States and scattered into their individual pods from there.

They followed El Sendero, choosing to vanish from existence, a tribe that for all intents and purposes had become extinct. They became like the chameleon, blending in. Imitating rather than assimilating. Their native language changed as they adopted a more common Spanish, which over the past forty or so years became mostly English. Naya suspected that in a few more decades they'd probably wind up in northern and then eastern Canada, adopting whatever language the locals spoke. French, more than likely. And after that? Alaska? The Arctic? What language did the Inuit speak? Maybe the Bororo would just keep going until they'd migrated their way back to South America so they could start all over again. Her grandmother said that the goddess had given Naya a gift and that's why magic sang to her. Whether or not any of it was actually true she didn't know. She simply did what she was told. Just like every woman in her family had done since the beginning of time. There were days, like today, that Naya felt more like a trained hunting dog than an actual member of a family. Paul had called her to heel, and here she was.

"Dude. You were about five minutes away from getting an armed escort over here whether you wanted one or not," Luz said as she skipped down the front steps to where Naya leaned against her car. "What in the hell are you doing out here, *loca*? You're staring at the front door like you're trying to blow the building up with your mind. Wait." Luz grabbed Naya by the arm. "You can't do that, can you?"

Naya laughed as she pushed herself away from the car and peeled Luz's hand from around her forearm. "Not yet," she said as she headed for the front steps. "But I'm working on it."

Luz snickered beside her, an aura of lightheartedness surrounding her slight frame. Naya loved her cousin, but sometimes the girl was too much. She was still more interested in sowing her wild oats than honing her skills. "Let's go out tonight," she said as they reached the front door. "There's a new club that opened in Redding I want to try and I need a wingwoman."

"I have no desire to drive four hours just to scope out a club. Take Santi," Naya suggested, and paused before she turned the knob. Something within her resisted every time she came here, as if urging her not to cross the threshold. "He'd be a great wingwoman. Er, man."

"Santi?" Luz said as if Naya had asked her to go out with her father or something. "I want to give the impression that I'm *un*attached. Come on, Naya. You know you want to go. You're wound so tight you look like your string's about to snap. You could use a little play."

Naya took a deep breath, turned the knob, and opened the door. "I live vicariously through you, Luz. You get enough play for the both of us."

"Seriously, Cuz, you suck. You act like you're a thousand years old already. You gotta flaunt it while you've got it, *chica*. Would it kill you to go out one freakin' night?"

Naya stopped dead in her tracks as Paul stepped into the foyer. She looked him straight in the eye for a brief moment before averting her gaze to the floor. It killed her that tradition dictated she should lower her eyes in his presence, but the tribal elders—all male of course—had no intentions of jumping into the twenty-first century. The Bororo men weren't without power. As shifters they could assume an animal form at will, but as far as *magia* was concerned, their males were impotent. For as long as their people had lived, certain Bororo females had possessed the ability to bend and manipulate magical energy. Naya and Luz were two of very few women left with that power. It made them special, revered among their people. But Paul and the other tribal elders still considered them beneath all males. And that was something that had stuck in Naya's craw since childhood.

"If I'm not mistaken, you're late for a training session, Luz." Paul's deep voice resonated with a rumbling growl. "José is waiting for you in the basement."

A cold lump settled in the pit of Naya's stomach. Out of all of the tribal elders, José was particularly sadistic. She'd trained with him when she was an apprentice and the bastard had gotten off on inflicting as much pain as possible. One of these days, she'd turn the tables on him, just to see if he could take what he dished out. A shadow of apprehension passed over Luz's expression, seeming to echo Naya's thoughts. José was an asshole and Paul knew it. Gods, how she hated tribal structure.

"Paul, you should let me train Luz." Naya chanced a look straight into the chieftain's eyes. "I can teach her just as well as José can. Probably better."

"*Cállate!*" Paul ground out with a slash of his hand. "Naya, you're not here to give orders. Luz, get your ass down to the basement. Now."

Luz took off at a trot, reminding Naya that no matter how cocky her cousin acted, she was still very young. And Paul could be downright scary when he wanted to be. "I'll be down as soon as I'm done here!" Naya called after her cousin. No way was Naya going to let Luz take José's abuse all afternoon without backup. Naya might not be a great wingman when it came to partying, but in a combat situation she was the best wingman you could get.

"You coddle her," Paul said with a disdainful curl of his lip as he turned and led Naya out of the foyer. "In the end, you're not doing her any favors."

"José is a bastard and you know it. The least you could do is assign her to another instructor."

Paul pretended to ignore Naya, which was nothing less than she expected, and she didn't waste her breath by trying to bait him into answering. If Paul wanted to ignore you, nothing short of poking him with a hot torch would get his attention. As she followed the high-and-mighty chieftain to whatever room he'd planned on meeting in, Naya couldn't help but wonder what the place looked like before the large house had been renovated to accommodate office space. It had probably been beautiful in its time, the floor plan open and inviting, furnished with gorgeous turn-of-the-century pieces. But now the rooms were too small, the hallways dark and foreboding, and the staircases sinister. Shadows dwelled in every corner, the light not quite penetrating, and the doors that led to the other office spaces were closed and locked, making Naya feel more than a little claustrophobic. She hated coming here, hated it right to the marrow of her bones, and Paul knew it. He'd made her come here to exercise his control over her. To remind her that no matter what she thought to the contrary, she was nothing more than a tool at the elders' disposal.

He took her to the back of the building and into the largest room besides the attic and basement. This was where the tribal elders met, made decrees, and decided the fates of their people as if they were all too stupid to think for themselves. Seated at a half-moon-shaped table, backs straight and expressions severe, were the rest of the elders. Naya tripped on her own feet as she walked through the door, and her jaw dropped in shock. What were they all doing here? A gathering like this only occurred when there was big business to discuss or if someone was in deep shit. And since Naya couldn't remember any big business coming up that pertained to her, she had to assume that the elders had gathered because she was about to get her ass kicked. *So* not good. Her heart raced as she took a seat opposite the gathering of males. Did they know about Ronan? Holy shit, she hoped not.

For the second time in the past twelve hours, Ronan woke up feeling like he'd been ejected out of the business end of an elephant. Though his mind was clearer now, he still couldn't remember what had happened the night before. She'd said that he'd told her he needed to protect her. From what? Had he known she was his when he tackled her to the ground last night? Was something after her? After them both? *Fuck.* She'd knocked him out and walked right out the gods-damned door. He had no idea where she was. He might not know anything about her, but she was his mate. She'd tethered his soul to hers. And it was his responsibility to keep her safe.

His muscles twitched involuntarily, causing his concentration to flag as the realization that he was still bound overcame him. Ronan tensed as he pulled the chains securing his wrists to the headboard. He inhaled sharply at the bite of pain. Though the silver had weakened him, he should have been able to at least bend the frame with his physical strength alone. So either his devious female chained men to her bed on a regular basis or she'd fortified the frame with a magical enhancement to prevent him from breaking free.

His female. Gods, even now the truth of it was a fist to Ronan's gut.

From the moment she'd tethered him, his body had turned traitor. His cock ached with the need to be buried inside of her and his fangs throbbed in anticipation of breaking the flawless skin at her throat. No matter what she thought to the contrary, he didn't know her name— had never seen her before—and yet she belonged to him. It was curious that she seemed not to recognize their tether. To her, he was nothing more than her prisoner.

Ronan thrashed against his bonds, welcoming the burn as the silver seared his skin. He needed to find her. Go to her. Make some sort of sense of why his soul had tethered itself to this unknown female who brazenly took a vampire captive. And he needed to know why he was here—wherever the fuck here was—and why. So many answers just out of his grasp, and worst of all, he had to relive the feelings of helplessness and anxiety he'd long ago put behind him as he lay here, chained and at someone else's mercy.

Did Mikhail know he'd left? Jenner? Ronan's stomach knotted up to the size of a baseball. *Fuck it all.* Did Siobhan?

He'd sworn a blood troth to the dhampir in exchange for a codex that had helped Mikahil unravel the mysteries of his mate, Claire. At the time, the bargain had been more than worth Ronan's while. He enjoyed bedding Siobhan well enough and he'd needed the codex. Now that he'd become tethered, his troth was at the very least problematic. If he so much as let another female touch him with intent, Ronan's blood would boil in his veins. Sex wasn't just off the table; indulging would literally kill him.

Ronan pulled on the chain once again, a forceful jerk borne of anger and his mounting frustration. A roar of pain built in his chest, but he held it in as the silver sizzled against his skin. The bed frame creaked under the strain. He pulled harder. Blood trickled down his arms and blisters marred his skin. The frame gave way, another inch.

Letting his arms fall back, he gave the chain some slack. Ronan drew a deep breath into his lungs and clamped his jaw down as he propelled his body up and forward. Damned near blind with pain, weak and shaking from the silver's effect on him, he fell back onto the pillow panting. He'd loosened the frame another inch, though.

On and on it went for a good half hour. Ronan steeled himself for one last tug. Blood stained his arms and his lip where he'd bitten down again and again. The scent of his own blood gnawed at him, further igniting his thirst to the point of frenzy. Something dark and foreboding rose up inside of him, sending icy tendrils through his bloodstream that spread out through his limbs. It awakened something primal within him. Wild. And with a shout Ronan propelled himself forward one last time. The frame groaned before it gave way completely with a hollow *pop*. The chain swung free of the broken metal bar and Ronan set to work freeing his legs in the same way, this time rocking backward as he jerked his knees up toward his chin.

His body grew damp with sweat and his breath sawed in and out of his lungs with his effort. The chill that overcame him caused Ronan to shiver, but he soldiered on until the bars at the footboard gave way and his ankles were just as bloody and ravaged as his wrists. He was free, though. More or less. He'd never been so gods-damned thankful for mobility.

Though his mate had been clever to use her magic on him, she'd been irresponsible in leaving the key to his cuffs behind. The weight of the chains was immense as Ronan reached up to rub at his bare arms. He couldn't seem to banish the chill that settled over him like an early-winter frost.

Need . . . blood.

Rage and mindless thirst overrode even his need to escape his prison. He wanted to rip, tear, savage the nearest available body. *Kill.* He wanted to hunt like a beast in the forest and take down his prey. Glut himself on his victim's blood and do it all over again. He'd never in all of his existence—even after his turning—been so gods-damned desperate for blood. The memory of the female's scent, clean and sweet, invaded his senses, and Ronan's fangs throbbed painfully in his gums. He stumbled to the dresser as his vision clouded and fell against it as his knees gave out beneath him. His hand searched blindly over the surface of the dresser, knocking over jars and a heavy mortar and pestle as he groped for the key.

There!

He scooped it up into his grasp, breath heaving in his chest. His vision continued to haze, darkening at the edges as his head swam with confusion. Where in the hell was he? How had he gotten here? It was so fucking dark he could no longer see. The smell of mildew and dirt invaded his nostrils. And with the damp air, the sharp tang of magic burned his lungs. What in the hell was happening to him? Gods, he was so, so *hungry*. His stomach *burned* with hunger.

Like a rag doll, Ronan toppled to the floor. The carpet did little to cushion his fall as his head smacked smartly on the floor. His limbs ached with cold and his teeth chattered as a violent tremor shook his body. The darkness pressed upon him taking him deeper, further away from reality. As he gave in to the force that steadily pulled him down, down, down, fiery dark eyes and creamy tan skin flashed in his mind's eye.

Naya.

Her name is Naya.

CHAPTER
4

Naya sat in her car, staring at her house, the only sanctuary she had, in a daze. Her cell phone buzzed quietly in the holster on the dash, the display flashing: "Luz." Naya had promised her cousin she'd check in on her when she'd concluded her meeting with Paul, but after being faced with all of the tribal elders in what she could only describe as an ambush she'd fled the moment after they'd delivered their mandate. Too shocked to stay long enough to check on her cousin's welfare. Some mentor she'd turned out to be.

Gods. Mated?

They might as well lock her away in a dungeon somewhere. Or just get it over with and kill her. Her life was over now anyway. Of course she'd known that eventually Paul would try to pair her off. But never in a million years would she have thought it could happen so soon.

You will be mated to Joaquin. The sound of Paul's voice as he laid down his mandate still bounced around in her head. *On the night of the blood moon, you will give yourself to him.*

But my job . . . ? Naya had barely recognized the sound of her own voice as she dared to question the chieftain. Once she was mated to Joaquin, she'd be forced to forfeit her position as the tribe's *bruja*.

Luz will become the tribe's bruja.

She's not ready! Naya had blurted. *You'll get her killed throwing her into the field so soon!*

Your opinion means nothing to this council, mujer. Paul had spat the word like it left a bad taste in his mouth. He'd never had respect for any female, and referring to Naya simply as "woman" was his way of devaluing her. *Bastard.*

She'd been forbidden to speak after that. One thing that guaranteed to make Paul crazy-pissed was having his authority challenged. By anyone. Insubordination from her was a hundred times worse. In the thousands of years her people had walked the earth, through the many countries, cultures, and generations, one thing had always stayed the same: The men retained all of the authority. It didn't matter that their women possessed the *magia* and the power to seek it out.

In the quiet of night, away from listening ears, her grandmother had told Naya that's why their males could shift. They resented their females for being so close to the gods and their power and so the first Bororo chieftain in his jealousy and rage had killed a jaguar and consumed its heart while it still beat, thereby joining their forms forever. The ability to shift had been passed to his sons and so on and so forth from that moment on.

Naya didn't care about the whos, hows, and whats of their history. But, damn it, it was about time the elders abandoned their antiquated ways and took a leap into the twenty-first century. Being what she was—being able to do what she did—should have made Naya feel special.

But all it made her feel was *trapped*. Her magic wasn't respected. Her abilities weren't revered. She was a *possession*. No better than the dagger at her back. She was a tool for someone else to use and direct and put upon a shelf when she wasn't needed anymore. Today Paul had taken the first step to shelve her. And she doubted that Joaquin would be anything other than thrilled about his father's proclamation. She'd never felt so invisible. So . . . inconsequential.

She couldn't just sit by and do nothing while her fate was dictated by the tribal elders. Didn't she have a say? Why would they want to put her out of commission so soon? She'd done a great job over the past decades since her mother had passed. And Naya was a far better enforcer than her aunt Marcella had been, perhaps only rivaling her own mother in skill. The steering wheel creaked in Naya's hands as she gripped it tighter, visions of her future as an obedient mate tightening around her like a noose.

Naya closed her eyes and focused her thoughts inward. If she continued to think about what had happened her energy would become volatile, and she wouldn't be worth a good goddamn to anyone if she wasn't centered. A heaviness settled in her limbs as she meditated, a peaceful urging toward calm and focus that she welcomed. She hadn't rested in almost twenty-four hours, as she'd been too uncomfortable to let her guard down with a volatile vampire chained to her bed. Gods, she was tired.

The tinkling chimes of magic stirred her senses, caused the tiny hairs on her arms and the back of her neck to stand on end. Wild, unfocused, the song lashed out at her senses, grating on her ears like metal scraping metal. Her eyes watered and her chest tightened until she couldn't take a deep enough breath to fill her lungs. Without thinking she snatched her sheathed dagger from the cubby in the center console, and it warmed her palm through the leather as though in warning.

"Shit!" Naya blinked to clear her vision. She threw open the car door, barely taking the time to slam it behind her as she ran for her house. Two at a time, she hopped up the steps to the front porch. Her hand shook as she fumbled with her keys, and after the third try she managed to slide the key into the lock. Tendrils of dread spread like poison through her bloodstream as she eased open the door and stepped into the living room.

How in the hell was he awake? She'd infused the *encanto el dormir* with her own magic, making it more than strong enough to keep a coven of vampires good and unconscious for another four or five hours. She'd been right to consider him a threat. Naya had underestimated his strength, and that bothered her more than anything. With the quiet steps of a hunter, she padded through the sparsely furnished living room to her bedroom. She pulled her dagger from the sheath. The blade pulsed, the citrine glow spreading over Naya's hand and wrist. It could sense whatever magic Ronan had stolen as well, and she knew by the way the handle warmed in her palm that the dagger was hungry.

She wrapped her left hand around the doorknob and took a deep breath. The sour taste of regret settled on the back of her tongue as she thought about what she was about to do. Whether he had no recollection of what had happened the night before or not, Ronan was a liability. She'd been anxious to unravel his mystery. She needed to know why his song could be so crude and ugly one moment and so breathtakingly beautiful the next. She wanted him to tell her how he knew her name and why he thought she was in danger. The male was a walking contradiction. A puzzle she longed to solve. None of that mattered, though. If the magic took him and he became a mapinguari, she couldn't allow for him to be loosed on the city. She had to neutralize him before he managed to free himself from his bonds. She turned the knob. The music changed, no longer wild and volatile but sweet with tinkling notes that caused her heart to swell in her chest. *Damn it. What a waste.* She was about to silence that beautiful sound forever.

Ronan stood with his back suctioned to the wall.

He'd felt her presence the moment her car had pulled up to the house, waking him from endless darkness. He blinked away the fatigue that pulled at his lids and worked the key, releasing his ankles and then his wrists from the manacles. He couldn't even take the time to appreciate the relief of being rid of the accursed silver. What would happen when she walked through the door? Would she finally run that scary-ass dagger through his heart? He felt like fucking shit and he wasn't even sure if his sorry ass would be worth a damn in a fight.

Guess you'll find out soon enough.

The doorknob turned slowly and Ronan tensed. His concentration was divided between controlling his mounting bloodlust and getting ready to neutralize the threat about to walk through the door. He'd feel a whole hell of a lot better if he were armed with more than his fangs, but there was nothing to be done for it. A low growl built in his chest. The feeling of vulnerability triggered an instinctual need to protect himself and his lip curled in a snarl. *Gods damn it, calm the fuck down.*

A sliver of light shone through the cracked door and cast a long, bright gash across the dark brown carpeting. She led with her hand, dagger extended, and Ronan suddenly felt the urge to chide her for coming in that way. What was she thinking? An attacker could easily disarm her and leave her defenseless. Ronan reached out and grabbed her wrist, twisting it behind her with ease. With his free arm he seized her around the waist, pulling her tight against him. It didn't take much effort to pluck the strange dagger from her hand when she was immobilized this way. Something she should have known had she been half as badass as she'd pretended to be.

With a quick flick of his wrist Ronan sent the dagger flying to the far end of the room. The blade lodged itself in the drywall and he hoped it stayed there. He didn't like the way it felt in his hand, the warmth pulsing from the handle like a heartbeat. His captive's ribs expanded under his arm as she took a deep breath, and he slapped his hand over her mouth to stifle her building scream. "Quiet." His mouth brushed the delicate skin behind her ear and Ronan's thirst blazed hot in his throat. "I can snap your neck with little effort. Don't make me do it."

She stilled for a moment as though she'd decided to play nice. But then she dug her teeth into Ronan's hand and bit down on his fingers, *hard*. He pulled his hand away with a yelp, shaking out his hand, surprised she hadn't bitten through the damned bone. And she didn't stop there. The bite was nothing more than a distraction, and she used it to her advantage. She threw her elbow into his stomach and Ronan grunted as she slammed her back into his chest. It put him off balance and he stumbled, his head knocking against the wall with a thump. Wow, that so didn't help the steady throb that made him think his brain was trying to escape his cranium.

Okay, so he *might* have underestimated his mate's fierceness in battle. But at least now the odds weren't tipped in her favor. He was free, she was disarmed, and despite the fact that he was still weakened from the silver, he had one up on her in strength. Problem was, he wasn't interested in hurting her. "Calm down!" he barked as he tried to catch his breath. She kicked her leg straight back, catching him in the knee. "Damn it, stop!" he shouted from between clenched teeth as he braced himself against the wall to keep from buckling. She reared back, slamming the back of her head into his face. The cartilage in Ronan's nose popped and a sticky trickle of blood ran down and dripped from his upper lip. His fangs throbbed and the scent of his own blood threatened to send him into a frenzy. "Naya! I said, stop!"

They both froze, and Ronan wasn't sure which one of them was more shocked. He released his grip on her and swiped at the blood trickling from his nose as the cartilage healed. That was her name: Naya. But how in the hell did he know that?

"I knew you were lying to me!" Naya seethed as she rushed to the wall where he'd thrown her dagger. Ronan wondered at the hurt in her voice. As if she couldn't believe he'd betray her. Perhaps she'd recognized their tether after all? She pulled the dagger out of the drywall and muttered almost to herself, "I should have taken care of this last night when I found you in that parking lot."

If she wanted to continue to fight, she couldn't possibly have felt their bond. Then again, maybe she was the sort of female who liked to play rough. A thrill chased through Ronan's blood as he tried to clear the haze of lust that settled on his brain. The situation had gone from zero to FUBAR in less than a second. He needed to contain her, to calm her down. He could've fought back, but what would that accomplish? One of them—more than likely Naya—would get hurt. That didn't mean he wouldn't defend himself if need be. Ronan could handle himself just fine, thank you very much. He leaned against the wall, watched as she advanced on him, dagger in hand, a look of pure malice on her beautiful face. This was a female who dealt in violence. Dangerous. And fucking *hot*. He had no intention of dying, though. Not today, anyway.

"Let's pick up where we left off, huh?" Naya leveled the tip of the dagger so it hovered over Ronan's heart. "Why are you here and how do you know my name?"

The time for playfulness and charm had long since passed. If Ronan didn't want the situation to escalate he had two options: One, he could disarm her yet again and show her just what it felt like to be bound in silver against her will. Or two . . .

With the speed of a cobra's strike Ronan seized the dagger from her grip and pulled her into his embrace. Practicality took a backseat to need as his bloodlust mounted, his desire for the female in his arms building to a fevered pitch. The scent of her blood drove him mad, her unyielding body held tight against him an unspoken challenge. She was an untamed thing, caught in his arms, and Ronan was determined to master her.

Her palms found his chest as his mouth descended on hers. She shoved at him before her fingers curled, her nails biting into his flesh. A flash of heat stole over Ronan's skin and he welcomed the burn that complemented the sting of Naya's nails. He flicked out with his tongue at the seam of her lips and she went liquid in his embrace, opening her mouth to deepen the kiss as she gripped at his shoulders to pull him closer.

His cock throbbed in time with his heartbeat and his fangs ached in his gums. The more he gave himself over to his lust, the hotter his blood coursed. Fiery heat licked up his spine, lashing out over his flesh like a whip. He pushed the pain to the back of his mind. Ronan held Naya, cupping the back of her neck with his palm. The tenuous grip he had on his control slipped another notch. Her scent was heaven. A rich bloom of tropical flowers, rain, and sunlight.

If he didn't taste her, he'd go out of his fucking mind.

He broke the kiss only to bury his face against her throat. Naya stiffened in his arms and he reached up, stroking gently over her jaw with his thumb. Too far gone to bloodlust for more than that single act of gentleness, Ronan jerked her T-shirt aside and buried his fangs into the tender flesh where her neck sloped down to meet her shoulder.

Ah, gods!

From the first deep pull on her vein he was lost. Thick and sweet, her blood spilled over his tongue, a heady nectar that had no equal. He wanted to glut himself on her blood. Lap every last drop from her skin. An almost inaudible sigh escaped Naya's lips and she once again became pliant against him. Her hips rolled into his and Ronan's sac tightened. With a grunt he shoved his free hand between them, plunging past the waistband of her pants and underwear to cup her heated sex in his palm. Her slick arousal coated his fingers and Ronan worked his fingers through the swollen folds as he continued to drink from her.

This was dangerous ground. Her touch on his bare skin was heaven and hell all at once. Once he crossed the line, gave over to his lust, the blood troth would put him in his place. Heat like the fires of fucking hell would swelter in his veins. He'd risk hell and all of its fire for the female in his arms, though. A hitch of warm breath caressed Ronan's cheek and a low, drawn-out moan that ended on a gasp when the pad of his finger circled her clit.

The air left Ronan's lungs as a fist made solid contact with his gut. His fangs disengaged from Naya's throat as he stumbled, his back meeting violently with the closed bedroom door. The haze of lust that burned through him quenched in an instant. He let out a quiet moan and cupped the back of his head; his brain had been jarred from his skull cracking against the molding that surrounded the doorjamb.

In the time it took him to gather his wits Naya had collected her dagger from the floor. She rushed at him, poising the tip of the blade over his heart. One hand wrapped tightly around the grip, the other palm braced against the pommel, she leaned in close and seethed, "How *dare you* take my blood!"

In his experience, women who wielded daggers didn't usually respond well to diplomacy, but he was willing to give it a shot. "Easy, Naya."

"Easy?" Her incredulous tone prickled over his skin. "What you did was a *violation*!"

The word sat heavy on Ronan's chest. Dirty. Shameful. As though the thought of it disgusted her. A warning growl gathered in his chest and Ronan bared his fangs. "What I did was my right as your *mate*!"

CHAPTER
5

Naya stared at Ronan. Dumbstruck.

Mate? Had the entirety of the male population lost their ever-loving minds today?

And, for that matter, had she?

Pleasure radiated through her body, suffused with a warmth that left her feeling boneless. Her core still pulsed with the need to finish what Ronan had started and her arousal dampened her underwear that clung to her heated sex. He'd wound her tight, bringing her to that place of mindless want so quickly that she'd lost herself to him before she'd even realized she was gone. Even now, she wanted to lower the dagger and resume where they'd left off. She gave her head a shake, as much to dislodge the music of the magic that clung to him from her ears as to banish the sensation of his touch from her skin.

He'd thrown her off her game. A feat very few males had ever managed to accomplish.

Her shock took a backseat to her anger as Naya brought her fingers up to the dual sets of punctures in her neck. There was magic in blood. A power that could be exploited by the right person. And by drinking hers, Ronan had consumed her *magia,* taking that power into himself. Had the vampire known what he was doing when he'd latched onto her throat? Did it matter?

"Let me close the punctures." His voice was as warm and smooth as dark chocolate. Silver chased across his gaze as he reached out and Naya pressed the tip of the dagger deeper into his flesh. He stilled. The tiniest shift in pressure would cause the blade to break the skin.

"Don't even think about touching me, vampire." Naya drew on her own power, concentrating her focus as it gathered within her. Warmth radiated from her fingertips as she brought them to her skin. Magic penetrated the wounded flesh that tightened and healed in a matter of seconds.

Ronan stared, rapt, at the spot where his mouth had just been, and a thrill chased through Naya's veins at the untamed heat in his gaze. *Dios mio. Get a grip.* She couldn't afford to let him get the upper hand again.

"A talented female." Ronan's voice was dark smoke that stole the starch from Naya's spine. She leaned in toward him, drawn in as though by gravity. "But you've denied me the pleasure of putting my mouth on you again to close the wounds myself."

"That will be the one and *only* time you put your mouth on me, vampire."

Ronan leaned toward her, but Naya held her ground—and the dagger still—refusing to move. The tip of the blade sank past the barrier of his skin. Her gaze flicked down to where crimson bloomed and spilled over the curve of his pec. The dagger grew hungry in her palm, eager to sink deeper, and she held the blade in check. Once it had a taste for the stolen magic that had secured itself to the vampire's blood, it would only want more.

"You've tethered me." His breath was warm in her ear

and Naya suppressed a shiver. "So believe me when I tell you, Naya. That it *will* happen again."

The air left her lungs in a shuddering breath. Until last night, Naya had been operating under the assumption that the vampire race was long extinct. She didn't know the first thing about them. "What do you mean, tethered?" Naya held her breath as she waited for a response that she was sure she wouldn't like the sound of.

Ronan's gaze settled on the dagger still pressed to his chest. "I'd be more cooperative if you considered sheathing your weapon." A rumble built in his throat and Naya cocked a questioning brow. He raised his eyes, gorgeous green gems rimmed with silver, to hers. "I don't respond well to threats."

"This isn't a threat," she assured him. The dagger dug itself deeper and Naya resisted the tug. Like the blade in her hand, some unseen force drew her to Ronan, urged her closer. "If I don't get some answers, soon, I'm going to run this blade straight through your heart. Understand?"

His gaze lit with fire, and a sardonic smirk accented his full lips. Cocky bastard. "For another go at your vein, I'd risk the blade."

Gods. They could go on like this for hours. Naya had a sinking suspicion that the vampire's stubbornness would equal her own and they'd be stuck like this, the tip of her blade embedded in his skin while he worked his overconfident charm. At this rate, she wasn't going to get any of her questions answered. But neither was she willing to let her guard down.

"I'll make you a deal. You lower the dagger, I'll behave myself. I give you my word. We'll sit. I'll answer your questions to the best of my memory."

She cocked her head to the side as if contemplating his angle. His mouth hitched in a half smile that caused Naya's stomach to do a backflip. It was almost as though he liked that she was suspicious of him. "You can sit. But not in here." Naya jerked her head toward the door. "The living room."

Ronan pushed himself away from the wall and she reacted, pressing the point of the dagger against his chest. His lips twitched again. "I like that you're feisty, but that doesn't mean I appreciate having that damned knife anywhere on my body." He raised his hands as if in surrender and shifted his weight from foot to foot. Naya mirrored his actions, ready to defend herself if he decided to attack. "I'm not planning anything, so cut me a little slack here. It'll be safer for both of us if you keep that blade at a respectable distance. Okay?"

His eyes grew serious as she assessed him. "And why's that? Thinking of going for my jugular next time, vampire?"

Ronan swept his hand toward the door in invitation. Cocky *and* high-handed. "Living room. Sit. Then we'll talk."

"Right," Naya scoffed. "Like I'm going to treat you as if you're nothing more than a docile kitten. No way are you dictating what happens here. You're my prisoner and I'm in charge. We do this my way. Got it?"

"You can cuff me if you want," he suggested as he followed her gaze toward the floor and the chains discarded there. "I won't fight you."

"All right," she said slowly. "Turn around, face the wall, and put your hands behind your back."

Naya backed away from Ronan, the dagger held in a defensive position. This had turned out to be one gut punch of a day. First the elders had smacked her with that insane mandate, and now a dangerous vampire was loose in her apartment. What could possibly happen next? *Don't answer that.* She approached the bed, her dagger trained on Ronan's chest.

"I said, turn around and face the wall." She wasn't going to leave anything to chance. He cocked a brow, a corner of his mouth teasing at a half smile. She flicked the dagger at him to urge him on and he sighed. "I usually stab first and ask questions later, so be thankful that I'm in a charitable mood today."

"This is charitable?" Ronan asked, that damn half smile returning to his face. His moss green eyes sparkled with a mischievous light and Naya couldn't help but admire the chiseled features of his handsome face and the way his tawny hair fell across his brow, almost brushing his long lashes. "I'd hate to see you when you aren't feeling so generous." He held his arms up again in compliance and turned toward the wall. He braced his legs apart and put his hands behind his back, palms facing outward. Apparently he wasn't a stranger to the command "assume the position." Figured. Naya had known from the moment she'd laid eyes on him that he was trouble.

Magnificent. But still trouble.

When she felt confident enough that she'd have the upper hand in the event he went back on his word and decided to attack, Naya slid the dagger into its sheath and retrieved the chains and cuffs from the floor. The incantation she'd used to reinforce the headboard had been a simple one and it took almost no concentration at all to release the spell, but that didn't mean she wasn't surprised as hell at the havoc Ronan has wreaked to release himself. The sturdy metal frame looked as though it was made of nothing more than flimsy wire, bent and curled backward until the slats of the headboard looked like a jagged metal crown.

The chains jangled as Naya gathered them in her hands. Ronan tensed, and every muscle on his well-built body went rigid. Naya wondered at his reaction and thought about drawing the dagger from its sheath. She'd seen

animals tense like that when they were cornered, and
Ronan was no harmless woodland creature. No, he reminded her more of a desperate wolf. "I'm going to cuff
you now," she said in a placating tone. "And I'd advise
you not to do anything sketchy, got it?"

"I already gave you my word."

"And you also promised me that you wouldn't hesitate
to sink your fangs into my throat again. Just don't move."

"Yes, ma'am," he drawled.

The words rolled off his tongue, smooth. Naya felt a
stirring in her gut that had nothing to do with fear. Who
in the hell was he? A gorgeous, powerful—not to mention bloodthirsty—stranger who knew her name and
was . . . what? Trying to *flirt* with her while she tied him
up? She reached down and captured one of his wrists in
her grip. He clenched his hand into a fist, and Naya could
practically feel the tension rolling off of him. Ronan's skin
was warm, warmer than she thought a vampire's should
be. The music that had been so riotous in her ears calmed.
He had an iron grip of control, the notes resonating in
Naya's soul one at a time, like a music box that needed to
be wound. Was he even aware of the power contained in
his massive form?

As she secured the first cuff, the pace of his breathing
increased. The muscles rippling across his back expanded
and contracted at a rapid rate, as if he were on the verge
of panic. She hadn't noticed his distress earlier, when he'd
been bound to the bed. *Don't feel sorry for him. In fact,
don't feel anything for him. Dangerous. He's a threat. Get
your shit together, Naya.* Quickly she grabbed the second
cuff and secured his other wrist. The chains were too long
for her liking. She didn't want to give him the benefit of
mobility. So she pulled the chains together, giving Ronan
only a few inches of breathing room, and with her free

hand retrieved the dagger from its sheath. Naya ran the blade through the links, joining the chain. She focused her magic, channeling it through her body, down her arm and wrist, and into the blade. It flashed white-hot for a single moment, just long enough to fuse the chains together.

Naya let out the breath she'd been holding and pulled back on her power, centering herself once again. It took a fair bit of energy to manifest her magic so quickly and it had taken a toll on her already-exhausted body. Without realizing it, she reached out, bracing herself with her palm on Ronan's back.

"Are you all right?" He turned his head to glance at her from over his shoulder.

"Living room," Naya ordered as she dropped her hand to the chain and guided Ronan toward the door.

True to his word, Ronan played the obedient captive and allowed Naya to direct him out of the bedroom and into her living room. The space was sparsely furnished with only one couch, but it was open and bigger than the bedroom, so if need be Naya had the space she'd need to fight if Ronan decided to retaliate. She turned him around and pushed against his shoulder with two fingers, urging him to sit down. He complied with that lopsided grin and Naya couldn't help but roll her eyes. Gods, he must have had women falling at his feet with that expression. Rather than sit and thereby put herself at a disadvantage, Naya chose to stand a good eight feet away at the far end of the room near the small fireplace, giving her plenty of space to prepare for an attack. She propped her elbow up on the mantle and cocked her head as she appraised her prisoner. "You said you wanted to talk. So . . . talk."

Ronan sighed, and again Naya pictured him running his fingers through the thick tangles of his hair. "I'm not even sure where to begin."

Great. She should have known he'd try to weasel his way out of talking. "You lied to me earlier when you said you didn't know my name."

"Not true." Ronan rolled his shoulders and Naya couldn't help but notice his discomfort. "I didn't know your name when you asked me, and to tell you the truth, I don't know how I know it now. It could be that I know it through our tether."

"That smells like bullshit to me." There were ways to get the truth out of him. But neither were options Naya was willing to explore just yet. "You're throwing some weighty words around, vampire. 'Mate' being one of them. And I don't know what in the hell a tether is, but if that's how you know my name and that I'm in some kind of danger, it's time you came clean."

He flashed another lopsided grin and she gritted her teeth, more to keep from smiling back than anything. He had the charming angle down pat. "I still don't remember anything that happened last night. Maybe if you filled me in, it would jog my memory?"

"See, your problem is that you think you can manipulate this conversation in your favor. That's just not going to happen, Ronan. So, you claim you can't remember anything that's happened since you breezed into town. Whenever that was. For the record, I'm not sure that I believe that, but we'll just skip over that for now. You have the answer to my next question and I want it. No more stalling. What is this tether? Does it have to do with the magic you've stolen?"

Ronan fixed her with a dubious stare. "Naya, I haven't stolen any magic. In fact, I wouldn't even know how to go about doing that. But I can guarantee you, pilfered magic or not, it has *nothing* to do with our tether."

Our. The word was spoken with a possessive edge that

caused chills to break out over her flesh. As if this tether was some shared thing between them, something that Naya had been a willing party to.

It wasn't unusual to encounter other witches or supernatural creatures that came by their magic naturally. But even witches who used their natural power to channel dark magic had to answer for it eventually. It wasn't Naya's business to police them, however. She paid them little mind unless their dealings affected the tribe directly. Those instances were few and far between.

In the course of her job as an enforcer she mostly came across thieves and usurpers. Creatures that could no longer be counted as human once the magic they'd stolen had corrupted them. Ronan was an anomaly to her. She knew nothing about vampires or what innate magic they might possess. Either way, the power he'd exhibited the night she'd first seen him had been volatile. He'd been damn near ready to blow. But the sound of his magic—the pure, perfect tune that could so easily become tainted—was in direct contrast to everything she knew. And the way the song spoke to her scared her more than she was willing to admit.

Ronan rolled his shoulders again in an effort to ease the knot that had settled between his shoulder blades. The slow, even breaths weren't doing a damn thing for the unease that had begun to coil in his stomach like a tightly wound spring. He focused on his surroundings, on Naya, the sound of her voice . . . but it wasn't doing anything for the panic that continued to creep up on him as he tugged against the cuffs that bound his hands behind his back. His bloodlust sparked anew, fire meeting dry kindling in his throat. What he'd taken from her was merely a taste, not nearly enough to satisfy his thirst. Her scent drove him mad; the rich bloom of her arousal perfumed the air. A fiery female with a tendency for violence. Just the sort of trait Ronan admired in a bedmate.

The cuffs chafed his skin and Ronan clenched his jaw until his fangs dug into his bottom lip. Blood welled from the punctures and he flicked out with his tongue. Deeply unsatisfied. Despite the silver that continued to blister the skin at his wrists, he'd break his bonds in an instant to get to her. To taste her again. To feel the petal softness of her sex as he teased her.

Focus, you lust-addled bastard. Keep your shit together. Do. Not. Lose. Control.

Naya quirked a brow at his low growl. "Agitated, vampire? Believe me, it's nothing in comparison to what I'm feeling now. In fact, I'm starting to feel a little stabby. So get to talking."

Gods, her fire. Ronan squared his shoulders, stamped the lust that threatened to master him to the soles of his feet. "Before I explain, tell me, Naya, do you feel our tether?" Ronan carefully gauged her reaction. Most people didn't realize that even when they tried to stay expressionless, the tiniest shift or twitch could give away their thoughts. Naya had a great poker face, though. She was obviously well practiced at keeping her face virtually impassive.

"There is . . . something," she answered with reluctance. Damn, her dark eyes bored right through him as if he were completely inconsequential. He didn't like it. "But I'm inclined to believe that what's drawing me to you is nothing more than the magic in your body and my own responding to it. Mates are paired in my world. And the last time I checked, no one gave me to a vampire."

Gave her? Like she was nothing more than goods to be traded. A territorial growl rose in Ronan's chest. Who were these people that they'd trade Naya like stock? "In my world," he countered, "a soul gives itself. Mine had been banished to oblivion. Yours called it back. My soul is tied to yours, Naya. Tethered. *That* makes you my mate."

Her jaw slackened, softening her luscious mouth. Ronan's eyes were drawn there, held captive by the rosy flesh. He needed to kiss her again. To taste the sweetness of her mouth. He wouldn't rest until her tongue slid across his. Until her mouth yielded to his once more. "You feel this tether?"

He responded to her dubious tone with a solemn nod. "My soul was returned to me the moment I laid eyes on you. The *only* thing I know with certainty right now is that you are mine."

Naya averted her gaze and her heart rate increased. The sound was music to Ronan's ears as he thought of the delicious blood pumping through her veins. Thirst scratched at his throat, but he pushed the sensation aside. He wouldn't gain any ground with her acting like an untamed beast, starved for her.

"I'm not sure what to do at this point. I know what I saw last night. Magic leached from your body. You could barely contain the power. If I'd come upon you a minute later it might have been loosed. It doesn't make any sense. There should be a corruption to it, the magic. And there is sometimes." She shook her head as though frustrated. "But instead, it speaks to me in a way that no other has in my entire life."

Interesting. Maybe she felt their tether and simply didn't know it. "Speaks to you how?"

"The song," she said. She kept her tone completely level, her emotions masked. "It's pure. But . . ." Naya paused as if trying to find the right words. ". . . only sometimes. Vampires don't come by magic naturally, do you?"

"There is an inborn power that connects all of vampire- and dhampir-kind," Ronan responded. "And I suppose that when you tethered me, it awakened a certain . . . magic." His smile grew as he regarded her serious countenance. "But I've heard no songs."

A gnawing doubt scratched at the back of his mind. The presence of cold darkness that had overcome him earlier had certainly not been a side effect of his transition. Something foreign was indeed trying to manipulate him. But until Ronan had a better grasp of just what that was he thought it wiser to keep the information to himself.

Grim passivity remained on her face and Ronan realized that he wouldn't be able to get a good read on her. She was too damn practiced at concealing her emotions. "I can assure you, Naya, that we are tethered. Is it really so hard to believe?" She shrugged and Ronan didn't know if he wanted to give her a nice rough shake or kiss her. Maybe both. "You're obviously attuned to magical energy. Maybe what you're sensing is our bond?"

"Why don't you like to be tied up?" Naya asked, her tone showing genuine curiosity.

She certainly knew how to deflect. "I doubt any vampire would appreciate being bound with silver," Ronan said with a smirk. "It's a knee-jerk reaction. Call it self-preservation. Now, about that song . . ."

Naya's eyes darted to the side, clearly to avoid meeting Ronan's gaze. Finally, he'd managed to rattle her. Looked like he wasn't the only person in the room who guarded their secrets. She lifted her gaze to his, her dark, almond-shaped eyes wide with worry. What didn't she want him to know? Something had her spooked and Ronan cursed his own foolishness that he wanted nothing more than to take that fear away. Problem was, he suspected that what she feared most was him.

"I think you're forgetting just exactly who the prisoner is here," she said, locking that passive expression back into place. "I don't have to answer *any* of your questions."

"True," Ronan conceded with a shrug. "But I figured, since we were having an amicable chat, that you'd be open to sharing."

"I don't have anything to share with you." Christ, that flat tone she used drove him bat-shit crazy.

He'd never met anyone so fucking *good* at putting up a front of ambiguity. As if nothing he said interested her in the slightest. "Come on, Naya. Let's play nice, yeah?"

Naya took a few more steps in his direction, pulling the crazy-ass dagger from behind her back. She stopped right at his feet and leveled the knife at his face. "See, the thing is, Ronan, I'm not playing."

Hot. Damn. Oh, she was playing, all right. She just didn't know it yet. "Take these cuffs off of me," Ronan said, giving her a taste of that no-nonsense tone she was so fond of.

"No."

Ronan sighed. This back-and-forth was getting them nowhere. "Look, Naya—"

A knock came at the door and Naya jumped as if she'd never heard the sound before. She looked around, frantic, and Ronan had to admit, he liked seeing her thrown off her game. Whoever was at the door deserved a tip of his hat, for sure. "Get up," she ground from between clenched teeth. "In the bedroom. Now."

"Naya, I know you're here. Your car's parked out front!" the male voice on the other side of the door called.

"Boyfriend?" Ronan cocked his brow in question. A wave of jealousy stole over him, congealing into an icy lump in his gut. He'd tear the throat from any male who thought to lay claim on her.

"Shhh!" Naya hissed as she pushed him into the bedroom. Ronan didn't even bother fighting her; this was just the distraction he needed. Once through the door, she gave him a none-too-gentle shove against his shoulder—*strong for such a petite little thing*—and he made a show of tumbling to the bed. "Sit. Don't move. You so much as whisper, I'm coming in here to gut you. Understand?"

Ronan pursed his lips together tight as if they were glued shut. Another round of door-rattling pounds came and Naya shut the bedroom door behind her. "Hang on, Santi!" she called in an airy voice. "I'm just getting out of the shower!"

CHAPTER
6

Santi looked her over, his mouth screwed up into a pucker. "I thought you were just getting out of the shower?"

Naya looked around for the first available hard surface to bang her head against. "I meant I was just about to get in the shower." She leveled her gaze, daring him to doubt her. "What's up?"

No one but Santi and Luz knew about Naya's house. And right now she wished neither of them did. The male's senses were keen. Hiding Ronan in her bedroom wouldn't do shit to keep his presence a secret. She needed to get him out of there. Like yesterday.

Santi narrowed his eyes as he regarded her. His nostrils flared. He'd be able to smell the anxiety wafting from her if she didn't calm the hell down. "Paul wants you tracking again tonight."

Another hunt? What in the hell was going on? It seemed that rogue magic users were running rampant lately. Tonight would mark ten straight nights of hunts. In a town that boasted fewer than ten thousand residents, Naya considered herself busy if she made one or two repossessions every six months. El Sendero drew the occasional magic usurper to their area, but the recent number of incidents to hit the area was unusual.

"Not a problem," she replied with a shrug. In fact, it was a huge problem. What was she supposed to do with Ronan while she was out working?

Santi walked deeper into the living room. Too close to her bedroom for Naya's peace of mind. His dark gaze flicked to the closed door and back to her. "Are you okay?"

Naya drew on her power and used it to project a façade of calm. "Of course I'm okay. Why wouldn't I be?"

Santi canted his head. "I *know,* Naya. There's no use trying to play it cool."

Shit! Shit, shit, shit. "It's not what you think. I was trying to—"

"For the record, I don't agree with Paul, or the council. Why the rush to pair you off? A mating with Joaquin is ill-timed. We need to neutralize these threats that keep cropping up first."

A sigh of relief built in Naya's chest, but she refused to let it out. Adrenaline flooded her system, a change in her scent and body chemistry that Santi was sure to pick up on. But perhaps her personal drama would be the diversion she needed to keep Santi from finding out about her new houseguest.

"I plan on dealing with it. When things settle down." Surely Paul wouldn't press the issue with mapinguari running amok. "I'll talk to Joaquin and we can go to the council together. Luz isn't ready to take over. They'll listen to reason."

She needed to quit babbling.

"Are you sure that's all?" Yep. Her stupid mouth and nerves had thrown up one too many red flags. "You're pretty nervous, Naya."

"You know I have zero interest in being *anyone's*

mate." It was the truth. The thought of being tied down made her break out into a cold sweat. "I want the opportunity to live a life outside of the tribe's parameters. And this mandate isn't exactly going to help it happen."

Santi was her friend. She could trust him. And yet she couldn't push the truth past her lips. Couldn't tell him about Ronan. He was a mystery that she needed to keep to herself for now. If Santi thought that the council's mandate to mate her to Joaquin was crazy, she could only imagine what he'd say when he found out she had a vampire in her bedroom who'd already claimed the honor.

It seemed that the town—hell, her entire life—was going to hell in a handbasket. And she had a feeling that the male currently cuffed in her bedroom had something to do with it.

Ronan forced every ounce of strength in his reserves through his arms. He tugged so hard on his cuffs that the links snapped with little resistance. A feral growl built in his chest. She might have wanted to keep his presence a secret, but he was ready to take the door right off the fucking hinges. He'd like to see someone try to mate her with another male. Ronan would cut a bloody swath before he'd let that happen.

Naya belonged to him as much as he belonged to her.

Pain radiated in his skull as myriad voices closed in around him. Ronan doubled over, clutched at his head as he squeezed his eyes shut. Images rained down on him: *Mikhail, searching the city for the female who'd awakened his power and saved their doomed race. Claire bloodied and unconscious, hanging lifeless in his friend's arms.* Ronan's mind grew hazy, as though a blanket of fog had settled over him, and he gave a sharp shake of his head to dislodge the hold of the Collective from his mind.

In quick succession a barrage of memories swamped

him. Mikhail, Claire, Jenner . . . Another bank of fog settled and cleared. Siobhan's dark raven hair and bright emerald eyes loomed in his mind's eye. She lay beneath him, writhing in ecstasy as he pounded into her. The sting of her bite was a welcome pleasure as her fangs punctured his skin. And a troth, freely given, that he was powerless to escape.

Ronan gasped as though breaching the surface of deep water, desperate for air. The Collective threatened to pull him under once again, but he fought its pull, forcing himself to remain in the present. A derisive snort filled the silent space as he gave his head one last violent shake. He was worried about someone giving Naya to another male? What about the blood troth *he'd* given to another female?

Gods fucking damn it. What a clusterfuck.

He focused his attention back on the conversation going on out in the living room. He knew little of the male with whom Naya was speaking, but her anxiety permeated the air with a sharp citrus tang that spiked Ronan's protective instinct. She'd promised to run her dagger through his chest if he stepped even a toe out of line, but he refused to cower in her bedroom while the scent of her distress burned his nostrils.

Fuck it.

He strode through the door without a thought to the silver cuffs still hanging from his wrists with links of broken chain. Naya turned to face him, the murder in her gaze doing nothing to cool Ronan's lusts. It seemed the angrier and more violent she got, the more he wanted her. Sick.

"Naya . . . ?"

The male standing beside her—Santi—took a defensive stance, legs braced as though in anticipation of attack.

His dark eyes narrowed as he assessed Ronan, and Santi's jaw squared as he clenched his teeth.

"I told you to stay put!" Naya seethed. The sharp, spicy scent of her annoyance banished that of her earlier anxiety. "Are all vampires this obstinate or is it just you?"

Santi's eyes widened. "Vampire?" He sprang to action, reaching out to guide Naya behind him.

Wrong move, asshole. Ronan's secondary fangs ripped through his gums. He wanted nothing more than to sink them into the other male's flesh. A predatory growl escaped from between Ronan's teeth and he let out a feral hiss. Santi's pupils elongated as he answered with a similar, decidedly feline snarl.

A shifter. Awesome.

"Everybody just calm down."

Santi made no move to release his hold on Naya. His fingers bit into her arm, and though she made no outward show of discomfort, it sparked Ronan's bloodlust and the need to commit violence burned through him. "If you don't want to die today, shifter, I'd suggest letting her go."

"Santi." Naya's tone was panicked and it served to further agitate Ronan. "You can't tell Paul he's here. You can't tell *anyone*. Promise me."

The shifter's eyes narrowed, the once deep brown irises now blazing gold. His pupils were narrow black slashes and his incisors had elongated in his jaw. "A vampire, Naya? They should be extinct. What is he doing here? Why? The elders need to know."

The tang of Naya's fear scorched Ronan's nostrils, and the icy cold that had penetrated his veins not an hour ago threatened to surface once again. Naya's brows gathered sharply above her eyes as though she sensed it as well.

"Ronan, put a lid on it," she warned. "I'm fine. You're

fine. We're all fine." She didn't look fine. Her scent sure as hell didn't smell fine. And you could bet that male's hands on her weren't doing a gods-damned thing to make Ronan feel fine. "Santi, let me go."

The male released her arm in an instant and some of the ice retreated from Ronan's veins. He resisted the urge to reach out and pull her to him, knowing it would do nothing more than spark her ire.

"Naya, what in the hell is going on here?" The gold melted from Santi's eyes, and with it more of the cold drained from Ronan's gut. "With everything on our plate right now, don't you think his being here is a little coincidental?"

"What *is* going on here?" Ronan needed answers, and maybe he'd finally get them. He turned to his tight-lipped mate. "Naya?"

"Our business is none of yours, vampire," Santi said with a sneer. In an urgent whisper he said to Naya, "We know nothing about them. *Him.* He could be creating the mapinguari for all you know, and you're keeping him in your *house*?"

Naya's jaw dropped as though words failed her. Ronan took a step toward her and she held up a staying hand.

"Look at him!" Santi said forcefully, throwing his open palm in Ronan's direction. "He's ragged and bloodied. Someone had him cuffed and bound, for the love of the gods!"

"I cuffed and bound him, Santi." Naya's tight-lipped response nearly coaxed a smile to Ronan's face. "I found him last night after I dropped off the repo with you."

"And you decided to keep him?" Santi replied in an incredulous burst. "This is beyond ill-advised, Naya. It's damned dangerous. Do you have any regard for your own safety?"

Ronan might as well have been a stray mutt she'd found

by the side of the road. "Naya's safety is none of your concern, shifter." Though Ronan had to agree that bringing a strange male back to her house showed a total lack of concern for her own well-being. Now that they'd found each other, he would make sure she'd not be so careless in the future.

Santi snorted. "Neither is it yours, *bebedor de sangre*. You are nothing to her."

"Oh no?" Ronan's gaze slid to Naya and her eyes grew round and wide. A deep blush colored her cheeks, and her jaw set with a warning expression that coaxed a smile to Ronan's face. "Naya, would you like to tell your friend exactly what I am to you?"

A wave of emotion rushed at Ronan through their tether, and it didn't fill him with anything even close to warm or fuzzy. In fact, he suspected that had it been in her scope of power, she would have incinerated him where he stood.

"Santi, I have this under control." Naya ushered the male toward the front door. "Let me handle this my way, okay? If Paul asks, tell him I'll start patrolling at full dark. And *please,* don't say a word about any of this."

She opened the door and Santi stood in the threshold. "Naya, this isn't a good idea. At least let me—"

"*My* way, Santi. Promise me."

"All right." He gave Ronan one last threatening glare over Naya's shoulder. "But only because I know you're capable. If you don't check in, I'm going to the elders."

Naya let out an audible sigh of relief that reached out through their tether, filling Ronan with the same sense of relief. "Scout's honor." She held up two fingers before moving to close the door. "I'll call you later."

Santi's golden gaze locked with Ronan's. The male's expression was pure menace as Naya slowly closed the door, shutting him out. Promised to one male, another beside himself with the need to protect her. It seemed Ronan's mate had drawn quite the pair of admirers. How many more waited in the woodwork?

"Mapinguari?" What he really wanted to do was question Naya about the male, Santi. Who was he to her that he could grab her by the arm and haul her behind him? But the thought of talking about the shifter set Ronan's fangs to throbbing in his gums. Discussing the creature she was supposed to be hunting seemed the safer course of questioning to take.

The term "mapinguari" was foreign to Ronan, and he thought he'd met everything that the supernatural world had to offer. Then again, he'd never come across anyone like Naya before, either. He'd met his fair share of witches. White witches who communed with nature, black ones who worshiped death. Humans who called themselves Wiccans and performed rituals in the hopes of manifesting a certain outcome. But he'd never in all of his centuries encountered a witch like Naya. She outshone them all.

"A demon," Naya answered with a resigned sigh. "When magic infects a body that it's not meant to reside in, it corrupts the host. Supernaturals generally know not to mess with magic that doesn't belong to them, so it's usually humans who get themselves into trouble. Trying to harness a power they can't possibly comprehend. The magic attaches itself to the host, and from there it takes over. It manifests into something dark and unnatural. A creature hell-bent on destruction."

Christ. "And you hunt these things?"

Naya kept her hand wrapped around the doorknob as though it anchored her. "I do. I can hear the magic. I can control it. I hunt down any creature that tries to run off with magic that doesn't belong to it. I repossess the magic and kill the mapinguari."

His mate was indeed extraordinary. "You hunt alone?" The thought of her chasing demons night after night without backup sent Ronan's protective streak into overdrive.

She rolled her eyes. "I do lots of things alone, vampire. Why? Worried?"

Yes. "How big are these mapinguari?" If they were the size of a house cat or a puppy, he could rest easy.

"Depends on the type of magic that's been taken," Naya responded with a shrug. "Sometimes no bigger than me, though once I fought a fully manifested demon that was pushing seven and a half feet."

Gods. Ronan's stomach tied into an unyielding knot. "And your elders, they expect you to do this? To hunt these demons and extinguish them on your own?"

"All by my lonesome." Her flippant attitude did nothing for Ronan's ratcheting nerves. "I managed to take a big, burly vampire captive last night with no one's help."

Ronan clamped his jaw down. She had, hadn't she? And damn it, she could have been killed. He had no recollection of last night, had no idea what sort of state he'd been in. Had he been in a state of bloodlust, he would have drunk her dry before his soul had even had a chance to return to his body. "You won't be going out alone tonight," he replied. "I'm going with you."

CHAPTER
7

"You can say you're going out with me until you're blue in the face, vampire. It's not going to happen."

"I *am* going with you and there's not a gods-damned thing you can do about it."

Naya sheathed the dagger at her back and tucked another into her boot. She bit down on her bottom lip to keep from letting slip the string of curses that she wanted to rain down on the very stubborn vampire blocking a path to her door, arms folded across his wide chest.

"It's not a good idea." She had no idea what she'd be tracking tonight. It could be someone in the early stages of corruption, or it could be a creature from a nightmare, hell-bent on mayhem. Plus, there was the issue of Ronan's own volatile state to consider. The magic hadn't manifested since she'd found him in the parking lot last night, but it could resurface at any time. Until she figured out what it was that had attached itself to him, he was a variable she couldn't be distracted by.

That was the only reason she wanted him to stay behind. It had nothing to do with the fact that she felt oddly drawn to him. That the music in her soul soared in a beautiful symphony whenever he was near. Or that the memory of his kisses still burned on her lips, seared every inch of skin that he'd touched.

And she absolutely didn't want him to stay behind because if he tried to sink his fangs into her throat again she didn't think she'd stop him no matter her claims otherwise.

Gods, what was *wrong* with her?

"Don't touch that." Naya snatched a ceremonial dagger used specifically for spellcrafting from Ronan's hand and set it back on the shelf. Her fingers brushed his and a current passed between them that sent delicious chills over Naya's flesh. His eyes flashed with silver and Naya wondered at his response. *Emotional? Physical? Both?* She swallowed down the lust that churned hot in her belly. She needed to get her head on straight and focus. No male had ever thrown her off her game to this extent.

The vampire was trouble.

"I'm not letting you go out there, unprotected."

Naya paused, the air essentially knocked from her chest with his words. She checked the clip of her SIG and stuffed the gun into a holster under her arm. Suffused with pleasant warmth that radiated from her belly outward, she tried to shut out the sound of the music that lulled her into a subdued state of peace and security. It was wrong. All of it. The music, the way it shifted from pitch-perfect to chaotic, the rightness that she felt just being close to Ronan. The way she trusted him without knowing anything about him.

He was a dangerous male who radiated power. A dark aura of death surrounded him. She knew that he would bring swift and painful retribution to any creature that sought to do him—or anyone he held dear—harm. And whereas that should have put Naya on high alert, instead it only made her want to lower her guard for the first time in her life.

And the thought scared the shit out of her.

"You're a liability, Ronan." He needed to lay low until she could decide what to do about him. Crescent City was a tiny town. He'd stick out like a sore thumb and the elders would know all about him by sunup. "I have to be on my toes out there and I won't be at one hundred percent if I have to keep an eye on you, too." She added under her breath, "I should just chain you back up to the bed."

He answered with a confident smile that showcased the wicked points of his fangs, "I don't mind being tied to your bed, but only if you stick around so I can reciprocate."

The flesh at Naya's throat grew hot at the memory of his mouth on her and she averted her gaze, focusing her attention on the knife she stuffed into her boot. Wicked male. "You saw how Santi reacted to seeing you. I can't risk you being seen by anyone else." It was best to steer the conversation away from either of them being on her bed. Tied up or otherwise. "And I'm already in enough trouble with the elders as it is."

Ronan's gaze hardened as it leveled on her. "What sort of trouble?" The words rumbled in his chest, a precursor to a storm.

The dark tenor vibrated over her skin and Naya suppressed a shudder. "None of your business. That's what sort."

"You're my mate, Naya." The words slipped from his lips as though he stated something as obvious as her gender. He continued to rifle through the shelves of weaponry, talismans, and powders, and Naya slapped his hand away. "Your trouble is mine. Tell me what it is, and I'll make it disappear."

The vampire was certainly cavalier. She grabbed two throwing knives from the bottom shelf and stuck one in her belt. "I'm not your or anyone's mate, so you can get that notion out of your head right now."

Ronan flashed her a confident grin that turned her body traitor and weakened her knees. "My soul knows it's been tethered to yours. You're mine, Naya."

Mine. The word snapped the meager hold Naya had on her temper. She brought the squat blade to Ronan's throat and choked up tight on the grip. "I belong to myself." His scent enveloped her, a bloom of rich aroma that reminded her of roasted coffee beans. It awakened her hunger, and this one wasn't for food. She pressed the blade into the flesh of his throat, nicking the skin. A drop of crimson latched on to the blue steel blade and Ronan's nostrils flared.

"I fucking love a female with a violent streak."

He was incorrigible. Obviously any threat of violence was just going to egg him on. Naya lowered the knife and sheathed it in her belt. Ronan closed the space between them, so close now that Naya had to look up to meet his face. Gods, he was a magnificent specimen. His very presence stole the air from her lungs; his sheer size crowded her until everything melted away but him. His scent enveloped her; his gaze swallowed her. In a heartbeat Ronan had become her entire universe. A tremor seized Naya's body. From fear or excitement she didn't know.

"We've been over this, Naya. Whether or not you choose to acknowledge it, we are tethered." He leaned down until his mouth hovered above her and his breath was warm in her ear. "Already I crave you like a drug."

She couldn't swallow. Her mouth had gone bone-dry. And forming a coherent thought was impossible when he was close enough to touch. His tongue flicked out at the hollow of her throat and her palm came up to steady her careening world, landing on the solid wall of muscle that was his chest. Her fingers tingled with the contact and she splayed her hand out as though to touch as much of him as possible.

"So if you think for one second that I'm going to let you go out there alone without protection, you've got another think coming, my beautiful little witch." He reached up and threaded his fingers through her hair, guiding her face up to meet his. His lips met hers in a slow, gentle kiss, and when he pulled away she could almost feel the pain that reflected in his expression. "Get used to having me around, Naya," he said as he released his grip on her and turned away. "Because I'm not going *anywhere*."

Ronan sucked in a sharp breath as he turned away. Fire raced through his veins with all of the heat of the sun in midday. A simple kiss was enough to set his blood to boiling, and it wasn't merely the beautiful female he was dying to fuck. The gods-damned blood troth was going to be the death of him. Honestly, death would be preferable to withholding himself from his mate. How could he possibly be expected to deny that essential part of their bond that demanded he touch her, taste her, sink his fangs into her flesh while he fucked her?

Even now, it took every ounce of willpower in his stores to withhold himself from Naya. She was reluctant. Stubborn. And oh, so fiery. But Ronan liked that about her. She was a challenge he couldn't wait to tackle. A puzzle for him to solve. He'd seduce her. Tease her. Discover what made her purr and relentlessly pursue her until she had no choice but to yield to him. He wouldn't be satisfied until she belonged to him: heart, body, and soul.

Siobhan would flay the skin from Naya's body if she found out about her.

On his list of concerns the vindictive dhampir was the least of his worries, and wasn't that saying something?

"Why don't you hunt in a pack?" If he didn't steer his mind from the lewd thoughts currently hardening his cock, he wouldn't be worth a shit.

Naya cocked a brow; the barest hint of a smile played on her full lips. "Only *brujas* track magic," she answered with a laugh. "But sometimes, I take Luz."

Ronan helped himself to a dagger from the top shelf, stuffing it into his waistband before Naya could take it away. "I just assumed that since your people are shifters, you would go out in a pack. Who's Luz?"

"My cousin." Naya's mouth formed a petulant pout as she watched him stow the dagger, but she made no move to take it from him. Point: Ronan. He was wearing her down. "You're just going to go out like that?" Her eyes dipped to his bare chest and Ronan's abdomen tightened with lust. "You might raise a few brows running around shirtless like that. And I'm not a shifter."

Who—and what—was this female who'd tethered his soul? She wielded magic like a witch and kept company with shifters. *Remarkable.* "The shifters employ you, then?" Ronan was determined to peel back her layers until he knew everything about her. He knew better than to assume that she was a simple employee. No hired hand would be forced into an arranged mating. "I don't need a shirt to fight," he replied. "But if it distracts you, love, I'm sure we can pick something up for me, no?"

She averted her gaze and pulled her bottom lip between her teeth. "We'll find you something," she said without denying that the sight of him distracted her. Ronan wanted to crow with satisfaction. "Are all dhampirs vampires?"

"No." Ronan smiled at her attempt to deflect.

She snatched a Ruger from a safe that sat next to the

shelves of assorted weaponry. She ejected the clip and checked the ammo before sliding it home and thrusting it into Ronan's hand. "If you insist on tagging along, you can at least make yourself useful. Or at the very least, protect yourself so I don't have to."

Ronan stowed the weapon in his waistband, opposite the dagger. Whatever had brought him to Crescent City, he obviously hadn't come outfitted for war. Unless . . . had someone divested him of his weapons? A tremor of anxiety rolled through him. Gods, he wished he remembered. "I'm touched that my mate is concerned for my safety." Naya's heartbeat picked up its pace, music to his ears.

"Don't call me that," she quipped. "I just don't want to have to explain how a dead vampire wound up on my turf when there aren't supposed to be any left."

Ronan swallowed down the snarky comeback that would assure their verbal sparring continued. She got his blood up with nothing more than her smart mouth. A mouth he wanted to savor at his leisure. He couldn't ignore the niggling feeling that whatever Naya hunted tonight was somehow connected to Chelle's disappearance. Ronan was a fixer. He was good at it. And if he could only earn Naya's trust, he'd take care of all of their problems and save them both a hell of a lot of stress.

Chelle . . . ?

Gods. Chelle!

"Naya, I remember something."

Her head whipped around, eyes wide with excitement. "You do? What?"

"I know why I'm here." His own excitement rushed through him like a spark. How could he have possibly forgotten his own twin?

He could kill two birds with one stone by going out with Naya. She knew the town and the outlying areas. He could look for Chelle while earning Naya's trust and showing her that he was capable of protecting her. He'd prove to her that she had no reason to be wary of him. In the hours since he'd woken up bound to her bed frame, Ronan had come to the conclusion that Naya was a strong female with an even stronger will. Reliance was a sign of weakness. She was the sort of female who demanded to be treated as an equal, rather than demonstrating her superiority complex the way that Siobhan did.

He wanted Naya more by the second.

"I came here to find my sister." The first step to earning his mate's trust: He had to confide in her.

Naya finished closing up the gun safe and the weapons cabinet and studied him, her brow furrowed over her dark eyes. "Vampires seem to be coming out of the woodwork," she remarked. "I'd know if there was another one of you in the city."

Ronan quirked a brow. "Would you?" He couldn't help himself. Getting her riled by challenging her authority was just too easy.

"Yes," she said. "I would."

"Chelle isn't a vampire. At least, not yet." What would his sister think of his transition? He hadn't had the chance to tell her before their phone call had been interrupted. "She'd appear human for all intents and purposes. She can tolerate sunlight. Silver. She'd blend right in."

Suspicion wrinkled Naya's forehead as she studied him. "How is it that you're a vampire and she isn't?"

How was it possible to be tethered to someone so different from himself? Someone with so little knowledge of what he was? Then again, Claire had been human when she'd tethered Mikhail's soul. You couldn't get much more different than that.

"Chelle is still a dhampir. I was only recently turned." It was explanation enough. He would only give so much.

Naya would have to quid pro quo if she wanted any more than that out of him. "She called me, said she needed my help. I left almost immediately after her call."

"Do you remember when she called?"

Ronan racked his brain. "The tenth, maybe."

"That was a little over two weeks ago." Fuck it all. He'd been here for two weeks already? "I left L.A. that night and that's the last thing I remember until I woke up on your bed."

Naya crossed the empty dining area to the kitchen bar and leaned against it, crossing her feet in front of her, one hand resting on the pommel of her dagger. "What did she need help with?"

He wanted to invite Naya's trust. Didn't mean he was willing to show his hand just yet. He wasn't ready to divulge too much about why Chelle was here, even to his mate. Just this morning Naya had knocked him the fuck out. Who knew what she'd do to him if she discovered his sister had been searching for a powerful vampire relic? "I'm not sure. Our call was disconnected before she could tell me anything. Chelle is a . . ." *Tomb raider–slash–Indiana Jones wannabe?* ". . . treasure seeker."

Naya tightened her grip on the pommel. "What sort of treasures?"

He wondered if she ever posed a question with genuine curiosity in her tone. So far, everything she'd asked him had been veiled with an answer-or-I'll-break-your-femur undertone. "The vampire kind."

For the most part, Chelle focused her talents on reclaiming vampire relics. The esoteric knickknacks of other cultures didn't interest her. That wasn't to say that there weren't other supernatural creatures out there who wouldn't give their left nut for what she'd been after. Namely, Set's chest.

A relic rumored to hold unimaginable power.

Power that someone as sensitive to magic as Ronan's mate would have no trouble tracking. Part of him hoped she'd lead him straight to it if it meant that he'd find Chelle. And another part hoped like hell that the chest stayed good and hidden. Naya feared unchecked power; his own state as her prisoner was proof enough of that. The chest might as well have been Pandora's box for all he knew. If Chelle—or anyone—managed to open it, all hell could break loose. Hell, maybe it already had.

His headstrong female might have been wary of magic in the wrong hands, but that didn't mean that she wasn't hell-bent on tracking it down. Protecting Naya would be problematic if she decided to hunt past sunrise. Which was why Ronan wanted to get a move on. "Don't you think we ought to—"

Icy cold crept up Ronan's torso and spread through his limbs. Naya's dark eyes grew wide with alarm and she pushed herself from the bar, her stance no longer relaxed but alert and defensive. She drew the dagger from behind her back and the blade glowed citrine bright.

"Whoa. Take it easy." Ronan swayed on his feet and his vision darkened at the periphery. The cold that snaked up his arms and around his thighs chilled him further, as though someone had dipped him in a vat of dry ice. "Na-ya." His tongue felt too thick in his mouth and the word slurred as he tried to push it past his lips. She approached him as one wary predator approaches another, the blade held high in front of her, ready to cut down.

A riot of color swam in his vision and Ronan's gaze darted to his arms. Color leached from his pores, running in fluorescent rivulets that dripped from his fingertips. *Jesus fucking Christ.* Either he was trippin' balls or the magic that Naya had insisted he'd stolen was making an unwelcome reappearance.

"You need to stay still." Her barked order cut through

him like a blade. She gave her head a rough shake, her brows knit together in pain. He took a stumbling step toward her and she jumped back. "Damn it, don't move!" Panic laced her tone and Ronan's own heartbeat echoed hers as the sound of it rushed in his ears. *Make it stop.* The cold was unbearable. Fire and ice at once. *Gods, make it stop!*

"Naya." His voice sounded foreign in his ears, far away and weak.

"I said, stop, Ronan, or I'll stop you."

Ronan fell to his knees as he lost all sensation in his limbs. A violent tremor shook him, the cold freezing him from the inside out.

"I'm sorry." Naya loomed above him, and the female who had tethered his soul raised her dagger high. "But you've given me no choice." His final thought as she swung her arm forcefully down was that he would never know the way it felt to hold her in his arms.

CHAPTER
8

Naya collapsed beside Ronan as she attempted to quell the tremors that rippled through her body. She was held tight in the grip of a fear she'd never known. Terror that tore at the fabric of her soul. Now that he was unconscious, the music had ceased its chaotic song. She should have killed him. Should have run the blade through his heart and let the dagger take the magic that infected his body.

The thought of taking his life had filled her with a sorrow so deep and so intense that she'd felt it in the very marrow of her bones. He was a stranger and yet, since the night he'd tackled her in that parking lot, she couldn't conceive of being parted from him.

She'd sworn she could feel his pain as the magic took its hold. Even now, her arms were slow to move and her legs ached with a bone-deep chill. How could the magic contained in his body sing to her with such pitch-perfect clarity one moment and become so corrupt the next?

She cradled his head in her lap as she combed her fingers through the locks of his tawny hair. The song quieted to a gentle melody and Naya hummed along to a tune she'd never heard but instinctually knew every note of. In the span of twenty-four hours, she'd begun to unravel. And it wasn't Paul or his stupid mandate or the corrupt magic running rampant through town that was the cause. No, it was the male in her arms who'd proclaimed with such unerring confidence that she belonged to him.

And that he, in turn, belonged to her.

Ronan let out a low moan and Naya quieted. "Don't stop."

A smile curved her lips and she let out a soft breath. "Don't stop what?"

"Touching me. Humming." His voice rolled over her in a wave that relaxed every muscle in Naya's body. "You're warm," he said on a breath. A tremor shook him and his shoulders tightened where he rested against her inner thighs. "I'm so fucking cold, I feel like I'll never get warm again."

"What can I do to help?" Truth be told, Naya hadn't felt so relaxed in a long damned time. Just sitting there, cradling his head, filled her with a sense of calm. But duty called and she wasn't going to find the source of the magical corruption infecting the town camped out on the floor with a vampire lounging in her lap.

His eyes came slowly open and the dark green irises were rimmed with silver. A lazy half smile tugged at his full lips, revealing the tips of his fangs. "You could give me your vein."

Opportunistic vampire.

His eyes drifted shut as though he'd expended too much effort to open them in the first place. A rush of adrenaline seeped into Naya's bloodstream and her heart renewed its anxious pace in her chest. "Will it really help, or are you working an angle?"

His lips twitched, but his eyes remained shut. "Both."

Twilight gave way to full dark, the only illumination in her tiny apartment coming from a single lamp in the far corner of the living room. His presence unnerved her, and not because she felt any sense of danger or malice from him. No, it was the ease at which he put her that shook Naya to her foundation. And the fact that she was about to give him the one thing she'd sworn, just hours ago, that he'd never have again.

"Here." She brought her wrist to his mouth. "But don't get greedy, vampire. This is only because I can't leave you here alone in case you have another . . . episode. And I need you mobile so I can get to work. I'm not an all-you-can-drink dinner buffet. Got it?"

Ronan's eyes snapped open and shone bright silver. Naya steeled herself against the trepidation that skittered through her as her heart leapt in her chest. His lip curled to reveal the dual points of his fangs and she recalled the pleasure that had raced through her veins like fire when he'd pierced the flesh at her throat.

"You're a sweet temptation any male would find hard to resist, love."

The quintessential charmer. "Just a sip," she reminded him.

His eyes locked with hers as he gripped her wrist in his large hands and brought it to his mouth. Naya's breath came in quick pants as he sealed his lips over her vein, the heat of his tongue like a brand as it flicked out at her skin. The sharp tips broke the skin and Ronan's eyes rolled back as a satisfied purr rumbled in his chest.

With the first strong pull of suction Naya melted.

His grip was firm, with a possessiveness to it that sent a thrill through her center. Fiery heat pulsed from her wrist outward, and Naya's stomach clenched with lust. Her breasts tingled as though Ronan's tongue stroked her tightened nipples and not her wrist. Swamped with sensation, her sex pulsed in time with her heartbeat and she couldn't stop the low moan that vibrated in her throat.

Ronan's grip slackened and he moved as though to pull away. "Don't stop." Naya didn't recognize her own voice, the pleading tone so foreign to her ears. She was getting off on nothing more than his bite, the deep suction a phantom sensation that seemed to settle on the most sensitive part of her sex. She threaded her fingers through Ronan's hair and held him to her wrist. Urging him to take more as her pleasure mounted to a fevered pitch that made her desperate to find release.

Ronan pulled away with a low growl that vibrated over Naya's flesh. In a flash of motion he was on top of her, settled between her thighs, his eyes alight with silver, wild and unfocused. Passion overrode good sense as his mouth ravaged hers and Naya gave in to the need that spurred her past reason. She opened up to him, deepening the kiss, and she tasted the tang of blood on her tongue. Both blood and sex could produce heady magic under the right circumstances, and Naya's senses were awash with the power that flooded her.

The rush was unlike anything she'd ever experienced, and all she could think was, *More.*

Ronan rocked against her, every roll of his hips moving in unison with each deep thrust of his tongue. A lascivious fucking of her mouth that drove Naya wild as she clawed at his shoulders in an effort to draw him closer. Raw energy buzzed in her brain, spreading outward through her body. She swore that she could feel every individual cell swelling, and through the silence a song began to play, plucking at her heartstrings until the beauty of it brought tears to her eyes. Still she cleaved to Ronan, kissing him as though she'd been starved for the contact for eternity, her hips rolling up to meet every sharp thrust as the length of his erection teased her through the barrier of their clothes.

"Naya." Ronan broke their kiss and she lurched up, desperate for him to give her more. "Naya." Again, more urgent this time as his weight left her. She bit back a frustrated cry. Lost to sensation. To want. To the power that filled her to bursting, Naya couldn't break herself from the spell he'd cast on her. And she didn't want to.

"Naya!" He gave her a gentle shake as she buried her face in the crook of his neck. Her tongue flicked out at salty-sweet flesh and she wondered what it would feel like to break the skin with her teeth as he'd done to her. "Naya. Stop. Something's happening. You're *glowing*."

Fear choked the air from Ronan's lungs.

A soft, rose-infused light emanated from Naya's skin, pulsing in time with her heartbeat. Lost to the moment, to the bliss of feeding from his mate's vein, Ronan had been swept up in a frenzy of lust that had robbed him of good sense. She'd been so responsive, so equally hungry, returning his ardor with a fervor that dizzied him. No longer punch-drunk from the magic that had laid him low, Ronan was infused with strength and power unlike anything he'd ever known.

A feat indeed, considering he'd been sustained by both Claire and Mikhail. Powerful creatures in their own right. This was different, though. There were no words for what coursed through Ronan's veins now. Was this the true power of a mate bond?

Naya's eyes came slowly open. Her brow furrowed as though she didn't understand the words Ronan had spoken. Her dark eyes were glazed, the pupils nearly pinpricks, and her full lips parted with her racing breath. "Don't stop, Ronan," she breathed. "I don't want to stop."

His cock twitched in his jeans, the stiff bastard more

than willing to give his female exactly what she wanted. Desire rolled through him like a breaker crashing over the rocks. His brain gave way to lust and he reached down to the fly of his jeans, ready to give in to his own desires.

She's fucking glowing.

Clarity blew the haze of lust from his brain. This couldn't be good. He pushed himself upright and Naya followed as though tied to him with a length of string. A drunken smile curved her luscious mouth and, *oh, gods,* how Ronan wanted to take her bottom lip between the tips of his fangs. She reached out for him and he took her wrists in both of his hands. "Slow your roll, honey." Jesus, since when was he the voice of reason? "Did you hear what I said to you? Your skin is *glowing.*"

Naya's eyes were slow to track as her gaze traveled down the length of her arm. She let out a low, seductive laugh that tightened Ronan's balls, and he damn near ached with the need to take her. "It's the magic," she replied. "It can manifest during sex under the right circumstances. Sort of feels like rolling around naked in feathers." A contented smile rounded out her dreamy expression. "A-ma-zing."

And it apparently made her high as a fucking kite.

"Has this ever happened before?" Ronan forced the words from between clenched teeth. The thought of her reaching this euphoric state with another male encouraged a murderous thought or twelve.

"Never tried it before." She blinked slowly as her fingers caressed his forearm. Through their tether Ronan had gotten a taste of Naya's magic, and it was like a shot of electricity to his nervous system with a Molly chaser. The female was a drug to him. And he couldn't help but feel a little smug that he'd had the same effect on her.

There were merits to being tethered to a witch, it seemed.

Later there'd be time for erotic play. And though it pained Ronan to part from her, to leave the heat of her body behind, there was still a lot to do before the sun rose. The gap still remained in his memory, Chelle was still out there somewhere, Set's chest was unaccounted for, and he needed to help Naya neutralize whatever threat ran rampant through the town.

Not to mention the small issue of her arranged pairing to another male and Ronan's blood troth to another female.

"Can you focus, Naya?" They were quite a pair. He'd been given a reprieve from the effects of infectious magic only to turn and intoxicate her to the point of giddy uselessness. How did you go about sobering someone up from a magical high, anyway?

He released his grip on her wrists. She reached up and traced his bottom lip with the petal-soft pad of her thumb. He'd sealed his troth to Siobhan with blood, and if he took Naya now the blood would boil in his veins, stealing any future he might have with this remarkable female. His cock throbbed with unspent seed, and the urge to throw good sense to the wayside and fuck her here and now was a temptation Ronan wasn't sure he could fight. He'd risk death and the heat that sizzled through him for one opportunity to sink into her slick heat.

The rose glow on her skin sparkled in the low light. Moonbeams and sunset. He let out a low curse under his breath. Siobhan had fucked him over with her games and demands. His only option at this point was to deny himself the one thing in this fucking world that he wanted or be burned alive from the inside out.

Gods, since when had his life become a Shakespearian tragedy?

"We need to get you five by five, Naya." As if she were the only one of them who didn't have a grip. "What's it going to take to get you square?"

Already her eyes appeared clearer and the soft glow of her skin had begun to dull. Naya pushed herself up to stand and Ronan followed, helping to steady her as she swayed on her feet. "I'll be okay in a minute." She let out a slow gust of breath. "I just need to meditate. Center my power and I'll be fine."

Sounded simple enough. "What can I do to help?"

She gave him a weak smile. "Just keep your distance. I'm still too wired for you to be so close."

He knew how she felt. Her proximity, coupled with the blood he'd taken from her vein, only made him want her more. A dry, gravelly scratch irritated his throat, though he'd taken more than enough of her blood to slake his thirst. After what had just happened between them, how could she possibly deny their bond? Surely Naya recognized their tether now. Ronan couldn't help but wonder if the realization would help to build a stronger foundation for a relationship with her or send her running in the opposite direction.

Ronan gave Naya the space she'd asked for and crossed over to the living room. She braced her arms on the countertop of the bar separating the kitchen from the dining area and let her head fall between her shoulders. Her breathing, slow and even, matched the beat of her heart, and Ronan let his own eyes drift shut as he allowed the gentle sound to lull him into a state of relaxation.

Gods, so much had been piled on his plate. How could he possibly handle it all?

"Ronan?"

He opened his eyes to find Naya standing beside him. Her skin was once again creamy brown and her gaze zeroed in on him, sharp and clear. The once dreamy expression had been replaced with a no-nonsense severity that caused his heart to ache. Though he knew she'd needed the clarity and self-control, he missed that lust-addled, reckless side of her.

"Ready to roll?" He tried not to think about how badly he wanted her. Or about what the consequences of taking what he wanted would be. Instead, he turned his attention to something he could control: finding Chelle and delivering a violent death to the bastards who'd taken her.

"I should apologize." The charge of energy that had sparked between them evaporated into an awkwardness that settled over Ronan like a black cloud. It ignited his already-volatile temper and he swallowed the emotion down, stuffing it to the soles of his feet. "I've never let magic control me like that and I won't let it happen again. I'm sorry."

She was fucking *apologizing* to him? As though what had happened between them was some shameful thing. The Collective scratched at the back of Ronan's mind and he pushed at the memories that threatened to crest over him. A blood exchange between a tethered pair was sacred. An act that always accompanied sex and was meant to solidify the bond between them. Had she been a vampire or even a dhampir, Ronan would have offered his vein to her in his eagerness to sustain his mate.

She wasn't a vampire, though. Just another obstacle that lay between them.

"Don't apologize." Ronan would be damned if he let her see how deeply her words cut him. "Let's just get a move on. We're wasting time and burning night." He pushed himself from the couch and stalked toward the door, his jaw welded shut. Trothed to a female he couldn't escape and tethered to another who wanted nothing to do with him.

"Sure, let's get moving." Naya gave him a nervous

smile that didn't shine past her lips. "We'll pick you up a few T-shirts on our way through town."

Fuck it all. What was the use in having his soul returned to him only to feel it crushed beneath the weight of his many disappointments? Oblivion would be a relief in comparison to the pain he felt now.

CHAPTER
9

Christian Whalen paced outside of the director's office, waiting for the imperious bastard to grant him entrance. It was easier to get an audience with the goddamned Pope, and Christian should know: He'd done business with the Vatican a couple of times. He flipped the bird to the two guards flanking the door and they each took a step in as though he'd actually try to muscle his way past them. *Whatever.* Like he'd waste his time with a couple of powerless pussies like them.

He was too antsy to sit down, so while he paced he checked the spread for the upcoming LSU/Georgia game on his phone. If he laid down his bet by the weekend and if LSU's defense could actually pull their weight, he might make a shit-ton of cash. A familiar tingle danced across his scalp and down his spine, the urge to make the wager like an itch he desperately needed to scratch. If he won, the high would be triple since the spread was so wide. If he lost . . . eh, it'd sting. But he'd make it up on the next game. Winning and losing didn't matter as much as the high he felt just taking the chance. Placing a bet was like walking through an alligator-infested swamp. Blindfolded. He felt a trickle of adrenaline just thinking about it.

"Christian?" The director's secretary poked her head out of the door. "He'll see you now."

Goody. Christian gave the secretary a flirtatious smile and raised both of his hands to the guards, giving them each the finger one more time as he walked past them. They actually thought they had a sweet gig standing in front of a door all day. *Morons.* Jesus, the director was so paranoid that Christian hadn't even been allowed to wait in the small foyer where the director's gatekeeper answered phones and directed calls. Christian wondered how much longer it would be before the director's gatekeeper's gatekeepers had gatekeepers. Jesus.

"Moneypenny," he said with a wink in his best James Bond British accent as he sauntered past the secretary's desk and into the director's office.

"What is it, Christian? I'm busy."

The director of the Sortiari didn't even bother to look up from his computer screen as he addressed Christian with less-than-casual disinterest. And why should the director give a shit? He'd been sitting in his ivory tower while agents like Christian risked their necks out in the field. Tristan McAlister had become obsessed over the past couple of years, stationing guards all around him and going nowhere without an armed escort. He used to be a damned good leader, but that was before a simple rumor reduced him to nothing more than a paranoid shut-in. *The guy hears one little rumor about his impending death and turns all single-minded, I-don't-give-a-fuck-about-anything-except-for-finding-my-rumored-killer obsessed.* Death threats or not, if he was that uptight about it he should have resigned from his position a long time ago.

"It's been over three weeks and Gregor hasn't checked

in," Christian said. "There's no trace of him or any of his men anywhere in the city."

"He hasn't left," McAlister replied with more of that wonderful disinterest. "Ian Gregor isn't going anywhere. He's in the city, Christian. Find him."

Christian gave a derisive snort. "Has being holed up in this office deprived you of oxygen, McAlister? This is *your* protocol he's violated. Gregor knows the consequences. There's no way he'd stick around. The bastard is probably halfway to Scotland by now." Along with an army of the Sortiari's berserker warlords. Christian didn't dare voice his concerns, but McAlister had to know that without Gregor and his brethren the Sortiari were as good as impotent.

McAlister paused and turned to face Christian. It wasn't exactly concern in his expression, but Christian hoped he'd gotten his point across. "He won't run. He's been harboring too much hatred for far too long to flee. Penalties be damned. Truth be told, I don't give a great hairy fuck about Gregor or his vendettas. What I am concerned about are the three hundred berserkers who would abandon their service with nothing more than a word from him. Find him. Kill him if he won't come back. Just bring me his army."

Well. It looked as though McAlister had priorities beyond saving his own ass after all. Christian folded his arms across his chest. "It's hard to win loyalty from men when you murder their general."

He was answered with more of McAlister's derision: "I'll buy their loyalty. I'm not concerned."

What an asshole. Christian wasn't about to let the director bait him into an argument, and so he stood stoic and silent, staring a hole right through the fucker's forehead.

The director sighed and turned away from whatever had kept his attention focused on his computer screen. "A purchased man can be just as loyal as one with an axe to grind. Gregor's men won't stand by and play along to his overinflated ego or skewed sense of vengeance for long. Get me my army back."

McAlister's arrogance rivaled Gregor's. That the director didn't recognize it was going to cause a hell of a lot of trouble for all of them. But the asshole was right. Gregor's men, whether his kinsmen or not, wouldn't entertain his madness for long. "I'll need at least a week," Christian said, turning on a heel. "If I can't track him by then, I'll assemble a team—"

"No!" The director barked out the word as if he was afraid Christian was going to evacuate the place and leave him unprotected. "You take care of this yourself. I'm not wasting personnel or resources on this. Gregor will expect me to send a force of men and that's not going to happen. *You* go. Alone."

What a crock of shit. If this wasn't a suicide mission, he didn't know what was. "It sucks balls that you just don't give a shit about this organization or its people anymore." Christian opened the door and turned to face the director before closing the door behind him. "Have fun hiding in your fortress, McAlister. If you think Gregor has fucked up by abandoning his post in favor of his own personal agenda, maybe you'd better take a look in the mirror. Because if you ask me, you're not interested in doing anything but saving your own neck. I just hope it's worth all of the lives you're putting in danger because of your own irrational fear."

Christian didn't give McAlister a chance to respond. He slammed the door behind him and stalked through the secretary's office. "Hope he lets you out of your cage every once in a while," he murmured as he passed her desk. "If I were you, I'd watch my back, though. No telling who he might use as a human shield."

You had to give it to her; the secretary was loyal. She didn't even bat a lash at Christian's harsh words. "Good day, Christian," she said in a stiff, professional way. "I trust you can see yourself out."

Yeah, he sure as hell could. He just couldn't understand what could prompt that sort of devotion. God knew Tristan McAlister didn't deserve it. Christian gave her a lazy salute as he stormed out into the hallway. He didn't even bother to heckle the apes standing watch at the door. He was too riled to get any real enjoyment out of taunting them.

Christian checked his watch as he continued down the dimly lit corridor. The track opened in a half hour; he could probably make it there by the second race. Nothing like a few harmless bets to take the edge off. And one fucking thing was certain: He'd need all of the calm he could get if he was going to single-handedly take down an immortal warlord while simultaneously usurping control of his army. Fuck the races. Nothing short of a trip to Vegas was going to level him the fuck out.

CHAPTER
10

"It's good to hear your voice, Ronan," Mikhail said through the line. "We were starting to worry."

"It's been a hell of a few days," Ronan said. His cell had gone missing. Presumably wherever his rental car had gotten off to. He used Naya's landline to check in, knowing that if he didn't Mikhail would send someone after him and he didn't want his king left without protection.

"What's going on up there? There's a period of time where there are no memories of you in the Collective. I've never experienced anything like it before."

Neither had Ronan. The blank space in his memory was a sore reminder that there was a mystery here for him to unravel and he needed to get his ass in gear. "Yeah, well, it's a long story. One I'll be more than happy to tell you when I get home. How's everything there?"

"Quiet," Mikhail said.

Ronan knew his friend. Mikhail was leaving something out. "The Sortiari?"

"Holding to a tentative truce, it seems," Mikhail replied. "No sign of Gregor, though."

The slayer was smart to stay off the radar. Once Mikhail found him, he was as good as dead. "Jenner will find him." The male was damned good at finding people who didn't want to be found. He'd worked as a skip tracer when he wasn't working for Ronan. Jenner could find anyone.

"Jenner is . . ."

"What?" Ronan asked. He knew Mikhail had been holding out on him.

"The transition has been difficult for him. I've tried not to pile too much on him until he's had time to adjust."

"How long has it been?" Gods, Ronan hated that he hadn't been there for Jenner's transition. To help him with his new senses. His magnified appetites.

"Only a couple of weeks," Mikhail answered. "Give or take. I thought he'd have a grip by now, but his control is tenuous. He hasn't learned to manage his thirst and Siobhan complains that he's rutting on all of the females in her coven."

Ronan's stomach sank like a stone in the ocean. "Is that all she's complaining about?"

"She's prepared to hunt you down to the ends of the earth," Mikhail said without humor. "And I think she'd gladly torture any soul she suspected knew where you were."

"Let me hire more people to watch over the house. I'd feel better if I knew that you and Claire and the little human weren't in danger of her doing something stupid."

"I can handle Siobhan," Mikhail said. "Don't worry. I'm making progress here. Dhampirs are coming to me now. Relationships are being formed. Plans made. In a few months' time I hope to see our numbers doubled. It would be nice to have you here for those who need help with the transition."

That had been the plan. Until his life had completely

run off the tracks. "I'll be back as soon as I can. Before a month."

"Have you found Chelle?"

Ronan dragged his fingers through his hair. "No. We're going out tonight again to search for her. You'd think she'd be easy to find in a small town, but there are thousands of acres of forest out here. She could be anywhere."

"We?" Ronan tried to ignore Mikhail's arch tone. "Who have you employed to help you up there?"

He wasn't ready to discuss Naya or his tether. "A local tracker, that's all."

"I suspect that isn't all, but I will allow you your secrets for now."

Of course, all it would take was a glimpse into the Collective if Mikhail wanted the truth. Weeding though millions of memories wasn't easy, but it could be done. Mikhail wouldn't do that, though. He kept his vows and wouldn't press the issue.

"You have this number on the caller ID?"

"Yes," Mikhail said. "I can call you there if I need to?"

"Sure, but only call if it's an emergency. Siobhan is shrewd and I wouldn't put it past her to find a way to track your calls. I'll deal with her when I get back as well. I need to go. The tracker is waiting."

Mikhail chuckled. "I can't wait to hear all about it."

"Tell Claire I said hi."

"I will. Take care of yourself, Ronan."

"You too. Later."

Ronan hung up the phone and let out a slow breath. He needed to get back to L.A., back to his king and his duties. Jenner needed a hand, and until someone kicked him in the ass Ronan doubted the male would settle down anytime soon. A quick glance at the closed bedroom door caused Ronan's stomach to knot up. Another night. Another hunt with Naya so close he could touch. The scent of her blood teasing his thirst.

Jenner wasn't the only one suffering from control issues right now.

A cool breeze kicked up the damp ocean air and the tangy brine was just what Naya needed to clear away the remnants of lust and want that once again fogged her brain. Over the course of the past week, centering her focus was becoming more difficult the longer she was in Ronan's company. They'd fallen into an easy rhythm, hunting after sundown, sleeping for most of the day—her in the bedroom and him on the couch—and then they'd start all over again. The search for his sister was proving as fruitless as Naya's search for the mapinguari. Either the magic that had infected Crescent City had moved on, using El Sendero to find a new home, or this current lull was simply the calm before the storm.

Likewise, the malicious magic that infected Ronan's body hadn't surfaced since the episode in her dining room a week ago. The music she heard in his presence was soft and melodious, a comfort to Naya's own soul. And though she'd exercised tremendous self-control over the past days, Naya felt that control slowly slipping. She didn't know how much longer she'd be able to keep herself from Ronan. And for that matter, she wasn't even sure she wanted to anymore.

Ronan had managed to awaken something within her that pulled the reins of her control taut. She'd never felt power in such a raw, visceral way before.

Naya was no novice. Not in magic or in sex. Tracking and repossessions were her specialties. She'd studied blood magic because it was part of her craft. Her heritage. Magic could corrupt a person through the blood. Spreading like a virus through the cells. Sex didn't usually enter the equation. And though she'd had a few romantic entanglements in her past, none of them had ever triggered that aspect of her power. It was a heady thing. Dangerous. And it made keeping Ronan at arm's length a damn near insurmountable task.

She could easily become addicted to the power he'd awakened in her.

Magic corrupted. Period. And it could damage those who inherently wielded it as easily as it did those who couldn't. Naya needed to be very careful in her dealings with the vampire. Their contact so far had been relatively innocent. She could only imagine what magic it might manifest if she gave herself fully to him or the emotional connection that it might forge. The elders had pledged her life to another male. And no matter the spark that ignited when Ronan touched her, Naya knew that there could never be anything between them. Tethered or not.

"This is where I found you." Naya put the car in park and turned off the headlights. They'd come full circle, hunting throughout the town and the forested areas surrounding Crescent City for any sign of demon or dhampir. "You were standing there"—she pointed to one of the broken floodlights—"and magic bled out of you."

"I don't remember any of it." Ronan gave a slow shake of his head. "I must have been looking for Chelle, but you'd think I'd remember *something*."

"Rogue magic takes a physical toll on its bearer. It could be the equivalent of an ethereal concussion."

"Vampires don't get concussions."

He'd gone from zero to broody in the space of a few minutes, and from his dark tone Naya suspected that his mood wasn't going to improve anytime soon. "Vampires might not suffer from head trauma," she remarked. "But a supernatural creature can definitely sustain a supernatural injury."

"Maybe."

His profile stood out as a finely cut shadow in the dark interior of the car. Naya's body warmed as she recalled the sensation of his strong hands on her. The way his mouth moved over hers. A week holed up with any female's living, breathing sexual fantasy was starting to take its toll. How much longer could she go on like this? Keeping him at arm's length when all she wanted to do was draw him closer. Her breath hitched as she recalled the intense pleasure of his bite and the heat that raced through her veins as—

"If you don't want to be stripped naked and fucked in the front seat of your car, I'd advise you to curb your thoughts, Naya."

She started at Ronan's words that ended on a warning growl. The sound cut through the silence, penetrated her skin, and left a flush in their wake. "You can hear my thoughts?" She had no idea what the parameters of Ronan's abilities might be. Gods, what else had he eavesdropped on?

"I can't read your thoughts." He kept his gaze straight ahead, but Naya didn't miss that his irises were rimmed with silver. "But through our tether, I can sense your emotions. And . . ." He shifted uncomfortably in his seat. "I can smell your arousal."

Naya resisted the urge to bang her forehead on the steering wheel. Smell her arousal? It would have been less embarrassing had she binged on chili dogs with extra onions and farted in the car! But like the aforementioned stench, pretending it hadn't happened wouldn't make it go away. "It's a residual effect of the magic that manifested when we were . . . uh . . . after you. . . ." *Nearly gave me an orgasm from biting my wrist before we dry humped on my dining room floor last week.* "I didn't realize your senses were so fine-tuned. I'm sorry."

Ronan, in turn, didn't seem to be any happier about it. A rumble grew in his chest as he turned to face her. His eyes had completely shed their green for vibrant quicksilver. "There's no need to keep apologizing."

Wasn't there? She was sending some pretty damned mixed signals. "Shifters can scent things I can't." As though babbling were going to help with the awkwardness that had settled like a heavy fog. "They can smell lies. Fear. Anxiety. Anything that changes someone's body chemistry."

"How is it that you keep company with shifters?"

They hadn't really talked about her life much up to this point and Naya had liked it that way. The Bororo were a complicated people, their ways rigid and set in stone over millennia. She didn't want to admit to Ronan that she felt trapped. A prisoner of her pod with no worth beyond the magic in her veins and reproductive organs. She didn't want to appear weak and there was nothing weaker than living a life you weren't strong enough to escape.

Ronan studied her with an intensity that stole her breath. If he could sense her arousal and other emotions through their supposed bond, she'd have to be either very honest or very careful in her responses to him. So far, he hadn't given her a reason to be distrustful of him. In fact, with each passing day she found herself trusting him more and more. And it was rare that Naya had the opportunity to form relationships outside of their pod.

"Only Bororo males can shift. Our females are the bearers of magic. Well, some of us are, anyway."

Ronan quirked a tawny brow. "Bororo?"

"My tribe."

His eyes narrowed as he continued to study her. "How old are you?"

She gave a nervous laugh. "Didn't anyone ever tell you that it's not polite to ask a woman her age? I'm probably older than you think, though I'd be willing to bet that you've got centuries on me."

"You're immortal?" Curiosity laced his tone. It was a far cry better than his previous sourness.

"More or less. Though really, Ronan, is there anything on this earth that is truly immortal?"

Like all supernatural beings, the Bororo were long-lived. They had an evolutionary advantage over humans in that they had more refined senses, could heal quickly, and were immune to most human diseases. But they were not infallible. Nothing in this world was.

"I suppose not," Ronan answered. "My own people were nearly extinct."

The conversation turned right down the road Naya had hoped it would. If he wanted information about her life, then it was only fair he reciprocate. "I've been wondering about that. I've never met a vampire before. I didn't think there were any left." The Bororo had hidden their existence well. Modern anthropologists had declared her people extinct decades ago.

"One," Ronan said. "For two hundred years a single vampire populated the earth." His tone dropped to a murmur. "Until recently, that is. Now there are four."

Wow. And she thought her own tribe was small, with little more than a thousand Bororo scattered across the world. "It must have been lonely for you," she replied. "Did you turn the others?" She had no idea how a vampire was made or born. Ronan's presence opened a door of information Naya couldn't wait to step through.

Ronan chuckled. "I am newly turned, Naya. Soulless for less than a month before you tethered me."

The words were spoken with such raw emotion that it caused a deep ache to settle in her chest. They hadn't talked about the tether for a week. Turning back down this road would only further weaken her resolve to keep Ronan at a distance. "What does that mean, you were soulless?" They should've been out hunting, but Naya's curiosity got the better of her. She found herself wanting to know more about Ronan. And sitting in the quiet car, talking like this, distracted her from the erotic thoughts that scratched at the back of her subconscious, as well as the need to experience the rush of magic his touch coaxed to the surface of her skin.

"When dhampirs are turned into vampires, we forfeit our souls to oblivion. When we find the one we're meant to be with, our souls become tethered to our mate's soul. You returned my soul to me, Naya. We are forever bound to one another."

She'd heard it before from him, but somehow it was different now. Her own body's response to him was unusual. The power that crested in heady waves when he touched her unlike anything she'd ever experienced. Still, whether she was starting to consider his claims or not, it didn't change the fact that the elders had already set her on a path that took her far from Ronan. Naya wasn't interested in tying herself to anyone. She wanted to be allowed the freedom to be—and belong to—herself.

She sensed that what she wanted didn't matter in the grand scheme of things. Paul would still insist that she be mated to Joaquin, and Ronan would continue to insist that she was already mated to him. Things were going to come to a head too soon, and when they did all hell would break loose. Either Ronan would have to get used to the idea of polygamy or they were all in for one hell of a fight.

Of course, none of it would matter if Naya couldn't first control the rogue magic that was infecting people throughout town. "We'd better get to hunting," she said as she opened her door. "The sun will be up soon."

CHAPTER
11

Ronan's mood slipped further into darkness with each passing hour. He hoped that they'd find some malicious beastie hell-bent on death and destruction so he could kill the fucking thing and hit the release valve on his pent-up aggravation.

The invisible tether that bound his soul to Naya's gave a tug and Ronan responded, closing the distance between them until he was mere inches behind her. The town was too small. Too quiet. The sights, sounds, and scents too unfamiliar. And Naya was much too exposed for his peace of mind.

"Do you recognize any of this?"

They'd been walking for miles, tracking residual magic that Ronan couldn't see or scent, which only furthered his frustration. How could he possibly protect her from something that eluded his senses?

"What?" His mind was wandering and he needed to get his shit straight.

Naya raised her hand and swirled it around. "Is any of this familiar? Anything triggering a memory?"

"No." So far tonight they'd canvassed the area of the town proper and the residential areas that skimmed the beach. Now, facing the crescent-shaped harbor, Ronan's gaze scanned through the darkness for any potential threats. Gods, *none* of this was familiar. It was like he'd just popped out of thin air and landed chained to Naya's bed.

"The residual magic is stronger here," Naya said as they continued to walk. The sound of waves lapping at the shore helped to lull his temper. He loved the ocean. Had never lived far from it. He wondered, did Naya love the ocean, too?

"How do you know?"

Naya cut him a look, her brow furrowed.

"I can't smell it. Can't see it. How do you know it's there?"

"I can hear it, remember?" Her quick smile punched straight through his gut. "Magic sings to me."

He'd stayed away from the subject of magic over the past week, opting to keep their interactions light. But after the night that he'd taken her vein, curiosity burned through him. His kisses, his touch had awakened a power in her and he was dying to know why. "Like actual music?"

Naya negotiated a wide pool of water that gathered in a low spot on the sand while Ronan crossed in a single graceful leap. Her mouth quirked in a reluctant smile. "I wish I could do that. You move like Joaquin. Graceful and powerful."

Joaquin. The male who was supposed to be her mate? Ronan swallowed down the predatory growl that rose in his chest.

"Anyway, yes, it's like actual music. Music in my head. My ears. My soul. I can feel it pounding in my chest. And the song is always different depending on who's using it and for what."

"That's how you know when it's corrupt?"

Naya jumped to reach the wood planks of the pier above them and missed. Ronan stepped up beside her and wrapped his hands around her waist. Gods, she was so slight that his palms almost completely encircled her and she was nothing more than a feather in his grasp as he lifted her up. As she began to climb, his touch lingered. He didn't want to let her go. Didn't want to sever the physical contact that he'd yearned for over the past days. "How did the music sound when you found me?"

"Chaotic," she responded without looking at him. "Out of tune." Her voice dropped to a whisper as she said, "And then so perfect and beautiful that it brought tears to my eyes."

Ronan's chest constricted and he let out a sharp breath as though he'd been gut punched with a redwood. Gods, how he wanted her! Every minute spent with her was torture. Every new detail revealed a secret he wanted to covet. Ronan jumped up beside her, so close that her exotic forest scent enveloped him. His want of her was a physical thing, digging in with barbed claws that wouldn't let go.

Moonlight shone on the curling strands of Naya's dark hair, lending a midnight blue hue to the locks. Ronan reached out as though he had no control of his own hand and lightly threaded his fingers through its silky length. His cock stirred with his emerging lust and his fangs began to throb. Needing her and never getting to have her would kill him as surely as his blood troth to Siobhan would. The question was: Which one would end him first?

His own life be damned, Ronan knew that he'd go mad if he didn't take Naya's vein again. Didn't taste the sweetness of her mouth again . . .

Naya's body went rigid in front of him and her scent soured as her adrenaline spiked. Ronan buried his face in her wild curls and whispered close to her ear, "What is it?"

"Trouble," she responded on a slow breath. "Up ahead. Maybe two hundred yards."

Ronan's own anxiety tightened his muscles. What if what had gotten to him had gotten to Chelle first and that's why they hadn't found her yet? What if the very creature they were tracking was his own sister, corrupted by foreign magic? "Let me go first." He stepped in front of Naya, tucking her close behind him.

She let out a soft snort and pulled away. "Oh no. I don't need protection, vampire."

The hell she didn't. He'd be damned if he let her put herself in the path of danger when he was there to take the first blow. "We don't know what's out there. It's not safe for you to go charging toward an unknown like that."

This time, the sound that escaped her lips was pure incredulity. "*You* don't know what's out there. I know exactly what we're dealing with." She took off at a jog, leaving Ronan to trail behind. "Just do me a favor and stay out of my way. I can't be worrying about whether or not you're okay. Got it?"

Without waiting for a response, she cut to the right, using the tall pilings as cover. Her shadow darted through the darkness, a graceful ballet of motion that Ronan couldn't help but admire.

Magnificent.

He took off after her, careful to follow her path. It took all of the self-control he could muster not to charge out ahead of her, but Ronan let her take the lead while he covered her back in the event of an ambush.

The screech of metal on metal grated on Ronan's ears and Naya took off like a shot, sprinting toward the source of the sound. His heart rocketed up into his throat as he pulled the Glock Naya had loaned him and a dagger from his waistband while he chased after her, prepared to kill anything that might do her harm.

Even Chelle?

Ronan's step faltered, but he stayed his course. If Chelle had been lost to infectious magic, he'd deal with it when—and if—he had to. But beyond that, his number-one priority was the female running headlong into danger as though she risked her life on a daily basis.

Fifty yards ahead of him, ripping through sheets of steel as though it were tissue paper, was a creature straight out of a nightmare. At least eight feet tall, with talons like sickle blades and razor-sharp pointed teeth, the creature couldn't have been any less human. Or dhampir for that matter. Ronan had no idea what he was looking at, but he knew whatever it was, it wasn't looking to take a peaceful midnight stroll. Globs of fluorescent color dripped from its scaly black flesh, landing on the ground with a splatter as it cut a swath of destruction in its wake.

One large arm swiped out at Naya, the talons flashing bone white in the moonlight. She ducked and rolled to her left, missing the blow by inches. In a beat her gun was drawn and she fired off three successive shots that whispered through the thick ocean air, quieted by the silencer. The beast's back arched with pain and it spun, its speed belying its height and bulk. Naya drew the dagger from behind her back and its canary glow was like a beacon in the foggy night as she gained her footing and charged at the creature currently trying to take her head off.

"Naya, look out!"

Gods. She truly was going to be the death of him, wasn't she?

The creature Naya fought was no longer human. Hell, it was no longer anything. A manifestation of malicious magic, it was an incarnation of evil and destruction. A force of nature in and of itself. Globs of residual ethereal energy seeped from its skin, landing on the ground in great puddles of colorful light. The music deafened her. A cacophony of riotous sound that caused her brain to pound in her skull and her vision to blur. Even the air was thick with magic, sticking to her lungs as she breathed it in and as difficult to expel as pudding. She fought as much against the sensory overload as she did the creature intent on killing her. Her own magic rose up from the seat of her power, glowing like a cinder in her belly. Naya drew on it, allowed the power to fuel her as it traveled down her arm like a conduit and into the blade of her already-hungry dagger.

Don't worry. You're about to be fed.

"Naya, look out!"

Ronan's voice snapped out like a whip. She turned toward the sound, ducking moments before the creature's giant claw swiped down at her. *Son of a bitch.* "Ungh!" The grunt left her chest as Naya swung her arm in a wide, sweeping arch. Power rippled through her as she funneled magic through the dagger and it severed the beast's hand from its wrist. The appendage turned to charred dust and evaporated before it hit the ground. She was answered with an enraged snarl as the beast turned on her, its giant maw of a mouth opened wide and ready to bite. Her breath sawed in and out of her chest as Naya brought her gun around, aiming with her left hand as she fired off three more successive shots that did nothing to slow the creature down.

Shit.

From out of nowhere Ronan launched himself at the mapinguari, taking its massive bulk down in a full-body tackle. Punches rained down as he wrestled with it, his fangs bared and eyes alight with deadly silver. Good gods, he was magnificent. A warrior, built to deliver death.

Powerful teeth snapped at him and Ronan grabbed it by the jaw, wrenching its mouth open with a shout; His body trembled with the effort until the hinges gave way and the beast's jaw cracked.

"Get the hell out of here, Naya!"

The creature was disabled, but what Ronan didn't realize was that there was no way to deliver upon it a physical death. It took magic to banish magic, and the only one of them who had a chance of defeating the demon was her.

A riot of sound assaulted her ears, the notes too sharp, too flat, disjointed and chaotic. Her vision further blurred and an acidic tang burned on the back of her tongue. If she didn't banish the magic soon, it would steal her senses completely. She'd be blind, deaf, her limbs numb and useless. And she and Ronan would both be dead.

"Hold it down!" Her strength was no match for the thing they fought, but with Ronan helping her she could get the job done. Ronan faltered and the mapinguari hurled him from its body. He flew in a graceful arc, landing on his back with a groan that sent Naya's heart toppling over her ribs to the soles of her feet.

Gods damn it.

She emptied three more rounds into the creature's black, leathery skin, buying Ronan the time he needed to regroup.

His speed astounded her. His strength was unlike anything she'd ever witnessed. He was formidable, intimidating, and with every passing second Naya only wanted him more.

The creature's inky black tongue lashed out at him, lacerating his biceps. Ronan didn't so much as twitch as he pinned it to the ground. Every muscle in his body strained, the veins standing out on his forearms in stark relief. His brows drew sharply over his silver eyes and he ground out from between his gnashed teeth, "Now what?"

So entranced by the beauty of his movement, Naya shook herself from her reverie and sprang into action. The heat of the dagger warmed her palm. She straddled the creature's body and stabbed down, straight through the heart. She twisted the blade at the same moment she sent a burst of her own power through the blade. Fiery heat licked up her arm and Naya cried out, but she gritted her teeth against the pain and drove the dagger deeper, cutting through the thick muscle to the center of the heart. Naya drew back on her power, funneling the corrupted magic out of the creature and into the dagger.

The transference of power blew Naya away from the disintegrating body with the force of an explosion. She braced herself for the landing that was no doubt going to result in a broken bone or two. Maybe ten. Time seemed to slow as she squeezed her eyes shut. The impact never came. Instead of crashing hard to the ground, she was jostled as she landed in the cradle of Ronan's arms. What could have been a very painful touchdown was only going to result in a few bruises. She could see an advantage or two to keeping a vampire around.

Ronan held her close and tucked her against his chest. The dagger dropped from Naya's grasp, falling to the ground as it sizzled with residual magic on the damp sand below. "Jesus Christ, are you okay?" He buried his face in her hair as he breathed the words. A light tremor vibrated through him into her and a sense of fear washed over her. *His?* He pulled back to look at her, his eyes still bright silver. "You do that sort of thing on a daily basis?"

"No. Not like that." Her tongue felt too thick in her mouth and the words slurred on her lips. She'd never fought anything so fully manifested by magic. And never anything so big and powerful. Whatever magic had corrupted it was beyond anything she'd ever encountered. The dagger had taken the brunt of most of the residual malicious magic, but not all of it. Her skin crawled as though insects burrowed just beneath the surface, and a sense of perverse darkness speared through her in icy cold shards that left her shaking. She clutched at Ronan's shirt, desperate for the warmth of his body as her vision darkened and the world careened around her.

"Try not to freak out," she murmured as darkness overtook her. "But I think I'm going to pass out."

CHAPTER
12

Jenner's fangs broke the skin of the female he was fucking—he was pretty sure her name was Naomi—and she let out a low, drawn-out moan. He pounded into her from behind, his jaws locked down on her throat while his eyes were locked on the second female writhing beneath her. She thrust her hips up to meet Naomi's mouth, ecstatic bliss glazing her silver-rimmed eyes.

Since his transition, his need for blood and sex had become insatiable. When he wasn't doing his king's bidding, Jenner was buried to his balls in a female. One, two . . . five a night. He fed more than he needed to, glutting himself to the point that his brain buzzed from the high.

"Fuck her harder, Jenner."

The female's heated words spurred him on as he gripped Naomi's hips and drove deep. What in the hell was her name? Mari? Melissa? He had no fucking clue. . . . *Marissa!* Naomi buried her face between Marissa's thighs, lapping with renewed vigor. His cock swelled inside of Naomi, his need for release bordering on desperation.

With a flick of his tongue he sealed the punctures on her neck, but what he'd taken from her had yet to quench the fire in his throat. His thirst was never ending. His desires unflagging. There wasn't enough blood or pussy on the planet to satisfy him and it was a state of constant need that was slowly beginning to unravel him.

"Oh, gods, yes. Yes. Yes!" Marissa threw her head back as she came. Jenner watched with fascination, taking in the sight of her quivering limbs and the points of her nipples that further hardened with each impassioned scream that tore from her throat.

Naomi rocked back, grinding her ass into his hips, and her pussy clenched his shaft. Jenner reached over her, molding his chest to her back as he fondled her swaying breasts, pinching the nipples hard as he drove as deep as he could go. Her head pulled back from between Marissa's thighs as a slow, mewling sound escaped her lips. Marissa came up on her knees and leaned over Naomi. She scored her bottom lip with a fang before she brought her mouth to his, but it wasn't enough for Jenner. He bit down, opening two more sets of punctures, and lapped at Marissa's mouth as he continued to fuck her friend.

Just a few more strokes and he'd get there.

Naomi shuddered, her body going rigid as she came. Her pussy squeezed him tight, holding on as Jenner increased his pace. The buzz in his brain reached a fevered pitch as his sac drew up against his shaft. He broke his kiss with Marissa as a shout erupted from his chest. He pulled out as he came, striping Naomi's pert ass with jet after jet as he collapsed on top of her. Waves of sensation crested over him, and Jenner shuddered as the last of his seed coated Naomi's soft skin. The myriad voices of the Collective quieted in his mind and the need that ate away at him like acid subsided, his body worked to the point of exhaustion.

Thank the gods.

The three of them tumbled to the bed in a tangle of limbs. The sun would be up in a few hours, and Jenner knew that before he went down for the day he'd need to fuck them both again as well as take their veins. His appetites had always been intense, but never like this. He'd welcomed the chance at transition. Yearned to find the feeling of completion he'd never had as a dhampir.

If he'd known that he'd be cursed with not only empty soullessness but also hungers that could never be sated Jenner might have rethought his king's generous offer.

For long, quiet moments, they lay atop the pile of blankets, hands petting, lips searching. He was spent, his limbs heavy, though his cock hadn't seemed to have gotten the memo. The bastard stood like a fucking mast, jutting lewdly from between his thighs. Naomi—or was it Marissa?—crawled down the length of his body and settled herself between his legs. Her eyes were limpid pools of silver as she took the engorged head of his erection in her mouth, sucking deeply before releasing her hold with a pop.

The thirst that had dulled to a warm glow in his throat blazed hot and fresh. Marissa—or was it Naomi?—joined her friend as she fondled his balls and Jenner pushed his head back into the pillow, gritting his teeth at the overload of sensation. His fangs pierced his bottom lip and his thirst rose to a frenzy as he was swept up in renewed bloodlust. Despair sliced through his heart as he gave in to his passions, winding his fists in both of the females' hair. This existence was no gift.

It was surely a curse.

"Where is Ronan, Mikhail?"

For all of her hatred and disdain, Siobhan was quickly becoming a permanent fixture in his home. He'd hoped that she would lead him to Gregor, but instead she'd become obsessed with Ronan's whereabouts.

"Contrary to what you might think, I do not keep Ronan on a leash." Mikhail leaned back in his chair, elbows propped on the armrest and fingers steepled in front of him. "He's free to come and go as he pleases. He asked to take his leave and I granted his request. That is all I know."

Not exactly true, but he wasn't about to give her any more information than she needed to be privy to.

"I don't believe you."

Mikhail gave an unconcerned shrug. "I don't care what you believe, Siobhan. You have a coven full of males. Ask one of them to warm your bed." Her eyes narrowed to emerald slits, confirming Mikhail's suspicions. "He's one of the soulless now, Siobhan. Release him of whatever troth he's made. Once his soul is tethered, he'll no longer be yours no matter what promises he's made."

She remained silent. Her expression unflinching.

"You can't hide him from me forever, Mikhail."

Gods, the female was infuriating! He pinched the bridge of his nose and let out a sigh of pure frustration. "I'm not hiding him. And if you think Ronan is the sort of male who would tuck tail and run after getting himself in a situation he no longer wished to be in, then you've greatly underestimated him. Likewise, you've underestimated *me* if you think my single focus is to control those I rule to the point of taking away their free will. Cease your stubborn foolishness, Siobhan. Now. We are not enemies."

Her coven was the largest in the city and possessed the strongest dhampirs. It would be a boon to them all if they could learn to be allies. If she'd put away her prejudices and allow those under her protection to be turned if they so desired.

"Do you still wish to banish the souls of dhampirs and turn them into thirst-driven beasts?"

Dear gods. The female certainly had a flare for dramatics. "I will offer the transition to those who desire it."

"Then we *are* enemies."

Mikhail's temper crested. Blind ignorance and hubris made Siobhan a threat to everything he sought to build. He thrust himself from the chair and brought the palm of his hand down on the desktop with a resounding crack. "Your constant whining and veiled threats grate on my ears. Be gone from my sight and don't darken my door again until you've *come to your senses!*"

As his voice faded into silence, the sliding doors of the study glided open to reveal the shapely form of his mate. A half smile puckered Claire's full lips and her eyes sparked with gold fire. "Everything okay in here?"

She was unflappable. Her control never ceased to astound him. A slight tang of fear wafted from Siobhan, and Mikhail smiled. His mate was indeed formidable. "Fine, love." The sun would be rising soon and he couldn't wait to take her to bed. "Siobhan was just leaving."

"All right. I promised Vanessa that I'd take her to school this morning. I'm making pancakes. Do you want some?"

Formidable and *unique.*

Siobhan's green eyes widened and Mikhail answered her astonished expression with a smirk. Unlike any other vampire on the planet, Claire's post-transition physiology shared more traits with dhampirs than vampires. One of those being that she tolerated sunlight.

Siobhan covered her surprise well with a smug pucker of her lips. A dark brow curved in a graceful arch over her eye. "I see you let your mate keep her pet?"

Mikhail bristled at the question. Vanessa's mother was still in a coma, and though she was expected to eventually recover from the head trauma, until then the child was under his and Claire's care. The Sortiari had expressed interest in Vanessa as well, which made her a pawn in a centuries-long power struggle. There was something other-worldly about the child, though Mikhail had yet to discern what. He planned to keep her close until he did, and the fewer who knew about her the better.

"Pancakes sound delicious," he said without acknowledging Siobhan.

She rose from her chair, but her step faltered as she headed for the door. Claire leaned against the jamb, her arms folded across her chest. A pleasant, though chilling, smile graced her beautiful face as she made no move to get out of Siobhan's way.

Mikhail watched with amusement as the female squared her shoulders, her spine starch stiff as she sidled past Claire, careful not to leave her back exposed. Claire looked at him and winked, an expression that sent the blood racing in his veins as the *click-clack* of Siobhan's stiletto boots echoed on the hardwood floors. He stood still, taking in the sight of his mate until the sound of the front door closing behind her signaled Siobhan's exit.

"Perhaps I should let you conduct business with Siobhan from now on," Mikhail remarked as he approached Claire. The heady scent of her blood intoxicated him as he took her in his arms and kissed her gently on the mouth. "She's certainly more intimidated by you than she is by me."

Claire giggled and kissed him back. "Please. It won't be long before I look like I swallowed a basketball. There's *nothing* intimidating about that."

Mikhail placed his palm over her belly, his fingers splayed wide. "You're lovely," he murmured close to her ear. "And the most formidable vampire I've ever encountered."

She nuzzled his throat and the scrape of her tiny fangs against his flesh sent a thrill through Mikhail's veins. "I don't know about formidable." Her tongue flicked out, bathing him in wet heat. "But I bet I could bring at least one vampire to his knees."

A rumble of pure lust vibrated in his chest. She could indeed. "Vanessa won't be up for at least another hour. Let me take you to bed." His hand plunged under her shirt to explore her bare skin. "We'll make pancakes together afterward."

Claire stiffened in his embrace but didn't pull away. "Jenner isn't back yet." Her concern warmed Mikhail's heart. That she would be a benevolent queen he had no doubt. "I'm worried about him. The transition's been hard on him."

Mikhail shared in her worry. It was true that the transition could be difficult for some and perhaps he had not done his due diligence in educating Jenner in what he could expect in his vampiric existence. Needs, hungers, passions intensified. For some, they became harder to suppress, to *satisfy*.

And whereas control could be mastered in a short period of time, Jenner seemed to always be on the brink of his. The male had begun to seek out fights; he searched the city for slayers to kill. His need for blood was unlike anything Mikhail had ever seen, and he suspected that Jenner bedded an excess of females on a nightly basis. But his loyalty was unflagging. His focus laser precise when Mikhail needed it to be. He could find no fault in Jenner save the tenuous hold on his control. Obsessions of any kind were dangerous and more so for vampires due to the intensity of their emotions. Mikhail could only hope that a female tethered Jenner soon. If not, Mikhail worried that Jenner's appetites might overwhelm him. And a vampire with no control was a vampire who would meet a swift and violent death.

"He'll be back by sunrise." The reassurance felt hollow as Mikhail spoke the words to his mate. "In the meantime, let me take you to bed. I have need of your skin on mine before the sun rises."

Claire sighed against his throat and he felt her smile. "I can't think of a better way to spend the remainder of the night."

Neither could Mikhail.

CHAPTER
13

"Naya!"

Ronan gave her a gentle shake, but she was down for the count. An icy chill clung to her skin and her warm complexion had gone ashen. Obviously in the grips of something he didn't understand, Naya had taken the brunt of that evil demon's magic and he had no idea how long she'd be out. Jesus, he had no idea how to help her. The sun would be up in less than a half hour and he needed to get them the hell out of there and somewhere safe.

The question was, where in the hell was safe?

Her house was a good thirty minutes away and he couldn't risk being caught unprotected. Gods, he felt so helpless! Had Naya been a vampire, she could have drawn on his power—on Mikhail's and Claire's—to fortify her. Ronan could have fed her from his vein to help her regain her strength. Not knowing what she needed was a dagger to his chest.

A tingle of sensation crawled over his skin with the on-coming dawn. At the edge of the harbor, he caught sight of a stack of metal shipping containers. With her body clutched tight to his chest, Ronan raced along the beach to where they'd first laid eyes on the creature that had tried to kill them. Shreds of curled metal littered the ground, containers torn nearly in half. The odds of finding safe harbor inside one of the containers weren't good considering someone was bound to notice the destruction. Ronan had run out of time and options, however. It was either this or burn to a crisp.

In a matter of minutes Ronan would fall victim to the daytime sleep that would render him virtually unconscious. He took off at a sprint to the far end of the harbor, negotiating hunks of twisted steel that littered the pier. Ronan wound a path to the far back through the rows of containers and chose a container at the top of a stack. Surely any investigation into the vandalized containers would be focused on the ground level.

Naya hung limp in Ronan's arms as he leapt to the top of the stack. He set her down as though she were made of finely spun sugar before dangling himself over the edge. He tugged on the lock secured to the double doors and it gave way with a groan of metal. Once he managed to pull the doors wide, he flipped himself over the edge of the container and landed on his feet inside.

Large crates were stacked from floor to ceiling with only a small row down the center that Ronan's wide shoulders barely fit through. He rearranged the crates as best he could, making a nest of sorts that would accommodate them both. By the time he made it back to the roof of the container to retrieve Naya, the first orange rays of the sun sparkled over the water, breathtakingly beautiful but as pleasant as acid on his skin.

Blisters boiled to the surface of his forearms and the back of his neck as he scooped Naya up. As the sun continued its unhurried ascent, he set her down in the area he'd cleared and pulled the doors closed to secure them both inside. Inky darkness enveloped him and cooled his fevered skin. He'd be healed before the sun set, but he wasn't so sure about his mate.

Her breathing was shallow but even. She'd begun to warm and Ronan took it as a good sign. Exhaustion tugged at his limbs, urged his lids to draw down. Every movement was a slog through neck-deep mud. He settled down on the unyielding steel floor, his back braced against the wall. He adjusted Naya so that she lay cradled against him, her head resting on his chest. She was a fragile, precious thing and Ronan vowed to do everything in his power to protect her.

As the sun rose higher in the sky, his thoughts became hazy. He combed his fingers through the silky strands of her hair, allowing himself to be comforted by the motion. The tether pulled taut between them and Ronan marveled at how close he felt to this female in his arms, though he barely knew her. A fierce sense of possessiveness gripped him and Ronan held her tighter against him. Or was it fear that shook him to his foundation and sent a tremor down his spine? Fear that another male had already claimed her. Wanted her for himself. That someone else would rip her from him, severing his now-restored soul in two.

The bone-deep exhaustion of daylight stole over him and Ronan fell reluctantly toward the death-like sleep that would own him until sundown. He made one last vow as he tumbled toward unconsciousness: No male save him would ever have her. Naya belonged to *him*.

Naya nuzzled closer to the source of warmth that enveloped her. She felt protected. Safe. As though nothing in this world could harm her as long as she stayed right where she was. Never had she known contentment the likes of which she felt right now.

Idly, she rubbed her palm against the contours of a

wide chest. Muscles flexed and released beneath her fingers as she traced over the swell of one pec and over a taut nipple. Farther down, she found the ridges of stomach muscles, little dips and valleys that she explored at length. Not a single detail was hidden by the tight black T-shirt. She might as well be caressing bare skin.

Naya kept her eyes closed as she continued her exploration. Gods, she was tired. And still cold as the grave. She sensed that she'd been through hell, but her brain was too logy for a well-rounded thought. Bare skin met hers as Naya's fingers skimmed a forearm that seemed to have been sculpted from marble. She traced her way upward, the crisp hair of his arms tickling the pads of her fingers as she went. Past the bulge of one biceps to the edge of the shirtsleeve she found the wide gash that the creature had cut into his arm.

Naya's eyes flew open on a gasp. Stagnant air and inky dark welcomed her as panic welled hot and thick in her throat. Beyond the absence of sight, what rattled Naya was the absence of music. Of any sound. Her soul was as quiet as the space was dark. And why did that terrify her more than not knowing where she was, how she got there, and what damage she'd sustained in the fight?

"Ronan?"

Her voice echoed in the enclosed space. Hand shaking, she reached up until she cupped Ronan's cheek in her palm. His skin was warm. But why had his song quieted into silence?

"Ronan." She gave him a rough shake, but he didn't stir. What in the hell happened after she'd passed out?

Naya reached for her back, only to find her dagger gone. *Shit*. Okay, so she was trapped in an unknown location, unarmed, with a male whose status was unknown. Whatever magic fueled his song was dormant now, but it could reemerge at any moment and Naya had no idea if the notes would fill her soul to bursting or grate on her ears.

First things first, light.

She centered her focus, drawing on the seat of her power. Warmth bloomed in her palm and Naya brought her hand to her mouth, cupping it like it was full of water. She concentrated, willing the magic to pool in her palm. A soft golden glow gathered there and she blew lightly as though fanning tinder to flame.

A flash of bright white light sparked to life in her palm and Naya shielded her eyes against the sudden glare. Closed in on all sides and surrounded by stacks of wooden crates, she had to assume that Ronan had hidden them inside a shipping container. Which meant that they were still on the pier. But why? Hand outstretched, Naya wound her way through the maze of boxes to the set of double doors at the far end of the crate. She eased open one door, cringing at the groan of the metal hinges. A swath of late-afternoon light cut through the dark, sending a rush of adrenaline through her veins. Gods, had she seriously been unconscious for almost twenty-four hours?

Ronan had hidden them inside the crate to take shelter from the sun.

He'd protected her. Held her in his arms. He could have left her if he'd wanted, but he didn't. Naya chanced a look back to find him as still as death. The only indicator he was still alive—or was it undead when dealing with vampires?—was the fact that his chest rose and fell with his breath. Something tugged at her center as though a length of string connected them and she'd reached its limit. Perhaps she couldn't leave him any more than he could leave her.

Gods, what was *wrong* with her?

Outside, water lapped against the pilings. The sound put her at ease. It was rhythmic. Peaceful. Nothing like the deafening screech that had assaulted her ears as she'd fought the mapinguari last night. Without Ronan's help, it would have killed her.

Naya returned to his side, remembering the wound she'd felt just below his shoulder. Though her knowledge of vampires was nonexistent, she had a feeling that he should have healed quickly. All supernatural creatures did. She knelt beside him, her gaze drawn to the way the shadows played against the angles of his face, sharpening them. A rush of breath left her chest and her heart pounded as she brought her fingers up and traced the square line of his jaw, rough with stubble, and up to his forehead. She plunged into the thick locks of his hair, reveling in the silky texture as she brushed it off his forehead, down his opposite temple and back across his jaw, her gut clenched as the pad of her thumb brushed over his lower lip. As if she couldn't help herself, Naya leaned into him and brought her mouth to his. The kiss was soft; a feathering of contact, and a tingle of sensation traveled through her, settling low in her core.

You're practically molesting an unconscious male. Gods, Naya, get a grip!

She didn't want to be tied to a mate. Didn't want to be nothing more than a sock or earring—something meant to finish a pair. She wanted her own identity and the opportunity for an existence outside of her pod—her tribe—and the responsibilities that weighed her down. The world was more than a series of trails she was meant to track and police. And she was more than the magic that sang to her.

Did Ronan, like Paul, consider her to be nothing more than an object whose sole purpose was to complete a matched set?

Naya shook herself from the maudlin thoughts that weighed down her soul. Instead, she focused her attention on the unconscious vampire, snoozing the day away beside her. The gash on his arm looked pretty nasty. At least two inches wide and six or seven inches long, it had yet to scab over.

The magic that infected him lay dormant, so trying to extract it without killing him wasn't possible. She could try to heal the wound for him, though. Or, at the very least, encourage it to begin to close so that it wouldn't get infected. From her boot Naya drew a short knife. She chewed her bottom lip, worried that she'd lost her dagger during the fight. Paul would pitch a fit and Santi wouldn't be much happier. The weapon was thousands of years old. Not exactly something you could run down to the corner market to replace.

Naya sliced the steel blade across her thumb and waited for the blood to well. She murmured an incantation under her breath and willed her own magic to the surface until the crimson staining her skin shimmered with flecks of gold. Warmth radiated from the cut as she swept the pad of her thumb across the gash on Ronan's arm. This was a dangerous game she played, joining not only her blood but also her magic with his. Inescapable bonds were made in such ways, and in using her blood and magic to heal him she'd be enmeshing her life's essence with his.

He'd had her blood twice already. Did a few drops on his skin matter that much more?

Ronan's eyes came open with a flash of bright silver. Naya started as his hand whipped out with the speed of a viper's strike to take her wrist firmly in his grip. His nostrils flared with an intake of breath and his lip pulled back to reveal the razor-sharp points of his fangs. A wildness accented his features as his feral gaze lit on the blood running from the pad of her thumb down her wrist.

"What are you doing?"

Voice rough with gravel, a crease dug into the middle

of his forehead as though in pain. His jaw squared as it clamped down and he drew in several ragged breaths through his nose.

"Y-your wound." Naya swallowed down the fear that rose in her throat. Even when he was a captive, chained to her bed with no recollection of his past, she'd never seen him so on edge. His limbs shook, the intensity of his gaze burned through her, and though he held her wrist in an iron grip, he didn't hurt her. "It hasn't healed," she continued to explain. "So I thought I should heal it for you."

The crease in his forehead dug deeper and his tawny brows drew down over his eyes that never left hers as he brought her hand to his mouth. He dragged the flat of his tongue up her wrist, taking the rivulet of blood that lined her skin into his mouth.

A swirl of butterflies took flight in Naya's stomach as Ronan's eyes drifted blissfully shut. For a long moment he held her still, the only sound in the enclosed space that of their mingled breaths.

"I'm mad with want." Ronan's voice pierced the silence. Warm and rich with an undertone of pain that sliced through her. "Your blood . . . your scent . . . your very presence blinds me with lust." He brought her thumb to his mouth and Naya once again brushed the pad across his bottom lip. It shouldn't have affected her, but her own body heated as his tongue flicked out to lap at the blood.

She repeated the action, mesmerized by the erotic sight. It didn't take much to become lust-addled in the presence of such a magnificent male. Instead of waiting for him to take her blood on his tongue, Naya leaned in and licked it away herself.

It appeared that Ronan wasn't the only one struggling with impulse control. Power sparked, arcing in a current between them. A week's worth of pent-up sexual frustration exploded inside of her and Naya reached out and clawed at Ronan's shirt, desperate to strip it from his chest as she thrust her tongue into his mouth.

He released his grip on her wrist, raising his arms and breaking the kiss only for as long as it took Naya to push the T-shirt up and over his head. A faint tingle of magic feathered over her skin and a pleasant, giddy buzz settled on her brain. When it came to the vampire, common sense didn't exist. Responsibility didn't exist. Her own obligations and safety didn't exist. There was only him and her and the passion that blazed white-hot between them. Not even the unanswered questions mattered as his tongue slid against hers in a wet tangle.

She wanted to lose herself to Ronan. Give him whatever he wanted. Her blood, her body, hell, he could have her soul if he wanted that, too. Anything to keep him there with her. To have his hands, his mouth, on her. Naya straddled his lap and the length of his erection brushed against her. Gods, she wanted him inside of her. Now. "Oh, gods, Ronan." The words tumbled from her mouth totally unfiltered: "Just fuck me already—"

Her cell phone rang in her back pocket, the theme song to *Charmed,* and broke the spell of lust that had clouded Naya's brain. Luz. *Shit.* Anxiety tied her stomach into a knot as she placed a staying palm on Ronan's chest and fished her phone out. Kisses rained down on her cheek, down her throat, and over one shoulder as he pulled her shirt to the side. His fangs scraped along her tender flesh and Naya shivered, her eyes drifting shut as she answered, "What's up, Luz?"

"What's up?" her cousin repeated, incredulous. "How about no one's heard from you in twenty-four hours, the police are investigating reports of some kind of animal ripping through the harbor last night, and there's some seriously bad juju on the horizon!"

Naya reached up to rake her fingers through her hair

only to have Ronan seize it. He took her thumb—the one she'd sliced with the knife—and drew it into his mouth, sucking gently on the digit. Her pussy clenched as though the wet heat of his mouth was a hell of a lot lower on her body, and she suppressed a moan. This was not the time to realize that her sex was slick and ready for him. *But oh, gods.* His mouth felt so good, she considered hanging up on her cousin and leaving the rest to fate.

"Naya, did you hear me?" Luz sounded as if she was about to blow a gasket. Not very reassuring, considering she was usually the carefree one. "Paul's freaking out. He's sent out a search party to find you." Her voice lowered to a conspiratorial hiss. "And Santi said you've got a new *pet.*"

That dirty, rotten promise breaker. She was officially screwed.

Naya cleared her throat, though it did little to banish the thick tone of desire from her voice. "I hear you loud and clear, Luz. I'll meet you at the house in an hour."

"Less than an hour if you know what's good for you," Luz replied. "And you are *so* busted for not telling me about this first!"

The call went dead and Naya's eyes met Ronan's. They were still silver, still glistening with desire, but she knew that he'd heard every word of her conversation. "I need to get you back to my house. Now."

CHAPTER
14

Ronan welcomed the opportunity to be found by whoever could frighten Naya into a state of panic. He'd sink his fangs in the bastard's throat and rip his jugular out.

"Ronan, get your shirt on and let's go." Her voice elevated with each word, the pitch tightening. His nostrils flared as a wave of bitter citrus hit him, Naya's lovely scent soured by the spike in her emotions. "I can't find my dagger. I must have dropped it in the sand before I passed out last night. If I don't find it—"

"Naya, calm down." If she didn't slow her breathing, she was going to hyperventilate. "What are you looking for?"

"My dagger." She headed for the double doors without looking back. The sound of her racing heartbeat echoed in Ronan's ears. "It's been a tribal asset for millennia. It's a sacred weapon. If I lost it and Paul finds out he's going to kill me."

Any male who sought to do her harm would meet a bloody end before he could even try. He reached behind a stack of crates and retrieved the weapon. It unnerved him, felt wrong in his hand. It contained magic that he didn't understand, but he'd kept it safe for her. "Here. It's not lost. Try to calm down."

She let out a sigh of relief as she turned back. "Thank you." Her voice shook with the words, further igniting Ronan's ire. "I was a mess last night. I'm a mess right now. My head isn't straight and I need to get it together."

Ronan scowled. Was she trying to make excuses for what had almost happened between them? That she hadn't been in her right fucking mind? Anger welled hot and thick in his throat as he pushed himself to stand. She was his *mate*. His soul belonged to her. Whether she wanted to acknowledge it or not. And Ronan was sick and fucking tired of being treated like a mistake.

Naya tucked the dagger into the sheath at the small of her back and headed back through the maze of crates to the double doors. She peeked outside and turned. "The sun's below the horizon. Will you be okay outside?"

He didn't want or need her concern. "Let's get out of here. Wouldn't want you getting caught doing something— or someone—you're not supposed to."

It was petty. And childish. Ronan hadn't been a child for a gods-damned long time, but he couldn't help it. He hadn't come to this tiny, secretive town to find a mate. He'd wasted precious time trying to win the affection of a female who didn't want him. So she'd tethered him. So what? His priorities had been out of whack for too long. It was time to find Chelle and get his ass back to Los Angeles.

A stab of pain shot through his chest. "Kiss my ass, Ronan!"

Through their tether, Naya's hurt sliced through muscle, eviscerated bone, and settled like ice over his soul. She jumped down from the container without a thought to her own safety and Ronan swore under his breath as he rushed after her. It was at least a twenty-foot drop to the ground, gods damn it. Did she not give a shit about herself?

He caught sight of her just in time to see her hit the pier below as she let her body fall into a graceful roll. She regained her footing and took off at a sprint without even a glance back. Twilight was quickly giving way to night, and who the hell knew how many more of those creatures were hiding in the shadows waiting to tear her to pieces?

"Naya!"

Her step didn't even falter. She leapt from the pier onto the sand with a feline grace that entranced him.

"Damn it, Naya, stop!"

Ronan took off after her, careful to keep his speed to an inconspicuous pace. What he wanted to do was overtake her, tackle her to the sand, and kiss her until she quit being so damned stubborn and acknowledged that there was something between them. The female tied him into gods-damned knots. Up was down and left was right when she was near. She flipped him on his axis and Ronan couldn't even trust his own feelings, wanting to be as far from her as possible one moment and needing her like he needed blood in the next.

Fifty yards ahead, she darted between the pilings of another pier. If she thought to lose him in the shadows, she had another think coming. The predator in Ronan rose to the surface, the thrill of chasing his prey spurring him forward. Seconds later, he ducked under the pilings and, with the cover of full dark, was no longer concerned with keeping a low profile or a level head. He darted between the pilings, Naya's scent fresh in his nostrils. Her blood called to him; her soul reached out through time and space, connecting them. She could try to hide, but he would find her. He would always find her.

Any reasonable thoughts were banished from his mind

by the instinct to hunt. To capture. To take what belonged to him. An unseen force knocked Ronan's feet out from under him and he slammed to the tide-hardened sand with a grunt as the breath was knocked from his chest.

He looked up to find Naya standing over him, her dark eyes flashing with indignant fire. Ronan struck out with his hand, catching her around the ankle. He took her down with a sweep of his arm, careful to cushion her landing with his own body. A low growl of outrage threatened to escape her throat and Ronan rolled her over in a flash, settling himself between her thighs. "What's the matter, Naya?" he ground out from between clenched teeth. "Are you worried that you might be seen with me?" Her lips parted as her eyes narrowed, but she made not a sound of denial. "That you might actually have to explain my presence to someone?" The hurt that constricted Ronan's chest now was the sting of his own rejection. "The female who called you, perhaps?"

Naya clamped her jaw down tight and her chest rose and fell in a rapid rhythm with her breath. She averted her gaze, looking anywhere but directly at him. Emotion shimmered in the dark depths, and the tether that bound their souls pulled taut.

"Answer me!"

"I'm not ashamed of you; I'm trying to protect you, you idiot!" Naya's head came up off the sand, close enough to Ronan's face that their noses nearly touched. "If Paul finds out about you, he'll kill you. You need to get the hell away from me, Ronan. They're out here. Looking for me!"

A bark of laughter escaped his lips. "Do you think I give a single shit about these males you work for or what they think?"

Her sadness weighed down the air, permeated his pores. "I don't work for them, Ronan," she said with a sad laugh. "They're . . ." She took her trembling lip between her teeth as though fighting for composure. "The tribe, it's more than family. When the elders give a mandate, it's followed. Period. If they find out . . ."

"What?" he demanded.

"If they even suspect how I feel about you, they'll kill you. Hell, they might kill me as punishment for my not killing you myself."

The Sortiari's slayers hadn't managed to do the deed. Ronan welcomed anyone else to try. His voice lowered to a murmur. "And how do you feel about me, Naya?"

They'd known each other for a little over a week. Mere days. Did that matter when compared to the complexity of the eternal soul? She met his gaze with a ferocity that set his blood on fire. How could Ronan ever think to keep himself from her? If she ever thought to leave his side, he'd hunt her to the ends of the earth.

"It's like finding peace after centuries of restlessness. I don't want to want you, Ronan. I can't afford to need you. Especially now—" She looked away as though she couldn't bear to make the admission.

He guided her face back to his. "What?"

Naya's brow furrowed and she released a heavy sigh. "Especially now that I'm about to belong to someone else."

He didn't understand her world. Covens respected the mate bond. A tethering was instant. Absolute. Fighting that bond would be like denying themselves blood. It was as much a part of their nature as feeding.

"That can't happen, Naya. Not when you already belong to me as much as I belong to you." Ronan wanted to laugh at his own foolishness. Covens as a whole might have respected a tethering, but there was a female who'd do her damnedest to see his severed.

Tears glistened in her eyes and the words slipped from

her lips in a desperate whisper: "I don't want to *belong* to anyone. I don't want to feel this desperate need for you that never goes away."

To Naya, the tether was nothing more than a collar around her neck. Something that made her subservient. Dependent. How could he possibly make her understand that their tether was so much more than slavery to desire?

"Naya, belonging is more than a simple statement of ownership." Ronan had never been very articulate. He was a male of action, not words. When a problem needed fixing, he fixed it. But he had no fucking clue how to make any of this right. "If you'd let yourself truly feel what this is between us, you'd know that."

Naya didn't want to feel. She didn't want her life—or any part of her—to change. And that's what scared her the most. Because from the moment he'd tackled her in that parking lot, Naya recognized that her life would never be the same.

The green of his eyes became rimmed with brilliant silver. So beautiful. His gaze held her rapt, the intensity of it sending a tremor through her body. "It's all too much. Too soon. And we have to stop pretending that the world is on pause around us." Malicious magic ran rampant and the town was too small to keep the secret for long. Ronan's sister was still missing and he'd yet to recover his recent memories. "We're being reckless. Irresponsible." And it had to stop now.

The sand gave way beneath her and the salt air filled her lungs as she tried to center her focus. An icy chill permeated the thin cotton fabric of her shirt, but above her the heat from Ronan's body left her skin flushed.

She wanted him so badly that she hurt. And right now all Naya wanted was for that soul-deep ache to go away.

"You might think it's all too much," Ronan replied, his tone as dark and rich as cocoa. "But for me, it's not nearly enough."

Proving once again that their bond was greater than both of them, Naya ignored common sense and let Ronan give her exactly what she needed. He lowered his mouth to hers, and instead of an urgent press of lips, his kiss was a slow, sensual tease. Soft. Gentle. But no less intense, as though he wanted nothing more than to linger in the moment and taste her.

His arms caged her in and Ronan's body remained still, cradled against hers in the sand. Darkness surrounded them, plunging Naya into a state of sensory deprivation where nothing existed but the sensation of his mouth caressing hers. His tongue flicked out at the seam of her lips and Naya opened up to him and the kiss deepened. An indulgent savoring of each other that she never wanted to end.

Magic pooled at the center of Naya's being and spread through her limbs in a pleasant tingle. The familiar giddy high settled in her brain and she twined her arms around his neck as she pulled herself up to mold her body against his. She rolled her hips, grinding against his erection. Ronan shifted, placing a staying hand on her hip that he eased back down to the sand. It was obvious who was in control here, and it wasn't her.

She broke their kiss, reaching up to scrape her nails over the stubble lining his jaw. "The way I want you right now . . . like I'll die if I can't have you . . . is that how it feels to need blood?"

The quiet of her mind was interrupted by song. A beautiful, trilling melody that filled her near to bursting. Silver flashed bright in his gaze and she nuzzled Ronan's throat, licking, kissing, nipping at the tender flesh. His scent swirled around her, warm and spicy-sweet.

"Yes." Ronan's voice was strained and raw as though he barely held himself in check. "I want to *ravage* you. Glut myself on your blood. Drink from your vein while I fuck you, and doing so would only chip the surface of sating my desire for both your body and your blood."

Naya had never felt anything so visceral with any other male. Urgency reared up within her, pulling her muscles taut and sending a rush of adrenaline through her bloodstream. A low growl of resignation vibrated in Ronan's chest and her pussy clenched as he thrust his hips, rocking her against the erection that strained against his fly.

"There's power in blood, Ronan." His mouth latched onto her throat, fangs scraping the skin. Naya shuddered as his tongue flicked out, bathing her in heat. "Magic in sex. You've awakened something in me that I've never been able to channel before." He went back on his knees and his palms traced a path down over her ribs to grip the hem of her shirt. Naya raised her arms above her head as he stripped the garment from her and tossed it somewhere behind him. The cool evening air kissed her bare flesh and her nipples hardened. "That power scares me. Because I want *more*."

"Naya." Her name was a prayer on his lips, spoken with the sanctity of a vow. "Your blood is *life*. It gives me breath. Makes my heart beat." His mouth found a sensitive spot beneath her ear and her pulse jumped. "And your body . . ." He continued the exploration of her bare skin, making his way back up her torso. A quick jerk pulled one cup of her bra aside and he smothered her aching breast with his palm. "Your body is the altar at which I pray. There's no greater power than that."

Gods, the way he spoke.

Ronan continued on his track, his mouth branding her flesh as it traveled down to her shoulder, over her collarbone, and lower between her breasts. Naya arched up to meet him, and when his mouth sealed over the pearled peak of her nipple a wave of pleasure crested over her. A soft rose glow infused the darkness that surrounded them and she bit back a whimper as his tongue swirled over her nipple, teasing it to an even stiffer point before he took it between his teeth.

Heat swamped her. Desire rose like a tide and crested within her. The rose glow of magic infused her skin and Naya was filled with a sense of power so heady, she felt as though she could take on the world, single-handedly. She shimmied her hands between their bodies and with shaking fingers unfastened her pants. It took only a moment to work them down over her hips before she abandoned the effort and went to work on Ronan's slacks.

Greedy for bare skin, she couldn't free him from his zipper fast enough. Ronan stilled, little bursts of breath feathering over her breast. Naya's hand plunged past the waistband of his underwear, her fingertips teasing the silky flesh of his engorged crown. Ronan sucked in a breath that was more reminiscent of pain than pleasure as he pulled away from her. In the soft glow of magic that encased them, Naya's gaze took in the crease that dug into his forehead above the bridge of his nose. His jaw squared and the sharp cut of his cheekbones made him look as though he'd been sculpted from marble. His nostrils flared as the breath sped in his chest.

She reached for him again, but Ronan seized her wrists. He eased her back onto the sand, his grip unyielding steel as he brought her arms high above her head. Naya struggled against his grip. Not because he was hurting her, but because she couldn't bear not to touch him.

"Don't move." The dark tenor of his command stopped her in an instant. He pressed her wrists into the sand. "Let me touch you. Taste you. Let me pleasure you, Naya."

Pleasure was a two-way street in her opinion. She

didn't want to simply be on the receiving end. But Ronan's insistence stilled her. His grip relaxed and then released. For a long moment, he stared down at her. Naya's back arched toward him and he reached behind her to unhook her bra. He pulled it away and slid the straps up her arms, leaving the garment to rest where her fingers were laced together above her.

"So beautiful." Ronan kissed a path from her wrist down her arm to the swell of one breast. Chills danced across Naya's skin. The thrill of him taking her under the pier where anyone could see them excited her almost as much as his mouth on her bare flesh. A trickle of anxiety raced through her at the realization that Paul, Joaquin, and a small army of shifters were out searching for them. If Paul found her here, writhing beneath Ronan's skilled fingers, they'd both be better off dead.

He swirled his tongue over her nipple, so warm and wet, before taking it in his mouth and sucking deeply. The tips of his fangs teased her sensitized flesh, banishing any worry that might have given her pause. She'd risk Paul's wrath for these moments with Ronan.

Gladly.

CHAPTER
15

When Naya's fingers glided over the head of his cock, his veins had raced with fire and his skin felt like rice paper held too close to a flame. Siobhan's blood troth claimed ownership over his body, and the moment another female had sought to claim him he'd paid the price for the bargain he'd made.

Gods, how he wanted his mate's hands on him.

Her touch was a glimpse of heaven from the pits of hell. A pleasure he'd considered dying for. But no matter how badly Ronan wanted to give himself to her, he vowed to bide his time. He'd free himself of Siobhan come hell or high water. And nothing would stand between him and his mate.

Her skin tasted like rain.

He took one breast in his opposite hand, plucking at the erect nipple while he teased the other with his mouth. Naya arched into his touch, quiet, desperate whimpers of sound escaping her lips. The soft glow of magic painted her skin blush pink with flecks of gold. Ronan held himself in check, aware of what their passion had built in her the last time they'd been together. He'd take his time, pace himself. Allow the power to build instead of burst upon her.

The agonizing burn that held him to his oath dulled to a slightly unpleasant fever. The cool ocean air helped to relieve the discomfort and he pushed it to the back of his mind. He abandoned the generous swells of her breasts, kissing a path down her stomach. His tongue dipped into her belly button and Naya's breath hitched as her muscles tightened beneath his lips. The sound of her quick panting breaths reached his ears over the sound of water lapping at the shore. He hooked his fingers into the waistband of her pants, slowly drawing them down. Her belt was laden with weapons, and an appreciative smile settled on his lips. A warrior. She had indeed been made for him.

Naya's body twitched with impatience as he slowly undressed her, but she did as he'd bade and kept her arms stretched high above her. He freed her stretchy pants and underwear from around her ankles and the scent of her arousal hit his nostrils. Bloodlust gripped him, his cock throbbed painfully in his jeans, and pacing himself became a feat that Ronan wasn't sure he could accomplish.

Gods, he wanted to bury himself to the hilt in her slick heat. Fuck her until they were both exhausted and sated. Ronan gripped her thighs, the creamy bronze of her skin dusted with sparkling particles that seemed to live and breathe, swirling up and over his hands as he massaged the toned muscles beneath her smooth flesh.

"Your hands feel amazing. Don't stop touching me."

Ronan's female wasn't one to beg. No, the words that left her mouth in a husky murmur were a gentle command that he had no choice but to obey. Fingers splayed, he gripped her and brushed his thumbs along her inner thighs that were already slick with want. A tremor shook her and Naya's knees fell open to reveal the dusky flesh of her swollen sex.

Gods, she was perfection.

He feathered the pad of his thumb over the stiff little bud that stood out proudly from between the glistening lips. A sound of unabashed pleasure caressed his ears and Ronan circled her clit with slow precision, loving the way it made her thighs twitch with every gentle pass. She was so receptive to his touch. So *ready* for him that it drove him mad with need. He teased the short nest of curls that covered her mound, and she let out a low moan. She thrust her hips upward, writhing as though she was as desperate to receive his touch as he was to give it.

The heady scent of her arousal enveloped him and Ronan breathed deeply, holding it in his lungs. He bent to her pussy and touched his mouth to the petal-soft flesh. A contented groan rumbled in his throat at the first taste and he lapped greedily, taking her sweetness on his tongue.

"Oh, gods, Ronan!" A desperate gasp accompanied Naya's words. "That's . . . so *good*." She bucked beneath him and he gripped her hips to keep her still. With the flat of his tongue, he explored her, delving into her channel before flicking out at her clit. The contact was slow. Soft. Deliberate in his tactics, Ronan prolonged her pleasure, drawing each desperate sob from her lips with a smug sense of male satisfaction. He pleased his mate. Made her purr.

And he wouldn't stop until he made her scream.

The rosy glow that suffused her skin brightened with each pass of his tongue. Desperate to have some part of him inside of her, he teased her opening with the pad of his finger, caressing in time with each pass of his tongue.

"Oooohhh." The sound was half relief, half desperation.

He thrust his finger deeper, though he kept his pace slow and measured as he took her stiff bud into his mouth and sucked. Naya's back came off the sand and her fingers plunged into his hair, holding him against her. A sizzle of heat crawled just under his skin, but Ronan bore the pain. It was worth it to have Naya's hands on him, gripping his hair in her fists as he pleasured her.

"I'm going to come." Her sharp intake of breath urged him on and Ronan increased the pressure, circling her clit with his tongue as he thrust a second finger deep into the tight heat of her pussy. "Oh, gods, Ronan. You're going to make me come."

Bloodlust cast a haze over Ronan's mind, ripped through his throat with a savage heat. He bit down at the juncture of her thigh and pussy, sinking his fangs into the sweet, tender flesh. A scream tore from Naya's throat as she came, and Ronan continued to thrust his finger deep inside of her as her blood flowed over his tongue. He sucked deeply and a sense of power and vitality filled him near to bursting. The light that infused her skin grew brighter, shining with the intensity of the rising sun. Magic crept over his body, igniting his nerve endings like sparks of electricity. Naya continued to sob her pleasure, her nails biting into his scalp as she held him fast against her.

The ecstasy of this moment had no equal.

Ronan brought her down slowly, glutting himself on the sweet nectar of Naya's blood while he caressed the slick, swollen flesh at his fingertips. The cold burn of magic intertwined with the pain of Naya laying claim to a part of his body. And through it all, Ronan continued to feed, suckling at her thigh until his limbs grew heavy and his mind cottony.

He could lie here in the sand until the sun rose, drinking from her vein while he caressed the silken flesh of her pussy.

Naya's thighs fell away from his face and her fingers released their grasp on his hair, falling lazily to the ground at her sides. He scored his tongue on a fang and sealed the punctures on her thigh and pulled away, his gaze mapping every hill and valley of her naked body as his fingers traced a pattern through the wetness coating her inner thighs.

A goddess bathed in gilded rose petals, Naya stared upward, her breath racing in her chest. "I've never felt anything like this." She rose up on an elbow, her eyes wild and unfocused. "I have to touch you, Ronan. I want my mouth on you. I need to feel you inside of me."

Though he needed release like a bottle of champagne that had been shaken, Ronan despaired that he wouldn't find it tonight. Gods, how he craved her, longed to join their bodies as one. She reached for him and Ronan's muscles seized. He welcomed the bite of pain, wanted nothing more than to spite Siobhan by giving himself to his mate. His fang nicked his lower lip and he licked at the blood that welled there. Her silken fingertips met the ridges of his abdomen and Ronan shuddered at the lick of heat.

To hell with his troth. To hell with Siobhan. His cock throbbed and his sac ached with unspent seed. He'd take Naya. Fuck her until this hollow sense of empty desperation was filled. He shoved his pants down around his ass and his stiff cock sprang free. He took the length in his fist and toppled over his mate, probing at the warmth between her thighs that welcomed him.

A warning growl came out of the darkness. It slithered up Ronan's spine, triggering his protective instinct. In a flash of movement he snatched Naya up and tucked her behind him, his gaze locked on the set of golden eyes shining with menace not twenty feet away. A scream pierced the darkness, feline and angry. Behind him, Naya scrambled for her clothes and swore under her breath.

"Don't hurt him, Joaquin."

Her tone was much too pleading and the sound of it speared through Ronan's chest. From the shadows a jaguar approached, his black fur as dark as the night sky. A long tail swished back and forth with serpentine grace and the animal bared his teeth, issuing a feral hiss. He crouched as though preparing to spring upon Ronan and he held his arms wide, welcoming the attack. He'd be damned if his mate saw him as the weaker opponent.

But instead of the cat pouncing, Naya jumped in front of Ronan. Her eyes were still wild, her skin bearing the luminescence of magic. She turned away to face his attacker. "I said, *no.*"

Naya tried to shake off the drunken haze that still clung to her mind. She'd known better than to linger where they might be found, and yet she'd given herself to Ronan where anyone could see, wasting precious time she could have used to hide him from the members of her pod. Common sense didn't exist where he was concerned, and she found herself wanting to live only in the moment. Even now, with Joaquin's deadly gaze fixed on them, all she could think about was how badly she wanted Ronan.

Get your shit together, Naya!

Joaquin wasn't the only one ready for a fight. Behind her a warning growl erupted in Ronan's chest, and she didn't have to turn around to know that the vampire's eyes were alight with silver and his fangs bared.

"Get out of the way, Naya." Ronan's voice was almost distorted with rage, every word stilted. They were all nothing more than highly evolved animals, and stepping in front of a territorial predator probably wasn't the best idea. Still, she couldn't simply hide behind him and do nothing!

Joaquin stalked in a wide arch around them, his tail swishing back and forth, head low to the ground. His silky black ears lay flat on his head as he raised his nose to the sky. Deep wrinkles cut into the fur as he sniffed, his nose no doubt burned with the tang of magic. He eyed Naya warily and she reached back to put a staying hand on Ronan's arm. Agitation pulled her muscles taut, but she knew that it was Ronan's emotions that she sensed and not her own.

The tether?

He was angry. It soured her stomach and left a bitter taste on her tongue. But this wasn't his world. And starting a fight with Joaquin would only make matters worse. Ronan's fingers tightened over hers, a brief, possessive squeeze before he let go. *Uh-oh.* The gesture felt a hell of a lot like an apology. "Whatever you're about to do," she warned, "don't."

A song, slow and rhythmic, pounded in her chest like a round of drums. The Bororo males might not have been able to manipulate or wield magic, but that didn't mean that magic wasn't an inherent part of them. The sound grew louder, for Naya's ears alone as Joaquin shifted, leaving his animal form behind.

The shift was painless as far as she knew, like slipping out of the water. And was it wrong that for a moment Naya had wished that the transition would have left Joaquin at a disadvantage? If only to buy her and Ronan time to get the hell out of there.

"Naya." Joaquin's dark brows drew sharply over his nearly black eyes. The pain in his voice was visceral, cutting through her in a bloody swath that left her feeling much too raw. How long had he been hidden by shadows, watching? How much had he seen? Naya's cheeks warmed with shame. Had he been witness to her unabashed passion as she screamed her pleasure while Ronan buried his face between her legs?

She didn't know what to say. Where to start. Excuses were trite and Joaquin would scent any lie she tried to tell him. Likewise, one misspoken word would just as surely cut Ronan down. Honesty was the only policy in this situation. She'd deal with the consequences of her actions.

"I know I haven't checked in, but—"

"Pensé que estabas muerto!" The words left his lips in a barely restrained shout. His lip curled into a disdainful sneer as his gaze raked her from head to toe. "And I find you naked in the sand, beneath that *pinche pedazo de mierda!*"

Naya cringed. The accusation in Joaquin's tone stung. She should have called someone. Told Luz to let everyone know that she was okay. Of course they'd assumed she'd been killed; she never went out on a hunt without checking in. He was upset. Worried. And betrayed. She got that. But any aggression against Ronan would be a bad idea. Joaquin had no idea just who—or what—he was up against.

Completely unabashed by his nakedness, Joaquin paced, his narrowed gaze flitting from Naya to Ronan. He was nearly as big as Ronan, his body corded with lean muscle. Sleeker than her vampire, but no less deadly. Joaquin's nostrils flared and a muscle at his jaw ticked. The sound of drums picked up its pace in Naya's soul and it was obvious that the male held on to his control by the barest of threads. If he shifted again, he'd attack. Naya was certain of it. She had to calm him down, diffuse his temper before it exploded. Joaquin rounded on her, his body shaking with unrestrained rage, and pointed an accusing finger. *"Eres mio!"* You are *mine*.

Oh, hell no. Naya wasn't some object to be passed

around and she sure as shit wasn't going to let *anyone* treat her like one. Ronan stepped up behind Naya, close enough that the heat from his chest soaked into her back. He rested a large palm on her hip, angling her body toward his. A low warning growl erupted into a full-blown snarl. Whether or not he spoke Spanish, Naya assumed that Ronan had gotten the gist of Joaquin's tone. *Great.*

She pulled away from Ronan's possessive embrace and stalked toward Joaquin, ready to take his fool head from his shoulders. There were monsters running loose in town. Malicious magic was infecting people at an alarming rate. They didn't have time for this bullcrap. "I am *not* your property." She stabbed a finger at his wide chest. "I've spent over half of the past twenty-four hours unconscious. And if not for the male standing behind me, I would be dead." Gods, she was so tired of being kept under someone's thumb. Of being treated as though she couldn't take care of herself when she was out patrolling every night, by herself and getting shit *done*. "And what I do with *my* body is none of your business, Joaquin. If I want to fuck the entire male population of Crescent City, I will! Got it?" She gave a final stab at his chest, knocking him back a pace.

Joaquin's eyes widened, his jaw slack. "*Dioses,* Naya. What has he done to you? *Usted está brillando!*"

Oh yeah. She'd forgotten about the magic that painted her skin with a brilliant rose light. Crap. Talk about a scarlet letter. Keeping her sex life on the DL was going to be a little tough when the evidence of a mind-shattering orgasm sent a charge of magic over her skin. Joaquin shoved her none too gently to the side, snatching a long knife from a sheath at her hip, and stalked past her.

"You're dead!" he seethed at Ronan as he brought the weapon high above his head, ready to strike.

Fuck. A. Duck. This was her fault. If she hadn't given

in to her passions like some sex-starved teenager, this never would have happened. Ronan would be tucked away at her house and she'd be getting an epic ass chewing from the elders.

"Joaquin, stop it!" She turned and grabbed his arm, but he shook her off as though she were nothing more than an insubstantial fly.

Ronan didn't share in Naya's concern. His eyes glowed like moonlight and he crouched in a defensive stance, his fangs bared. Joaquin's speed was impressive as he launched his body at Ronan in a graceful arch. Impressive, but Joaquin was no match for a vampire.

Ronan caught him in midair and slammed him to the ground.

Never one to cower, Joaquin rocked on his back, kicking his legs up to propel himself upright. Sand kicked out from under his feet as he dug in, charging for Ronan with his dagger drawn. The two went down in a tangle of limbs and a cloud of sand. Their movements were nothing more than a smudge of color against a dark backdrop, leaving Naya no hope of entering the fray to break up the fight.

"Ronan, stop it!" Her plea fell on deaf ears as he landed a wicked right hook to Joaquin's face.

A flash of blue winked from Joaquin's stolen blade and Naya's stomach did a backflip as Ronan batted the weapon away. He was stronger than Joaquin. Faster. But Ronan's size and bulk of muscle made him less limber and Joaquin was able to outmaneuver him more than once. The tiny hairs on Naya's arms and the back of her neck prickled as though in warning of a coming storm. Electricity charged the air until she swore she could smell the ozone in the distance. Her eyesight blurred, and the sound of the fight faded to the back of her mind as her ears were filled with staccato notes, wild and raucous, so sharp and disjointed that goose bumps rose on her skin.

No. Gods damn it. Not now!

Malicious magic leached from Ronan's pores, covering him in a vibrant war paint. A shout of unadulterated pain shook the pier above them on its pilings as Ronan threw Joaquin from his body. Joaquin landed thirty feet away, sprawled out on the sand face-first. Fear gripped Naya, chilling the blood in her veins as Ronan went to his knees, his head clutched firmly between his hands.

Without a thought to Joaquin's well-being, she rushed to Ronan's side, collapsing beside him. The music was deafening, drowning out everything around her until she was overwhelmed and disoriented. She had to do *something*. The magic was volatile and, if left to run its course, would mutate him into a creature that Naya would have no choice but to kill. No way was that going to happen. She closed her eyes, centered her focus—

The click of a hammer engaging caused her eyes to fly open in an instant. She turned to find Joaquin standing above them, Ronan's gun drawn and pointed at his head. Joaquin was all about pilfering weapons tonight. *Bastard.* Before she could think it through, Naya drew her own gun and leveled it at Joaquin's face. "Drop it," she said, as cold as ice. "Or I'll drill a silver round straight into your brain."

CHAPTER
16

Apparently Christian wasn't the only one trying to get his hands on Gregor. If he was still in the city, like McAlister thought, the son of a bitch was certainly laying low. Christian had been tracking the berserker warlord for a little over a week and had yet to find a sign of him or any of his kinsmen anywhere in L.A. If the bastard knew what was good for him, he'd have been tucked away in the Highlands of Scotland by now, licking his wounds and devising a plan to get back in the Sortiari's good graces. As it were, he'd face a harsh punishment if Christian managed to get his hands on Gregor. The Sortiari didn't take betrayal lightly.

Christian watched the woman with interest. She was any hot-blooded male's wet dream: tall, lithe, dressed in leather and lace with a river of curling black hair and creamy porcelain skin. Her green eyes were like emeralds, sparkling in the low light of the club. Heads turned when she walked by, both male and female alike. The attention meant nothing to her. She obviously knew she was the shit. He could get behind—on top of, under, beside—a woman like her.

He kept his distance as she made the rounds. So far, she'd beat him to anyone who could be considered a potential contact, and the proprietor of this particular club happened to be a mage who kept a finger on the supernatural goings-on in the city. This was the third club she'd been to tonight, and those she spoke with treated her with a certain level of respect or even reverence. Who was she? She looked like a fucking porn star and good enough to eat. But Christian doubted it was celebrity status that elevated her in the opinions of those she interacted with. An aura of lethal power surrounded her, and he knew by the hard expression on her face that she demanded obedience.

Damn. What he wouldn't give to be brought into line by such a woman.

His skin prickled and Christian leaned back in his chair, letting the shadowed corner swallow him. The woman turned, her hawkish gaze drilling into him. Her irises flashed with silver and Christian swallowed down a groan. Not a woman. Dhampir if he had to guess. *Fuck.* So much for stealth, she'd probably been aware he was tailing her all night.

McAlister had warned Christian that the vampire king would want to see Gregor and all of his kinsmen dead. It served to reason, what with the berserkers nearly wiping out the entire vampire race. So who was she? She didn't look like the type who took orders from anyone. An assassin, maybe. Hired help so that Aristov wouldn't have to get his hands dirty. A trait all of those in power shared. Why bother when you could send someone else out to do the grunt work?

The female's gaze locked on Christian and she stood, unmoving. Those around her gave her a wide berth, and still as a statue amongst chaos, she stared as though she could see straight through him. But rather than unnerving him, Christian found the attention electrifying as a tingle raced down his spine and settled low in his balls. *Hot. Damn.* Her full lips curved into a disdainful smile as though she'd sized him up and found him to be . . . uninspiring.

Awesome.

He took a sip from his Jack and Coke and dragged his gaze away from her. It took a serious fucking physical effort. The female was a high-powered magnet and he was nothing more than a helpless hunk of metal. He kept her in the periphery of his vision, watching as she continued to chat with this person or that for a half hour or so. Christian took note of several sets of silvery gazes scattered throughout the press of people, one of them belonging to a mammoth son of a bitch sporting dual sets of fangs. Vampire. And definitely not Aristov. Looked like the orphaned king wasn't wasting any time in repopulating his race. Which meant that Christian needed to get a move on if he wanted to get his hands on Gregor before the berserker's enemies did.

Jenner tossed back his drink with a scowl. Siobhan was supposed to be leading them to Gregor, but all she'd managed to do so far was ask a few random, useless questions. Finding the berserker had taken a backseat to a more important quest: finding Ronan. *Jesus fucking Christ.*

Not only was Siobhan wasting Mikhail's time; she was also wasting Jenner's. Sunrise was a good six hours away and he didn't want to spend it following her all over the gods-damned city. His throat burned with thirst and his body ached with the need to fuck. If he didn't find a female to service him soon, he was going to crawl right out of his fucking skin. But until the would-be dhampir

queen exhausted her efforts for the evening, Jenner was
obligated to keep an eye on her.

"You're wound tight as a spring, Jenner. What's the
matter? Has soullessness got you down?"

The pain-in-the-ass female in question sauntered up to
him with feline grace, a wry smile painted on her dark
red lips. She made no secret of her disdain for vampire-
kind, and Jenner refused to take the bait.

"What do you want, Siobhan? I'm busy."

"Yes," she said with a sneer. "You certainly look it."

He wasn't in the mood to deal with her haughty bullshit
tonight. From the corner of his eye, he caught sight of a
female with short blond hair and a pert ass that was barely
concealed by the skirt that skimmed her upper thighs.
Easy access and less time wasted getting undressed. Their
eyes met and she smiled. *Promising . . .*

"How is it that Ronan has suddenly vanished into thin
air?" Her tone rang with accusation and Jenner tried hard
not to roll his eyes. The female had a one-track fucking
mind. "He's not answering his phone, and no one seems
to be very forthcoming in providing his whereabouts."

Ronan hiked an unconcerned shoulder, his gaze still
locked on the blonde at the far end of the club. "Did it
occur to you that maybe no one actually knows?"

Siobhan's eyes narrowed. "No."

The blonde's fingers flirted with the hair that brushed
the back of her neck. Her eyebrows rose in question over
brilliant blue eyes as she inclined her head toward the
back of the club where the restrooms were. An invitation?
Jenner gave a nod of his head. *Hell fucking yeah.*

"Where is he, Jenner?"

He dragged his attention back to Siobhan and let out a
sigh. "No fucking clue." That was the truth, too. He suspected that Mikhail knew, but if he did, he wasn't letting
the cat out of the bag.

Siobhan studied Jenner, her nostrils flaring almost imperceptibly as she scented the air. She'd know he spoke the truth and he hoped she'd leave him the hell alone and go back to her coven for the rest of the night. Because he had better shit to do than follow her around.

"Don't forget who pulled you out of the gutter and gave you a home, Jenner. You owe me at least some small amount of allegiance. He'll check in with you if he's at all concerned about keeping his business afloat. I want to know when he does."

It was true that Siobhan had given Jenner shelter when he'd had none. Station when he deserved none. And yes, the female had introduced him to Ronan and Jenner's relationship with the male had changed his life. But Jenner had sworn an oath to his king. No amount of past loyalty would sway him from that.

"I suspect that Ronan will call when he's damned good and ready," Jenner remarked. "Not much I can do about it, though."

"You know that I treat my friends well. But my enemies get exactly what they deserve."

If she thought idle threats would spur him into action, she was mistaken. "Everyone knows that, Siobhan."

She smiled as though it pleased her to have her reputation confirmed. "And in the interest of friendship . . ." Her gaze roamed to the back corner of the club. "There's a werewolf on the prowl. I'm not sure if he's following me or you. I just thought you should know."

Jenner thought he'd smelled wet dog. The male watched them with interest from his shadowy corner, his posture relaxed. "Thanks for the heads-up."

With their many loose ends currently dangling in the wind, it was hard telling what the werewolf might be after. The Sortiari's reemergence in the city had stirred up a hornet's nest of activity. Mikhail would want to know about it no matter who the male was tracking. Werewolves were territorial. Even more so than vampires. If a pack had moved into the city, it could have some political impact. If the male was a rogue—meaning he had no pack—it could be even worse.

Males without allegiance were dangerous no matter their creed.

"I'll keep an eye out," Jenner said. "And my ear to the ground."

"Thank you, Jenner." He had no idea if Siobhan assumed he was speaking in regard to Ronan or the werewolf, but Jenner didn't much care. And humbling herself by showing appreciation was about as transparent as a Ziploc bag. Over Siobhan's head, he watched as the blonde took off toward the back of the club. Time for him to make an exit.

"You have an escort tonight?" Siobhan rarely went out alone, and though Jenner knew she could take care of herself, he didn't want her alone in case the werewolf's intentions weren't so innocent.

"Carrig is with me." Her narrowed gaze followed Jenner's and a sly smile stretched her lips. "Have a good night."

"Go home, Siobhan." Jenner brushed past her, anxious to relieve the ache that had settled in his throat as well as between his legs. "There's no need for you to stir up any trouble tonight."

He didn't wait for a response. Instead, he let his dick lead the way as he plowed through the crowded club to get to the blonde. The door to the women's bathroom swung open and she slid inside, and Jenner picked up his pace. Gods, his throat was on fucking fire. His sac felt like someone had secured it with a drawstring and pulled it tight. The unending feeling of emptiness stole over him, filling him with a desperation that caused his heart to pound in his chest and his stomach to knot up.

Unconcerned with the crowd of females loitering in the space, he shoved past the door. He beelined for the blonde and hoisted her up on the counter, his mouth ravaging hers with a fierceness that left the tang of blood in his mouth.

The tiny skirt hiked up around her waist as she wrapped her legs around his torso and Jenner reached between them, a groan of pure relief rumbling in his chest as his palm found her slick and heated sex. He twined his fingers in the short strands of her hair, jerking her head back as he buried his fangs in her throat.

She came in an instant, her cries echoing off the tiled walls as he drank from her. *Gods damn it.* She'd be through with him before he even got started. And despite the blood that flowed over his tongue, quenching the fire in his throat, Jenner knew that it wouldn't be enough to satisfy him. It was going to be another long fucking night.

CHAPTER
17

Cold unlike anything he'd ever felt before chased through Ronan's body. Like an intricate web, the tendrils spread through his brain, his heart, even his lungs. It raced through his veins, making the burn from his blood troth seem like a dip into tropical waters by comparison. A ragged shout of unmitigated pain erupted from his throat as he fell to the ground, his back bowing to the point that he thought his spine might snap.

"If you think I'm kidding, Joaquin, make a move."

Naya's voice was a beacon in his pain-hazed mind. Her tone promised death and Ronan almost felt sorry for the poor bastard on the receiving end of her words. A force of pure energy swelled inside of Ronan and he gnashed his teeth until he felt his fangs puncture his bottom lip. Blood welled in the seam of his lips and he swore it froze in a crystalline ribbon. Gods, if whatever the hell was trapped in his body didn't release soon he was going to fucking explode.

"Ronan? Can you hear me?" She was the *only* thing he

could hear. The center of his entire gods-damned universe. "Stay calm and try to focus."

Oh, he was focusing all right. On the icy shards that were currently spearing his liver. The Collective intruded on his stream of consciousness, pulling him away from the present. A tidal wave of memories crashed over him, images flashing in super fast-forward as though he sped through time. Ronan clutched at his chest as he relived the memory of a slayer driving his silver-tipped stake through some poor vampire's heart. Bloodlust flared in Ronan's throat as he relived another's first feeding, post-transition.

"Ronan?"

Naya's voice grew quieter, more distant, and panic seized him. He thrashed his head from side to side as though it would somehow dislodge the hold of the Collective on his mind. There was no refuge for him there with the dead. His salvation was right here in the present.

With *her.*

"Siobhan." He wasn't sure if he spoke the word aloud or not. His mind spun in a dizzying haze, the voices of the Collective scratching at his psyche. "Belong. To her. I'll break the troth, Naya. Only you. Want . . . only you."

His world spiraled into darkness and he fought its seductive pull. Visions of Jenner prowling nightclubs for a fresh vein caused a pang of concern to stab through Ronan's chest, and another of Claire voicing her concerns to Mikhail. His king worried for Jenner; a vampire who couldn't master control would be a vampire with a very short life span. Mikhail worried that he would be the male to put Jenner down if he couldn't get a grip on his lusts. The world Ronan had left behind was unraveling, and the world that lay before him was a dark void that sent a jolt of unease through him.

Break free from the Collective. Leave the past where it belongs.

Ronan surfaced from the memories as though breaching an ice-covered lake. Power pulsed within him, an unnatural presence that his body fought to reject. It pooled in his gut and his stomach heaved. A riot of color filled his vision as blinding as midday. Hands, warm and soft, cupped his face and he leaned into the contact. She was the sun. A pinpoint of light in a dark, fathomless universe.

"Naya."

He gripped her upper arms in an attempt to steady his careening world. The tether that bound them gave a forceful tug and Ronan lurched forward as though it were a physical thing. A blanket of warmth covered him, banishing the bone-deep chill until he no longer felt as though he were freezing from the inside out.

Exhaustion weighed him down and Ronan toppled forward, the hard sand grating against his cheek upon impact. Gods, he could sleep for a year. Just lie there on the beach, not giving a single fuck whether the tide took him out to sea or not.

He was rolled over onto his back and his head came to rest in a nest of soft warmth. Her fingers slipped through his hair, brushing it off his forehead as she murmured words of reassurance. "You're going to be okay. Just try to relax."

Relax? Shit. Just call him Jell-O.

One lid cracked and then the other. The blinding colors were gone, thank gods, but from the corner of his eye Ronan caught the shadow of an enormous black cat pacing near the edge of the pier. Looked as though his mate's boyfriend wasn't ready to throw in the towel yet, which was fine by him, because the second Ronan was back to 100 percent he planned to pick up where they'd left off.

Fucking hell, he was sick and tired of feeling sick and tired.

"Here. Drink."

Naya pressed her wrist to Ronan's mouth. The cat laid his ears back and issued an angry hiss, but she paid him no mind. Ronan felt as though he'd been run through a meat grinder, but he mustered just enough energy to flash a superior smirk in the male's direction.

"You. Quit being so smug." Naya gave Ronan a nudge and he suppressed a grunt of pain. Yup, through the meat grinder.

He crooked his neck back until his gaze met hers. Still a little fuzzy, she appeared to be surrounded by a halo of light. "Gods, how I love a feisty female." The cat growled and Ronan reached up to take her wrist in his hand. His fangs broke through the skin and an almost imperceptible sigh slipped from Naya's lips.

The moment wasn't half as intimate as Ronan would have liked. They had an audience after all, and he never was one to share. He didn't linger at his mate's vein. It was a utilitarian feeding meant to restore his strength and nothing else. There would be time to enjoy her body while he drank from her later. Now he needed to be prepared to protect her from not only the threats running rampant through the town but also the one currently staring her down from the shadows.

Ronan sealed the punctures, swirling his tongue over Naya's flesh. He stole a glance upward to find her eyes heavily lidded, her lips parted. A rich bloom of scent perfumed the air and it stirred Ronan's lust. Odds were good that he wasn't the only one who'd noticed his mate's arousal.

He reached up and cupped her cheek in his palm. "Curb your thoughts, love. If the cat scents you, one of us is bound to kill the other before the night is out."

Naya quickly averted her gaze, focusing her attention on the jaguar that continued to pace several yards away. "He'll tell the elders about you," Naya said. The cat swished his tail back and forth as he returned her stare. "I can't keep you a secret any longer."

Ronan's temper surfaced. "I never asked you to."

Christ. That she would once again treat him as though he were some shameful thing she needed to hide away. She was his mate. *His.* Not the male who continued to watch them with his feline eyes.

"I know."

Sadness accented her features, but Ronan held fast to his anger. He shoved himself upright, his head still so gods-damned heavy it felt like a boulder atop his shoulders. Naya's gentle care of him no longer gave him comfort. Instead, it made him feel weak. Dependent. A male who thought himself more worthy of her watched as Ronan crumpled like paper at her feet, helpless against the force of magic that sought to overtake him.

"Easy, Ronan. The magic is still—"

"I don't give a fuck-all about the magic!" Ronan railed. The cat growled from where he stood watching them and Ronan rounded on the beast with bared fangs. "Bring your elders!" he shouted. "She"—he jabbed his finger at Naya—"belongs to *me!*"

A little blood went a long way when rejuvenating a vampire, it seemed. And being the blood donor hadn't exactly been a hardship for Naya, either. Embarrassment flushed her cheeks as anger burned in her stomach at Ronan's heated words. Why was he treating her so harshly? As though any of this were her fault. By rights, she should have killed him that first night. She'd spared his life. And now he was treating her kindness as though it were something reprehensible, taking the care she'd shown him and throwing it right back in her face.

She sat in the damp sand, stunned, as Ronan continued to shout at Joaquin. His eyes were fully silver, shining like the moon in an endless midnight sky. Her vampire was quick to temper. A foolish tantrum that would do nothing but coax Joaquin to violence.

As if it hadn't been humiliating *at all* for her to have the male she was supposed to be paired with notice her raging desire for the one resting in her lap. Ronan acted as though she allowed her lust to master her on purpose. As though the pleasure of his bite were something that she could turn on or off like a light switch. Gods, her entire life had gone into a fiery tailspin. She no longer had control over anything, least of all her own emotions. And Ronan threw them in her face as though they meant nothing.

She belongs to me!

His words cut deep. Once again, a male equated her with nothing more than a bauble to be put on a shelf until needed. And who in the hell was Siobhan? Naya's teeth clamped down at the thought of his incoherent ramblings. Was there another female in his life? One who perhaps thought she had a claim on *him*?

There was much Naya's vampire hadn't told her, it seemed.

As Ronan continued on his tirade, shouting at Joaquin, daring him to attack, the control that Naya exercised over the power swirling within her was held by the barest of threads. A pittance compared to what was still contained inside of Ronan, but no matter how she'd tried, she'd been unable to extract the magic from his body. Like a malicious parasite, it refused to leave its host. His volatile temper was proof enough that the darkness inside of him was growing in power. Cold dread settled on her heart at the realization that, as with every usurper she'd hunted, the only way to banish the magic would be to kill Ronan.

If she didn't, he'd become a monster.

Hours seemed to pass in the minutes they'd been under the pier. The moment Naya had threatened him, Joaquin had shifted. It was hard to tell at this point if he was planning to kill them both. Knowing the chieftain's son, Naya realized he'd try to take them both before the council. Joaquin was nothing if not a stickler for the rules. But if she didn't do something to diffuse the situation now, he wouldn't get the chance to play it by the book, because Ronan was going to kill him.

"Ronan, let's go." As much as his words stung, she didn't want to be out here, exposed, for another minute. It wouldn't be long before Santi or one of the elders showed up. They rarely went out alone in their jaguar forms. And whereas Naya had no doubt that Ronan would win in a one-on-one fight, she doubted he'd fare as well if he fought a handful of Bororo warriors.

"I'm not going anywhere," Ronan grated. He jerked his chin toward Joaquin. "I'm not afraid of him. I'm not afraid of *any* of them."

Exasperating male! "I never said you were! But this is going to get ugly fast if we don't leave. You're still volatile. I can hear it. And I'm not doing much better. We're at a disadvantage here. We need to regroup."

"*We* don't need to do anything," Ronan stressed. "I need to find my sister. I need to get rid of whatever this is inside of me. And I need to get my ass out of this backward fucking town and back to L.A. Come on!" he shouted at Joaquin. "Are you going to stand there all fucking night or are you going to fight me, you cowardly son of a bitch!"

Deafening music punished Naya's ears, so loud that she wished she could do something to soften the offending song. Ronan's fury washed over her like a winter-ocean spray and she sucked in a sharp breath at the chill that permeated her skin.

Joaquin's dark ears perked up and he took off down the beach, letting out a loud cry as he loped through the sand. *Not good.* There would be a force of Bororo descending on the beach in a matter of minutes.

"What in the hell is the matter with you?" The music of corrupt magic had begun to quiet in Ronan's body though his anger had yet to subside. "Are you out of your mind? It's like you're looking for a fight!"

"Maybe I am." Ronan rounded on her, his eyes bright with silver. "I don't need your protection, Naya, and I don't need you to fight my battles for me. I'm more than capable of taking care of myself."

"You think I'm trying to fight a battle for you?" *Seriously?* Testy vampire was testy. "I'm trying to save you! Ronan, the magic inside of you is feeding on your anger; can't you see that? You're only accelerating the process by giving in to that aggression. I'm trying to save you, damn it! Hanging around and waiting for a fight isn't going to do us a damned bit of good."

He raked his shaking fingers through his hair and let out a measured breath. Every muscle in his body rippled with tension, pulled taut and hard as granite. His chest heaved and his lip pulled back in a feral snarl revealing the wicked points of his fangs. "You are tethered to *me,* Naya. *Mine.* Any male who thinks to claim you is going to meet a violent and bloody end."

"Do. Not. Treat me like I'm a possession!" Naya snapped. "Who is Siobhan, Ronan? You seem so bent out of shape that another male would claim me as his, but the words from your own lips suggest that you might not be as free as you've let on, either."

His jaw flexed as he gnashed his teeth. "When did I speak of her?"

Naya's question seemed to drain some of the fire from Mister Intense and High-Handed's commanding tone. Tears prickled at Naya's eyes, but whether from anger or hurt she didn't know. It shouldn't matter to her if Ronan had pledged himself to someone else. It did, though. Gods, it did.

"Never mind," she said, defeated. "Let's just go. I'm weak and I need to meditate and center my energy. And I need to discharge the dark magic from my dagger."

Ronan stood immobile, a deep furrow creasing his brow.

"Please."

She could leave him here to his fate, but that's not what she wanted. As angry as Naya was with him, there was still that part of her that couldn't bear the thought of being separated from him. Long moments passed as they stood in the surf, the tide rising up to meet their feet. He let out a long ragged sigh and started toward the car.

Relief flooded her. Gods, she was so lost to him that she'd rather argue with him for the rest of the night than spend a single moment apart. There was still so much between them that needed to be settled. So much about him that she didn't know. She just hoped that she'd get the chance before the magic that influenced him took what was left of the male who claimed to be her mate.

CHAPTER
18

Ronan slammed the door with enough force to take it off the hinges, stalking through Naya's living room as though he had someplace to go. *Gods.* He had nowhere to go. No idea how to find Chelle so he could get out of this miserable place. Away from *her*. The tether that bound them pulled taut and Ronan wished he could take a blade to it. Sever it. Free himself from the inescapable *want* that was slowly eating him alive.

The rational side of him knew that she didn't understand. She wasn't a vampire. Naya didn't feel the tether in the same way that he felt it. But the irrational side of him didn't give a fuck-all about that. She'd given her body to him. Her blood. And when push came to shove, she'd tried to get him to run and hide like he was some sort of fucking coward. As though he were in the wrong for laying claim to what was rightfully his.

She was *his* mate!

The past twenty-four hours had passed in a flurry of emotion and Ronan's world refused to stop spinning. Neither of their tempers had cooled on the drive back to

Naya's house, and if anything, they were simply looking for reasons to perpetuate a fight. Was that better than the alternative? Of Ronan coming clean with her and admitting that he'd trothed his body to another female and sealed the bargain with blood? *Christ.* How could he have been so stupid as to ramble on about Siobhan while his mate offered her vein to replenish what the damned foreign magic had stolen from him? Magic that turned people into demons, no less.

That creature could have killed her. Would have had she been out hunting alone. The energy she had expended to kill the thing had dropped her unconscious onto the sand. She would have lain there until someone had the good sense to look for her or another creature came to finish her off. How could her own people risk her life so callously? Ronan might have been angry with her. He might have wanted to shake some sense into her. But ultimately he wanted nothing more than to protect her. To keep his mate safe from harm, and that included her own kin.

"I want an audience with your chieftain." Ronan kept his voice to below a shout, but barely. "You're all living in a bubble, Naya, and it's about to burst." If the Sortiari got wind of the goings-on in Crescent City, it would only be a matter of time before they intervened. Those bastards didn't take prisoners. They wiped out entire species. The Bororo might have wanted the world to think they were gone, but the Sortiari would make it a reality if it fit into their agenda. "There is no way—*none*—that you can fight whatever this is on your own."

"That's not the way this works, Ronan." Naya's curt tone wasn't doing anything for his escalating temper. "You can't just show up out of nowhere and demand that your voice be heard. You're not in the position to change something that hasn't changed in centuries."

"For fuck's sake, Naya! Have you ever considered that your inability to join the twenty-first century is part of the problem?" It happened with supernatural creatures. Hell, Mikhail was still having trouble adjusting to the modern world. "You're being manipulated by your own people and you're too damned blind to see it!"

Naya's jaw took a stubborn set and she palmed the dagger sheathed at her side. Ronan wouldn't put it past her to use it if she got angry enough. His anger flared that she would treat her own life and safety so carelessly. If he hadn't been on that pier last night, that monster would have killed her. And she was more than ready to run right back out there and single-handedly take on more of the bastards because a roomful of antiquated bastards said so!

"You have no right to say that! And what I choose to do—what's my *responsibility* to do—is none of your gods-damned business."

Her dark eyes sparked with indignation and her chest heaved with her breath. Ronan took a moment to admire her fierce beauty before he shot back, "You. Are. *Mine!*"

Her expression fell into blank indifference with the words, a calm before the storm. Gods, he hadn't intended to say it yet again. Didn't even want to admit it to himself. He wanted nothing more than to find Chelle and put this miserable place behind him. So why did the thought of Naya belonging to another male send him into such a jealous rage that he had no choice but to assert his ownership of her? Talk about living in an antiquated past. He was such a hypocrite.

"I *will* protect you, Naya." It seemed that Ronan couldn't keep from running off at the mouth. "I won't stand by while you go out into the night and hunt something that you have no chance of defeating. And likewise, I won't allow you to be punished by a council of blind fools who are not even male enough to go out and hunt this evil by your side."

Naya snorted, her eyes wide with disbelief. "Buddy, I was out doing this—on my own—way before I met you. I can hold my own. You don't know anything about me. What I'm capable of. And I won't sit here and listen to you not only insult my abilities but undermine them."

It was true. He knew virtually nothing about her and it rankled. Had she been dhampir, he would have turned her. Had she been a vampire, they would share a history of knowledge of their kind through the Collective. She was neither of those things, though, and it was stupid to keep falling back on it as an excuse. They were tethered. Ronan's soul knew hers. That should have been all that mattered.

But gods damn it, it wasn't good enough.

"You could have died!" he railed.

"And if I can't stop whatever this is, and find the source of the magic that's causing it, you're going to die as well!" Silence followed on the heels of Naya's emphatic words. Her eyes met his, shining with unspoken emotion. She let out a slow sigh and her voice became soft and sad. "There's something inside of you, Ronan, and I don't know how to banish it. It might be dormant now, but it won't be for long. And when it truly wakes, it won't stop until it's clawed its way out. Paul, Joaquin, they'll kill you if I don't. How can you possibly expect me to sit by and not do something—anything—to protect you just like you want to protect me?"

Her worry echoed his own. At least they were on the same page about one thing. He'd felt that force within him tonight. Clawing, scratching, expanding inside of him, and anxious to be let loose. If that happened, what then? Would he turn into a monster as well? Kill his mate? Despair choked the air from his lungs and Ronan crossed the sparse living room to where Naya had collapsed onto the couch.

"If that happens," he said, his gaze unwavering, "*you* kill me."

He'd rather die than see any harm come to her. Especially at his own hand.

She let out a soft snort. "If you think I could possibly do that, you're kidding yourself, Ronan. I can't even make myself leave the room when you're in it."

Ronan sat down beside her and let his head fall back on the cushion. He stared up at the pattern of plaster on the ceiling. The sun would be up soon and he'd be forced to sleep while Naya faced the firing squad over everything that went down tonight. Gods, he'd waited so long to become a vampire, and now he felt nothing but disdain for the weakness that would keep him from her until the sun set once again.

"Why don't you like to be restrained?"

The question came out of nowhere and Ronan brought his head up to look at her.

"That first night, when you offered to let me handcuff you, I could tell that it made you uncomfortable. Your body went rigid when I secured the cuffs. Was it the silver?"

She studied him as though she wished she could climb into his head for the answer. For a moment Ronan took in the sight of her: her soft bronze skin, lush, full lips, and eyes that were as deep and fathomless as the night. Dark, wild curls framed her face and Ronan reached out, unable to stop himself as he took the strands between his thumb and forefinger, stroking the silky length.

"I was a warrior," he said, low. "I fought for a vampire lord against the Sortiari when they waged war on the vampire race over three hundred years ago." Naya's expression softened and Ronan gave her a rueful smile. "I had yet to be turned and the slayers were killing off vampires at an alarming rate. We were losing. And there were those vampires in the aristocracy who chose to hide rather than fight. To send detachments of dhampirs into battle while they fled for safety. I'd sworn a blood oath to a lord who promised to turn me and many others. Instead, he took us as slaves." Ronan took a deep breath, raked his fingers through his hair. "I was trained to fight. To show no mercy."

"He sent you out to die?" Naya's wide eyes shone with emotion.

"I don't think that was his intention. I think he hoped we'd beat down the berserker warlords that the Sortiari sent. Not all vampires were honorable," he said. "Nor are all dhampirs. But they were afraid. And they were dying at the Sortiari's hand. I suppose my lord did what he thought he had to do. When we weren't fighting, we were kept like dogs in the bottom of the keep. My sister refused to leave me there. She attended to our lord's mate. A gentle female who spent most of her nights sobbing in fear of her impending death."

"Gods," Naya breathed. "That's awful."

Ronan supposed there were worse fates. "I was good at war," he said with a shrug. "But I was equally willful and worried for Chelle. My temper got the best of me more times than not, and when I wasn't fighting I was chained."

Naya reached out and smoothed her fingers over his wrists. "I never should have cuffed you. Ronan, I'm so sorry."

"You couldn't have known." All of his previous anger and agitation melted under her gentle touch. "It was a price I would have paid a thousand times over. Worth my soul. Worth *you*."

Naya's lips parted and she looked away, but Ronan heard the way her heart raced at his words.

"They were turbulent times, and in the chaos Chelle

and I managed to escape. We sought out a coven that had hidden itself deep in the forests and far from battle. The Sortiari continued to wage their war against the vampires and it wasn't long before they were gone. Wiped from the earth. I could never be turned. I resigned myself to my fate. But there were rumors. And so I left Chelle in the care of our coven and set off to find any vampire that might have survived."

"I wondered," Naya said. "I'd never seen a vampire until the night you tackled me. I thought you were all dead."

"I searched for Mikhail for almost a century. I found him in Russia. Starved. Weak. Feral." Ronan gave a rueful laugh. "It's a wonder he didn't kill me."

"Paul steers clear of the Sortiari," Naya remarked. "He calls them *reyes de las tineblas.*"

Ronan quirked a brow.

"The kings of darkness."

Ronan snorted. "Fitting." He wondered what sort of history the chieftain had with the guardians of Fate. "What do you know about them?"

"Not much," she replied. "Just that they're bad news. We follow *El Sendero* and don't bother with what the rest of the world is doing."

"The Path?"

Naya pursed her lips and cut him a look. "Very good, vampire. *Caminos de la magia* are roads of ethereal energy that stretch across the earth." Ronan lost himself in the smooth timbre of her voice. When Naya spoke, he swore he could feel the power that thrummed around her. "We police it. Magic. My grandma used to say that it was a gift given to us by the gods. But more and more, I only see it as a curse."

Naya had never spoken so openly with anyone. Ever. Not Santi or even Luz knew how Naya felt about her lot in life.

But being with Ronan filled her with a sense of peace and comfort. Trust. Even though they'd fought, she didn't worry about laying herself bare to him. Deep down, she sensed that he could see everything she sought to hide anyway.

"Paul keeps a tight rein on our pod."

"Pod?"

"You know. It's the Bororo equivalent of a . . ." Naya swirled her hand around as she tried to find the right word. " 'Pack.' "

Ronan quirked a brow. "Vampires don't live in packs. We live in covens."

She pursed her lips. "Potato, potahto. You know what I mean."

He continued to fiddle with her hair, his gaze pinned to it as he ran the strands through his fingers. Naya suppressed a pleasant shudder. Something so simple shouldn't have felt so good. "There are other Bororo pods?" The sound of his voice lulled her, low and warm.

"A few." She leaned into his touch, angling her body until her shoulder rested against his. She wanted to lay her cheek against his chest, but she held herself in check. She couldn't afford to lose herself to him again. His pull was too strong, too absolute. And until she knew more about this Siobhan and what she was to Ronan, Naya had to guard her heart as best she could. "Smaller pods are less conspicuous. The size of the pod depends on the size of our location. Crescent City is a tiny town, so our pod is relatively small in comparison to some of the others."

The pads of his fingers caressed the shell of her ear. A rush of liquid warmth suffused her and settled in a soft thrum between her legs. It seemed even innocent touches from the vampire made her ache with desire. "Are you the only hunter?"

Pride swelled in Naya's chest. That he would acknowledge her in such a way was more than even Paul could do. He called her tracker. Or *bruja*. But she wasn't worthy of the title hunter as far as the elders were concerned. "I am. Each pod only has one at a time. Though there is always an apprentice. My cousin Luz is mine."

"How does an apprentice move up in the ranks?"

Ronan's interest in Naya's life—and *who* she was—warmed her heart. He was genuinely curious, not simply placating her. The tightness that had pulled her entire body taut for the past few days loosened and something rose up inside of her as though an empty pocket of her soul had been filled. Beside her, Ronan's eyes drifted shut and an enigmatic smile settled on his full lips.

"An apprentice moves up when the pod's *bruja* either dies or becomes mated."

"Hmmm." Ronan didn't open his eyes. "They plan to put you out to pasture, then?"

Naya laughed. As though her head acted of its own volition, she laid it on Ronan's shoulder. Her palm found his thigh and he captured her hand in his, twining their fingers together. Naya marveled at how natural it felt to settle her body against his. To allow the strength of his body to support her. This was dangerous. She couldn't afford to feel anything for him.

"More or less," Naya responded with a sigh. Ronan's thumb traced a lazy pattern over her finger as she tucked in closer to his chest. "I just don't understand the rush. Luz isn't even close to being ready to take over and it's not like I've been botching up any of the repossessions I've done lately. If I had to guess, I'd say that Paul's nervous about the fact that I've tried to put some distance between my life and the pod's tight-knit circle. He probably thinks that mating me to Joaquin will bring me back into the fold."

"Why bring you in at all?" With his free hand Ronan

guided her chin up until their gazes met. "Why not let you leave to live your life as you wish?"

Naya gave him a sad smile. "There are few Bororo females who can hear the music of *magia* anymore. Paul needs me to stay. To make babies with Joaquin. Girls with the ears to track and take the magic that's been stolen or loosed upon the world."

A territorial growl built in Ronan's chest. "If he thinks to keep you like a common brood mare, he'll find your current mate to be an obstacle in seeing his ambitions to fruition."

Jealousy flashed hot in Naya's chest, followed by a rush of fierce protectiveness that left her muscles aching with the need to fight. By her physical reaction, the emotions gripping her might as well have belonged to her, but she knew that Ronan's emotions swirled in a violent whirlwind inside of her.

The tether?

"So . . ." Control seemed nonexistent when it came to Ronan. The urge to get closer—and with a hell of a lot less clothes on—consumed her. Naya's mind wandered to the incredible high she felt when he touched her. The magic and power that it evoked in her. If she didn't keep their conversation rolling, she'd be naked and begging him to do wonderful and delicious things to her before another minute passed. "Are you allowed to live your life the way you want, Ronan? When you're not busy losing your memory or searching for missing sisters?"

His lips twitched in a reluctant half smile. All she could think about was kissing the corner of his mouth, coaxing him to kiss her back. Gods, she was *hopeless*! A slave to her own desires. Weak.

"I own a firm that specializes in fixing problems for anyone with enough money to buy a solution," he replied.

"Mostly celebrities. And I only have one sister. Chelle is my twin, actually."

Naya kept her attention focused on their joined hands and how his much larger one swallowed hers. A problem solver. She had a feeling that Ronan's business dealings ventured just left of what was legal. "Do you look alike?"

"I suppose. Though since my transition there are differences that weren't there before."

"I've never seen a dhampir, either. There must not be many of them."

"There are a few covens peppered up and down the coast," Ronan said. "But most of them live as close to Mikhail as possible."

"A mandate?"

Ronan chuckled. "A necessity."

Naya was struck with a sense of rightness as she sat and talked with Ronan, exchanging bits and pieces of their lives. That rightness was also dangerous. If she let her guard down, she'd allow Ronan to wiggle his way into not only her life but also her heart. There was no room for him within the Bororo, and likewise, Paul would never, *ever* let her go.

"Why a necessity?" A sense of grief overtook her, weighing down Naya's heart.

Ronan's brow furrowed as though he felt it, too. "We're all interconnected," he replied. His voice twined around her and Naya angled her face up so she could look into his eyes. "We draw strength from each other."

"Has it weakened you to be away from your coven?" What was Ronan's family like? Did they manage him with a choke hold the way Paul did with her?

"No." Ronan leaned in until his lips hovered over hers. Naya's breath hitched and her heart raced in her chest. "I have you now." He touched his mouth to hers, the barest of contact. "My mate and our tether give me strength."

The kiss was soft. Slow. A tantalizing tease that awakened her want of him. His tongue met hers in a silky glide. She sighed into his mouth and their breaths became one. How could she possibly agree to Paul's arranged pairing when in her heart of hearts she already knew that she belonged to the male cradling her in his arms?

Magic trickled over her skin like warm, tropical rain. Ronan's palm cupped the back of her neck. He deepened the kiss as he eased her back, stretching her out on the couch. As he settled himself between her thighs, Naya thrust her hips up to meet the hard length of his erection concealed by his pants. Gods, she needed him naked, his bare skin on hers.

"Naya!" A palm pounded on her front door with all the subtlety of a jackhammer. "Naya, I know you're in there!"

Luz. *Shit.*

Ronan pulled reluctantly away, a half smile pulling at his lips. "Your secret lair doesn't appear to be so secret, you know."

"Tell me about it." Between Santi and Luz coming and going as they pleased, Naya figured it was time to move. Of course, in a town of around ten thousand people no "secret lair" was going to stay secret for long. She disentangled herself from Ronan and crossed to the front door, throwing it open. "You know, Luz—"

"Oh. My. Gods." Luz waltzed in past her and stared at Ronan, mouth agape. "It's true!" Luz looked at Naya with wide, excited eyes and gave her a nudge. "You *do* have a new pet!"

Ronan smiled with amusement, but Naya was ready to get her cousin out the door. Butterflies swirled in Naya's stomach. If Santi hadn't already told Luz about her houseguest, she would have heard it from Joaquin. Which meant that by now Paul and the elders knew about Ronan as well. "Luz, this isn't a good time." Naya's attention wandered back to Ronan. His pupils were rimmed with silver and his gaze was hungry. Gods, he flipped her world on its axis. She couldn't think straight when he looked at her like that.

Luz snorted. "I bet not. But my party crashing is the least of your worries." She jerked her chin in Ronan's direction. "Paul's furious. He's put a bounty on the vampire's head. One hundred pieces of gold for his fangs."

Ronan's amusement dimmed as he arched a brow. "Just one hundred pieces? Surely I'm worth more than that."

How could he be so cavalier? Icy shards of dread speared Naya's chest. If the parasitic magic didn't kill Ronan, then Paul would certainly get the job done. And she was powerless to stop any of it.

CHAPTER
19

Luz was quite a spitfire. She resembled her cousin in many ways, but she lacked Naya's maturity and self-control. Not to mention any sort of a mental filter. Luz flipped the length of her dark curly hair behind one shoulder. Her lips pursed in concentration and she cocked a hip as she studied him. Shorter than Naya by four or five inches, she gave the appearance of a petulant teenager, not a powerful witch who hunted down demons.

"So . . . Is the size of a vampire's fangs in direct proportion to the size of his, uh . . ." She flashed him a mischievous smile. "You know."

Ronan laughed and Naya cut him a look.

"Luz." Naya didn't sound as amused. "Get a grip."

"What? When am I ever going to get the chance to ask again?"

"We've got to get you out of town." Naya ignored her cousin's antics in favor of her worry. The smell of it tainted her usually sweet scent and Ronan wrinkled his nose. A wave of anxiety vibrated through him—hers.

"I'm not going anywhere until I find Chelle." That was only half of it, though. Finding Chelle was definitely a priority, but Ronan wasn't leaving Crescent City. Not without Naya.

"Ronan." Naya threw up her hands in frustration. She paced through the sparsely furnished living room while Luz hoisted herself up on the bar countertop that separated the kitchen from the dining area. "Paul put a price on your head. And not just money. *Gold.*"

"And . . . ?" Ronan didn't give a fuck-all about the bounty. He'd take on anyone who thought they could kill him.

"Gold is big mojo, bloodsucker." Luz swung her legs back and forth, making her seem younger. "It's the only precious metal that can safely hold residual magic."

"Bororo gold isn't like regular gold, I take it?"

"Nope."

Naya shot a glare Luz's way, but the younger girl seemed not to notice. "For non–magic wielders, it's like getting one hundred wishes from a genie. Naya and I can conjure up what we need with our own power. We don't need Paul's gold or his wishes. But everyone else . . ."

"Will be more than ready to put a stake through your heart for the opportunity to get their hands on the gold." Naya's dark gaze met his and another wave of anxiety caused his chest to tighten.

"You can conjure up *anything*?" Ronan fixed her with a stern eye and cocked a brow. Apparently his mate had been holding out on him.

"Luz is overexaggerating."

As though she couldn't wait for the opportunity to show off, the younger woman closed her eyes and opened her palm. Naya gave a derisive snort as quiet settled on the room. A lavender glow pooled in Luz's hand. "It's raw." She slowly opened her eyes. "But with the right intent and maybe an extra ingredient or two, I can make it do almost anything I want it to."

"Stop it, Luz," Naya groused. "You're an apprentice for a reason, so stop being so cocky."

The barb bit deep and Luz shot back, "Not for long. You're being retired, remember?"

They stared each other down for an uncomfortable moment before Naya resumed her pacing. "You can take my car, Ronan. I'll look for Chelle. You need to get back to L.A. before Paul—"

"I'm not leaving, Naya." That she expected him to tuck tail and flee grated. "Not until *all* of my loose ends here are tied up."

"Paul is sending out hunting parties to take you out, Ronan!"

Her exasperated tone and the sour scent of her fear ignited his temper. "Do you think I'm afraid?" he railed. "Let them come after me!"

He was fucking sick and tired of hiding. The gap in his memory was yet to be filled and he had no idea where to find Chelle. Hell, for all he knew, Naya had killed his sister on the pier last night. Sorrow crested over him. A feeling of helplessness that had no end. The key to finding her was lost with his memory. He had no doubt. And he'd be damned if he'd let a few closed-minded, self-righteous shifters get between him and *anyone* he held dear.

"Is it me, or did the temperature in here drop by about thirty degrees?" Luz rubbed at her arms and her comment wasn't simply an attempt at levity.

Power rose to the surface of Ronan's skin. The magic that attacked him like a parasite thrived on negative emotions.

"Ronan?"

He crossed the room and seized Naya roughly against

him, bringing his mouth to hers. She melted in his embrace, her lips soft and warm, yielding to him. Her fingers threaded through his hair, her touch soft and reassuring. The cold that blanketed his skin abated until all that remained was a pleasant glow that left his limbs heavy with content.

"See." Luz snickered under her breath. "A Bororo *bruja* can do *anything*. Even tame a raging vampire. Big mojo."

Prying himself from Naya was a greater feat than he'd anticipated. But the physical contact had managed to calm his temper and sent the magic back to whatever dark place it hid inside of him. Luz studied him, her dark eyes shrewd and missing nothing.

Her gaze didn't leave Ronan's as she said to Naya, "You're in some deep shit, *chica*."

Naya tried to pull away, but Ronan kept his hold on her. He brought her back tight against his chest and settled his hand at her hip. "Do you trust her?" Ronan trusted fewer than a handful of people. Inherent power or not, he didn't trust Naya's cousin not to collect on the bounty herself.

Naya remained rigid in his embrace. "I trust her. Luz, there's something going on here and it goes way past what we've been entrusted to take care of."

"You fucking think so?" Luz hopped down from the counter, giving Ronan a wide berth as she headed for the living room. "You heard that, right, Naya? *Mis dioses! La musica es muerte.*"

"No." Naya's word cut through her cousin's panic. "It's volatile, but I can control it."

Luz's disbelieving laughter echoed off the bare walls. "Control it? Pretty ballsy coming from someone who just took me to task for being cocky. You heard what I heard. There's no controlling that *magia*. It's *oscuro*. It'll kill you if you try to control it. I think we both know there's only one way to get rid of it."

A ripple of fear trickled through the tether that bound him to Naya and soured the air. "That's not going to happen, Luz."

Her eyes went wide with disbelief and Ronan stayed rooted to his spot on the carpet, his arms wrapped around his mate. He tried to put her at ease as best he could and pushed calm emotion through their bond. Calm that he didn't necessarily feel.

"Fine." Her jaw took a stubborn set, making Luz look more like Naya's twin than her cousin. "Sorry, tall, dark, and vampy. No hard feelings, but I don't have a problem with killing you before the mapinguari takes you."

Luz drew a citrine dagger from behind her, almost identical to the one Naya carried. She jumped into action and Naya shouted, "No, Luz! He's my . . . my mate."

On the one hand, Ronan's heart soared with her admission. On the other hand, Luz looked as though her head might launch right off her shoulders.

"Unless you're thinking about starting a polygamist cult out in the forest somewhere, you'd better rethink that statement. Because if Paul finds out you're saying crazy shit like that, he's gonna have your ass."

"Luz—"

"Don't even start with me, bloodsucker." She pointed her dagger at his face. It glowed an angry yellow as though echoing her emotions. "I don't know what you've told her, but you need to quit with the crazy talk. Wait—" Luz looked at Naya, horrified. "You didn't actually let him sink his fangs into you, did you?"

Naya's silence sparked Ronan's ire. Was it so shameful to admit that she'd given him her vein? A string of angry Spanish followed, and Naya volleyed back, breaking away from Ronan's hold as she rounded on her cousin. Luz brandished the dagger for emphasis, pointing it at his face as she continued to shout. The sun would be up soon.

Another night wasted. Another day spent in useless unconsciousness.

Another twenty-four hours living with this damned dark force inside of him, slowly trying to claw its way out.

"That's enough!"

Having grown up with a sister, he knew that this fight between them wouldn't end until someone drew blood, and Ronan wasn't interested in playing referee. The two stopped immediately and turned. Naya looked annoyed while Luz flashed an amused grin.

"Don't get your fangs twisted, vamp-a-licious. This is *familia* business. *Prendé?*"

"Oh, I understand," Ronan replied. "And since your argument is with *my* mate, and about *our* current situation, I think that your business includes me. *Prendé?*"

No one outside of the elders ever put Luz in her place. Ronan not only took her snarky comments in stride, but also had managed to shut her up with a few terse words. Impressive.

"It has to feed, Naya." Just because Ronan had shut her down didn't mean she wasn't going to keep running off at the mouth. "And once it's consumed him, it'll move on to the next host. We have to banish it. Now. Before it gets any stronger."

"Don't you think I know that, Luz?" A chill snaked over Naya's skin and she instinctually reached for Ronan, twining her fingers with his as though it was the most natural action in the world. As long as they touched, she could keep him calm. Calm kept the magic dormant. "But he doesn't have to die. No one else needs to die. I just need to sort it out, find a way to beat it at its own game."

"Magic isn't sentient, Naya." She was getting pretty tired of Luz treating her as though she needed to be schooled on the nature of magic. "It doesn't think. It doesn't feel. You can't outwit it. It's like fire. It consumes and it destroys if it's not properly contained."

True. "Luz, go home."

"Oh no. No freaking way, Cuz." Luz shook her head with so much emphasis it was a wonder it was still connected to her neck. "Town is crawling with little black kitty cats out looking for you and your boy toy."

Naya's spluttering laughter escaped despite her attempt to remain stoic. "Exactly. I need someone to run interference. If you disappear, Paul and Joaquin will turn to Santi. He'll cave like a Las Vegas casino on demolition day. No one can know about this place, Luz."

"Santi's game is tight. No way is he going to rat you out. You have a plan. I can see it in your eyes. Knowing you, it's risky and not a little dangerous. And you're on crack if you think I'm going to let you do anything on your own."

Ronan's grip tightened around her fingers. *Ouch.* "She regularly harbors a blatant disregard for safety, does she?"

"Oh," Luz scoffed. "You have no idea."

"Really?"

By Ronan's stuffy response, Naya sensed that putting her life on the line in the name of protecting innocent people from dangerous malevolent magic didn't fill him with pride and joy.

"I'm always safe," Naya interjected. Even at her most reckless, she followed protocol. "And stop trying to change the subject. All I need is for you to keep Paul and Joaquin off my back at least for a couple of days."

"A couple of days?" If Luz's eyes bulged any bigger, they'd fall right out of her head. "I'll be lucky if I can keep them off your back for a couple of minutes. We don't live in a metropolis, Naya. We're talking a few thousand people. The fact that Paul doesn't know about this house is a damned miracle."

Not if you considered the fact that Naya had cast a concealment charm over the place. "He's not going to find me here. But if you go off the grid, too, it's going to throw up a red flag. He sent you after me, didn't he?"

"Yeah, but he also sent ninety percent of the pod after you, too."

"I'm not leaving. Use Santi to throw him off." Luz pulled her cell from her pocket. "Better yet, I'll take care of it."

Before Naya could stop it, Luz was jabbering away to Santi. Ronan stiffened beside Naya and she turned to face him. Luz's presence was a buffer. Naya didn't have to worry about throwing herself at him when her cousin was there to run interference. And what did that say about her that she actually needed a chaperone to keep her from attacking Ronan like an Atkins dieter in a room full of chocolate cake?

"We need to talk."

His severe expression caused tiny butterflies to swirl in her stomach and she had a feeling she was in for an ass chewing. And really? What gave him the right? She'd been a tracker and hunter for decades. Had been taking care of herself from the time she was a girl. The Bororo life wasn't an easy one by any means and her responsibilities within the pod didn't leave room for weakness. She was capable, damn it! Strong. She didn't need a male to worry or fuss over her.

She left Luz to her conversation with Santi and followed Ronan into her bedroom. She opened her mouth, more than ready to lay into him, when he grabbed her by the arms and hauled her against his wide chest. His lips brushed hers, a soft, open kiss that drew a contented sigh from her. So much for putting the vampire in his place.

"The sun is about to rise," he murmured against her

mouth. "And I want to taste your mouth before I'm forced to sleep."

The words, spoken with so much heat, made her melt in his embrace. She kissed him again, a glancing of lip to lip. "I thought you were angry with me."

"Oh, make no mistake." He ventured down, crossing her jawline and dipping to her throat. His fangs scraped the delicate skin and she shuddered. "I'm *furious* with you. But I know better than to give in to my ire right now."

"The magic feeds on negative emotion." Naya's voice was thick as his tongue flicked out, so hot against her throat.

"It does. I feel it rise up when I'm angry."

"I guess that means I need to keep you happy." Was it wrong that she wanted him to bite her? To sweep her up into that frenzy of sensation that caused all rational thought to take a vacation from her brain?

"If you want to keep me happy, don't send your cousin away."

Naya pulled away and studied his guileless expression. "You can't be serious."

"If I could meet this Paul now, I'd wring his neck for allowing you to hunt alone. Taking backup doesn't prove that you're weak, Naya. It shows that you're smart. Only fools and characters in horror movies go it alone."

She bristled at the implication in his words.

"Gods, but you're a willful female." Ronan stroked her hair and brushed his thumb along her temple. "I'm not saying that you're foolish, either. Just promise me that you won't make a move without having someone at your back."

Naya sighed. "Whatever."

"I'm going to take that as a yes." Ronan took her by the hand and led her toward the bed. "Lie with me until the sun rises."

Ronan was a male who expected nothing less than to be obeyed, and where he led she found herself helpless to not follow. Naya didn't want this tenderness, the soft emotion that urged her to take down her walls. The tether that bound them drilled through her cold apathy, and despite her best efforts to keep him at bay, Ronan had wormed his way into not only her soul but also her heart.

She lay down on the bed, tucking her back against Ronan's chest. He hooked one arm round her waist and rested his mouth near her temple. "Luz is telling your friend Santi that she's afraid I'm going to use you as my own personal Slurpee," he said with a gentle laugh.

"You can hear her?" Naya had assumed that all of Ronan's senses were keen. *Impressive.*

"She thinks I'm using mind control on you."

Leave it to Luz to jump to the worst conclusions. "Can you do that?"

He idly kissed her temple, the outer shell of her ear. "More or less. But I doubt it would work on you."

Ronan was more powerful than she'd given him credit for. Vampires had their own magic, it seemed. Magic she couldn't comprehend or understand. "Why don't you think it would work?"

"You're strong willed. Your magic is *powerful.* More so than mine."

Naya's chest swelled with emotion. For most of her life, she'd felt so weak. Her magic seemed paltry in comparison to the Bororo males who were stronger, their senses sharper. She'd wanted the ability to shift when she was a girl. Run through the woods with Joaquin and Santi. See the world through the jaguar's eyes.

"I don't feel powerful." She felt like a slave. Trapped in a life she didn't want to live and tired of blindly following orders that she'd begun to question. What scared her most about Ronan's sudden presence in her life wasn't the mystical tether that pulled at her soul or the way he evoked raw emotion and a magic she'd never known existed. It wasn't the instant emotional connection or ease at which he put her. She understood the importance of mate bonds. Knew how they forged a male and female together. No, what truly terrified her was the glimpse of a life outside of everything she knew. A life that she'd never, ever be allowed to live.

"You are so powerful, Naya. The very essence of life." Ronan's voice became lazy and thick. "And I will tell you every day until you believe it."

The arm holding her went limp as the first rays of sunlight peeked through the blinds. Naya disentangled herself from his embrace and took the comforter off the bed, draping it over the window as a safeguard to block any daylight from coming in. Her gaze wandered back to the male sleeping like the dead, his well-muscled frame taking up the bulk of her bed. So tall that his feet touched the footboard.

She crossed the room and leaned down over him, brushing his tawny locks from his forehead. "I'm going to fix you, Ronan," she murmured against his skin. "I promise."

CHAPTER
20

"Okay, what the fuck is going on? I know I told you to sow some oats, but I didn't think you'd plow the field with so much gusto."

Naya fixed Luz with a stern eye and placed her hands on her hips. She brought her finger to her lips and shushed her cousin as she eased the door closed behind her. Who knew how much vampires heard when they slept?

"You think he's using mind control on me?" Naya hissed.

Luz was taken aback, but she recovered quickly, masking her expression with passivity. "Well, is he?"

"Do you actually think I'd be able to answer that if he was?"

"Good question. I never thought of that. I should do a cleansing ritual on you, just in case."

Naya shook her head and plopped down on the couch. She was too damned exhausted to stand in the middle of the living room and fight. "Luz, seriously." Naya rubbed at her temple in an attempt to banish the painful throb that settled there. Her body was overloaded with magical energy and it needed to be released.

"I *am* being serious." Luz settled down beside Naya, tucking her legs underneath her. "I've never seen Joaquin so pissed off. He told Paul that the vampire was controlling you."

Naya let out a soft snort. Of course Joaquin would have opted to see it that way. Anything to save face and preserve his injured pride. "Joaquin found us in a . . . um . . . compromising position."

"Doggie-style?" Luz asked, waggling her brows. Naya should have been appalled, but Luz's questions only managed to steer her thoughts down an erotic path. Warm magic tingled on her skin and Naya rubbed at her arms as though she could banish it. Luz's eyes grew wide. "Holy shit. No wonder you're banging him."

"Gods, Luz. Do you have to make it sound so dirty?"

"Isn't it?" she asked in an arch tone. "Don't hold out on me, Cuz. I got a *good* look at him. Did the vampire ring your bell right out of its belfry?"

Naya propped her feet up on the coffee table. "That's none of your business."

"Damn. Sex magic." Luz's appreciative tone made Naya smile. "What's it like?"

"I haven't used it for anything." Honestly, Naya found the magic too powerful to wield. "It's a high. I can't even think straight." Even now, she practically vibrated with the residual energy. "I don't know what to do with it."

"I bet I could give you a suggestion or two on how to use it." Self-control had been the one hurdle Luz had yet to overcome. They were taught to harness their power. Use it sparingly and only in service to the tribe. Luz didn't buy into any of that crap. She thought the rules were Paul's way of keeping them under his thumb. Luz was probably right.

"Something's coming down the pipes and it isn't good." If Naya was going to let Luz stick around, then she was going to help her find a solution to her—and Ronan's—problem. "I fought a mapinguari last night. It was huge, Luz. And more powerful than anything I've ever had to take down before. If Ronan hadn't been there, it would have killed me. Whatever found its way onto *El Sendero* is bad news."

Luz's brow furrowed. "Let me see your dagger."

Naya crossed to the hutch that doubled as her armory and retrieved the blade. It glowed with the heat of a star, pulsing with a bright pale lemon light. "The magic needs to be discharged." She'd yet to funnel the magic into the gold box that would need to be turned over to Paul and the other elders.

"Uh, you think?" Luz's eyes grew wide as she took the dagger from Naya's outstretched hand. "Holy shit, Naya. It's practically nuclear. My arm is numb all the way to my shoulder."

"What do you think they do with it?" Naya asked. This was a dangerous subject to breach. One that would be considered treasonous if heard by the wrong ears. "I mean, neither of us has ever witnessed the actual banishing ceremony." Something she regretted now. "How do they do it? The elders are all males. They can't manipulate magic."

"Oh, they banish it all right," Luz said with a rueful laugh. "Right into the pieces of gold they're using to buy your boyfriend's death."

According to the elders, the gold pieces had been infused with the magic of *brujas*. White magic. Benevolent. "If that's the case, that gold isn't going to bring anyone anything but a world of darkness and grief," Naya remarked.

"Preach." Luz examined the dagger, worked the grip in her palm. She was a powerful witch in her own right.

With the proper discipline, she'd be more powerful than Naya in two or three decades. "This isn't like anything we've dealt with before. The magic is *old*. Did you notice?"

No. She hadn't. Naya's curiosity piqued. "When I found Ronan, he was bleeding magic. He tackled me to the ground and said my name. Then he passed out. He doesn't remember anything that happened before he woke up chained to my bed almost two weeks ago."

"Kinky," Luz said with a grin.

"I was going to kill him," Naya said, low. "I planned to. But . . ."

"But how could you possibly run a dagger through your mate's heart?"

Naya wasn't ready to address her feelings for Ronan with herself, let alone her cousin. "He said he was looking for his sister. That she told him she'd found a relic."

Luz's eyes narrowed. "What sort of relic?"

"He wouldn't tell me." Naya let out a long sigh. "But if we're dealing with vampires, it's got to be old. *Ancient*."

"Did you ever think you'd see one?" Luz sounded like a kid at the zoo. "I mean, holy shit. A real freaking vampire! The white whale of the supernatural world."

Not only did Naya never think she'd ever see one; she also sure as hell never thought she'd find herself mated to one. "I thought they were all dead."

"Everyone does," Luz said. "This will change our world."

"He mentioned the Sortiari. Paul won't be happy if he thinks they might find out about what's going on up here."

"No. It'll make trouble. And I'm not interested in trouble that doesn't start with Cuervo and end in the company of a well-muscled male." Luz handed Naya the dagger and she tucked it back into the cabinet. She'd need to siphon the magic out of it before she went out hunting again.

"Do you think Ronan's relic has something to do with the influx of magic on *El Sendero*?"

"I do." She just didn't have enough information to connect the dots yet. "We need to find his sister. I think she's the missing piece."

"She might have been the mapinguari you killed last night."

Naya had already thought of that and it made her heart ache for Ronan. "She could have been. I sure as hell hope not, though."

"You do realize that none of your theories or plans will matter if Paul gets his hands on your vampire first." Luz gave her a pointed look. "You can't hide from him for much longer."

"I know." She was surprised she'd gone this long. "I'll go to him. I'm not turning Ronan over, though. What happens from here on out has to be on my terms."

"Good luck with that." Luz looked away, her expression sad. The reality of their life within the pod could be harsh at times. Their esoteric existence left little in the way of freedom. "When word gets out, it's not just our pod you're going to have to worry about."

"Yeah, that's what I'm afraid of." And why she needed to get to the bottom of this mystery before anyone else got hurt. Or died.

"What's your plan?" Luz patted the cushion beside her and Naya sat down. "Let's hatch something while Prince Charming is sleeping."

If she didn't find Ronan's sister and her relic soon, Naya had a feeling that she'd be forced to kill Ronan before Paul had the opportunity to get his hands on him. Sorrow bloomed with a deep stabbing pain in her chest. If Ronan died, Naya wasn't sure that she'd be able to live without him.

"We need Manny." A magic sensitive—not to mention

a human—would be the perfect bait for rogue magic looking for a host. "Do you think he'd help us?"

Luz flashed a smile. "I think he'd be game."

"Good."

Something dark and powerful festered in Ronan's soul.
His body had succumbed to the daytime sleep, but his
mind was wide awake. A turbulent storm of thought and
worry that swirled through his consciousness in a dream-
like haze.

Sharp claws raked at his skin as though trying to break
through. A need rose within him, stronger than the thirst
of the newly turned, more intense even than the lust for
his mate. A deadly desire that made him yearn to sink his
fangs into the nearest body and tear the flesh. Want to glut
himself on blood.

Rage pooled like gasoline in his gut. All he needed was
a spark to transform it into an inferno. His body was lifeless. Useless. Trapped until sundown, the force within him
paced like an anxious wolf in the confines of a cage. It
wanted out. *Needed* out.

A roar of anguish echoed in the confines of Ronan's
mind. He fought against himself and the urges that rose
up inside of him like a tide. In order to protect Mikhail,
Claire, and Jenner, Ronan had closed himself off from the
Collective, building a wall between them. He'd relied
solely on Naya's blood and their tether to sustain him, but
if he couldn't control the force trying to breach the surface of his psyche he'd have to block her out as well.

He'd throw himself on her blade before he'd allow the
evil inside of him to harm a hair on her head.

Limbs heavy with fatigue, Ronan tried to fight against
the hold of daylight over his body. A chill snaked up his
legs, winding like icy vines over his torso and chest. The
darkness within him surged, rising to the surface of his

psyche once again. His throat burned. The thirst consumed him. There wasn't enough blood in the world to satisfy his lust for it.

Anger. Fear and panic constricted his chest. He couldn't let it win. Couldn't allow it to hurt Naya. She'd calmed the darkness before, sent it back to wherever it lay dormant with the simple touch of her hand. Her fiery heat was like a summer sun over a blanket of snow. Through the tether he sought her out despite every instinct screaming at him to keep her at bay. Her blood was a heady nectar that he couldn't resist. Her body beautiful round curves and supple flesh that he couldn't wait to touch. In the darkness, her soul was a beacon that called to him, kept him anchored to the earth.

Naya.

Yessssss! The darkness seethed, hungry.

No! Violent spasms shook Ronan as the cold took root. He instinctually reached out for Naya, desperate for the comfort of their bond, of her body, her heat. The darkness rose inside of him like a thick fog, clouding his mind and intent, stealing the sensation from his limbs.

"Oh, gods. Ronan, you need to calm down!"

Blind, his limbs useless, Ronan had no idea if the sweet tenor of her voice was real or in his mind. The warmth of her body buffeted his and the darkness lapped greedily at it. She smoothed his hair from his brow. The daytime sleep that made him all but useless gave way to the command of the darkness that threatened to swallow him whole. Ronan's eyes snapped open and he saw the world through a haze of red. Naya loomed above him, concern etched on her beautiful face.

"Ronan? Stay with me, okay? You need to focus. Try to calm down."

Feed. Need. Blood.

Like a whip his arm struck out, his fingers curling

around her throat. Naya's eyes went wide with panic as she tried to pry his grip loose.

Drain her. So hungry. Need her blood.

The dark voice seethed in Ronan's subconscious and he was helpless to fight it. Icy tendrils traveled up the length of his throat, past his jaw, and into his brain. He gnashed his teeth together as he fought the pain, the influence he couldn't seem to shake. Naya gasped for breath and he flipped them around until she lay on the bed and he hovered above her.

"Ro-nan." The word was nothing more than a pained gasp. "Stop."

Don't stop until you've taken every drop of blood she has to give.

Ronan's mind resisted the command, but still his grip tightened. If only the sun would shine through the window, burn him to a crisp. Anything to save her from this parasitic *thing* that had attached itself to him. She struggled beneath him, the scent of her fear fouling the air. His stomach turned, knotting itself as he lowered his mouth to her exposed throat.

"Kill me, Naya." His voice was sandpaper scraping its way up his throat.

A blast of heat struck his chest and Ronan flew backward. He slammed against the far wall and crumpled to the carpeting. The force within him stilled, but Naya had failed to rout it.

"Again!"

The darkness roared its agony in a blast of icy cold as Naya attacked again. Crimson stained his sight and she was nothing more than a smudge of color in the darkened room. Ronan's back arched off the carpet with such force that he felt a vertebra snap. It healed in an instant, but his body continued to contort, bones snapping and knitting over and again. His pained shout shook the walls that surrounded them and through the agony he heard Luz's frantic shout as she urged Naya to drive her dagger through his heart.

"Yes!" he shouted. It was the only way to protect her. "Do it! Now!"

"No!" Her impassioned cry rang with sorrow and desperation.

Luz stepped into Ronan's field of vision, her face an impassive mask. "If you won't do it, I will."

"If you touch him, you'll regret it!" Naya barked. "Back off, Luz."

His mate was fierce. Another shock of heat infused his body and the darkness retreated deeper inside of him. Naya's mouth caressed his, soft. Slow. So damned warm. A silky glide that heated Ronan's blood and hardened his cock. He rose up to sit and she settled in his lap, wrapping her legs around his waist.

"Naya, are you out of your fucking mind?"

Her cousin's alarm took a backseat to Ronan's lust. He couldn't be bothered to care about keeping a level head. About anyone's safety. Or about having a gods-damned audience as he kissed Naya.

He couldn't get close enough. Couldn't kiss her deeply enough. There were too many damned clothes between them and not enough bare skin. Gripped by lust, Ronan ignored the sounds of Luz's enraged shouts and buried his face in Naya's throat. She tilted her head to the side, an invitation, and he buried his fangs in her soft flesh.

The skin popped beneath his lips and blood welled sweet and hot in his mouth. Ronan groaned as he took pull after long pull. His mind cleared. His body flooded with heat. The darkness that threatened to consume him retreated completely as though sated, returning to its dormant state. Naya cleaved to him, her nails biting into his shoulders as she held his body to hers. Ronan disengaged with a roar, lapping at the trickles of blood that ran from the two sets of punctures. Naya held him tightly, her head nestled close to his shoulder. The breath sped in her chest and she trembled in his embrace.

"Don't you *ever* tell me to kill you again."

The bond between them flared and the fear that shook her was Ronan's own. He pierced his tongue and healed the wounds on her throat, kissing the soft, smooth flesh. Gods, he could have killed *her*. What she'd done was too damned cavalier. With featherlight strokes he brushed the backs of his fingers over the skin around her neck, marred with ugly welts and raw; his stomach clenched at the sight.

"I'm sorry, Naya." The words were a mantra, barely audible even to him. "I'm sorry, Naya. I'm sorry." He took a deep, shuddering breath and hugged her to him. "I'm sorry."

Moments passed and the world fell away. There were only the two of them, the sound of their soft breaths, gentle touches with seeking hands. Ronan couldn't bear to be parted from her. Inches of space were too much. As long as he could touch her, kiss her, inhale her sweet scent, he'd be all right. He could do anything as long as he had her.

"You've got to be fucking *kidding* me!"

Luz's incredulous outburst broke the spell and the reality of their situation crashed around him. Ronan looked over Naya's shoulder at the sight of her enraged cousin. Her stance was battle ready and she gripped a wicked citrine dagger in her palm. His mate might not have wanted to kill him, but Luz sure as hell wanted to see him dead.

"Are you seriously going to just sit there in his lap and pretend that he didn't want to suck you dry right now?

And like a crazy person, you just *gave* your throat to him?"

"That's exactly what I'm going to do." Naya didn't move, didn't even turn to face her cousin. "I can't live without him, Luz. I won't."

CHAPTER
21

Naya didn't understand this tether that bound her to Ronan, but one thing was certain: Come hell or high water, nothing would come between them. And that included her family.

"Call Manny. It's time to end this."

"*Estás loca*," Luz said. Naya didn't have to look at her cousin to know a piteous expression had settled on her usually chipper face. "I'll call him, but you'd better deal with Paul before sundown. I love you, but he won't hesitate to put the vampire down. I hope you know what you're doing, Cuz."

"Yeah. Me too. After you call Manny, tell Paul that you found me and that I'll be over to see him soon. I don't want anyone else to get hurt, and if Joaquin or any of them are searching after sundown it'll invite trouble."

An uncomfortable silence descended and Naya's skin prickled. She wouldn't put it past Luz to do something rash. "Luz?"

"If you so much as lay a threatening finger on her while

I'm gone, I'll run my dagger through your heart myself, vampire."

The door closed behind her and silence once again settled over them like a too-warm blanket.

"I'm sorry, Naya."

His words caused a fissure in her heart, so full of tender emotion. Tears stung at Naya's eyes and she willed them to stay put. The last thing she needed was for him to see her fall apart when he was so clearly hanging on by the barest of threads.

With her face still buried in the crook of his neck, Naya couldn't help but wonder what it would be like to sink her teeth into his flesh. Take his blood on her tongue. "What's it like?" she asked. She needed to keep him in the moment. Negative emotions—even regret—could trigger the magic to reawaken. If she didn't extract it from Ronan's body soon, he'd become a mapinguari, a demon with an unquenchable thirst for chaos. If that happened, Luz would get her wish and there wouldn't be a gods-damned thing Naya could do about it.

"What's what like?" He held her so tight, as though he was afraid she'd slip away. His fingers teased the strands of her hair and she shivered.

"Drinking my blood."

Ronan pulled away and stared into her face. His irises flashed with silver and a furrow marred his brow. "It's *everything*," he replied in a hoarse whisper. "I've fed from dhampirs, taken my king's own blood the night he turned me. But even my first taste as a true vampire can't compare to the experience of taking your vein, Naya." He stroked his fingers through the hair that framed her face as he studied her. "I am in love with the locks of your hair," he remarked with a quiet laugh. "Like threads of raw silk against my skin."

"I could cut some for you to carry around in your pocket." She looked away with a nervous laugh, afraid that he might see the shameless want shining in her eyes. "You know, if you're into that sort of thing." She'd used the joke to deflect from the fact that what she wanted to hear from him was that he was in love with more than just her hair. Though she decried the idea of belonging to anyone, Naya wanted a male to love her. Even if she was bald, ugly, too thick, or too thin. And most of all, she wanted a male to love her even when she was *powerless*. When she had nothing more to offer than herself.

"To cut even a strand of your hair would be a travesty." He continued to stroke her as though the act itself kept him grounded. "I want it long and wild."

Naya's lips hitched in a half smile. "It's not long enough, huh?"

"Hardly. I want it cascading down your back, covering your breasts. I want your hair to brush my chest, the tops of my thighs as you ride me."

Heat swamped her, pulsing low in Naya's abdomen. She wanted him so badly that she ached and nothing short of joining their bodies would make that hurt go away. It wasn't normal to want someone so badly. This went beyond obsession. It was a need that couldn't be sated.

"The sun is still up." Naya swallowed down the lump that rose in her throat. She needed to put some distance between them, but her body refused to move. "Shouldn't you be out for the count?"

His brows pulled together as Ronan searched her face. "Cold darkness woke me." Pain marred his handsome face and Naya smoothed her thumbs over the furrows that lined his forehead. "It's growing stronger. Harder to fight. Luz might be driving her dagger through my heart sooner than either of us thinks."

"That's not going to happen."

"It might. My thirst is unquenchable, Naya. The darkness is insatiable. I'll gladly die if it keeps you safe from me. My only regret will be not having the opportunity to join with you in a true mate bond and enjoy your body while I take your vein."

The idea of having Ronan's fangs buried in her throat while he fucked her sent a thrill through Naya's bloodstream. "Is that what a vampire mating entails?" Bororo matings were more ceremonial than physical. Always performed at the full moon and witnessed by every member of the tribe's pod. It was an unbreakable contract. One that, if broken, would gain swift retribution. The Bororo were big on shame. And breaking sacred vows was as shameful as it came. "Sex and blood?"

"Can you think of anything better?" Ronan asked with a flirtatious grin. It turned Naya's insides to mush and caused her heart to beat wildly in her chest. "The tether is sacred for so many reasons, Naya. When tethered, our souls are returned to us from an empty oblivion." He cupped the back of her neck, his artful fingers loosening the tight muscles there. She let out a soft sigh, her lids drooping. The sound of his voice, his touch, his very presence, was a comfort unlike anything she'd ever known. "And though we can gather strength from our covens, from that bond that connects us all, the blood of our mate is an elixir of life and power that has no equal. It makes us stronger not only as individuals but as a whole. The tether is revered among vampires."

"And the sex?"

"Isn't sex a sacred act no matter your creed? Is it not the one thing that solidifies any mate bond?"

Naya smiled. "So true. But . . ." She worried her lip between her teeth. "You seem to want to bite me when we're intimate. Is drinking blood and sex tied?"

Ronan's lips curved in a sensual grin that revealed the

sharp tips of his fangs. "My mate is so curious." He searched her face and silver chased across his gaze. "It warms my blood."

A flush crept to Naya's cheeks. She wasn't a vampire, but even she sensed the connection. Wanted his bite as he pleasured her. It supercharged every sensation in her body. Heightened her sensitivity. "It makes me . . ." She paused. Let out a nervous breath as she looked away.

Ronan guided her chin up until she had no choice but to meet his eyes. "There isn't anything you can't say to me. Ask me. For you, Naya, I'm an open book."

For you, Naya. Did he have any idea how his words affected her? "The bite. It makes me feel so *good.* Is it the same for a vampire?"

A low purr vibrated in his chest and Naya swore she felt it in her pussy. The ache in the center of her core intensified until she thought she'd go mad with want. "It's the same. For us, sex and feeding are closely tied. They're both acts of intimacy. To take your mate's vein—to have your vein taken by your mate—there's no equal."

Despair settled in Naya's stomach like a stone. How could he ever be truly happy with her then? She wasn't a vampire. Wouldn't ever be a vampire. If they stayed together there would always be an essential part of their relationship that was missing.

"What are we doing, Ronan?" The words burst from her lips, unbidden. "This is ridiculous. How can we use words like 'bond' and 'tether' and 'mate' when we're about as compatible as a sheep and a wolf?" Anger burned in her chest, banishing the warm glow of her arousal. "Who's Siobhan, Ronan?"

His jaw squared as he met Naya's gaze. "A dhampir. Leader of one of the city's most powerful covens. And . . ."—he took a deep breath—". . . the female Chelle and I took refuge with when we fled England. I made a blood troth to her in exchange for a codex that I gave to Mikhail. If any female save her lays claim to my body, my blood will boil and the heat of my betrayal will burn me alive."

"We're both promised to others for the love of the gods!" Rueful laughter bubbled in Naya's throat. "I can't even touch you the way I want to without the risk of you burning from the inside out?" She pushed herself away, but Ronan held on to her, refusing to let her go. Gods, he was a stubborn male. "Is that how you want to live? Without ever being able to solidify our—"She snorted. "I can't even call what this is a *relationship*. Our tether? I don't need your blood to live, Ronan! We can't even have sex!"

Magic pooled in her cells and trickled from her pores. Ronan jerked and released his hold on her as though he'd been stung. A sob rose in her throat and Naya swallowed it as she scrambled to stand. She had to get out of there. Get away from *him* before she lost it.

She reached for the doorknob and turned, only to have the door slammed shut. The heat from Ronan's chest buffeted her back. He surrounded her. Overwhelmed her. His presence sucked all of the breathable oxygen from the air and Naya's head swam with his clean, masculine scent.

"Let me go, Ronan."

His response was a low growl. "No."

"I want to leave. Damn it, let me leave!"

Again, "No."

Did he want to see her fall apart? Her world was crumbling around her and Naya would be left with nothing but ruin. "This tether is going to destroy us both. Gods, Ronan, don't you understand? I can't *ever* be what you need!"

There was no doubt that their situation was a fucking mess, but Naya was sorely mistaken if she thought he'd simply let her walk out that door and out of his life. "I thought you were a fighter, Naya."

She bucked her chin in the air. So defiant. How could she possibly think she couldn't be what he needed? Naya was the *only* thing he needed in this gods-forsaken world. "What in the hell is that supposed to mean?"

Ronan kept his palm planted firmly on the door. Naya seemed reluctant to let go of the knob. As though it were the only thing keeping her from reaching out to him. "You know what it means. You're bailing. You're making excuses so you don't have to deal with this. With *us*."

"There is no us, Ronan!" She pulled on the knob, desperate for an escape that he refused to give her. "There's just you, and me, and this desperate, crazy, all-consuming want that's destroying us both!"

"Naya."

"No!" She released the knob to shove at his chest, but Ronan wouldn't be moved. "I belong to Joaquin. You belong to Siobhan. You deserve to be with a female who can make you feel whole. Who can pierce your skin with her fangs. Drink from you! Do all of those things that you say are so vital. And I . . ." A tortured sob escaped her lips ". . . I have to stay here. I have an obligation to Joaquin. To Luz. To all of them."

"Those are bullshit excuses and you know it, Naya!"

Tears glistened in her eyes and the air soured with her sorrow. Ronan's heart ached in his chest. A deep, stabbing sensation that stole his breath.

"What do you want from me?"

"I want you to fight for us, damn it!"

"How many times do I have to say it? There is no *us*, Ronan!"

She shoved at him again and he captured her wrists, pinning them against the door, high above her head. With his free hand he snatched her around her waist and hoisted her up, pressing Naya's body against the closed door. Her breasts rubbed against his chest and Ronan couldn't help but thrust into the cradle of her open thighs. Naya let out a desperate moan that was more pain than pleasure, but she didn't fight him. "I can't keep going like this." Her voice was a ragged whisper in the darkened room. "I'm unraveling. I can't think straight. It gets worse every minute that I'm with you, and I'm afraid that if I don't leave you now we'll both pay for it."

"I'm not afraid, Naya." He leaned in close until his mouth rested at her ear. Ronan inhaled her tropical scent, the rain forest in full bloom. "As long as we're together, nothing else matters."

"I'm terrified." Her voice quavered with the murmured words, sending a spasm of anxiety through him. "You apologized to me for succumbing to a force that you have no hope of controlling. When it's me who should be apologizing for being unable to control it for you. If I fail . . ." She rested her forehead on his and her breath hitched. "If I can't save you from this *thing*, I won't survive it. How can I possibly feel that way, Ronan? When we're so clearly *not* meant for each other, why do I feel like dying when I picture an existence without you?"

"Gods, Naya." Why was she fighting so hard what he'd known from the moment he laid eyes on her? "We *are* made for each other." He kissed her cheek. Her temple. The corner of her luscious mouth. "Allow yourself to feel the truth of it for once."

"I can't." She trembled in his embrace. "I don't want to love you, Ronan."

Every ounce of her fear and doubt weighed down their tether. Naya had lived in a tiny bubble for so long. Everything that she was had become enmeshed with her pod. If she could just learn to let go. "Loving someone doesn't mean that you give up any part of who you are." The backs of his fingers brushed her ribs on their journey to the hem of her shirt. They found bare flesh and Naya's lids became hooded, her dark eyes shining with unspoken emotion. "It's about sharing who you are with the only other soul on the face of the earth who understands you and accepts you without condition. Love is a gift, Naya. One that makes you better because of it. It's not a curse that weakens you or tears you down."

A tear trickled down her cheek and Ronan released his grip on her wrists to swipe it away. His other palm cupped her bare torso and he reveled in her comforting heat. "I felt myself slip away that first night." She swallowed against the emotion that cracked in her voice and looked away. "I'm losing myself to you, Ronan."

"No one has lost anything, Naya. We've simply *found* one another."

With her fingers still wound in his hair, Naya pulled him close. Her mouth met his, soft, warm, inviting. His grip on her tightened as Ronan pinned her against the door with his body. There was nothing rushed or frenzied about this moment. It was different. *She* was different. The tether that connected them no longer tugged at his soul as though resisting, but rather, it enveloped him.

"Paul might have thought he could give you to his son, but Joaquin will never have you," Ronan murmured as he rained kisses down her throat. The sound of her heart racing in her chest sparked his bloodlust and he nuzzled the throbbing vein at her throat. "And though Siobhan has my troth, I will never give myself to her again."

Naya's head fell back on her shoulders and he scraped his fangs along her skin, resisting the urge to pierce her flesh. A shiver traveled the length of her body and her response caused a delicious ache to settle in his sac. Gods, he needed release. Needed to bury his cock in Naya's wet warmth and solidify their bond once and for all.

"I am for no other female but you. This is my vow to you, Naya," Ronan said. "Give me yours. Tell me that you are for me and me alone."

"Yes," Naya gasped as she pressed him tight to her throat. "No other male but you will ever have me, Ronan. I'm yours."

His fangs punctured her skin and Naya's low moan coupled with her warm breath in his ear tipped Ronan over the ledge of his control. He'd burn himself to a bloody fucking crisp right here and now, because he refused to withhold himself from his mate for another gods-damned second.

No more stolen moments. No mere glimpses of her naked body before someone or something intervened. And no more wanting—*needing*—her and knowing that he would end up unfulfilled. *Fuck Siobhan and her troths.* The thing seething inside of him grew more powerful by the hour. Either way, he was dead. Ronan refused to go into whatever afterlife awaited him before he held his mate in his arms and made love to her. Bound himself to her. Forever.

Ronan kissed Naya deeply, his tongue sliding against hers. She tasted like heaven, sweet, fresh spring rain. She kept her legs wrapped around his waist and she released her grip on his shoulders only long enough for him to strip off her shirt.

"We can't, Ronan." He kissed a path across her collarbone and over the swell of one tantalizing breast. "Your troth." He jerked the cup of her bra aside and captured her hardened nipple in his mouth. Naya gasped, her nails biting into his shoulder. "We have to wait."

He pulled away, scraping his teeth over her sensitive

flesh as he went. Her answering moan vibrated down his shaft and he reached behind her, his fingers fumbling in his haste to rid her of her bra. The scent of her arousal bloomed around them, a rich, exotic perfume that dizzied him. "Let the blood burn through my veins. I will not wait another gods-damned second to have you."

CHAPTER
22

Ronan dragged the straps of Naya's bra down over her shoulders and she shucked the garment as though it were on fire. She reached for his T-shirt, clawing at the soft cotton in her effort to shove it up his chest and get it off him. She could no longer deny this bond between them, the connection that burned with the heat of a solar flare whenever she was within touching distance. His words. The vow he'd made. The tether that had once been so tight and was now an open doorway between them convinced her once and for all that it was time to stop resisting what her heart had been telling her all along. The vampire had been made for *her.*

She could understand why Siobhan had tricked Ronan into promising his body to her. He was magnificent. What female—dhampir or otherwise—wouldn't do anything in her power to keep him? Naya's palms traced the topography of defined muscles, over the swell of his pecs, down the ridges of his abs that twitched and tightened in response to her touch. He held her as though she weighed

nothing, and Naya had never been more painfully aware
that he would never, ever let anything harm her. Even
himself. Ronan would die—would let Luz run her dagger through his heart—before he'd let the darkness inside
of him win.

"I want you to take off all of your clothes and lie
down on the bed, Ronan."

A wide grin lit up his face, showcasing the dual points
of his fangs. Naya suppressed a pleasant shiver. *Sex per-
sonified.* She couldn't let him shake her focus. At least,
not yet. "Gods, how I love a commanding female." She
slid down from his embrace and Ronan's brow furrowed.
Silver rimmed his irises, so beautiful. "Commanding is
one thing—cruel is another." He lunged for her, but Naya
skirted his reach.

"Do as I say," she instructed.

He unfastened his pants and slowly lowered the zipper. "Going to cuff me to the bed again?"

Dear gods. The mental image sent a pleasant rush of
sensation that settled between her thighs. "Would you let
me?" Her gaze was riveted to his body as she backed
slowly away toward the dresser at the far side of the room.
She memorized every bulge, every groove, from the cut
of his torso to the taper of his lean waist and the trail of
hair that plunged below his waistband. He shucked his
pants with a wide sweep of his arms and Naya sucked in
a sharp breath as she took in the sight of his erection
jutting from between his thighs.

*Fan-freaking-*tastic.

He was a masterpiece, cut from marble. Her gaze drank
him in and she swore he grew even harder from her unabashed attention. "I'm at a disadvantage here. Quid pro
quo, don't you think?"

He wanted to watch her undress? Naya wasn't exactly
self-conscious. The Bororo might have mandated their

pairings, but they didn't force their people into celibacy. Still, to be held in place by his intense silver gaze while she undressed? Naya would probably burst into flames before he managed to put even a finger on her.

"Quid pro quo," she agreed. If her plan was going to work, she needed an arsenal of magic at her disposal. She didn't think that a blood troth was something easily thwarted.

Ronan stretched out on the bed and tucked his arms behind his head. *So confident. So damned smug.* Naya didn't think she'd last the time it would take to call on her magic. The sight of him, hard and ready for her—gods, she wanted to ravage him.

Naya took a deep breath. Held it in her lungs. She'd never harnessed sex magic before. Hell, up until Ronan's appearance in her life she'd sort of thought it was a myth. Blood magic carried more weight, but since it was sex that Siobhan wanted from Ronan, it stood to reason that the best way to skirt the troth was to fight fire with fire.

Naya's breath left her lungs in a rush. Ronan propped himself up on an elbow as he settled down on the bed, his expression etched with concern. "Naya?"

"I'm okay." Power tingled across her nerve endings, a pleasant warmth that relaxed her too-tight muscles. "Give me a second."

He watched her with an intensity that sent a tremor from the top of her head to the tips of her fingers and toes. His irises were solid silver now, glowing in the low light of the bedroom. Her breasts became heavy, the nipples puckered tight under the heat of his gaze, and Naya kept her attention focused on Ronan as she eased her leggings down over her thighs.

Ronan drank her in as though it took a sheer act of will to stay put. Urgency stretched between them through the tether. Would this desperate want ever go away?

"Slower." His voice was a rough command that caused her sex to clench around nothing. She wanted him inside of her so badly. He was unlike any other male she'd ever known. Strong, protective, fierce. Commanding. And the fire blazing in his eyes as he looked at her was enough to unravel her.

His Adam's apple bobbed as he swallowed hard, his fist clenching and unclenching at his side. Propped up on the pillow, sprawled out on the bed, his body was on display for her to enjoy as well, and the proud length of his erection was enough to cause a deep hollow ache to radiate from low in her belly outward.

She eased the leggings over her hips, down the length of her thighs. She bent at the waist and removed them from around her ankles before she straightened, clad in nothing more than her underwear.

"Put your palms flat on your stomach." Naya felt Ronan's words in every nerve of her body, a pleasant vibration like she was a tuning fork and he the perfect note. She did as he told her, elbows out, one hand below her breasts and the other over her belly button, her palms horizontal. "Slide them down, over your hip bones to your thighs."

Her lids fluttered, her body hyperaware of her own touch as Naya slid her hands down. "Keep your eyes on me," Ronan instructed. "Now, slide your fingers around to the insides of your thighs; trace your underwear all the way back up to your hips."

Her fingertips feathered over the lace, tracing the fabric at the juncture of her thighs. Naya sucked in a breath, her sex clenching at the light contact. Power bloomed inside of her, the intense rush causing her to sway on her feet. A rose glow rose to the surface of her skin, tingling like static electricity. She followed the hem around to her outer thigh and back up to the waistline, skimming the lace just below her belly button.

Ronan shifted on the bed and his erection bobbed as though straining toward her. Naya swallowed and licked her lips as she wondered what it would feel like to have his hard length glide between them.

"Cup your breasts."

The words were rushed, forced through his lips on a sharp exhalation of breath. Naya couldn't help the moan that accompanied the tingle of sensation that traveled to the tips of her hardened nipples when she took herself in her palms. Her eyes were riveted to Ronan and his hips surged, thrusting into air. Without being told, she took her nipples between her fingers and rolled the hardened peaks, her head falling back on her shoulders as she let out a deep sigh.

"Fucking hell, Naya." Ronan pressed his head into the pillow, his fists clenched so tightly at his sides that the veins stood out in relief, cording his arms. "Are you wet?"

She ventured down past the waistline of her underwear, desire raging in her body with the pounding force of thunder. "Yes," she moaned as her fingertips met her wet core. "Gods, yes."

"Get on the bed."

Each encounter with Ronan was better than the last. More erotic. A thousand times more intense. Sensual. She climbed up on the bed and went to her knees beside him. The words pushed past her lips in a thick, husky murmur when she said, "This might feel a little strange, but just bear with me, all right?"

"An adventurous female," Ronan replied with a cocky grin.

Magic pooled in her gut, gathering in the center of her body. It pulsed and grew within her. Thriving. Contrary to Luz's opinion, magic once manifested was no different from any other living thing. The trick was controlling it and manipulating it to her will. Giving it purpose.

She climbed up on the bed and straddled Ronan. His erection pressed against her barely clad pussy and Naya worried she'd come before she even had a chance to put this magic to the test. Her head swam in a giddy haze and a lazy smile tugged at her lips. If every encounter with Ronan produced such an intoxicating side effect, she'd have to master her control or quickly become a hopeless addict. Already she felt her grip begin to slip.

Keep it together, Naya. Business before pleasure.

She swallowed down a giggle and laid her palms on Ronan's chest. His eyes grew wide and he hissed in a breath, his back arching off the bed as his head pressed into the pillow. "Gods, Naya," he panted. "That feels amazing."

Power crested over her and Naya let her head fall back. Focus was becoming harder—another giggle—by the second when the pleasure coursing through her was so *intense*. Clarity scratched at the back of her lust-addled mind, reminding her that if she didn't do something to neutralize Ronan's troth to the dhampir his pleasure would be short-lived when the blood boiled in his veins.

Ronan's body went rigid beneath her as he reached up to take her hips in his hands. His grip was firm and he pressed her down on his cock and then thrust up to meet her. "You're so wet," he said through shallow pants. "So hot, it's like fire. Get rid of these"—he tugged at the fabric—"now, before I rip them off."

Yes. Oh, gods yes.

No! Not yet. Clarity returned to once again blow the drunkenness from her mind. "Wait." Her own voice sounded foreign in her ears. Every inch of her, every cell, was infused with magic. Naya let her eyes drift shut as she focused the power to funnel through her into Ronan, past his skin and into his veins.

"Fucking hell!" Ronan shouted. His fingers dug into her hips. His cock hardened and pulsed, rubbing against her clit through the dampened lace with every thrust of his hips. The foreign magic inside of him pushed at Naya's intrusion, resisting the power she funneled into him. She pushed back, harder, sending it back to the darkest part of Ronan's being, where she forced it to sleep. *One battle at a time.*

Ronan rose up and brought his mouth to Naya's. The kiss was furious and demanding as his tongue thrust into her mouth. He kept his palms wrapped around her hips, guiding them to rock over his erection. Naya itched to let her fingers dive into the thick locks of his hair, but she resisted. *Focus, damn it.*

But gods, he made her feel so good!

Ronan didn't know what she was doing to him or how she was doing it. But one thing was certain: He wanted *more*.

His cock was like a steel rod between his legs, swollen and throbbing. Just the thought of having her hands on him caused the blood to heat to a painful level in his veins. But the moment she'd laid her palms to his chest, the fiery heat abated to a warm, tingling glow that ignited every nerve ending on his body.

"Oh, gods, Naya. Do that again."

The scrap of lacy fabric that separated their bodies was a tease that frustrated him to the point that his teeth gnashed together. Wet, and so hot, the contact was just a taste of what he could expect when he sank his cock inside of her. Death would be a paltry price to pay for such a sweet reward.

Her fingertips danced over his skin from his chest to his torso. Naya let her head fall back, and the silky curls of her hair cascaded over her shoulders. Her lips parted with her shallow breaths and his gaze was drawn to her full breasts. The erect nipples were a rosy brown in the low light of the bedroom and straining toward him as Naya arched her back in invitation of his touch. Sparks ignited on his flesh, the same rose and gold glow that infused her skin. Ronan continued to rock his hips, shallow thrusts that frustrated more than satisfied him. He sealed his mouth over one nipple and Naya started in his grasp, a low moan vibrating through her as he swirled his tongue over the pearled peak and sucked.

Her skin tasted like spun sugar, sweet with the barest tingle as the residual magic touched his tongue. Ronan seized her by the waist. Naya let out a quiet squeal as he hoisted her up and settled back on the pillows, adjusting her position so she sat on his chest. Guiding her legs up beside her, his palms caressed a path to the tops of her thighs. "You smell so good." His tongue flicked out at her sex through the lace of her underwear. A tortured groan rumbled in his chest. "You taste *so* good."

"Ronan." The word was a desperate gasp. He flicked out with his tongue once again and her thighs trembled against him. "Not yet. I have to be sure it worked."

"Oh, love. It *did*." He had no idea what she was saying, but he'd agree to anything she wanted.

She looked down at him, her brow furrowed. Concern rippled through the tether. This wasn't simply teasing erotic play. She was truly trying to do something to him. "I'm serious, Ronan." A sensual grin curved her full mouth. "I can't risk you getting hurt."

Her eyes were glazed and slow to track, but her words were sharp and clear. Coupling with Naya—even relatively innocent contact—seemed to have a powerful effect on her. Power built and sizzled in the space between them. His mate was truly extraordinary.

"Tell me what you need from me." A sly grin tugged at his mouth as Ronan traced the pad of his finger over the barely concealed pearl of her clit. Naya's breath caught and her gaze went liquid. Gods, he loved her responsiveness.

"The troth," she said on a gasp. He continued to pet her, rapt with her reaction. "I'm using magic to block it." A low moan followed the words and his cock jumped at the sound as though trained to respond. "Is it working?"

Clever witch. She'd used her magic to thwart Siobhan.

"The only pain I feel is my aching cock," he said with a grin. "And the only death I'll suffer will be at your hands if you don't let me taste your gorgeous pussy again and fuck you until sundown."

A rush of pure lust replaced the earlier anxiety he'd felt from her. It went straight to his head, damn near shutting down his brain completely. Naya had reduced him to an animal with base needs. Ones that demanded to be met. Now.

"Tell me the truth, Ronan." She leaned back, bracing her arms on his thighs. *Ah, gods!* The angle gave him an unhindered view of the soft flesh he sought. Barely concealed by the transparent lace, her swollen bud protruded from between her glistening lips. "I need to be sure."

"Can't you feel it?" It was time that she quit relying on only what her eyes and ears told her. They were connected on a much deeper level than that. "All you have to do is reach through the tether and you'll know."

She cocked her head to one side and her eyes narrowed. Ronan reveled in the weight of her atop his chest, the warmth of her body as he used his fingertips to paint over the creamy skin of her inner thighs. Her power was unlike anything he'd beheld. Her body without equal. Her fire, the very spark of her soul, was like a beacon calling out to him in the darkness.

And this remarkable female, this force of nature and beauty and sex, belonged to *him*.

"I feel it, Ronan," she said with an enigmatic smile. The expression transformed from one of bewilderment to joy. "I did it. I beat that bitch at her own game."

Gods, how he loved a strong-willed female.

CHAPTER
23

Ronan trembled with need. His thirst blazed hot in his throat, but it was nothing compared to the desire that coursed through him. With Siobhan's blood troth temporarily nullified, he could enjoy Naya at his leisure. Make her truly his once and for all. How could he possibly be patient after wanting her so badly? With such raw desperation?

Restraint seemed an insurmountable obstacle. He didn't want to wait another moment. Especially when he knew that it was only a matter of time before that bastard Joaquin and his father found her. Before reality and their obligations intervened once again in a cruel effort to separate them.

With shaking fingers, Ronan grabbed either side of her underwear and gave a tug. Naya brought her hips up so he could pull it down, and the view was so gods-damned erotic that Ronan feared he'd come before he ever got a chance to sink into her. He'd never wanted anything—anyone—so badly in all the centuries of his existence.

Naya rocked back, the bare skin of her ass caressing

his chest as she brought her legs together and up in front of him. Ronan paused, her underwear tangled around her knees, and swallowed down the grunt that rose in his throat. *Such a gorgeous view.*

"Don't move." He could barely push the words out.

For a moment Ronan simply stared. The sight of her, bare and on display for him alone, sent a zing of electricity through his bloodstream. Her lips were swollen and wet with arousal and her clit protruded proudly from between them. His gaze ventured lower, to her tight opening and the crease of her ass. "Fuck." The word was nothing more than a whisper that rushed from his lungs on a ragged breath. He supported her outstretched legs with one hand and with the other traced along the crease, circled her opening with the pad of his finger, before dragging his slick finger through her lips and over her clit.

A shudder rippled through her and Naya's moan filled the quiet of her bedroom. His sac ached as it pulled up tight. A pleasant sting of pain to complement his pleasure. Naya bent her knees and he removed her underwear, inhaling the sweet scent that clung to the lace before discarding it somewhere beside him. He guided her legs to open and settled them on either side of his head. The globes of her supple ass fit perfectly in his palms as he angled her hips toward his face, opening her up to him. *Fucking beautiful.*

Ronan reached up and gathered the length of her hair in his hand. He pulled it over her shoulders, letting the length fall down her chest until the silky strands brushed the swell of her breasts. His gaze locked with hers and his muscles tightened as he angled his head up toward her. With the first languid pass of his tongue, Naya cried out, her thighs shaking as he flicked out at her clit. He could spend the day in bed, teasing her like this, building her slowly to the point of abandon.

She threaded her fingers through his hair. The scrape of her nails against his scalp coaxed a chill to the surface of Ronan's skin. With the tips of his fingers still clutching the soft skin of her ass, Ronan urged her closer. He sealed his mouth over her sex, sucking, licking, nipping at her sensitive flesh. The tip of one fang nicked her labia in his fervor and a drop of blood welled to the surface of her skin. Naya sucked in a sharp breath and her body stilled above him. He hadn't meant to be careless with her. Had he hurt her?

"Oh, gods, Ronan." The words left her mouth in a desperate, heated rush. "Are you going to bite me there?" As though she couldn't wait for a response, she answered for him, "Yes. Do it. I want you to."

She gripped his hair tighter, the tug bringing with it the slightest bit of pain. Ronan's cock pulsed in time with his heart, bobbing against the flat of his stomach as he shifted on the bed. His fangs throbbed in his gums and his throat blazed with renewed thirst. It seemed as though there hadn't been a day since they'd met that he hadn't taken her vein, and still he wanted—needed—more.

He would never, ever get enough.

With soft, teasing strokes, he lapped at her pussy. Naya's hips thrust in a shallow rhythm as she attempted to increase the pressure against his mouth. Ronan gripped her ass, to hold her where he wanted her. She was dripping wet; an easy wiggle of her ass only managed to spread her slick warmth over his chest. Gods, he wanted it hard and urgent and messy with her. Wanted to spend his seed on her taut stomach, round ass, stripe her mound with it, and mark her as his. He wanted to fuck her as though today would be their first and only time together.

Her soft sobs of pleasure further stoked the fires of Ronan's lust, each one more ragged and desperate than the last. Her thighs vibrated as he circled her clit with his tongue and her muscles tightened. Ronan's eyes met hers and he took in the sight of her, mad with lust and her body shimmering with the rose gold hue of magic. She was close.

Ronan sealed his mouth over one swollen lip and bit down. The moment his fangs punctured the delicate flesh, Naya screamed. She threw her head back, bracing her arms on his thighs as she came. Blood flowed hot and sweet over Ronan's tongue and his fingers dug into her flesh, holding her to him as he sucked. She reached out, winding her fist in his hair once again as her hips continued to buck and roll. The world melted away as Ronan sated his thirst. The only sounds in the room were those of Naya's pleasure and his own greedy gulps as he drank from her.

His thirst wasn't even close to being sated. His need for her body built to a fever pitch that rivaled the boiling heat of the blood troth.

Her orgasm ebbed and the violent jerking thrusts of Naya's hips were now nothing more than lazy rolls. Her head hung limp on her shoulder and sweat beaded her skin, setting off the residue of magic and making her look like a luminous goddess in the presence of a lesser creature.

"Ronan." Naya's breath came in quick pants. His gaze followed the path of her hand as she let go of his hair and clutched at her own chest. Her fingers splayed out and particles of rose and gold magic dispersed into the air like dust stirred by a breeze. "That was amazing." Her gaze was still wild and unfocused, and a lazy smile graced her lips. "I've never felt anything like that in my entire life."

Ronan kissed the inside of one thigh and then the other. She let out a slow, contented sigh and he kissed the apex of her pussy, just above her clit. *Mmmm.* He'd bite her there next time.

If he had a next time.

Through the warm glow that penetrated his skin, the cold foreign magic stirred in the center of his being. Though dormant for now, it was becoming harder to fight, and Ronan worried that it would only be a matter of time before the magic overtook him completely. He shoved the thought from his mind, refused to let that piece-of-shit force of dark energy take anything away from this moment with Naya.

He continued to place lazy kisses over her flesh, wishing he could lay her down and nuzzle against her thigh and sleep. If he made it out of this alive, he'd hole them up in his bedroom in L.A. and they wouldn't leave for days. Until then, Ronan needed to make every single moment with her count.

"I feel tipsy." Giddy laughter bubbled in Naya's throat as she listed to the right. She reached down and cupped his face in her palm, her eyes wide and wondrous. "You make me drunk, Ronan. Drunk on power, and sex, and . . ."

"And what?" Ronan pressed.

She averted her gaze, unwilling to meet his eyes. "You," she said low. "Just *you*."

He sensed that she'd meant to say something else, but even drunk on power, Naya didn't let her walls completely down.

Ronan wrapped his hands around her waist and lifted her from his chest. He rolled them over and settled her down on the mattress while he cradled himself between her legs. The head of his cock brushed her slick center and he shuddered. "Gods, Naya. I want you." The muscles in his ass contracted as he rolled his hips, teasing himself as he slid through her folds. He was used to rough and rowdy. Hell, he preferred it that way. But Naya was different. A quick, hard fuck wasn't what she deserved. He gnashed his teeth as he stroked himself against her sex. The urge to drive home was almost too much to resist. "I ache, I want you so badly."

She rolled her hips up to meet him and Ronan jerked at the ripple of pleasure that crested over him from the contact on his oversensitized flesh. The head of his cock pulsed, swollen and tight, and his shaft was like marble. If he didn't come soon, he was going to fucking explode.

"What are you waiting for, then?" Her expression was gentle, her brow furrowed. She reached up and brushed the hair away from his forehead.

He swallowed so hard, he felt his Adam's apple bob in his throat. "I'm waiting for the necessary restraint to treat you with care." The words were rough in his throat. "And not fuck you like I'm starved for you."

"Oh, gods, Ronan." A gust of breath escaped from between Naya's lips. "That's exactly how I want you to fuck me."

Her words knotted his stomach tight and Ronan slid home in a single thrust that caused them both to cry out with relief. The rightness of it stole his breath.

He was home.

Naya was past the point of coherent thought. She was nothing more than a tangled knot of sensation, need, and longing. Ronan stretched her inner walls until she felt deliciously full. Complete. As though some missing part of her had finally been returned. For a moment they lay still and quiet, wrapped in each other's arms. She'd never known such bliss. The world could've burned down around them and Naya wouldn't have noticed. Nothing mattered but this moment and the male who made her feel things she'd never known she could feel.

The power that swirled within her was without comparison.

Ronan put his mouth to hers and Naya opened to him. Their tongues met and parted in a sensual dance as he began to move above her. The first hard thrust caused Naya to gasp, but she didn't break their kiss. She could taste herself on his lips and it only served to further ignite her desire. Ronan pulled almost completely out and she whimpered into his mouth, desperate that they stay connected. His engorged head teased her opening and he plunged back in, knocking the headboard against the wall from the force.

Gods, yes.

At this point, she wouldn't care if he brought the house down around their heads. He kissed her like he fucked her—as though he was starving and she was the only thing he needed to stay alive. Naya wrapped her legs around his waist and dug her heels into the tight globes of his ass. There wasn't a single part of Ronan's body that wasn't cut from stone. He was a magnificent male.

And he belonged to *her.*

Harder. Deeper. Faster. Mooooore. Talking would require her to separate their mouths and that wasn't going to happen. He tasted so good. Felt *so* good. Words would do nothing but interrupt the feeling and Naya didn't want anything to get in the way of the sensations that danced over her skin and built inside of her much like the magic that manifested from his touch.

Ronan pounded into her, his tongue thrust into her mouth with the same desperate intent. He nipped at her lip and blood welled there. He licked it away, but not before Naya tasted the coppery tang. What would it be like to take Ronan's blood? The magic that manifested from any sexual contact with him was practically nuclear. To ingest his blood, to draw on that part of his innate power, could be the equivalent of a supernova. Would she be able to withstand it? Gods, she wanted to find out.

Blood and sex were closely tied in Ronan's world. In fact, she doubted there were very few occurrences where a feeding didn't end in sex or vice versa. She didn't need his blood to sustain her. But maybe just a taste . . .

"Ronan." she broke their kiss and he lunged at her mouth. She put a staying hand between them and marveled at the play of muscles against her palm. "I want your blood on my tongue."

His eyes flashed brilliant silver and Ronan smoothed her hair away from her face, searching her expression. "You do?" A low growl rumbled in his chest.

"I do." She couldn't think of anything she wanted more. "I want it."

Ronan's thrusts became shallow and Naya urged him deeper with her heels, rolling her hips up to meet him. His lips formed a half smile before his jaw locked down. When his mouth parted to kiss her once again, crimson stained his skin.

This time, Naya lunged for him. His blood added a sweetness to his mouth that she hadn't expected. Rich and heady like an aged burgundy. A trickle of power pooled in the pit of her stomach, not enough to manifest magic, but it gave her a taste of what dabbling in such mediums could yield. Ronan was like an electrical outlet, and Naya was some inanimate thing, useless until plugged into a power source.

She'd never known true power until now. And it came from this inexplicable bond that tethered them.

Naya lapped at his mouth with the starvation that spurred Ronan. She licked his bottom lip, his tongue, taking every last drop of blood into her mouth. The act drove Ronan into a frenzy and he renewed his pace, thrusting hard and deep, each jerk of his hips more powerful than the last. He pulled away as he drove into her, incoherent grunts echoing in the quiet room as he fucked her with mindless abandon. Naya gripped his biceps, her nails digging into the flesh as she rolled her hips up to meet his.

Naya's eyes drifted shut and she let her head fall back. Ronan cupped the back of her neck and her eyes snapped open to find his wild and silver, trained on her face. "Look at me, Naya."

His voice was gruff, commanding, and a thrill chased through her. Pleasure built within her, cresting like a tidal wave that threatened to sweep her out to sea. "Oh, gods, Ronan, don't stop." If she didn't find release soon, she'd burst out of her skin. "Please. Don't stop."

He drove hard and deep and Naya's nails broke the surface of his skin. The orgasm swept her up, rocketed her past her own body, her own consciousness, leaving her floating in a vast universe. A formless mass of never-ending sensation.

"Ronan!"

His name burst from her lips as wave after wave crashed over her. Each sobbing cry intensified with her pleasure, and just when she thought she couldn't take another blinding second, Ronan buried his face in her neck and bit down. Another orgasm came on the heels of the first, sweeping her world out from under her once again.

Ronan pulled away from her throat with a roar, pounding into her with such force that it rattled Naya's teeth. She held on to him, met him thrust for desperate thrust as her voice grew raw and ragged from her impassioned cries. His body went rigid and a shout burst from his lips. He pulled out as he came, striping her stomach with jet after heated jet. So hot on her already-sweat-dampened skin.

Quiet settled over them and the sound of Ronan's music carried to Naya's ears in lilting tones that brought tears to her eyes. It occurred to her that the pitch-perfect tune wasn't the force that had attached itself to Ronan but the magic that was their *bond*. The tether itself was a mystical force, and it served to reason that where Ronan felt that bond as a vampire was meant to feel it, Naya *heard* it. That beautiful music that made her chest swell with emotion was the sound of their tether.

Amazing.

"You're so quiet." Ronan nuzzled her ear, kissing a path down her throat. Chills broke out over Naya's skin and she smiled against his shoulder.

"I'm listening," she murmured.

"To what?"

"Our tether. It makes the most beautiful music I've ever heard."

Ronan guided her chin up and searched her face. "You can hear it?"

"Mhhm," she replied dreamily. "It's . . ." She swallowed the lump that rose in her throat. "It's the perfect song."

Ronan kissed her softly. Once. Twice. And again. "Your words are too lovely to offer to someone who rutted on you and marked your skin like a horny beast."

Naya smiled. "Mmmm. Is that what that was about? Marking me?"

"You drive me mad with desire. I couldn't help myself. It was all I could think of—seeing my seed spread across your stomach."

She knew the feeling. Her fingertip traced over his shoulder, down into the valley that curved his biceps, and back up over the hill of muscle. In the wake of her touch she left a blush-and-gold-colored trail. "Well . . . ? How does it look?"

He rose up on his knees and her stomach flipped as his eyes raked her from head to toe. "It looks as good as I thought it would. Makes me want to do it all over again."

Again, and again, and again. A contented sigh slipped from between her lips. She'd never get enough of him. "I like it, too. And if you haven't noticed, I've put my mark on you, too."

He looked down at his body and a very male, very satisfied smile spread on his lips. "That you have, love. And I'm more than happy to bear your mark."

Love. Somehow, that word, no matter how innocently he'd used it, no longer filled Naya with fear.

CHAPTER
24

Ronan had never known a more extraordinary female. Naya was everything he could have ever asked for in a mate: strong, fierce, sensual. She was a warrior and a protector. Brave.

And ah, gods, when she'd asked for his blood . . . The request alone had nearly made him go off. Naya wasn't a vampire. Neither magic nor biology would allow for her to be turned. Ronan had despaired of ever experiencing that aspect of the bond with her: The sharing of blood was a sacred act between mates and lovers alike. But perhaps he and Naya could overcome that hurdle. It was a small thing in comparison to the many obstacles that still stood in their way.

"I need to go talk to Paul."

Her voice was little more than a whisper in the darkened room. Ronan shifted, rolling over and tucking her back against his chest. He slung one arm over her torso and she wove her fingers with his while she traced his knuckles with her free hand. Such a peaceful, blissful moment. And it fucking sucked that one of those obstacles he worried about would interrupt the intimacy that had begun to grow between them.

"Wait for sundown. I'll go with you."

Naya let out a soft snort. "The hell you will. Did you forget there's a bounty on your head? You're not going anywhere near Paul or Joaquin."

Her tone didn't carry the usual sharp edge. Ronan reached up to comb his fingers through the dark tangles of her hair. Gods, he loved the way it slid against his skin like silk.

"Tell me about Siobhan," Naya said just above a whisper. "What sort of female is she?"

A twinge of jealousy and hurt flared through their tether. It pissed Ronan off that the spiteful dhampir would affect Naya in such a way. Siobhan should have been a part of his past, already forgotten. Not a glaring presence that would have to be dealt with before their relationship could move forward.

"The sort that would eat her young," Ronan said with a soft laugh. "She's a fighter. Intelligent. Calculating." Obviously. She'd secured his troth, hadn't she? "She's loyal to those who are loyal to her."

"Is she beautiful?"

Siobhan's beauty was fierce, like a fire burning through dry forest. "Yes." It wouldn't do either of them any good to lie for whatever reason, and Ronan knew that Naya would consider it an affront if he tried to spare her feelings. "But so are roses. And yet, they're riddled with thorns."

"Heh," Naya chuffed. "True." A pregnant pause followed and Naya continued to trace up and over his knuckles. "Did you love her?"

Ronan had felt many things for Siobhan, but none of them was love. "No. Siobhan is not a female who you love." In fact, Ronan couldn't imagine her feeling a tender emotion for anyone or anything.

"I see," Naya said. Pity rippled through the tether and it turned Ronan's stomach. "She's just a female you fucked?"

He supposed the context of his relationship with Siobhan came off as callous. They'd both been aware of the terms, though, and Siobhan had never been the sort of female to cleave to any male. She was above the sort of weaknesses created by love and attachment.

"Naya." He'd never been an articulate male. Ronan took action and asked questions later. He'd never had to explain himself to anyone. "If you knew Siobhan, you wouldn't feel sorry for her. What we had was a mutually beneficial relationship with no strings attached." That is, until she'd felt the need to claim ownership of him. "Siobhan didn't demand the blood troth because she harbored a deep affection for me. It's because she hates to lose. Anything. And she knew I was slipping away."

"I don't feel sorry for her." Naya turned in his embrace to face him. Her expression was etched with so much tender emotion that it settled as a deep ache in Ronan's chest. She reached up to cup his cheek in her palm. "I feel sorry for you. You must have been lonely to seek out such a cold and emotionless relationship with a female who would treat you like you were some sort of possession."

Had he been lonely? Ronan had never thought about it. He existed. Worked. Though his line of business was hardly morally rewarding. He spent time with Jenner and Mikhail. Fed when his thirst crested. Fucked when there was a willing female. Siobhan had satisfied his needs well; she'd been a skilled lover and never held back in bed. But there had not been an ounce of tenderness between them. He'd never held her in her arms. Never stroked her hair. He'd never searched her emerald and silver gaze and wondered what she might be thinking.

"Perhaps I was lonely," he admitted. "Empty." He let the pad of his finger follow the curve of Naya's shoulder and the magic that dusted her skin scattered in its wake. "But not anymore, Naya. Now, I'm full. Complete."

A sad smile curved her mouth. He brushed her bottom lip with his thumb, full, almost pouty and petal soft. "It can't always be like this," she said. Her gaze darted to the left before she looked at him once again. "There will always be obstacles, Ronan. My people. Yours. I have a feeling that non-vampire pairings aren't the norm. Non-Bororo pairings sure as hell aren't."

Three vampire males spoke for an entire race at this point. And so far, the tetherings had been anything but normal. Ronan found no evidence of non-vampire matings in the Collective, but perhaps nature and evolution had compensated for the vampires' near extinction.

"Mikhail and Claire will love you." Claire shared Naya's fiery spirit. Ronan had no doubt that the two would like each other. "Jenner too." The male was like a brother to Ronan. He could have been tethered by a seaweed-covered sea nymph who had to live in a giant tank and Jenner would have approved. "They are my family. No one else matters."

That was the truth. The rest of the world could go to hell. He didn't give a good goddamn what anyone else thought. Even if Mikhail treated Ronan's tether with disdain, he wouldn't care. Naya belonged to him. And he was hers. There was no being, no force on this earth, that could break their bond.

And that included Siobhan.

"You're my family, Naya. My tribe. My pod. My coven. Whatever you want to call it. I don't give my vows lightly. And I've given mine to you."

"And you gave it to Siobhan."

"I did. For Mikhail. "

"You got in a little over your head, I'd say." There was no more pity in her sympathetic tone.

"That's an understatement. But I'd do it again," he said.

"I know you don't think so, but you're a very selfless male, Ronan. You sacrificed your body for your king and your friend. You sacrificed your memory and possibly—" Naya broke off abruptly as though the words were too painful to say. "—your life to find your sister. You're brave. A male worthy of admiration and love."

"You make me sound like a saint." He snorted. "Believe me, love, I'm not. I needed the codex. Ensuring that Mikhail's mate bond with Claire was secure was worth the sacrifice, but it wasn't selfless. I did it to be sure that Mikhail would give me his bite. That he'd uphold a centuries-long promise and turn me."

"Why was there any question? You said vampires recognize the tether immediately."

"Claire was human."

Naya quirked a brow. "Was?"

Ronan smiled. "Mikhail turned her."

"Ronan." Fear soured Naya's fresh rain scent. "I don't want to be turned."

His laughter echoed in the quiet room. "And I don't want to turn you. Claire is an anomaly. She was rare as a human and is even more so as a vampire. Typically, only dhampirs can endure the transition. I have no intention of trying to make you anything other than what you already are."

"A stubborn *bruja* with a laundry list of hang-ups and familial obligations with a penchant for violence?"

The air left his lungs in a rush. Gods, she was perfect. *"Exactly."*

She rose up on an elbow and put her mouth to his. The kiss was slow, sensual, deliberate. Her tongue flicked out at the seam of his lips and Ronan opened up to her, reveling in her dewy sweet taste. Her lips wandered to the corner of his mouth, and she murmured, "I'm lost to you, Ronan. Addicted. I don't have any control when it comes to you." She kissed across his jaw and took his earlobe between her teeth. "Nothing else matters. No one else. The way you make me feel I can't get enough. And it scares me."

Naya's palm wandered down Ronan's chest and the flat plane of his stomach. The muscles contracted and rippled under her fingertips as she ventured lower. Every word she'd said was the truth. She needed to go and talk to Paul and Joaquin before the situation with Ronan got even more out of control, but for the life of her she couldn't make herself leave his side. The magic generated by their coupling would wear off soon and his blood troth to Siobhan would remain intact. When would Naya get another chance to be with him like this?

If the magic overtook him, there wouldn't ever be a chance.

I'll have no choice but to kill him.

Naya's hands shook with fear. Roan would no doubt sense it and she focused instead on the work of art that was his body. If Luz had done what Naya had asked, Paul would be momentarily placated. Sunset was still hours away and Ronan was virtually a prisoner here until evening came. There was no telling what Paul would do once she showed up at the house. Hell, she might be the one to wake up handcuffed to a bed. He wouldn't want to hear what she was going to tell him: She was leaving. With Ronan. As soon as the magic creating the mapinguari was banished and they found Chelle. Naya was leaving the Bororo, her people, for a life with a vampire.

"Naya? What's wrong?"

Ronan wrapped his fingers around her wrist to stay her progress. She could hide nothing from him. Through their bond, her feelings were laid bare. She looked at him, her lips curving in what she hoped was a reassuring smile. "I'm going to talk to Paul before the sun sets. But before I leave I need this." She tugged against his hold and Ronan released her. "Let's both be selfish, just for a while longer."

His brow furrowed and his eyes flashed brilliant silver. The most breathtaking male she'd ever laid eyes on. "When it comes to you, Naya, how can I ever be anything but selfish?"

This wasn't normal. It wasn't even close to sane. They'd known each other for barely a couple of weeks, and already Naya couldn't imagine another day without him. Her need surpassed obsession. Hell, it went way past addiction. There wasn't a word to explain what this was between them. He was the air she needed to breathe. Water. Food. Ronan was *everything*.

The rough stubble of his jaw brushed her lips as she kissed him. Naya worked her way down his throat, nipping at the flesh before kissing his collarbone, over the swell of his pec, and down his chest. She ventured lower, down the trail of dark hair and the juncture where his thigh met his hip. The silky flesh of his erection brushed her cheek and Naya turned to kiss there as well. A groan vibrated in Ronan's chest and Naya kissed her way up and around the long shaft to the crown.

"Fuck, Naya," Ronan grated. "You're driving me crazy."

She took him in her hand—her fingers barely met—and stroked. He was marble encased in silk as her hand glided over his thick shaft. Ronan's hips bucked and he pressed his head back onto the pillows. She watched the play of muscles, contracting and releasing across his body as she stroked him again. Fascinating. A living, breathing work of art. With her free hand Naya cradled his sac, massaging the tender flesh as she took the head of his cock into her mouth.

She swirled her tongue over the engorged flesh and Ronan wound his fist in her hair, giving shallow thrusts of his hips. His breaths came in ragged pants, and as she took him deeper those pants turned to desperate groans. "Gods, yes." His thrusts became more forceful, though he didn't push any deeper into her mouth than Naya could take him. "That feels so good. Don't stop."

She had no intention of stopping. The giddy haze of the unique magic created by their coupling coursed through her veins and burst on Naya's skin like myriad bubbles. He filled her mouth, the salty-sweet taste of his skin causing her own moan of pleasure to vibrate over his shaft.

Power consumed her. Not only the magic but also the power borne of giving someone pleasure. Ronan writhed beneath her, the veins stood out on his arm as he worked his fingers against her scalp. She'd meant what she'd said to him. She was starved for Ronan and she would never get enough.

She took him deeper into her mouth, allowing the blunt ends of her teeth to scrape gently over his shaft. Ronan shuddered and an incoherent moan conveyed his pleasure in a way that words never could. The sound drove Naya mad with want. She worked her mouth over his shaft in earnest, sucking with greedy attention. She held the base of his cock firmly in her grip, stroking him as she worked her mouth back up to the swollen head.

Without warning Ronan sat up and seized Naya in his embrace. He flipped her around so that she lay on her stomach and jerked her hips up in the air. Her fists wound in the sheets and she moaned at the shock of heat as he entered her. Naya cried out as Ronan molded his chest to her back, his powerful thrusts sending her to a state of ecstasy that caused her limbs to tremble and her mind to go blank.

"Harder."

The word meant nothing, yet it came to her lips as though by instinct. Ronan wrapped one large arm around her waist to steady her, and his free hand cupped one swaying breast. He rolled the tight nipple between his thumb and finger, and Naya cried out, a desperate sob of pleasure that caused her sex to clench around his hard length. His mouth sealed over her throat and she came as his fangs broke the surface of her skin. Waves of sensation pulsed inside of her, the ebb and flow of which stole her breath and caused her limbs to go limp in his embrace.

Ronan disengaged, his hips jerking as he thrust wildly into her. Naya sensed that he was about to pull away and held on to him, gripping his thighs from behind. "No. Stay with me," she said through pants of breath.

His body went rigid as he came, his low, drawn-out moan coaxing delicious chills to the surface of Naya's skin. Heat flooded her body as his cock pulsed inside of her. He collapsed over her, holding her tight against him as he rocked back to rest on his knees. Their bodies still joined, Naya sank back, enjoying the way he filled her so completely. His heated breath raced in her ear and Ronan trembled around her. "Our child would be a dhampir," he whispered. The words bore such deep emotion that her heart ached. "A dhampir with the ability to hear the music of magic, perhaps. I wasn't sure if—"

"Ronan." Maybe they should have talked about issues like pregnancy before they'd attacked each other like mindless animals. Though supernatural beings didn't contract human diseases, they shared one sentiment with the mundane, and it was obvious Ronan was worried. "I'm not fertile, if that's what you're worried about. One of the benefits of wielding magic. I'm in control of every aspect of my body."

"I wasn't worried." He kissed behind her ear. "I love babies. I plan to have several of them someday. But we didn't talk about it and I didn't want you to think that I would be careless with you."

Several of them? Good gods. "I appreciate your concern." She laughed. "But there's no reason to be. And Ronan . . ." She might not have wanted to discuss the prospect of children with him while their relationship was so new, but it needed to be said. "I would love my child if it was a dhampir, *bruja,* or anything else."

He continued to hold her, his chest brushing her back with every breath. "The complications of a tether are many, it seems." The words were spoken with humor, but Naya sensed his worry.

"But nothing we can't manage." She meant that, too. Their relationship was definitely unconventional, but in comparison to the obstacles that still stood in their way— the mapinguari for starters—a conversation about birth control was a walk in the park.

Ronan pulled out and a profound sense of loss overtook her as their bodies separated. He urged her to turn and Naya settled in his lap, wrapping her legs around his waist.

"You're right." He kissed her once, slow. "There's nothing we can't manage."

Gods, she hoped they were right.

CHAPTER
25

"Naya. Wait for sundown."

Ronan raked his fingers through his hair as frustration churned in his gut. Two hours, that's all he needed from her, yet Naya refused to wait another second.

"I've already waited too long." She slid the yellow blade of her dagger into the sheath at her back before she secured a wide leather cuff bracelet around her left wrist. "It's not fair to Luz to make her run interference for this long, either."

"Seems fair to me." She'd threatened to run her blade through his heart. Ronan didn't want to be anywhere near Naya's cousin right now.

Naya turned a caustic eye on him and continued to get ready, retrieving a pair of boots from the nearly empty closet. "Paul already has it out for her. I'm not going to give him any more ammo."

The more Ronan learned about Paul, the more he sounded like the type of male that Ronan would like to stomp under his boot. "What did she do to get on his bad side?"

Naya grinned. "What didn't she do? Luz harbors a general disdain for authority. Doesn't really do her any favors with our tightly woven social structure, know what I mean?"

Ronan couldn't imagine any female feistier than Naya, though Luz had definitely served to rub him the wrong way. It appeared that the female was always looking for an excuse to commit violence on someone's person. Come to think of it, she'd be great to have on the payroll.

"Regardless, I think she can take care of herself, don't you?"

Naya's mouth formed a hard line. *So stubborn.* "That's not the point. Whether or not she can hold her own with Paul and Joaquin, she shouldn't *have* to. This is my responsibility, not hers."

"I'm a responsibility?" Ronan knew he was acting like an ass, but her words stung.

She let out a huff of breath. "You know what I mean, Ronan."

"What if you're attacked on your way?" He couldn't simply sit here, imprisoned until sundown, while she was out there, unprotected.

"Mapinguari are nocturnal." Her matter-of-fact tone drove him crazy. She cocked her head to the side and flashed him a superior grin. "Sort of like vampires. Nothing's going to attack me as long as the sun is up."

Infuriating! "There are more than demonic forces that could do you harm, Naya." Her own gods-damned people for starters!

"Paul's not going to hurt me."

Again, so fucking confident. "You don't know that."

"Ronan, Paul's power isn't absolute. With Bororo pods, every decision is made by the elders. We don't have a king. This isn't a monarchy."

As if Mikhail would ever make a decision without

counsel. But aside from that, did she think he was an idiot? "And I suppose the thought that he'd go rogue never occurred to you?"

"No," she said flatly. "The tribal structure relies on community. Why do you think this house is a secret? I have an apartment downtown. We all do. We're required to live on the same city block, Ronan. A sacred circle. If Paul broke that circle, he'd violate the tribe's trust. And he'd be punished for it."

So apparently the Bororo tribe was a lot like the Mafia. Once you're in, you're in for life. Where did that leave them, then? If he wanted to be with his mate, he'd be forced to stay in Crescent City? Become a part of Naya's life and sit in the prison of her home during the daylight hours while she was out doing gods knew what with gods knew who? Would he remain a secret—like this house—a part of her life protected from the tribal circle?

"Stop growling," Naya said as she slung a jacket over her shoulders. "I'll be back before you know it."

"I might not be here when you get back." In the back of his mind, common sense screamed for him to shut his fool mouth. But anger, frustration, and helplessness had taken control of his words.

Naya's annoyance flared and the sulfuric tang of her anger scented the air. "There's a bounty on your head, Ronan."

Did she think he gave a single shit about that? He was no coward. And he certainly wasn't afraid of a pack of shifters. "My sister is still missing, Naya." He matched her scolding tone, unwilling to back down. "I've done little to find her since the day I woke up cuffed to your bed."

Her eyes widened with shock and hurt and Ronan wished he could take back the accusing words. "Stay. Go. Whatever. You're not my prisoner or anything else, Ronan."

A stake to the heart would have been less painful than her dismissive words. Naya spun on a booted heel and strode for the door, slamming it behind her. A moment later the front door followed suit and a sickening silence settled over the tiny house.

"Gods damn it!" Ronan ground out from between his clenched teeth. Cold snaked up from the pit of his gut, fanning out in tendrils that wove around his limbs like lengths of ribbon.

The dark force within him surged up, glutting itself on his negative emotions like he'd glutted himself on Naya's blood. That insatiable hunger chilled him to the bone and Ronan shivered violently as he fell back to plant his ass on Naya's bed.

Fight it.

You're not my prisoner or anything else. She'd discarded him. Treated him as though he were as inconsequential as the boots on her feet. Icy cold snaked up his neck, winding to the base of his skull. Ronan clenched his head between his hands, the low growl in his chest building to a pained roar.

Let go. Don't give it fuel.

He wanted her. *Needed* her. She belonged to him, damn it. How could she treat their tether as though it were nothing? How could she leave him behind, trapped within these fucking walls until the sun set?

"Arrgh!" Ronan slipped off the bed and crashed to his knees on the floor. His fangs punctured his bottom lip and a trickle of warmth dripped down his chin. His limbs went numb, the cold unbearable. Fluorescent greens and blues rose to the surface of his skin like beads of sweat and Ronan panted through the pain. Darkness rose up like a tide and his lungs seized up as he was dragged away from consciousness by the undertow.

No.

If he gave in, let the darkness take him, Naya would be left unprotected. He couldn't let that happen.

Ronan sought the shelter of the Collective. Its presence had been all but nonexistent in his mind with the amount of blood he'd taken from Naya over the past few days. The power lent to him by feeding from his mate fortified his mind against its pull, but now he needed to lose himself, to hide from the magic that threatened to eat him alive. Perhaps submerging his psyche in potentially unhappy memories wasn't the best idea, but at this point Ronan didn't think he had any other choice.

Weeding through centuries of memories for only happiness wasn't as easy as you'd think. Ronan's concentration was shot to shit thanks to the effect of the dark magic that coursed through him, coupled with hours of intense sex and the blood he'd taken from Naya buzzing around in his skull until he wanted to bash himself with a hammer in order to quiet the shit down. The blanket Naya had thrown over the window kept the room dark. Still as a tomb. But he wouldn't be trapped here for long. Twilight was fast approaching, and with any luck Ronan would be five by five and ready to hit the streets in search of Chelle—and Naya—once the sun set.

Myriad voices called out, accompanied by the visions that were gossamer things in his mind's eye. Ghosts of lives lived, tragedies endured, happiness enjoyed. Escaping the more tortured memories became easier than he'd expected. It was the visions of joy and contentment that ensnared him. Like a fly caught in a web, he found it almost impossible to free himself from the tangle. His heart was too full, and the icy cold that raced through his veins, froze his muscles, and rendered him helpless began to retreat. Warmth infused his skin. Contentment swelled in his chest. The darkness fled and was replaced by a strength and light that made him feel as though he could overcome any obstacle in his path. He wanted to live in these moments forever.

The Collective was a wormhole from which there was no escape.

Slowly, as though waking from the deepest sleep, Ronan disentangled himself from the Collective. His eyes snapped open and a surge of strength coursed through him with the setting sun. He ripped the blanket from the window and jerked the cord that pulled up the blinds. A mantle of gray settled on the landscape outside and a feral growl rose in Ronan's throat.

No more hiding. It was time that these sly shifters knew what it felt like to be stalked.

Ten minutes had passed and both Paul's and Joaquin's silence had become unsettling. An intimidation tactic to be sure, and though she wasn't necessarily scared, that didn't mean it wasn't unnerving as hell. They wanted her to break. To panic and beg and blather on until she inadvertently supplied them with Ronan's whereabouts. Too bad for them, that wasn't ever going to happen.

Paul let out a slow, disapproving sigh. He didn't look a day over forty, though he had a good three centuries on her. His nearly black eyes narrowed as his gaze raked her from head to toe. A disdainful sneer pulled at his upper lip and a low growl echoed in the quiet.

Naya didn't budge. Didn't so much as let out a deep breath. She simply gave him stare for stare.

"What would your mother say if she was alive to witness your behavior?"

So, he was leading with a guilt trip. *Fabulous.* "I suppose she'd say that I should never let any male diminish my worth or power and that no wrong could ever be found in protecting those you care about." Paul didn't know shit about the female her mother had been. Pilar Morales had been revered not only by their pod but throughout the Bororo. Paul wasn't going to bullshit Naya with some conjured shame he thought she should feel.

"So you care for this creature?" Paul spat the words at her, his voice quavering with disgust. "He means as much to you as your own people?"

She couldn't show her hand. If Paul knew that she felt anything for Ronan, he'd hunt him with a fervor that would make the mapinguari's rampage seem tame in comparison. "Have I somehow failed in my duties as *bruja* to this pod?" She let the question hang in the air as Paul regarded her. Beside him, Joaquin's expression was that of veiled hurt and damaged pride. Out of everything that had happened in the past few days, the one thing she'd change was the way Joaquin had found her with Ronan under the pier.

"You've been satisfactory," Paul replied.

Wow. Don't go out of your way with the glowing praise. Naya ignored the barb, refusing to let him bait her. "Then what I do when I'm not on the job is none of your concern."

"*Everything* you do is my concern!" he snapped. "Especially when you've chosen to defile yourself with a vampire. Not to mention one that's been tainted with dark magic."

Defile. Taint. Trigger words made to make Naya feel as though she'd done something wrong. Paul could talk until he was blue in the face; it wasn't going to change the fact that she was tethered to Ronan. No amount of bitching or guilt-tripping would sever that connection.

"I need the vampire." The context of that need was none of Paul's gods-damned business. "Mapinguari are running rampant. I've never seen such a concentration of malicious magic. Ever. His sister was searching for a relic before she disappeared. I think it has something to do with this negative influx."

"A convenient story," Paul said with a shrug. "No doubt concocted to stay his execution. You've grown soft, Naya. We do not show mercy."

Wasn't that the freaking truth? For decades she'd done her duty, killed indiscriminately, extracted cancerous magic, and turned it over to Paul's keeping without batting a lash. No questions asked. It was she and Luz and other *brujas* in the vast tribe who could hear and manipulate magic, and yet time and again they'd entrusted it to elders who didn't know the first thing about what they were handling. They *brujas* had followed the elders' mandates without question.

Maybe it was finally time for a damned change.

"Ronan's sister and this relic she hunted is the key to the disruption. I'm sure of it. But I'm not going to find her without his help."

Joaquin let out a derisive snort and folded his muscled arms across his chest. "Your judgment is clouded by lust, Naya. It can't be trusted."

Of course he'd choose to see it that way. "You're making assumptions that aren't based on the facts, Joaquin. You don't know anything about him—"

"Tú mismo diste a él como una puta de mierda!" The words exploded from Joaquin's mouth in an angry shout that left him shaking with rage. "You are *mine!*"

Accusing her of whoring herself off to Ronan wasn't exactly the best way to win her favor. "I. Am. *His.*" Her gaze locked with Joaquin's. Despite her and Ronan's differences and the obstacles that still lay in their path, their bond was the one and only thing in Naya's life that rang with truth. "The vampire is my mate."

"Mentiras!" Paul shot out of his seat and pointed an

accusing finger at Naya. A static charge thickened the air
that caused the hairs to rise on her arms and the back of
her neck. Wild drums echoed in Naya's ears. *Curious.*
The air was thick with magic. More than what should accompany the presence of shifters.

"I'm not lying." Naya kept her composure. It wouldn't
do any of them any good to shout. "A mate bond is established through a tether. The vampire's soul is tethered to
mine."

"Impossible!" Paul seethed.

"Is that what he told you?" Joaquin said with disdain.
"And you believed him, no questions asked, just rolled
over and spread your legs for the *bebedor de sangre.*"

Naya had officially reached her breaking point. "I get
that your pride is hurt, Joaquin, and I'm sorry about that.
But insult me one more time and I'll be more than happy
to show you how that makes me feel with the tip of my
dagger."

"Enough." Paul's hand sliced through the air with the
word. "The vampire lies, Naya. There is no tether. Where
is he? Turn him over now and you'll receive no punishment for your decidedly foolish actions. We'll take care of
the *blood drinker* and you will return to your duties hunting
the mapinquari until the blood moon, at which time you'll
be *properly* mated to Joaquin. Do you understand?"

Naya was past the point of blindly following. For centuries their traditions had been upheld without question.
They'd lived in a bubble, a society within a society. Paul
might not have understood her tether to Ronan, but that
didn't make it any less real. Change was inevitable. If not
by Ronan's appearance in her life, something else would
have triggered it. "No, Paulo." The use of his given name
caused his lip to curl. *"El vínculo es real."* The bond was
real. She doubted that her words would sway him, but she
had to try. There were far more important things to deal

with than whom she chose to give herself to. "I can hear it. Our tether. It's woven with *magia*. There is no doubt in my mind, my heart, my soul. I'm bound to the vampire."

Paul's dark eyes glistened with gold and his pupils elongated. His canines grew in his jaw, protruding past his lip. Once he shifted, their discussion would be officially over. No use in trying to win an argument with an angry jaguar.

"I'm sorry you feel that way, Naya." His voice was roughened by the onset of the change, an inhuman growl that shivered over her skin.

The door burst open and fifteen of Paul's armed guards filtered into the room, their expressions fierce. Naya gathered her power in the pit of her stomach, ready to call on it if need be. The sound of something zinging through the air preceded a sharp sting at the back of her neck. What in the actual hell? One of them had shot her with a dart?

"You son of a . . . bitch." Her words were thick, slurred as whatever drug they'd hit her with took effect. "Gods damn you," she said to Paul as she crumpled to the floor. "You'll never find him."

A gold and black form leapt up onto the long table that lined the wall and a powerful tail flicked with annoyance. The jaguar hopped down to where she'd collapsed on the floor, her limbs all but useless. Naya called on her magic, but it wouldn't respond. Darkness descended and the cat sniffed at her face, issuing an angry hiss before he ran from the room.

If they hurt Ronan, she'd make them *all* pay.

CHAPTER
26

Christian stared up at the night sky, the moon heavy and round above him. It would be full in two nights' time, and after that he'd succumb to the change until it began to wane once again. *Fuck the moon.* Fuck this gods-damned curse that he couldn't escape. And fuck the bloody fucking animal that squatted under his skin, always present in his mind no matter if the moon was full or nothing more than a sliver hung high above his head.

Two nights left to find that son of a bitch traitor Gregor and Christian was no closer to pinning down his location than when he'd started.

Fuck.

He scented the air, disappointed to find it devoid of the dhampir's delicious jasmine aroma. Who gave a shit about finding Gregor when he could watch her tight ass and the sway of her hips hugged in the tight leather pants she had a penchant for wearing?

Just thinking about her raven hair and supple curves made his cock hard.

The hulking vampire who never seemed to be far from

the female was flying solo tonight. What was he to her, anyway? A bodyguard? Lover? A territorial growl rumbled in Christian's chest. The thought of any male touching her perfect body made him want to break something.

Jesus, obsessed much?

The night was quickly turning into a bust. Christian checked the scores for the USC game on his phone and cursed under his breath. He's missed the spread by three motherfucking points. One gods-damned field goal and he was out five grand. With a growl he tossed back what was left of the whiskey in his glass and slammed it down on the bar. Perfect ending to a shitstorm of a week.

He watched as the vampire made the rounds. If he was the dhampir's lover, then he was definitely playing the field. *Asshole.* The male was big enough to break Christian in half, and he wasn't exactly petite. Again, the thought of the vampire rutting on the dhampir sent Christian's blood to boiling.

Fuck this shit. I'm outta here.

Christian threw a twenty down on the counter and pushed away from the bar. If tonight's activities followed the trend, the vampire would be chasing pussy until sunup. All of this was a monumental waste of Christian's time.

The night air helped to cool his rising temper as he stepped out of the club, and Christian took several cleansing breaths. A faint scent piqued his curiosity, a deep woodsy musk. *Gregor.* Or at the very least a berserker. Christian took off at a clip, tracking the scent out of the club district. Ten blocks passed under his feet and he continued on, his attention focused solely on his quarry. Streetlights illuminated the sidewalk, but Christian kept to the shadows. He sidestepped a group of humans who were a little too drunk for sure footing, and stepped into an alley to keep from being knocked on his ass.

"McAlister must be desperate to send a tracker after me."

Christian was snatched by the collar of his shirt and whipped around. Gregor took hold of him by the shoulders and slammed him into the alley wall with enough force to crack the building's façade. His head knocked against old stucco and Christian let out a grunt. *Fuuuuck.* He was strong, but an angry berserker could put Christian on his ass without batting a lash.

"Take it the fuck easy," Christian said from between his teeth. "He doesn't want you dead. He wants you back."

Gregor chuckled. A cold, emotionless sound that got Christian's hackles up. "Sure he wants me back, but not before he teaches me a lesson for my disobedience, right?"

Christian shrugged. Well, gave as much of a shrug as one could while pinned against a wall. "You know how the director is. His pride took a hit when you left. He's gotta get a piece of it back. Doesn't mean he's not willing to let bygones be bygones. The Sortiari is always looking at the bigger picture, right?"

Black bled into Gregor's eyes, inky tendrils that swallowed up all of the color. It was fucking chilling when berserkers gave themselves over to rage. Even his wolf crept deeper into his psyche as though to take cover.

"They're nothing without their army," Gregor replied with a derisive snort. "And McAlister is an impotent coward."

True. Christian wasn't going to argue that point with him. "Wouldn't you rather be the right hand of Fate than another one of their targets?"

Gregor's eyes narrowed as he studied Christian. There was no use in trying to gauge his loyalties. He was a private contractor and McAlister had him by the balls.

"The Sortiari's plans no longer fit into my agenda."

"What does that matter?" Christian had one job, and

that was to bring Gregor in. He doubted McAlister would care how he got it done. "Why not use their resources to get what you want? You play nice with the director, knock some heads when he asks you to, and continue on the path you're already on. Wouldn't it be easier for you to accomplish your goals if you're not looking over your shoulder all the time?"

Gregor slammed Christian into the wall, rattling his teeth. Gods, that fucking hurt. Berserker strength wasn't anything to scoff at. "Let's get one thing straight, were-wolf. I'm not afraid of the Sortiari."

"Why would you be?" Tough to sweet-talk a male with the disposition of a badger. Why couldn't McAlister have sent Christian after the sexy dhampir? He would've liked the opportunity to sweet (or dirty) talk her into compliance. Still, he wasn't throwing in the towel yet. "I'm just saying. The Sortiari is after you; the vampires are after you. Why not knock one enemy off your list?"

"So now I'm the Sortiari's enemy?"

Fuck my life. How did one reason with a mindless beast hell-bent on violence? "Don't be thick, Gregor. You're an *asset.* I'd be willing to bet McAlister will turn a blind eye to your extracurricular interests as long as he gets you back."

Gregor snorted, his lip turned in a sneer. "And what's in it for you if I come crawling back?"

Another debt forgiven, as usual. "Money." No use lying; the berserker would smell it on him.

"Is that all?" Gregor did nothing to hide the disgust in his voice, but what did Christian care? There were worse sins than selling one's services for a few bucks. "So, you sell your skills to the Sortiari. Why not sell them to me?"

Gregor's grip eased up and Christian eyed him warily. He never said no to money, but he wasn't sure if he wanted any part of the vendetta that had supposedly caused Gregor to break faith with McAlister. "What would you need me for?" Christian was a damned good tracker, but there wasn't anything he could offer Gregor that the bersker couldn't do himself. The bastard definitely had one up on him in the strength department.

"A diversion. Maybe. I'll let you know." Gregor pushed away from Christian and turned to leave.

"What about McAlister?" No way was Christian going to let the berserker slip through his fingers. It would be his ass otherwise.

"I'll pay him a visit," Gregor replied. "On *my* terms. Don't worry, wolf. You'll get your paycheck."

Thank. Fuck. With the tanked USC game, he'd need the cash. His debts were starting to pile up and he wasn't interested in going on the run. Not again.

The black faded from Gregor's eyes and the aura of violence that enveloped him mellowed. He flashed Christian a cocky grin before taking off in a smudge of dark shadow. Fast. Strong. Deadly with a temper that ran south of hot *all the fucking time*. Why would Gregor possibly need a diversion?

Did it really fucking matter as long as Christian got paid?

With the werewolf gone, Jenner finally felt as though he could relax. Or relax as much as his desires would allow. It wasn't unusual to encounter a rogue every now and then, but this one kept popping up wherever he—or Siobhan—was. And Jenner didn't believe in coincidence.

"Jenner," a smooth female voice purred from behind him. "I was hoping I'd see you out tonight."

A smile grew on his face and he caressed the point of one sharp fang with his tongue as he turned to face Isla. The female looked good enough to eat in a flimsy white tank that gaped at the sides, revealing the lacy turquoise bra beneath and a skirt so short it was almost criminal. He'd be willing to bet she was going commando tonight. He could set her on top of his cock and go to town right here and now if he wanted.

And Jenner was sorely tempted.

The dhampir gave him a flirty smile, revealing the petite points of her fangs. His cock twitched at the sight. He hoped that she was hungry tonight. She swayed on her feet as she leaned in toward him, and her pupils were blown. It was a little early in the night for her to be so far gone. Drugs and alcohol had little effect on Jenner since he'd been turned. The only downside to his transformation. Now he found his highs by glutting himself on blood and burying himself between some female's thighs. Just as fun, though the downside was waking up the next morning with a clear head and even clearer memories.

Addicted to blood and pussy and willing to do or say anything to get it. Gods, he was as pathetic as any junkie.

The scent of Isla's arousal was almost too delicious to resist. But the female wasn't in any state to make a logical decision, let alone get her ass back to the coven. She'd become one of Jenner's frequent bedmates, but even so, he wouldn't take advantage of any female too fucking high to remember what had happened between them. She was Siobhan's responsibility and it made his gut churn with anger to think that the female was too fucking obsessed with Ronan's whereabouts to give a single shit about those under her care.

Who are you to condemn someone for their obsessions, asshole?

His own had mastered him from the moment Mikhail had turned him. "Are you alone tonight, Isla?"

She pursed her lips and they turned up at the corners coyly. "Yes. But I bet I could get Marissa to join us. I know you like her." Isla reached out and rubbed her palms over his chest. "Just say the word."

Jenner grabbed her by the wrists. He resisted the urge to pull her to him and bury his face in her fragrant throat. "Not tonight, honey."

Her bottom lip trembled in an almost pout. "What about Carrig? I heard him tell Siobhan that he wanted to have a go at you."

Carrig was one of Siobhan's lovers and everyone knew that the male's tastes ranged wide. Any other night, Jenner might have taken Isla up on the offer, just to see if mixing up his routine would do anything to quell the never-ending want that ate him alive. But knowing the werewolf had been following him again prevented Jenner from taking it easy. The male's constant presence could mean danger for Mikhail, and despite Jenner's own needs, protecting his king was more important.

Jenner released his grip on Isla's wrists and tucked her under his arm. "Come on, I'm taking you back to your coven."

"But it's early!" Her petulant tone made Jenner feel like a scolding parent. *Awesome*.

"You need to sleep it off, sweetheart. Siobhan wouldn't like it if she found out you'd let yourself get out of control."

Secrecy was paramount in their world. Getting too high, too drunk, too whatever opened the door for mistakes to be made. For secrets to slip. And Siobhan didn't spare the rod when it came to punishing the members of her coven.

"You're not going to tell her, are you?" Isla's horrified tone made Jenner feel bad for having scared her.

"I'm not going to tell her as long as you let me take you back so you can sleep it off."

She relaxed against him and Jenner led the way through

the club. He got points for not being a selfish bastard when the opportunity presented itself, right?

Jenner couldn't be happier to no longer be living with Siobhan's coven. For a group who considered themselves royalty in the dhampir hierarchy, he couldn't understand why they insisted on living as squatters in the condemned building. It wasn't as though they hadn't done what they could to make the space not only livable but also comfortable, but it was sort of like putting lipstick on a pig. Not the best use of their time and resources in his opinion.

After he tucked Isla into bed, Jenner tried to make as hasty a retreat as possible. He didn't want to be on the receiving end of another of Siobhan's interrogations. He still had no fucking clue where Ronan was or when he was planning on getting his ass back to L.A. The fucker needed to get back, too. Not just because of Siobhan, but because they had a shit-ton of work backed up and Jenner couldn't do it all alone.

"She won't remember in the morning, but she owes you one." Carrig stepped out of the shadows toward Jenner. "Little twit doesn't know when to stop."

Jenner gave the male a blank stare. Isla was young and careless but no twit. "Yeah, well, she's home now and won't be causing any trouble. That's all that matters."

"Any word on Ronan?"

Was there anyone in Siobhan's coven not burning the midnight oil to track him down? "No. And like I told Siobhan, I suspect he'll be back when he's gods-damned good and ready."

Carrig shrugged as though he could care less, and Jenner figured the male hoped Ronan would stay away for good. Being Siobhan's lover carried with it a certain station. With Ronan out of the picture, that made Carrig her main consort.

"Thanks for bringing Isla home," the male said, and headed down the hallway.

"Yeah, no problem," Jenner replied under his breath.

Tonight was officially wasted. Sunrise would put him down for the day, leaving him aching with a hunger he couldn't sate. A thirst he couldn't quench. For the first time in the weeks since his turning, Jenner was starting to think that the only thing to give him peace would be a Sortiari stake through the center of his heart.

CHAPTER
27

Ronan rifled through the cupboard in Naya's empty dining room. His head pounded and a dry, raging fire burned in his throat. After he woke from yet another epic battle with the magic trying to take over his body, his only option had been to draw on the communal power that Claire and Mikhail supplied to the interconnected web of vampirekind. It had certainly helped to get him back to fighting condition, but what he really needed was his mate's blood to nourish him.

Where in the hell was she?

Icy shards of panic speared Ronan's chest. The fear that gripped his heart in a vise was unlike anything he'd ever felt before.

Was she in danger?

Ronan reached through their tether, his frustration mounting as he was greeted by a dark void of sensation that left him shaken. First things first, he needed to find Naya. Then Chelle. And then he was getting the hell out of this town. He only hoped that that it wasn't too late for all of them.

Ronan stepped out on the porch without a clue as to where he should start. For a town the size of a cracker, he was surprised how tough it was to find his way around. Beyond the town proper lay acres of rain forests. To the other side, the ocean. The Pacific Coast Highway sliced it all in half, a beautiful tourist stop on the drive to SoCal. He supposed it was beautiful in the light of day. Green, lush, quaint. The perfect contrast to the blue waters of the Pacific in the distance. In the dark of night, however, Ronan was reminded that monsters lurked in the shadows. Demons intent on creating havoc. A cold, dark, evil presence that stole the cheer from this small town and turned it into something corrupt. Had Chelle had anything to do with that?

The presence of someone lurking in the shadows at the edge of Naya's property put Ronan on high alert. He kept his demeanor relaxed as he continued to stroll down the driveway as though unaware. Steps, barely audible despite the graveled driveway, overcame him and Ronan darted to his left, grabbing his assailant's arm as he tossed her body to the ground in front of him.

"Where is she, you son of a bitch?"

Ronan pursed his lips as he regarded one very enraged witch. Luz's chest heaved with her breath and her eyes sparked with a vengeful fire. Damn it, he'd hoped that Naya would be with her cousin. The fact that she wasn't caused the cold lump of dread in his gut to grow. "I thought she'd be with you." Ronan reined in his anger, though what he wanted to do was break the nearest available object. *Where in the hell is she?*

"Well, she's not." Luz pushed up from the ground and dusted herself off. "I've been trying to track her down for over an hour. Paul said that she never showed up at the house and she promised me—"

"Never showed up? She left here before sundown to turn herself in."

"So she lied?"

"No." Ronan would have smelled the deception had she lied. "Something happened to her. I can't feel her through our tether."

Luz pursed her lips and gave him some serious side eye. "That's just creepy, vamp boy. But I'm inclined to agree with you. Naya is no fan of tribal structure, but when it comes to protecting those she cares about, she does what has to be done."

"Then Paul's lying." A growl vibrated in Ronan's chest. He was going to get that bastard in a corner and the male was going to answer for his unreasonable mandates and harsh treatment of Ronan's mate.

"Honestly, I wouldn't put it past him," Luz remarked. She looked around as though trying to decide her next move. "I could see him lying to an outsider like you." She gave him an apprising look. "But why lie to me?"

Exactly.

Ronan took off down the driveway, his mind spinning with myriad scenarios. Naya wasn't dead—he would have recognized their tether being cut—but that didn't mean she wasn't in a shitload of trouble.

"Hey, bloodsucker!" Luz gave a sharp whistle and Ronan spun around. "Are you seriously going to hoof it twelve miles into town when we can drive?"

Ronan could have covered twelve miles on foot faster than they could drive. But with a force of Bororo warriors presumably out hunting him, perhaps stealth would be the better choice.

"This way." Luz headed back the way she'd come around the back of the house. An older-model Toyota 4Runner was parked several yards down the road.

"Trying to sneak up on me?" Ronan quirked a brow as he climbed in.

"Just wanted the element of surprise on my side in case you were slurping my cousin dry."

"I know my current state is volatile, but I would never hurt her."

"Yeah, I know," Luz said as though disappointed. "Sort of a bummer I won't get a chance to test my hand-to-hand combat skills with a vamp. Anyway, I suspected she wasn't here when I pulled up."

"Why's that?"

"I think she's unconscious," Luz said. "If she were awake, I'd be able to hear her."

"The magic?" Ronan asked.

"Yeah. I can hear hers from really far away. She's über-powerful." His mate was indeed powerful. "Even if she were asleep, I still think I'd hear it, but it would be faint. So she's either down for the count or she's . . ."

"She's not dead," Ronan said. "*I* would know if that were the case."

"Well, guessing isn't going to do me a damned bit of good if I can't track her."

Luz couldn't track Naya, but maybe Ronan could. It was a long shot—she'd only taken a small amount of his blood on her tongue. It might be enough for him to find her, however, if he was in close enough proximity.

"We'll start out in town and fan out from there. Is it possible that any other members of your pod have houses or properties that are secret, like Naya's?"

"It's doubtful," Luz said. For the most part, we're one big happy family if you know what I mean."

Somehow, Ronan doubted that. If Naya resented being under Paul's thumb, there was a good chance others did, too. "Where does your loyalty lie when it comes to her?" Ronan had to be sure that Luz wouldn't stand in his way if someone from their pod had taken Naya. They were a tight-knit group, and in those circumstances family strife was dealt with internally.

"My loyalty is to my girl," Luz replied. "Everyone else can piss off."

Ronan sensed no deception in her words; her scent was clean, reminiscent of a spring forest. Like Naya. His heart clenched in his chest as a fresh wave of anxiety-fueled rage came over him. He would rip the throat from any creature who sought to do her harm. And he would revel in the kill.

A twinge of pain stung at Naya's neck. Not the pleasant bite that suffused her with warmth when Ronan fed from her, but more like she'd been zapped by a hornet the size of her fist. *Ouch.* Her lids were heavy, and though she wanted to reach up and massage the spot on her skin that burned with a pulsing fire, she couldn't get her arm to co-operate. Gods, she couldn't remember the last time she'd been so exhausted.

"Ronan?" Her voice was unfamiliar in her ears, thick and slurred. Even her tongue refused to work correctly as it stuck to her too-dry mouth.

She was answered by silence, and a ribbon of anxiety unfurled in her stomach. Where was he?

The scratch of synthetic fibers abraded her cheek. Not the downy softness of her own pillow. Her last memory was of lying next to Ronan on her bed. Naked, deliciously sated, and feeling more whole and content than she had in her entire existence. Had she rolled off the bed onto the floor? And if so, why was she so damned helpless to get up? Talk about some serious lovin'. He'd rendered her completely useless.

Even the smile that grew on her lips was slow to form. This wasn't right. Something was seriously wrong with her.

Naya attempted to center her focus, but her mind wandered. A meditative state was essential to draw on her power. Images swirled, and a collage of the past several days played like a slide show in her mind's eye. Ronan, standing in the rain, magic leaking from his pores and his expression pained. The hard lines of his body as he fought against the silver chains she'd used to bind him to the bed. His fierceness as he fought the mapiguari. The concern and gentle care he showed her by hiding them in the storage container on the pier. The passion that lit his eyes with brilliant silver as he'd made love to her.

Love.

Could she love Ronan? His concern, his protectiveness, and his interest in *her* that went beyond what she could do and how it might benefit him caused her chest to ache with tender emotion. He'd laid himself bare to her as well, trusting her with the most painful memory of his past. An undeniable connection flared between them, an arc that ran soul deep, and a sense of comfort enveloped her just from being near him.

If those things weren't the very seeds of love, she didn't know what was.

Naya tried to open her eyes, but all she wanted to do was sleep. It didn't matter that the floor was hard beneath her or that her skin was chilled without the heat from his body beside her. Who needed a pillow when exhaustion weighed so heavily? And the pain that pulsed steadily in her neck . . . yeah, it was a little more than annoying, but maybe she could sleep it off without drawing on her power to heal it.

Sleep would make everything better. . . .

As she floated toward oblivion, a sense of unease scratched at the back of Naya's brain. Whatever she was forgetting, it was important. An entire chunk of hours that had been replaced by darkness in her mind. Sort of like the gap of time that was missing from Ronan's memory.

Where was he? Why couldn't she move? *What in the hell is going on?*

The fear that seized her helped to clear the fog that had settled on her brain. Her limbs were still heavy and weak and there wasn't enough saliva in her mouth to swallow against the dryness coating her tongue. She didn't bother trying to open her eyes again. Instead, Naya turned her focus inward as she attempted once again to center her power.

Warmth gathered in her stomach, a tiny sphere of energy the size of a marble. She envisioned it as a pinpoint of blue light that pulsed at the center of her being. *There it is.* Now that she had a grasp of the magic, growing and manipulating it would be easier. The marble gained in mass like a snowball coasting downhill as Naya drew on her power. Her breathing became deep, even, and her heartbeat slowed. *Thrump. . . . Thrump. . . . Thrump. . . .* Thoughts that thwarted her focus were sucked away like water down a drain, and the world around her dropped away as she achieved the perfect meditative state.

The blue orb that pulsed in her center exploded.

Power flooded her body, saturated her pores, and coursed through her veins. The pain in her neck disappeared, and though her memory still failed her, her mind became sharp and clear. Naya no longer felt as though she could sleep for hours. Instead, she was ready for a fight.

Her eyes snapped open and her vision was hazed over with a gossamer web of blue. Flooded with the magic inborn to her, Naya stumbled as she pushed herself to stand. Maybe her focus had been a little too sharp. Her brain buzzed and her ears rang in the silence that enveloped her. Adrenaline coursed through her veins and her once nearly still heartbeat kicked up its pace.

Whoa.

She'd been introduced to several new facets of her power over the past few days. And of all things, she had a vampire infected with parasitic magic to thank for it. A smile crept to Naya's lips, but her amusement was short-lived. She looked around the empty room—one of many in the large house the elders used for day-to-day business.

How did she get here? And when?

She reached around to her back; her dagger was gone, as were her sidearm and the knife she kept tucked in her boot. A search through her memory turned up nothing, as though an impenetrable wall blocked her path. She never would have left her house unarmed, which meant someone had divested her of her weapons or she'd been brought here against her will. Either option left her shaken. Because in order for anyone to do that, they would have had to go through Ronan to get to her.

Naya sprang to action, unwilling to remain static for a moment longer. A quick search of the house confirmed that she'd been left here without anyone to keep guard over her. *Interesting.* Familiarity tugged at her memory, as though the key to the missing chunk was just within her grasp. A cold chill snaked around her arms, residual malicious magic. She hadn't done an extraction since the night she'd tried to banish it from Ronan. Or had she?

Damn it. Not knowing what had happened stressed her the hell out. Her worry for Ronan overrode even her own sense of self-preservation. She needed to find him, make sure he was safe. If Joaquin or Paul or anyone else had laid a finger on him, her wrath would rival any punishment the gods could conjure. She'd make them all pay.

Naya wandered down the hallways, poking her head into this doorway and that only to find more of the same unhelpful nothing. She might as well have wandered in after hours and fallen asleep on the floor without any help from anyone. At the back end of the house, Naya stopped at the entrance to the council room, the very place where the elders had made their decree that she was to be mated to Joaquin. She let out a derisive snort as she walked into the room, remembering how she couldn't help but think that their order signaled the end to her marginally happy life.

Now the prospect of being mated to a male didn't fill her with dread. Rather, it filled her with a sense of hope. A future of companionship and a connectivity that she'd never had with anyone else. In hindsight, she realized that it wasn't the idea of being mated that was so unsavory. No, it was the command that she be mated to a male she hadn't chosen for herself.

But really, had she chosen Ronan?

Yes. Her *soul* had chosen his.

In the far corner of the room, a citrine glow drew Naya's attention. She made her way to a small desk and the drawer that had been left open just a crack. She yanked it open to find her dagger, gun, and knife tucked away inside. *Paul. That son of a bitch.* It had to have been him. Who else would have kidnapped her and taken her weapons without exacting any bodily harm. He had to keep her in good breeding condition for his son, after all.

Anger churned in her gut as she snatched up her dagger and sheathed it at the small of her back. She holstered her gun and tucked the knife back into her boot where it belonged. First things first, she was going to find Ronan. And after that, she was going to get some damned answers. Even if she had to threaten the entire elder council to get them.

CHAPTER
28

"What is this place?" Ronan asked as he stared up at the façade of the large, weathered house that loomed over the darkened street.

"The center of the village circle," Luz replied with a shrug. "This is where the elders conduct business. Sort of home base, if you get my drift."

And Naya was inside.

It hadn't been as difficult as he'd thought to track her. With even a minuscule amount of his blood in her system, he'd been able to sense her. It had taken a fair amount of concentration, but then, a few blocks from the house, their tether flared and he was acutely aware of her presence. Luz had noticed it in an instant, too, and Ronan marveled at these witches and their innate attunement to magical energy. Naya was finally conscious. And if she was anything less than 100 percent, whoever had harmed her was going to pay.

Ronan leapt from the car before Luz could bring it to a complete stop. His steps didn't even falter when she called out to him, "Hey! Slow your roll, bloodsucker!" Whatever danger he might face inside, Ronan would meet it head-on. Nothing mattered to him but Naya, and he had to assure himself that she was safe.

The front door splintered on the hinges as Ronan barged through. He rushed past the foyer and smashed straight into Naya. Before she could fall, he wrapped her in his arms and spun to settle both of their footing. She let out a desperate cry, holding him to her with a fierceness that struck him like a punch to the gut. "I felt you," she said through panting breaths. "Everything was still and quiet and then I knew you were here before I even heard the music of the tether. Oh my gods, Ronan, I was so worried! I thought that Paul or Joaquin had gotten to you!"

"Naya." Her name was a prayer of thanks whispered into her hair. Ronan cradled her against him as he tried to slow his racing heart and control the shaking in his limbs. A rumble of anger vibrated in his chest. "What happened? What did they do to you?"

"I can't remember." The fear that permeated her words caused his gut to tighten with worry. "I was lying in bed with you and then I woke up here. Everything in between is a blank."

"You left the house to meet with Paul," Ronan said. "You told me you'd be back by sundown, but you never showed up."

"I did?" Her brow furrowed and a ripple of anxiety reached out to him through their tether. "I don't remember any of that. I don't remember talking to Paul. When I woke up, the house was empty."

A fresh wave of rage clouded Ronan's vision. "We're going to find Chelle, and then we're out of here." He kept Naya tucked under his arm as he steered them back toward the door where Luz stood, one hand placed on her cocked hip.

"Girl, you scared the shit outta me!" she all but shouted at Naya. "There is some seriously shady shit going on here."

Understatement of the century. It wasn't a coincidence that Naya was experiencing the same type of memory loss that he was. Her own people—the family that was supposed to love and care for her—had done something to her. The betrayal wouldn't go unpunished, either.

"I'm not leaving until I get answers, Ronan." Her determination was admirable, but for safety's sake he wanted to put this town behind them as quickly as possible. "I felt the presence of foreign magic in my body when I came to. Someone put it there just like they put it in you. I need to know who. And why. If I don't, I might not ever be able to banish it from your body."

He had to admit, not dying would be good. And unless they got rid of whatever was currently squatting in his body, he was as good as fucked. Protecting Naya was his number-one priority, however. Tonight's events proved to him that her supposed haven was no longer safe.

"This is too dangerous. Too many variables."

From the doorway Luz snorted, and Ronan cut her a look. "The knight in shining armor routine is cute. Do you use it on all the females?"

"Don't start." She had a smart mouth, that was for sure. It was a wonder the feisty younger witch hadn't taken control of the pod long ago. She didn't strike him as the sort that took orders from anyone. She and Naya were certainly cut from the same cloth. "We need to get the hell out of here before someone notices she's missing."

What Ronan really wanted to do was to wait for the fuckers to come back so that he could show those cat-shifting bastards what it felt like to tangle with a truly formidable male.

Naya paused and regarded the door that hung on its hinges before turning to Ronan and quirking an amused brow. "Overzealous?"

He hugged her tight and flashed a confident smile. "When it comes to you, love? Never."

Luz hustled down the stairs ahead of them and down the driveway to her car. She stood with the door open, her brow furrowed as she chewed on her bottom lip. "Naya, *magia alimenta de magia. Es peligroso.* If you've both been infected—"

"I don't give a shit if it's dangerous or not," Ronan said before Naya could respond to her cousin. "We'll just have to deal with it, because we're not separating again."

Naya turned to him, her eyes narrowed and lips pursed petulantly. "*Habla Español*, Ronan?"

He gave Naya a peck on the cheek before depositing her in the backseat and climbing in after her. When they were settled, he gripped her chin gently between his thumb and finger and guided her face to his for a slow kiss. "One of several languages, actually."

"Impressive," Naya replied with a wry smile. "Obviously I have a lot to learn about my mate."

My mate. Gods, Ronan felt like the fucking Grinch at Christmas, hearing those words from her. His heart swelled near to bursting in his chest and he was overcome with emotion. He kissed her again, her face cupped between his hands as he slanted his mouth hungrily over hers.

"All right, knock it the hell off back there." He peeked from the corner of one eye to see Luz staring at them from the rearview mirror. "You're grossing me out."

Naya pulled away and smiled. The open, joyful expression stole his breath. "We need a game plan," she said as she settled back into the seat. "There isn't a lot of ground to cover, and I'd be willing to bet there's another mapinguari raising hell somewhere."

"We're not splitting up," Luz said. "So we need to decide what to track first. Paul, or the demon."

It was a no-brainer for Ronan. "Paul. The demon can wait." Ronan wanted to meet this male who thought he could control Naya and give her away as though she were nothing more than a commodity to be traded.

"No," Naya replied. "If we want answers we need to find the mapinguari, and I know how to lure one in. Luz, did you get ahold of Manny?"

"I did," she said from the front seat. "He's waiting for us."

"All right, then. It's settled."

"Why is this the first I'm hearing of this plan? And who in the hell is Manny?"

Naya grinned at Ronan's overprotective tone. Maybe it was a vampire thing to need to control every situation down to every finite detail. "You were down for the count when Luz and I discussed it," she said. "And Manny is our friend. He's human, but a magic sensitive. The mapinguari will be looking for a body to transfer its magic to. Manny would make the perfect host. The magic could just slip right in with little to no resistance."

"And what if your plan backfires?"

From the front seat Luz snorted. "Why don't you leave the magic to the experts, tall, dark, and vampsome?"

Naya nudged the back of Luz's seat with a knee. "Magic—and that includes dark magic—is just like any other living thing, Ronan. It needs to be sustained. Nourished. Magic becomes corrupt when it's stolen and manipulated by someone or something that it's not born to. Corrupt magic is like a parasite, and it needs a host to feed from to continue to thrive. Manny will be like a big, fat cheeseburger to this particular etheric force. It won't be able to resist him."

"Exactly," Luz chimed in. "Manny acts as bait, and we annihilate the pain-in-the-ass bad juju once and for all." She reached behind her for a high five and Naya obliged. "Be in awe of our badassedness, Nosferatu."

"And what if your badassedness isn't badass enough?" Ronan countered. He turned to Naya, his expression severe. "What if that magic targets you instead?"

"Silly vampire," Luz said. "Why don't you relax and let the big girls handle this."

His gaze flashed silver as he ignored Luz and kept his attention focused on Naya.

"It won't," Naya explained. She reached out and squeezed Ronan's hand, hoping to reassure him. "Our own magic makes us sort of immune."

"You said you felt it in your body."

"I'm not saying it doesn't affect us," Naya explained. "I'm almost certain that dark magic is what's caused my memory loss. But it can't overtake us. It just dissipates in our bodies, dilutes like a drop of food coloring in a glass of water. It can't grow or thrive inside of us."

"Because we're awesome."

Naya rolled her eyes. Luz was too cocky for her own good.

Aside from the tension that Ronan threw off, Naya was confident. If she could pinpoint the source of the dark magic, that might make expelling it from Ronan's body easier. At this point, it was her last resort. She couldn't let it take him. Wouldn't let it. She'd fight to her dying breath to save him.

"Tell me about the relic Chelle was searching for." It was all connected. Had to be. And the sooner everything was out in the open, the better their chances.

Ronan raked his fingers through his hair and let out a gust of breath. "It's a vampire relic," he said after a moment. "The origin of our race is rumored to have begun with it."

"The suspense is killing me, dude." Naya nudged Luz's seat again, but she either didn't notice or didn't care. "Spit it out already!"

"What Chelle was looking for—has been searching for over centuries—is Set's chest. And the last intact memory I have before waking up in Naya's house was getting a phone call from her, telling me that she'd found it. Here."

"Set as in the Egyptian god?"

"The one and only," Ronan replied.

"How does an Egyptian deity tie into vampire lore?" Luz asked. "You're a little too blue-eyed and white to be from that part of the world. KnowwhatImean?"

Ronan ignored Luz's snarky observation, but he did give his head a rueful shake as his gaze met Naya's. Apparently she wasn't the only one who noticed that Luz acted like a sixteen-year-old most of the time. "Set constructed the chest as a coffin for Osiris. He tricked him into laying in it and sealed him inside. Isis found the chest and rescued Osiris. Set consequently hunted Osiris down and ripped his body into pieces, scattering them throughout Egypt."

"Yikes. Can you say overkill?"

Naya laughed at Luz's rib and Ronan gave a lopsided grin. "After that, the myths fork into separate legends. As vampires are told, Isis tasked the god Thoth with placing a resurrection spell on the chest that Set had constructed to be Osiris's tomb. And after Isis collected the pieces of Osiris's body, she placed them inside the chest. When he emerged, he was whole but there were noticeable changes."

Naya leaned forward, rapt. "Such as?"

"Fangs," Ronan said with a grin that showcased his own sharp dual points. "An insatiable thirst for blood and an aversion to sunlight. For starters."

"Cool!" Luz exclaimed with all of the enthusiasm of a kid at a magic show. "If that's true, then you're, like, descended from a *god*. Pretty impressive, bloodsucker. Also, can I just point out that without the help of magic you probably wouldn't be here right now?"

Naya laughed her agreement. "She's got a point. Why was Chelle looking for it? And how did she track it here?"

"I have no idea how she tracked it here. Our phone conversation was brief. She said she needed me to come and that someone was following her. After that, the line went dead. Chelle's a bit of a tomb raider, but only where it pertains to vampire relics. She takes private contracts, but the chest has been her own personal obsession. For centuries, Mikhail was the only vampire and our kind teetered on the brink of extinction. Without a mate, he wasn't strong enough to turn a dhampir."

"And she thought if she found the chest she could make vampires without Mikhail's help?"

Ronan cocked a brow. "It was a hopeful notion when we had no hope."

"But you don't believe it?" Naya asked.

"As much as I do any myth. Who can say? There isn't any evidence of it in the Collective, and neither I nor Mikhail is old enough to have witnessed it."

"The Collective?" Luz asked.

"Vampire memory," Ronan explained. The memories of every vampire living or dead are shared among all of us."

"Creepy," Luz said with an exaggerated shudder.

"It can be a challenge, but it can also be very useful."

"You bet! Especially if you thought your girl was steppin' out on you."

Leave it to Luz to give the vampire race's collective memory a Jerry Springer twist. "If the legends are accurate, the chest would hold an immense magical charge," Naya explained. "Especially if it carries the power of resurrection."

"A god's magic? Big mojo."

Naya met Luz's gaze in the mirror. She had a point. "Magic can only be used for its intended purpose. If someone who didn't know anything about it was trying to make that magic work for them it would certainly corrupt it."

"And whoever has Set's chest might have Chelle." The hope in Ronan's voice was like a dagger to Naya's chest.

"That would be my guess." Unless, of course, Chelle had been one of the first to be corrupted. In which case, odds were good that Ronan's sister was already dead.

Luz pulled to a stop in front of a storefront at the edge of downtown with the sign *Occult Books and Curiosities*. From inside, the low light of a single bulb illuminated the space, and Naya noticed Manny leaning over the counter, his nose buried in a book. "We're here," she said to Ronan. He opened the door and she put a staying hand on his arm. "He's human, Ronan. He knows a lot, but he doesn't know everything. We need to go easy on him, okay?"

Ronan's brow furrowed for a moment before he swept the worried expression away with a smile that showed off his fangs. Naya rolled her eyes. Not exactly what she'd been hoping for. "Don't worry, love. I deal with humans on a regular basis. I know how to behave myself."

Somehow, Naya had a feeling that her idea of Ronan behaving was way different from his.

"Hurry up, losers!" Luz called as she beelined it for the front door. "We're burning darkness and we need to get this wrapped up before Prince Fanging goes down for the count."

Ugh. Luz. Always so impatient.

CHAPTER
29

After trekking around the world with Chelle for decades, Ronan now had a tendency to stay away from the occult. He preferred to deal in what he could control. Keeping an A-list celebrity's mistress's damning pics off of Twitter or Instagram was a hell of a lot easier than dispelling a curse or transporting a charmed item. The blood codex he'd acquired from Siobhan had been the deepest Ronan had been willing to dig into vampire lore in a long time. He supposed if he was going to get back involved he might as well go all in. Start at the motherfucking origin of their very existence. And they were going to rely on a human to lead them to it.

Fucking nuts.

As they walked through the door, a man—presumably Manny—looked up from a leather-bound book. He was tall and wiry, clean-cut, with short hair and thick black-rimmed glasses. His eyes lit up when he saw Naya, and Ronan swallowed down a territorial growl as he remembered his promise to behave himself.

"So, Luz says you want to use me as bait." His voice

was mellow and even, full of confidence. "You gonna make it worth my while?"

He winked and Ronan's body went taut. Luz reached up to pat him on the shoulder as she walked past, chuckling. "Heel, boy."

Ronan wasn't used to feeling so territorial, and so far his time spent with Naya had been mostly one-on-one. Now that they were in the presence of another male—one who obviously found himself charming—Ronan had a hard time suppressing his natural impulses.

"Manuel Esparza, you sexy thang," Luz drawled as she approached the counter, "I'll make it more than worth your while."

Everyone enjoyed a laugh, except for Ronan. He stood stoic at the door, arms folded across his chest.

"Who's your bodyguard?" Manny asked with a jerk of his head. Luz snickered, but Naya flashed Ronan a radiant smile that almost made him forget the tension that pulled like tightly wound string through every muscle in his body.

"Naya's new boy toy," Luz responded. "He's broody."

Luz spoke about him as though he should be carrying a pickaxe and keeping company with Sleepy, Grumpy, or Doc. "Ronan," he said by way of introduction.

"Manny," he replied with an amicable smile. "All right, what's the game plan? Want me to stand outside with a sign around my neck? *Free body. You possess.*"

Luz's peal of laughter cut through the relative silence of the little shop.

Ronan suspected that the younger female's interest in the human went a little beyond simple friendship. He wasn't *that* funny. "I'm curious as well." He might as well jump in now, because he wasn't going to be the broken wheel that slowed this hunt down. "We have a limited amount of time to see this through, and it's counterproductive to wander the streets and beaches for the rest of the night."

"Ronan's a night owl," Luz explained. "You'd think he was allergic to the sun or something."

As Naya stepped up to the counter she shot her cousin a look. "I'm not interested in wandering around town all night, either. We'll scry for the mapinguari and track it that way. It's a little complicated, but much more efficient."

"Woo-hoo!" Luz exclaimed. The volume of her voice seemed to crank up with every word spoken. "Blood magic. Bring. It. On!"

Blood magic. Ronan didn't like the sound of that.

"With the two of you, it shouldn't be difficult," Manny said. "It's a great idea, actually, and will save tons of time."

"Why not just listen for it?" Ronan was in favor of saving time, but not at the expense of Naya engaging in anything that might be risky.

"We could," Naya said with a shrug. "But that could take longer than the time we have. Luz and I have good ears but not so good that we could hear the magic from miles away. And a mapinguari could easily been hiding in the forest somewhere."

"Gah!" Luz let her knees give out in dramatic fashion. "That would take for-ev-er! Scrying will be quicker. Easier. And it's fucking *cool*."

Well. As long as it was *cool*.

"Trust me, Ronan. This is our best option. And I know what I'm doing."

She sounded confident, but Ronan wasn't so sure. The magic that manifested inside of her during sex was something she barely had a grasp of. Who was to say she could control blood magic any better?

"And besides," she continued, "you're going to help me."

The words shouldn't have evoked such a strong sense

of lust, but gods, she spoke as though for him alone. As though the act would be something intimate between them.

"Uh-hum!" Luz cleared her throat with overexaggerated gusto. "I'd tell you two to get a room, but we really don't have the time. So keep it in your pants. Both of you."

Ronan exchanged a look with Naya. A whip of sensual heat snapped out at him through their tether as their bodies angled toward each other, mere inches separating their parted mouths.

"I'm not kidding," Luz said. "I do *not* want the live show."

Naya took several steps back and brushed her fingertips across her bottom lip. Rosy gold bloomed on the surface of her flesh, and Ronan marveled at the play of color against her dark skin. He'd never, ever tire of seeing that physical evidence of his effect on her.

"Okay," she said on a rush of breath. "Let's get going. We're wasting time."

As Luz and Manny set about gathering what they'd need for the ritual, Naya grabbed a bag of salt from one of the shelves and used it to draw a circle on the rough wood planks of the floor. "Sit." She indicated a spot on the floor and Ronan lowered himself down. Luz and Manny joined him, dividing the circle into what he assumed would be quarters once Naya sat down. A squat candle was placed in the center of the circle along with a shallow copper bowl.

Ronan was a throw-punches-first-and-ask-questions-later male. He'd never been one for patience. Or ritual. However, as he watched Naya pace clockwise around the circle, eyes hooded as she chanted low under her breath, he found an appreciation for her measured steps and serene expression.

Lovely.

"Almost ready," she said under her breath. As she came around to the starting point, Naya entered the circle and took a seat near Ronan, her legs crossed in front of her.

"Luz."

From behind her back the younger female produced a dagger similar to Naya's. Luz held the grip in her palms, the blade's tip just below her chin. Her eyes drifted shut, and with a few murmured words the dagger glowed with all of the intensity of the sun. Her lids snapped open and she held out her hand, slicing across her palm with the blade. Blood welled from the deep wound, the aroma awakening Ronan's thirst. His fangs punched down from his gums and his throat ignited with a dry fire.

"Try to focus, Ronan," Naya said from the corner of her mouth. "I can feel you wandering."

Remarkable. Ronan steeled himself against the mounting bloodlust. In his fledgling state, he still felt the urge to drink overwhelming. Sitting in a circle where the participants willingly opened their veins in front of him was a lot like being forced to hang out at an all-you-can-eat buffet without filling your plate.

Luz turned to Manny and he held out his hand. She ran the blade across his palm and a ribbon of crimson flashed against his skin. Ronan's nostrils flared and he pierced his tongue on a fang in an effort to master his thirst. Tonight's experiment would be a test of his fortitude, that was for damned sure. Luz bent over his palm and put her lips to the wound. After a moment she guided Manny to press his bleeding palm to hers. They held their joined hands over the bowl and Ronan watched, rapt, as thick drops of bright red splattered onto the worn copper. Rather than spread out in the bowl, the blood pooled like mercury, a shining crimson bead that rolled with liquid grace. It leapt and bounced like a living, breathing organism waiting to be let loose.

Naya drew her dagger from behind her back and repeated whatever ritual awakened the magic in the blade. It glowed with a bright, blinding yellow and she held out her hand. Ronan gave her his, palm up. When it was her turn to bring the blade to her own flesh, he knew he was going to lose it. How could he sit back and watch the lovely crimson bloom from her skin and not take it on his tongue? But instead of repeating Luz's actions, Naya brought the blade to Ronan's wrist. She leaned toward him and he mirrored her actions, his breath sawing in and out of his chest as he waited for her to act.

He hissed in a breath as the blade bit into the skin at the heel of his palm. The burn of magic kept the wound— which should have healed almost instantly—open. Blood welled from the two-inch slice and Naya bent over him, her beautiful lips parted. Her mouth sealed over the spot where she'd cut him, and a groan of pure pleasure rose up in Ronan's throat.

Ah, gods!

His head spun with each deep pull of suction. To have his mate drink from him was bliss, the greatest pleasure he'd ever known. This wasn't some playful act like the moment he'd scored his tongue to allow her to kiss the blood away. No, there was purpose behind the act. An intent that stirred his lust and hardened his cock. He'd never wanted her more than in this moment.

Naya blinked lazily and the corners of her lips tilted up as she drank. All too soon she pulled away and a black hole of need opened up inside of Ronan, demanding that he take her. Her body, her blood. He wanted to lose himself in her.

A flash of light caught his attention and he watched as

she sliced her palm. She joined their hands, and their mingled blood dripped into the bowl to form a separate bead that rolled and hopped alongside the first. Ronan couldn't peel his eyes from her. Didn't give a single shit that they sat in the circle with others. When she pulled away and moved to break their joined hands, Ronan wrapped his fingers around her wrist and hauled her palm to his mouth.

Secrecy be damned. He *needed* his mate's blood.

A ripple of energy flooded Naya. Not the giddy, drunken magic that coursed through her veins when she touched Ronan, kissed him, fucked him. What she felt now was something entirely different, though no less heady. Blood magic was sacred and practiced very rarely for a reason. Naya was blinded by power. Bursting with it. A sense of invincibility crested over her, and she felt as though she could take on the world. Luz's eyes nearly bugged out of her head, and Manny watched with fascination as Ronan snatched Naya's hand tightly in his grasp and brought it to his mouth.

Quid pro quo, it seemed.

She did nothing to stop him. Her heart pounded against her rib cage and her pulse rushed in her ears, nearly drowning out the riotous sound of magic that echoed all around her in a symphony. Ronan didn't simply take from the wound she made with her dagger. That was much too civilized for her vampire. He claimed her with his fangs, the flesh yielding to his bite.

Fire chased through her veins, igniting every nerve ending in her body into a heightened state of sensitivity. Pleasure pulsed low in her core and a deep, needy ache opened up inside of her. She wanted Ronan inside of her. Wanted him to pound into her without mercy. She needed him hard and fast, and with an urgency that echoed the desperation pulling her muscles taut. Naya wanted to tell the world to go to hell, and leave here. Go back to her house and lock themselves inside forever. Ronan was her universe. The sun at the center of her existence.

"Ronan." Naya's voice was thick with want and emotion. She had to break the spell of this moment now, before she was too far gone to him to do anything about it. Luz squirmed uncomfortably opposite her and Manny averted his gaze. She'd let this go too far and it was time to get back on track.

Ronan's tongue flicked out at the wounds before he pulled away and a shiver chased across her skin. She flashed Luz an apologetic grimace, which she responded to with a dramatic roll of her eyes. "Let's just get on with it," she said as she sheathed her dagger at her back.

Luz and Naya held their cupped palms over the bowl as though warming their hands. Magic glowed, rose and lavender, and after a moment the blood reconstructed itself into a three-dimensional image. A relief map of sorts. Fascinating.

"That looks like one of the trailheads at Del Norte," Luz said. "The one at Mill Creek Campground that we partied at last June."

"It does," Manny agreed. "That's only about ten minutes from here."

"Remember how wasted Jules Everett got?" Luz snickered. "Oh my gods, she totally—"

"Later, Luz," Naya interrupted. She swiped her hand over the bowl and a flash of heat hit the blood, incinerating it. "Let's get moving."

Powerful witch. Ronan stared at his mate with wonder. So full of surprises.

CHAPTER
30

Naya didn't like to start a hunt at midnight. Her mother had always said it was a bad omen, but Naya didn't have a choice. The cusp of time where night bled into day. Sunrise was still several hours off, but they couldn't waste a second, let alone a few minutes. And so she swallowed down the ominous feeling that rose in her throat and set out for Del Norte.

Manny was quiet in the backseat beside Luz. He was the most at risk in this endeavor. Being human was a definite disadvantage. Among the three of them, however, Naya was confident that they could keep him safe.

"Here's how it's going to go down," Naya said as she drove. "Manny, it needs to look like you're alone, so you'll go out first. But we're going to be close and Ronan is faster than any of us. The mapinguari won't get the chance to latch on to you."

"I'm not worried." The words belied the quaver in his voice. "I trust you, Naya."

The air was thick with tension as everyone filed out

of the car at the Mill Creek Campground ten minutes later. Naya handed Manny a short dagger that wouldn't do much in a fight but might distract the mapinguari if need be. He took a steadying breath and gave Naya a shaky smile. "Well, looks like I can cross 'act as demon bait' off of my bucket list."

He was the bravest human she knew. Not many others would put themselves on the line like this. "I've got your back," Naya said. "We all do."

"I'll run point," Luz announced. She was noticeably wound up, and the music of her magic played at a frenzied clip. Naya had always suspected that Luz's feelings for Manuel were a little more than friendly. This confirmed it. It also made for a complication.

"No. You're too emotional." This wasn't a seek and destroy mission. They needed to contain the mapinguari and use it to lead them to whoever was creating demons. If Luz let her fear and feelings for Manny rule her, she'd kill first and ask questions later in an effort to protect him.

"Bullshit," Luz argued. "I'm not the one who almost got it on in the middle of a scrying ritual."

Low blow, but Naya was willing to let it slide. Luz was worried about Manny, and Naya felt the same way about Ronan. Which was why she was willing to use Manny as bait in order to track down the source of the dark magic. But that didn't mean she was going to give her cousin her way. "No, Luz. This is my responsibility. I'll run point. You flank the path that leads to the trailhead. It'll give you a straight shot to Manny if this goes bad."

Luz's gaze bored through her. "You drank vamp boy's blood," she said after a quiet moment. "What did it do to your *magia*?"

"Supercharged," Naya admitted. "Like the Red Bull of magic."

"Good," Luz said. "You're going to need it. Come on, Manuel, you gorgeous hunk of man meat, let's get going."

Even overcome with worry, Luz was able to keep things light. Naya wished she could do the same.

"Are you ready for this?"

Ronan's breath was warm in her ear. His presence at her back was a welcome comfort, and Naya fought the urge to lean into his chest and guide his arms around her. Right now she needed to be hard. Tough and emotionless. She wasn't going to be any good to anyone if she let her more tender emotions get the better of her. "We've only got one shot at this. There's no room for mistakes. Just remember, don't kill it. I need to find the source and that won't happen if we extinguish the dark magic."

"Naya, I need you to know—"

"Don't, Ronan." She refused to look at him. If she saw the emotion undoubtedly shining in his eyes, it would undo her. "We'll talk after."

"There might not be an after."

How could he say that? She whipped around to face him, this time fueled by anger and frustration. "You don't get to say that." Her voice was nothing more than an angry hiss. "I'm doing this for you. For *us*. I'm going to rid that poison from your body and then we're going to find Chelle."

"You said it yourself, Naya. This magic, it needs to feed. I can feel it rising up in me, and my thirst for blood is *nothing* in comparison to the hunger of this darkness that's eating me alive. If it comes down to it, I want you to kill me. Do you understand? Don't hesitate. And when it's done I want you to get the hell out of this town. Go to L.A. and find Jenner. He'll know what's happened and he'll protect you."

A sob worked its way up Naya's throat, but she forced it down to the soles of her feet. Damn it, why was Ronan doing this to her now? It wasn't fair of him to force the reality of their situation in her face when she was trying to keep a freaking optimistic outlook. She hadn't wanted to admit it to anyone, not even herself, but Naya knew that their odds were bleak. The mapinguari were stronger than any she'd ever faced.

"Drink." Naya had used Ronan's blood to fortify her magic; now she was going to give him hers to fortify his body against the magic's dark influence. She gathered her hair up and secured the length with a hair tie. Standard procedure when she was going out on a hunt. Hair could be pulled, snagged easily. She tilted her head to one side to give Ronan unhindered access to her throat. "I need you strong, Ronan." She refused to let him succumb to this evil force. Wouldn't let him go without a fight. "Do it."

The scent of Naya's blood was a siren song he couldn't resist. Her heart beat steadily, filling his ears with the only music he needed to hear. A beautiful sound as its rhythmic thrum pushed the blood through her veins. His need left Ronan shaking, and his fangs throbbed painfully in his gums. When would enough be enough? When would his thirst for her slake? And why had she so quickly become his drug of choice? An addiction he'd never, *ever* be able to kick. He doubted even Mikhail thirsted for his mate with such dire intensity. It was the magic inside of Ronan that hungered for Naya. For the power inside of her.

In the pit of his gut the cold chill of dark magic ate away at him like a cancer, and malicious thoughts picked at his brain, digging in like a tick. *Drink. Drain her.*

Ronan seized Naya in his grasp and pulled her roughly to him. He buried his face in her throat and bit down with abrupt force. She cried out, clutched his shirt in her fists. Blood flowed warm and sweet over his tongue and Ronan took gulp after gulp, groaning against her flesh as he drank. Naya went limp in his arms, her own heavy breaths bordering on desperate gasps. "More."

Gods, when she ordered him like that, her tone forceful yet breathy, he was helpless to do anything but obey. As he sucked, Ronan fought the urge to answer to the darkness inside of him. To drain her. To take everything she had to give. Through their tether, strength flared within him, helping to banish this insanity from his mind. Naya was his strength. His life. And there wasn't a force on this earth that could convince him to harm her.

He scored his tongue and sealed the punctures, kissed and nuzzled her fragrant throat when he was through. The gods only knew what he and Naya would be facing tonight. The dangers, the sacrifices they might be required to make. "I love you, Naya." Ronan didn't know if he'd get the chance to say these words again and he wanted her to hear them and know that they were true. "Gods, I love you."

It was too soon for words like "love," but that didn't make them any less true. Sure, they hadn't spent enough time together for him to learn the little, inconsequential things like whether she liked chocolate or vanilla ice cream, scary movies or action flicks. Did she prefer to shower or take a bath? And most important, pretzel or peanut butter M&M'S. Because everyone knew that peanut butter were the best. The pretzel ones just didn't cut it.

Those weren't the things that determined whether or not you loved someone, though. Ronan knew that Naya was fierce, strong, and protective. Passionate. Smart. Demanding when she needed to be and giving when she wanted to be. She was loyal. Tough. So yeah, Ronan could say without a doubt that he loved her. Those were the things that mattered. They'd have time enough to learn each other's nuances. *Maybe*.

Hopefully.

Fuck.

"Do you hear it?" It wasn't going to do Ronan a gods-damned bit of good to lament his impending death like a sniveling pussy. If these were his last moments, he was going to live them to their fucking fullest. Dark magic be damned.

"It's faint. The mapinguari has to be pretty deep in the forest. Without Manny, we'd be out here chasing it for hours. Once it catches his scent, so to speak, we'll be golden."

"What then?" If Ronan had it his way, he'd kill the fucker. "How do we subdue it?"

"I'm going to bind its power," Naya said. "And if it works, the mapinguari will be as helpless as a little kitten."

"If?" Ronan didn't like ifs.

"It's going to work." Naya hopped over a moss-covered log as she headed farther up the trail, and Ronan followed. The scent of the forest enveloped him, so similar to Naya's natural scent.

"What makes you so sure?"

"Because I drank your blood, vampire," she said in a teasing tone. "Big juju. My *magia* is *strong*."

"You think so?" Ronan wanted to believe it, but fear for her safety, and a nagging doubt, ate through any confidence he might have felt.

"Oh, I *know* so. Can't you feel it through the tether? I'm practically vibrating with power. If I'd known vampire blood would supercharge my magic, I would have been out looking for you, not waiting for you to tackle me to the ground in an unconscious heap."

Had he known about Naya, he would have begun searching for her, too. "What can I say, I know how to make an impression." They came upon some heavy foliage and Ronan reached over her to clear the way. She turned back and beamed. *Gods.* Just looking at her made his chest ache. Ronan reached out through their tether, searching for some evidence to her claim that his blood had given her magic a power boost.

There it is.

Holy. Shit. Naya hadn't been kidding. Ronan didn't know how he'd missed it. Power pulsed through their bond to fill him with a sense of strength and vitality that rivaled what he felt when he drew on Claire's and Mikhail's stores of power. *Amazing.*

Maybe the future wasn't as fucking bleak as he thought.

"Watch out!" Naya's arm shot out behind her. Ronan's heart rocketed up into his throat as Naya's throaty laughter surrounded him. "You almost got beaned in the face by that limb."

Jesus. He was a fucking wreck. So worried about Naya's safety that he could barely put one foot in front of the other. *Focus. You won't be protecting shit if you can't get your head straight.* Instead of letting her truck out ahead of him, Ronan reached out and took Naya's hand, gently urging her toward him. He put his lips to hers for a slow, gentle kiss. Her mouth was so damned sweet.

"Oh, gods!" Naya pulled back with a gasp. "I can hear it, Ronan. It's close."

Naya took off at a sprint, negotiating the steep forest trail as though she could see as well as Ronan in the dead of night. The canopy above blocked out the starlight and they were shrouded in a fragrant, damp darkness that chilled his skin as he chased after her.

Ronan was kidding himself if he thought it was simply the late-autumn air that made his blood run cold.

Despite the blood he'd taken from Naya, the strength that she offered him through their bond, the darkness inside of him had woken.

And it was hungry.

CHAPTER
31

Naya's vision blurred and the cacophony that assaulted her ears nearly brought her to her knees. But she pressed on, running like a wild thing through the forest, focused on capturing the mapinguari before it had a chance to infect Manny with a healthy dose of dark magic. Ronan was close behind her, his own footsteps pounding on the earth as he chased after her. With him at her back, she didn't have to worry about an ambush, though it left him vulnerable. There was no place for worry or anxiety right now, though, and Naya refused to acknowledge the fear that pierced her chest like an arrow.

Magic pooled in her gut and the dagger warmed her back through the sheath. She drew on her power as she pressed forward, dodged tree branches and bushes, tangled with thick ferns as she raced to cut the mapinguari off before it got to Manny. Gods, she hoped he'd had enough time to surround himself with salt.

She drew her dagger as she came upon the footpath that led to the trailhead. Manny couldn't have been more than ten or twenty yards ahead and Luz was somewhere to the south, ready and waiting to jump in. The trap was set. Now it was time to spring it.

"Naya!"

The urgency in Ronan's voice stopped her dead in her tracks and she turned. In an acrobatic move he launched himself in a graceful arc, his boots barely clearing her head as he flew past her. She whipped her head around in time to see him clash with a massive black and orange form as he took the massive jaguar to the ground.

"Get the hell out of here! Run!"

The scream of an angry cat pierced the night and Naya's lungs seized. Indecision gave her pause. Ronan was strong. A warrior. A supernatural creature with speed and quick healing. Virtually immortal. Manny, on the other hand, wouldn't last if the mapinguari got ahold of him. Each step that took her away from Ronan was like wading through sludge. Her body resisted, urging her not to part with him. But in truth, he was safer in a tussle with a Bororo shifter than he'd be with a demon.

Naya didn't have time to worry about which member of the pod Ronan fought and, more important, why he was out here. Hunting a vampire, maybe? And was he alone? *Shit.* Her boots dug into the soft earth as Naya propelled herself forward. The sound of limbs breaking and wood splintering behind her caused her heart to stutter in her chest, but she pressed on.

Stay on task. Get to Manny. Bind the demon.

She covered the next thirty yards at a hard sprint, her step only faltering once as she tripped over a rock. How much farther? Where was he? Where in the hell was Luz? Naya spotted the dark outline of a body up ahead and she slowed her pace to a careful jog. She pulled her dagger from the sheath, massaged the grip in her palm until it felt like an extension of her hand. Riotous music burst in her ears, wild drums and screaming horns.

"Naya . . . ? Luz . . . ?"

The dark shadow of Manny's body didn't so much as twitch. Through the darkness, Naya made out the white outline of a circle on the ground around him. The salt would deter the mapinguari but wouldn't stop it.

"I'm here. Luz?" Silence answered and Naya's heart stuttered in her chest. "Luz?"

Damn it.

Another complication to draw her focus. Nothing was going according to plan so far, and her watertight plan was beginning to leak like a sieve.

"I don't know what this thing is, but it's packing a punch." Manny's words were muffled as though he spoke from the corner of his mouth. "My skin is crawling with magical energy and the damned thing isn't even in sight. Not gonna lie, Naya, this is making me nervous. And where's Luz?"

That made two of them. Her nerves were pulled as taut as a guitar string. One hard pluck and she'd snap. She couldn't let herself think about Luz right now. Between her safety and Ronan's, Naya's concentration was shot. She needed a clear and level head to center her own magic. She wasn't going to be of any use to anyone otherwise.

"Luz can take care of herself, Manny." Naya could barely hear her own voice over the din of the music. She crept closer, keeping to the foliage until she stood off the foot trail, just to the left of the salt circle that surrounded him. "Where is it? Can you tell?" The music was already too loud for her to discern the location of the source.

Please don't say south.

"To the south I think. That's where I feel the most intense concentration of energy."

Naya's teeth gnashed and she gripped the dagger tighter in her palm. Luz had flanked Manny from the south. *She's okay. She can take care of herself.*

The trees rustled several yards ahead and Naya tensed. She'd feel a hell of a lot better about the impending fight if she'd known everyone she cared about was safe. *Focus, damn it.* Naya crouched low, ready to pounce as she waited for the mapinguari to approach. Power gathered in her gut, the magic snaking through her limbs with silky warmth. She shook with pent-up energy and her head pounded from the cacophony of music that blared in her ears. Just a little closer. A few more steps and she'd have it. A sleek, dark shadow crept down the trail toward Manny. A chuff of breath fogged the air as the mapinguari approached. A little closer. A few seconds, that's all she needed to wait before she could attack.

Whatever Ronan fought, it wasn't a shifter. At least, not anymore. The cat was larger than the jaguar he'd fought a couple of nights ago. Its eyes glowed feral green in the darkness and its incisors were unnaturally long. Likewise, its body was bulky with heavy muscle, the animal's shoulders larger and out of proportion with the narrow taper of its body. Powerful haunches flexed as the beast moved to pounce and Ronan shifted on the balls of his feet, ready to dodge an attack if need be. This was a planned distraction. Something engineered to separate him from Naya. He needed to put the animal down and get to her ASAP.

"You're the second male I've fought too cowardly to meet me face-to-face."

The cat snarled, revealing its long, sabered teeth. It lunged at Ronan and he started, a prebattle ritual a lot like playing chicken. Armed with one of Naya's long daggers and a .45 Ruger loaded with silver-tipped rounds, the obvious solution would be to shoot the fucker Indiana Jones–style and walk away. The gun remained holstered at Ronan's side, though. He doubted a bullet would slow the mutated cat, let alone stop it.

This was going to have to be hand-to-hand combat. Well, hand-to-giant-fucking-paw. *Damn it.* He needed to get to Naya. Now.

The cat lunged again and Ronan crouched low, the dagger held firm in his grip. "You aren't the only one with fangs, you big bastard," he goaded. "So quit posturing and *do something!*"

In a single graceful leap, it attacked. Rather than dodge the tackle, Ronan met it head-on, the dagger poised to stab. The blade slid between the cat's ribs, buried to the hilt. Its scream echoed in the night as they fell to the ground, breaking tree limbs and smashing bushes as they rolled down the embankment. Their downhill progress was stayed by a large boulder, and they crashed into it in a crunch of tangled limbs.

The jaguar was stunned and even Ronan was a little slow to move. A large branch jutted out from his right pec and the scent of blood was thick in the air. He might have been quick to heal, but he hurt like a sonofabitch. He wrapped his hand around the branch and yanked. "Motherfucker!" Ronan's shout echoed around him and he panted through the pain as the wound began to close on its own. He rolled over, the bloodied dagger discarded a few feet beside him, and scooped it up.

The jaguar slowly came to. It rolled to its stomach and shook out its massive head. Ronan didn't have time for this bullshit. He stabbed down quickly, driving the blade between the animal's shoulder blades. It let out a pained yowl before its head slumped to the ground. He pulled the dagger out with a yank and scrambled back up the hill, his speed making him a smudge of shadow in the dark as he raced back to the trail that would lead him to Naya.

"Don't move, Manny. Stay in the circle, understand?"

Naya's tone was wary but not frightened as Ronan approached. He kept his steps light, though what he wanted to do was rush to her. Hold her. Get her the hell away from anything that could hurt her. But in her soul, his mate was a warrior. Brave. Stalwart. He could no more ask her to back down than he could ask the wind not to blow. Naya was a force of nature, and he had to trust that she could take care of herself.

That didn't mean he wouldn't fight by her side, though. And it looked like she'd need all the help she could get.

The mapinguari towered over her. *Huge.* Much larger than the one they'd fought two nights ago. Covered in coarse, dark fur, this one looked a lot like a bear on steroids. Freakish, supernatural steroids. Each of its massive claws resembled daggers affixed to its paws, and its beady crimson eyes were barely noticeable on its face. The damned thing smelled like death warmed over, and gooey, thick saliva dripped from its maw of a mouth. It regarded Naya with a frightening intensity, much too calm for Ronan's peace of mind. This wasn't some mindless beast with an appetite for chaos. The mapinguari had a plan and it simply bided its time before putting the plan into action.

A demon with a brain. Great.

Luz was nowhere in sight, just one more kink in an otherwise perfect plan. Considering the circumstances, the human seemed to be holding up well, which earned a fair share of admiration from Ronan. Because on a scale of one to a hundred, their situation ranked somewhere near fucked beyond repair.

"Behind you, Naya." Ronan kept his voice even so as not to startle her. "I'm right behind you."

She let out an audible sigh of relief but didn't turn. "Are you all right?"

"Five by five, love. You?"

"I will be once I bind this thing and find Luz."

The beast canted its head to the side, looking over Naya's head at Ronan. It sniffed the air and a low growl rumbled in its chest. A giant gob of spit dripped from its mouth and landed on the ground with a wet plop. This was seriously fucked up, and Ronan had seen some hair-raising shit in his life.

"What's the plan?" The thing was obviously sizing them up and Ronan didn't think that giving it time was going to work in their favor. They needed to put it down before it got tired of waiting around.

Naya turned the dagger over in her palm, a quick twist that Ronan imagined she did subconsciously. "I need to bind it. But it's bigger than I thought it would be. I don't know if I can do it without Luz's help. What about your trouble? Is it taken care of?"

He hoped it was. The cat was at the least incapacitated, if it wasn't dead. "Think so. Though I have a feeling that someone from your pod has been drinking the Kool-Aid, if you know what I mean."

Naya cursed under her breath, "Fuck."

Yup. Pretty much.

The mapinguari shifted and Naya mirrored its movement. It looked past them to where the human stood confined in a ring of salt, and a hungry rumble bubbled from its gut. It brought its enormous snout up to scent the air before its gaze landed on Ronan.

"I can immobilize it." *Probably.* The fucker was *big.* "Just say the word."

The mapinguari swayed, craning its thick neck once again to see around Naya and Ronan to Manny. Naya followed its movement and listed to the other side. She blocked the demon's view. It swayed again. Like a cobra and a snake charmer, their strange battle dance continued for another few seconds. A jolt of energy snapped out at Ronan through the tether and a burst of battle-fueled adrenaline dumped into this system.

"Get ready, Ronan. On my count. Three . . . two . . . one."

Ronan sprang into action, but before he could lay a finger on it the mapinguari crumpled to the ground like a puppet whose strings had been cut. Fluorescent light bled from its lifeless body, oozing and winding down the footpath toward them. The dark magic inside of him surged, a blizzard of icy cold that raged. He snatched Naya by the waist and spun, keeping her clear of the viscous substance headed their way.

"Holy shit!" she exclaimed. "What in the hell just happened?"

The demon's essence, blood, or whatever the fuck it was continued on its path, surrounding Manny. The salt circle kept the magic at bay but officially turned the human's sanctuary into an island. No way in—or out.

"Sit tight, Manny," Naya said. "I'll get you out of there."

"Yeah. Let's work on that." From the quaver in his voice, Ronan suspected that if they didn't get Manny to safety soon the human was going to lose his shit. "The faster the better."

"I need Luz." The worry Naya was throwing off buffeted Ronan's senses with the prickle of a cactus. "Where is she? Without the mapinguari, we're screwed. I've never tried to contain or control dark magic outside of a body. Hell, I don't even know if I can banish it on my own."

Ronan's grip tightened on her waist and his fingers curled like claws. A powerful urge to sink his fangs into Naya's throat overwhelmed him. And he wouldn't stop there. No. He'd rip the flesh. Tear. Bathe in her blood. *Kill*.

With an abrupt shove Ronan cast her from him. Naya grunted as she stumbled, her expression severe as she turned to face him. The anger melted as he went to the ground. He collapsed to his knees and cradled his head in his hands. Cold enveloped him. Cold and darkness and hatred unlike anything he'd ever felt.

"Ronan?"

"Don't come near me, Naya," he ground out from between his teeth. "Don't fucking touch me!"

CHAPTER
32

Naya didn't have to ask Ronan what was wrong to know that he was in the grips of the infectious magic. It vibrated around her. Crawled on her skin. Soured the air until she didn't think she could take a decent breath. And gods, the sound of it. She slammed her hands over her ears in a desperate attempt to block it out.

"Naya, this is bad." There was too much going on for her to manage on her own, and Manny's panicked words weren't doing anything to decrease her stress levels. "We need to find Luz and get the hell out of here!"

No shit. But with one member of their party trapped inside of a cleansing circle, the other in the grips of dark magic, and the other currently MIA, there wasn't a whole hell of a lot Naya could do. Her *magia* was tight, but it didn't give her powers of teleportation.

"Manny, you're safe in the circle. Don't move." Without a physical body, the dark magic that evacuated the mapinguari's form would have a tough time breaching the salt circle. Of the four of them, Manny was definitely the safest. "You need to hold tight until I can form a plan of action." Her attention was divided between the trickle of magic that surrounded Manny and the male buckled over and cradling his head in his palms not ten feet from her. "Ronan, can you hear me?"

Like the first time she'd laid eyes on him, Ronan threw his head back in agony. Magic leached from his pores as though his body rejected it. His chest heaved with labored breath and a shout of pain erupted from his chest with enough force to cause the branches of the surrounding trees to quake.

"He is *not* okay, Naya."

"Yes, thank you, Manny. Don't you think I know that?" Her own frustration and anger was past the point of containment. She needed to go to him! Touch him. Soothe him until that dark force had no choice but to crawl back in its hole and sleep.

She took several rushing steps forward and Ronan's head snapped to attention. His eyes glowed with silver light and his lips pulled back to reveal the twin tips of his elongated fangs. "Not another step, Naya, not until your dagger is ready to strike. Do as I say, damn it!"

She'd never been one for following the rules. "Listen up, Ronan. I'm not giving you what you want. Understand? I'll die before I kill the male that I love."

A pained howl burst from Ronan's lips, as though he couldn't bear to hear the words. Well, too damned bad. Naya didn't think she'd ever say them, either. But there it was; the truth of it couldn't be denied. Their souls were connected, bound forever. How could she not love him?

"That's right! I love you! So you'd better fight, Ronan, because I'm not letting you go. Not now. Not *ever.*"

The rustle of foliage in the distance drew Naya's attention from both the crisis on her left and the one on her right. She spun, dagger in hand and ready to fight. A large jaguar stalked out of the forest and onto the path. *Holy shit.* The cat was enormous, a hulking sinuous body with silky fur and rippling muscle. Dangling from his jaw was an unconscious Luz, her limp form looking very much like a mouse caught in the grip of a simple house cat.

Ronan hadn't been kidding when he'd suggested that someone from the pod had been drinking the Kool-Aid. *Good gods.* He'd fought that thing and walked away? This was no mapinguari. He looked like an animal right out of ancient history. He could have easily kept company with mammoths.

"Let her go." Naya squared her shoulders and willed her spine to stiffen. That one of her own people would betray them was as good as a dagger through her heart. "If you've hurt Luz, I'm going to kill you."

The Bororo males carried recognizable traits that made them easy to identify in their animal forms. Joaquin, for instance, had a black coat with a white spot that marred the fur below his throat. Dark magic had turned this particular shifter's form into something unidentifiable. He might as well have been a stranger to her.

Luz groaned as the cat deposited her in an unceremonious heap to the ground. She was alive. And for now, Naya would count it as a blessing. The cat craned his neck, taking stock of everything around him. Surrounded by crisis and unable to help anyone, Naya had never in her life felt so utterly alone.

Magic sizzled in the air, a deafening pop and hiss to accompany the din of music in Naya's ears. The sensory overload threatened to take her down, but Naya forced herself to remain stalwart. She could end this. Now. She simply needed to stay strong.

The shift was usually a fairly painless transition, from what she'd been told. Sort of like slipping into a pool of warm water. But the enormous jaguar screamed and thrashed his massive head as he left his animal skin behind. Clawing at the damp ground as he writhed.

Naya used the momentary distraction to grab Luz. She was weak but conscious. "I . . . I'm okay." Luz pushed the words out in a slur. "This is some serious shit, Naya."

That was the freaking truth.

She dragged her cousin several feet away from the epicenter of danger and tucked her in the bowl of a towering redwood. "Don't move," Naya instructed. "Just sit tight and keep quiet, got it?"

"Mm-hhmm." Luz couldn't manage more than a sound of acknowledgment, but it was good enough for Naya.

"Is she okay?"

"She will be," Naya said to Manny. He sat in the middle of the circle, arms rested on his knees. "I owe you for tonight. Sorry everything went to crap."

"It's all good," Manny said in a less-than-convincing tone. "Just get rid of this magic before it harms anyone else."

That was the plan.

She approached the shifting cat with caution, one tentative step after another. Her dagger held at the ready, Naya said, "Toss me the box, Manny. Just toward my feet."

"Got it."

The gold box landed on the ground beside her with a muted thud. A simple square with a slot on the top just big enough for her dagger to be inserted, it looked more like an elaborate piggy bank. She hoped it was big enough to contain the amount of dark magic that surrounded them. It was more than she'd ever had to banish before. What happened next would be a test of power and endurance that Naya refused to fail.

It didn't matter who he was. The male was tainted by the darkest of magic. She didn't know if he controlled the magic or it controlled him. Hell, maybe he was another unfortunate victim. Either way, she needed to bind him before it was too late. Naya was done with killing.

The last traces of the animal disappeared, and with it a strong wave of natural magic dissipated into the air. Naya let out a deep breath as some of the tension left her body and she shook out her shaking limbs and she continued to approach. He lifted his gaze to meet hers and the shock sent her stumbling back a step.

"Paul?"

Though really, should she have been the least bit surprised? He'd always been a bitter, power-hungry male who found immense satisfaction in lording his authority over the pod.

"Evolution is inevitable," Paul said through heavy panting breaths. "And the *magia* is no longer yours to control, *bruja*."

Ronan might as well have been encased in ice. The Collective was beyond his grasp; there was no shelter to be found there. Even his tether with Naya appeared to have weakened. When he tried to reach her through it—to pull from her strength—the bond felt tenuous and thin. As though it might snap with the slightest jostling.

His thirst was too intense. His need absolute. Nothing save a stake through his heart would save him now.

"Had you simply allowed yourself to be given to Joaquin, you wouldn't have put so many in danger. But as always, Naya, your stubborn willfulness proves that you are worthless to this pod."

The male who spoke wasn't the human. Blind to everything but the cold that numbed his body, Ronan scented the air and found that the male who disrespected his mate with his callous words was the shifter he'd fought on the foot trail. The bastard who had dipped into the stores of dark magic to give himself an edge. And Naya faced him alone.

"You've betrayed *us,* Paolo." Naya's voice thickened with her anger, the heat of it melting some of the chill that seized Ronan's body. "And you *lied* to me. *Used* me. It's time for you to answer for that."

"You think you're in the position to take me to task, *mujer*?" The male laughed, and through the tenuous thread of their tether, Naya's anger further heated. Her rage cleared the icy fog in Ronan's head. "The pod listens to me, not you. I've found a way to circumvent nature, stupid girl. You and your ilk—like the legends of our people—are about to fade into obscurity. Dark can't exist without light. I'll pass this power on and with your help we'll breed a new race of our people. Mankind will tremble in our presence and we'll take this world back from the pathetic mundane who've disregarded their stewardship of the earth in favor of their own useless greed."

"The earth isn't our responsibility and neither is policing humans. We follow *El Sendero*. It's what we've always done. You're crazy if you think any of the pods will follow in your wake. I won't let that happen."

"Truly, Naya, I'd hoped you'd cooperate. But the truth is, I don't need you. Not as long as I have Luz."

Ronan's soul howled in agony at the threat inherent in the male's words. Instead of fighting the grip of debilitating cold, Ronan let it in. Magical energy surged within him, a dark, sickening power that made his stomach turn. He couldn't let it take him. Not completely.

Ronan's vision cleared in an instant. A tall male, naked and enraged, rushed at Naya, catching her off guard as he took her to the ground. She cut crossways with the dagger, dragging the blade across his chest. He let out a rough shout as he rolled them over. The male's bulk pinned Naya to the ground and he wrapped his hands around her throat.

Ronan rolled to his hands and knees, his joints stiff as though frozen solid. He worked the tension loose as he pushed himself to stand, wobbling on his feet as he tried to find a balance between the dark magic that threatened to overtake him and his own consciousness that fought for control of his body, mind, and soul.

Until Naya was safe, not a gods-damned thing was going to take him down.

The balls of his feet dug into his boots and Ronan gained his footing and pushed off the ground at a dead run. Manny sat inside of the salt circle, surrounded by bright blue liquid light that poked at the perimeter of salt as though looking for a way through. Five feet ahead, the male looked up, his hands still wrapped around Naya's throat. Any male with balls enough to put his hands on Ronan's mate was guaranteed to meet a violent end.

Despite the chill that stiffened his joints, Ronan overtook Paul with ease. Like plucking fruit from the vine, Ronan swept him away from Naya and threw him to the ground. Behind him Naya coughed and spluttered, gasping for breath. "Ronan, don't kill him!" she rasped. "Paul's infected. We need him if we're going to find the chest and your sister."

Could this be the son of a bitch who'd taken Chelle? "Where is she?" Ronan grabbed Paul by his hair and dragged him up until he was at eye level. His dark eyes gleamed with malice and his full lips pulled back into a sneer that revealed a row of straight, white teeth.

"The dhampir?" he asked with a superior chortle that made Ronan want to rattle his brain inside of his head. "You mean you don't remember? You were with her after all."

His disbelieving chuff of breath steamed the night air. Could he have actually found his sister? Been with her before someone had infected him with this fucking dark magic? What else had happened that he couldn't remember? He tossed Paul back to the ground, as inconsequential as a discarded rag doll, and pressed his knee into the male's back as he pinned him face-first to the earth. "Where is she?" Ronan leaned in close until his mouth rested near the male's ear and railed, "Tell me!"

Magic rose up inside of him, a charge of power that left him feeling damn near invincible. His thirst raged—with an urgency that far surpassed anything he'd felt thus far—and demanded he glut himself on blood. *Do it,* the darkness urged. *Drain him.*

Ronan clamped down on his control, pushing back the cold, the *need* that threatened to master him. Soft, warm skin slid over his arm and he looked up to find Naya standing above him, her touch so gentle that it caused his heart to constrict in his chest.

"Stay with me, Ronan." Her pleading tone nearly did him in. "Fight it. Be strong for me."

Anything. He'd do *anything* for her. He couldn't push the words past the gods-damned lump that settled in his throat. He gave Naya a sharp nod of acknowledgment and kept his eyes focused on her. His powerful mate. Warrior. Goddess. *Mine.*

"Okay." She let out a slow sigh of relief. "Just hold him. I need Paul immobile so I can bind him. Once that's done, I'll banish the magic attacking Manny and we'll get Luz and get the hell out of here."

The sooner they got the fuck back to town the better. The sooner they could find Chelle.

"He's trying to shift, Ronan. I've got to do this now."

Ronan watched as Naya knelt on the ground beside Paul. He struggled against Ronan, but the bastard could fight all he wanted. He wasn't going anywhere. Beneath Ronan's hold, the male's muscles bulged and grew as his body sought to leave its human form. Naya's eyes met Ronan's, shining like water at midnight. She clenched her dagger in both fists, the tip pointed down, and drove it into the earth with a forceful shove.

Paul thrashed beneath Ronan's hold and let forth a string of profanity in English, Spanish, Portuguese, and another language that Ronan couldn't decipher.

"Shut the fuck up!" Ronan barked as he pressed Paul harder against the ground. "The only thing keeping you alive right now is the female you're disrespecting. One more word and I'll rip out your throat. Understand?"

Naya didn't acknowledge Ronan—her concentration was absolute—but her lips quirked at his words. Warmth rushed through their tether, chasing away the cold. Gods, she was extraordinary.

He watched with fascination as a soft blush light gathered in her palms. The serenity of the moment filled him with an odd sense of comfort. She was so calm: eyes closed, expression soft, her lovely mouth parted slightly with her measured breaths. The light spread from her cupped hands, engulfing her body in a halo of light. *Beautiful.* The sight of his mate bathed in magic was so lovely that it caused a lump of emotion to grow in Ronan's throat.

Naya tipped her hands and the pooled magic poured over Paul's body. He jerked against Ronan's hold, struggling as threads of magic twined around him, binding him as though with a length of rope. Her softly murmured words reached Ronan's ears, an ancient language that he didn't understand.

So in awe of her, Ronan could do nothing but stare.

"Okay, you can let him go now." Naya slumped backward, one shaking arm bracing her. In an instant he was by her side and scooped her up into his embrace. "I'm okay." Her words were meant to reassure, but her voice was weak. Quick, panting breaths rose and fell in her chest and she trembled in his arms. "Besides, I can't get too cozy. I still have to banish the mapinguari's essence and we need to make sure Luz is okay."

What about making sure *she* was okay? "You're exhausted, love." Ronan put his lips to her temple, her jaw just below her ear. In the pit of his gut the cold rose once again, but he forced it down. He refused to let that dark force control him when Naya needed him. "Rest. For a couple of minutes at least."

"No rest for the wicked," she said with a laugh. "There is one thing you could do for me, though. . . ."

Ronan smiled against her skin. Didn't she know he'd do *anything* for her? "Name it."

She let out a shuddering breath. "I need a little of your blood to replenish my magic."

Gods, how he loved an assertive female.

CHAPTER
33

"What my mate wants she gets."

Ronan's voice was a sensual purr in her ears. Naya's stomach did a little flip despite her exhausted state. His pleasure radiated through their tether, leaving her warm and relaxed in his arms. Binding Paul had taken every last bit of energy in her stores and the night was far from over.

Ronan's smug satisfaction didn't go unnoticed. Until she'd met him, she'd never experienced the magic that could be harnessed through sex or blood. Ronan had given her both. Just like he claimed her blood was an elixir of life for him, his body, his blood, was a source of power for her. It seemed with each passing moment the universe was proving to her how perfect they were for each other. A fated match to be sure.

Tethered.

"You have to promise to behave yourself." Ronan nuzzled just below her ear and inhaled deeply. They weren't clear of danger yet. It was *way* too early for him to get comfortable. "This is business. Not pleasure."

"You've got that wrong, love." Another delicious shudder rippled through her. "Because the business of nourishing my mate—giving her *whatever* she needs—is indeed a pleasure."

Gods, he could crumble her resolve with nothing more than a few heated words. "Ronan."

"Naya," he replied in the same chiding tone.

She felt him smile against her skin and it caused her chest to swell with tender emotion. "Work first. Play later."

His thumb brushed her jaw. "Promise?"

She smiled. "On my word."

He refused to let her leave his lap as he scored his wrist and offered it to her. The moment was entirely too intimate for their current situation and audience, but Ronan didn't seem to care.

"Let him watch." Ronan jerked his head to where Paul lay, immobile. "I want the world to know that you are mine, and I am yours. And that *anyone* who seeks to come between us will suffer for their efforts."

Who could argue with that logic? Naya sealed her lips around Ronan's wrist and sucked. Before she met him, Naya never would have dabbled in blood magic, let alone taken blood straight from someone's vein. But with Ronan it was comfortable. A natural evolution of their bond. She was careful not to take too much. She needed to be stronger, not buzzed. The punctures closed as she pulled away and Ronan flashed a very male, very self-satisfied smile.

"Do you need to feed?" She could only imagine what having such dark magic inside of his body was doing to him.

"Later." His brow furrowed as though in pain.

"Are you sure? We have time if you need—"

"Later, love." Ronan smoothed her hair back and gave her a smile that didn't quite reach his silver-rimmed eyes. "Let's finish this, yeah?"

"Yeah." Naya sighed. Still so much to do for so many. Could she come through for all of them?

With the mapinguari gone, containing the residual magic was an easier task than she thought it would be. Naya gathered it with the aid of her dagger and stored it within the gold box. Manny was shaken but otherwise unharmed. He muttered under his breath something about staying out of *bruja* business for a while, and though she didn't say anything, she definitely agreed with him. He took off toward the redwood where Ronan tended to Luz. Aside from a nasty bump on the head, she was going to be fine. *Thank the gods.*

"Dude. I missed all of the action!" Luz wasn't so hurt that she couldn't let loose the snark. "The least you losers could have done was wake me up."

"Don't get your panties in a bunch, Luz," Naya said. Manny stepped in to help Luz to stand and supported her weight as he guided her back to where Paul lay. She let out a low whistle. That pretty much summed it up. "Because we're not even close to being done for the night."

"All right then," Luz said with *way* too much enthusiasm. "Let's get the show on the road."

Ronan hauled Paul up and tossed him over his shoulder. He led the way down the foot trail with Naya following close behind and Luz and Manny bringing up the rear. There was no telling who else Paul might have corrupted, and they weren't out of the woods yet. *Heh.*

Naya had used every ounce of magic in her stores to bind her chieftain. And though she and Paul had their *many* disagreements, he was still the leader their pod looked to. His actions tonight would ripple throughout not only their pod but the entire Bororo. What in the name of the gods could have prompted Paul to allow himself to be corrupted by foreign magic?

Her gaze wandered to her fingertips and the sparkling light that clung to her skin. When she was a girl, she used to pray to the goddess to take away the music that never ceased in her ears, and instead make her stronger. She wanted to shift like Joaquin. To run at night in the forest, stretch her powerful legs. She wanted to hunt. To prowl. Naya wanted to be respected as a warrior.

Perhaps she hadn't been the only one in her tribe who wanted what they couldn't have.

"Luz, I need a truth powder. Do you have the ingredients to make one at your place?" It would save time if Luz could blend the powder rather than drive to Naya's house on the outskirts of town.

"I think so. I haven't made one since I caught Eric Randall stepping out on me a few years ago, though. Valerian doesn't have an expiration date, does it?"

Naya gave a little laugh. "You're not supposed to be using powders for your own personal use, Luz. Especially on human ex-boyfriends who don't know any better. But no, as long as it's dried, it's fine."

"Not for personal use, huh?" Ronan piped in from the head of the line. "If I recall, a certain witch used a powder on me to make me nice and drowsy a couple of weeks or so ago."

"Oh, snap!" Luz giggled. "Vamp boy's got you, Cuz."

Har, har. Whose side was Luz on, anyway? "When we get to town, go straight home. Make the powder and then get back to the main house ASAP. Got it?"

"Fine." Luz's pouting tone would have made a four-year-old proud. "But once everything's wrapped up, you're totally spilling the sleeping-spell story."

"You don't have to wait until later," Ronan said. "I'll tell you all about it in the car."

"Turncoat," Naya mumbled under her breath.

Ronan chuckled. The sound of his amusement coaxed

a grin to her lips. Damn it, she couldn't even bring herself to be mad.

Luz's 4Runner came in handy with their extra passenger. Ronan deposited the immoble Paul into the cargo area and climbed into the backseat.

"Are you okay to drive?" Naya was still a little wired, but she or Manny would probably be the better choice to hop behind the wheel.

"I'll drive." Manny grabbed Luz's hand and led her around the front of the truck. "You need to sit and relax for a while." Luz started to protest, but Manny shut her down. "Don't argue. Just do it."

Naya had never seen Manny put her cousin in her place before. So either Luz was more addled than she'd let on or they truly did have feelings for each other. Either way, it was one for the record books.

The trip back to town passed in quiet reflection. Ronan sat still beside Naya, tension pulling every muscle in his body taut. He fought an internal battle. The sound of his music that vibrated through their tether was erratic, like an orchestra warming up before a performance. Neither sharp nor flat, the pitch was true. Simply . . . off.

Aside from banishing foreign magic to the gold boxes she turned over to the elders, Naya had no experience with it. She didn't study other supernatural races or their powers, nuances, individual magic. If what Ronan had been infected with had in fact come from Set's chest, perhaps it was safe to assume that it wouldn't transform Ronan into a mapinguari. The chest was a vampire relic; Ronan was a vampire. But if the legends were true, the chest contained a very intense power, very ancient magic. One that hadn't been in contact with any member of vampire-kind aside from Osiris, the rumored father of the vampire race.

She'd never felt so damned useless. So helpless. What if she couldn't do anything for Ronan? What if that power was doomed to live inside of him forever? Icy shards of dread speared Naya's chest. Reaching over, she took Ronan's hand in hers and squeezed. The reassurance was trite, but it was the only comfort she could offer him right now.

Hell, it was the only comfort she could offer herself when she was overcome with so much fear and uncertainty.

When Naya offered her vein to him, it had nearly snapped the meager control Ronan had on his composure. The darkness required blood. And though Ronan had taken care with his mate in all the times he'd fed from her, he worried that there would come a time that he would succumb to the urging voice of that darkness and drain her.

To be responsible for the death of his own mate—was there a worse torture to put upon himself?

Her touch was gentle, reassuring, as she gripped his fingers and gave a light squeeze. When it came to relics, Chelle was the expert. In all of their adventures, Ronan's role had been that of the muscle and little else. His knowledge was minimal; he'd only ever learned what pertained directly to whatever treasure they happened to be hunting. The only dhampir with more knowledge of vampire lore and legend was Siobhan, and Ronan would cut his own throat before he'd ask that viperous female for help.

"What do we do with Paul once we get to the house?" Luz's voice broke the tense silence. "There's a hunting party out right now searching for your vampire so they can get their hands on that hundred pieces of gold. The entire block is going to be like a ghost town when we roll up. Sort of defeats the purpose of turning Paul over to the elders in dramatic fashion, don'tcha think?"

"I doubt we'll have to call in the troops," Ronan remarked as they rounded the corner that began the block of buildings that the pod occupied. "Looks like they're already here."

"Shit."

Naya's sentiment echoed Ronan's thoughts exactly. Naya and Luz were technically keeping company with the enemy and they currently had the pod's leader bound and tossed in the back of the truck, looking very much like a hostage. Assumptions would be made and there wouldn't be a damned thing anyone could to do sway the elders' minds. "What do you want to do?" Ronan asked Naya.

"How do you feel about letting me tie you up?"

The sparkle in her dark eyes set Ronan's blood aflame. He flashed her a smile despite the seed of anxiety that took root deep in the pit of his gut. Being bound definitely triggered his fight-or-flight instincts—mostly fight—and he worried that it might wake the darkness that he'd managed to quell. "You're thinking that if they perceive me as a prisoner it'll buy you time?"

"More or less. It's our best shot at this point."

He could definitely see the merit in her plan. "No silver."

Naya's gaze dropped. "It'll be suspicious otherwise." If she bound him with silver, it would weaken him and he'd be unable to protect her if Naya's plan went south. Ronan ground his teeth and the tips of his fangs nicked his bottom lip. He swiped out with his tongue and licked the blood away. "I'm sorry, Ronan. I don't know another way."

"I have a pair of gold cuffs in my glove box," Luz offered. They were approaching the house and needed to act quickly. "If they think he's been tainted by magic, gold would be what you'd use, right?"

Interesting. Up until now, Ronan hadn't considered the possibility that gold might contain the magic inside of him. He looked at Naya, his brows raised in question.

"Taking prisoners into custody isn't exactly part of the job description, if you know what I mean." Naya spoke for Ronan alone as he bent her head close to his. "But since gold is a conduit for magic, the cuffs will hold a charm. Paul has asked me on occasion to charm gold cuffs for the elders to use if one of the male members of the pod has committed some sort of offense. It prevents them from shifting. No one should know that gold doesn't disable vampires in the same way. You're sort of a rare breed, you know."

Naya winked and it coaxed a smile to his lips. "Let's do this, then." He held out his hands to her palms up. "I'm your prisoner."

Her gaze heated and she didn't look away as Luz handed her the cuffs from the glove box. With the gentlest of touches, she secured the wide bands of gold around each of Ronan's wrists. When she finished, she bent over him and kissed the gold. "I'm your prisoner, too."

"Gag." Luz shifted in her seat to turn and look at Naya. "Time to ditch the love-struck routine and get your badass bitch face on, *chica*. And you'd better make it convincing, because Joaquin just showed up."

The male took up a place near the group of twenty or so who had gathered outside of the elders' building. His dark brows drew down severely over his eyes and his mouth formed a hard line. Arms folded across his chest as he braced his legs apart. He carried himself with the air of one who held authority, and it was obvious that in the absence of their chieftain they looked to the younger male for guidance.

"Okay, Luz, get ready to make a break for it." Naya shifted in her seat as Manny brought the truck to a stop on the opposite side of the street. "Make the powder as quickly as you can and get your ass back over here."

"What are you going to do?" Luz reached for the door.

"I'm going to wing it. Now, go."

Manny cut the engine and hopped out to chase after Luz. Naya took a deep breath and let it all out in a forceful gust. She wasn't facing this alone, though.

"Leaving the chieftain where he is?"

She hiked a shoulder. "Seems like the best idea for now. When Luz gets back, we'll haul him out of there."

"All right." When the others discovered that Naya had bound their leader it would only ruffle the shifters' fur. "What's our play for now?"

"Now," Naya said as she reached for the door handle, "we distract them."

CHAPTER
34

No way would Joaquin buy that Naya had brought Ronan in to turn him over to the elders. Not after admitting to him that she was Ronan's mate. She didn't really need Joaquin—or any of them—to believe her. She just needed to stir enough curiosity and confusion among the elders gathered on the street to buy Luz enough time to make the truth powder.

Naya gathered magic in her palm. Without intent it was simply raw energy. How she used it would be up to the elders and Joaquin. Because one thing was certain: She wasn't taking shit off of anybody else tonight.

"Naya, you captured the vampire?" Diego, one of Joaquin's closest friends, asked with an insulting amount of surprise. She hunted demons, repossessed rogue magic, and protected her people as she patrolled *El Sendero* night after night. But the thought of her capturing a vampire was a gods-damned *shock*?

Joaquin didn't waste any time setting the record straight. "He's not her prisoner." Joaquin's lip curled with disdain and he spat at Ronan's feet. "She thinks the vampire is her *mate*. She's playing at something."

"I smell magic," another of the elders spoke from the rear of the group. "A fair amount of it, too."

Naya brought her palm up and regarded the golden light glowing there. "I am a *bruja*. Wouldn't you agree that the scent of magic clings to me?"

Beside her Ronan stood stoically, but from the corner of her eye she noticed the flex of his jaw and the angry muscle that ticked there. Luz needed to hurry the hell up before the situation went south.

"The vampire has slaughtered innocents and, through the spread of corrupted magic, created mapinguari to ravage this town. He has taken lives and he has violated the secrecy that protects not only his kind but ours as well. For whatever reason you have come here tonight, Naya, it is your duty to hand him over to us so that we might mete out justice."

Twenty angry Bororo shifters against one enraged vampire? Naya already knew who she'd put money on in that fight.

"Hand him over." Joaquin stepped forward, every bit his father's son. "If you don't, you're proving that you're in league with the vampire and a betrayer to our people." His brow furrowed as she kept her gaze forward, her face impassive. "Do you want to die alongside of him, Naya?"

Joaquin's anger prickled over her skin, abrading with each shouted word. Drums pounded in the depths of her soul, a precursor to the magic that initiated a shift. Joaquin was tired of talking, it seemed. He'd always been a rash male with a too-short temper.

"Luz is coming." Ronan murmured the words under his breath for Naya's ears alone. That he could hear Luz approaching from around the block renewed Naya's admiration for his keen senses. "Time for a new distraction."

"What? No."

Ronan threw himself at Joaquin. With a quick snap of his head the sounds of their skulls cracking together echoed in the space of the nearly deserted street. Joaquin whipped back from the force, his shock apparent in his wide eyes. He righted himself much too quickly, though, and swiped at the blood that trickled from his nose before charging at Ronan with a violent battle shout.

Others moved to come to Joaquin's aid, but one of the elders raised his hand to stay them. "They'll fight to the death!" he proclaimed over the din of the fight. "The truth will lie with the victor."

Useless, antiquated logic. Why not dunk them underwater? Set them on fire? Drive them off the edge of a cliff? That sort of thinking worked well in the witch trials. Why not use it here, right? The stupidity of it all made Naya want to scream. Ronan had been right. Her people needed to step into the damned twenty-first century.

Even with his wrists bound, Ronan was a formidable opponent. His speed was beyond impressive as he dodged each swing of Joaquin's fists. The dagger he clutched in his right hand flashed silver under the streetlights as he stabbed down at Ronan's shoulder. It was a wasted effort, though, as the weapon made contact with nothing but air. Ronan used the other male's misstep to his advantage and brought his knee into Joaquin's gut.

The static charge of magic thickened the air as Joaquin gave himself over to the shift. In his jaguar form, he'd be even more formidable. Faster. Stronger. As deadly as Ronan, with sharp canines more than capable to rip out a throat. Her mate would lose the upper hand, and in the court of warriors Ronan would be found guilty, his sentence delivered before the verdict could even be made.

Magic pooled in Naya's palms. Her own worry and anger fueled her power. It built in her body, and her limbs quaked with the effort to contain it. Change was going to come to the Bororo and it would begin with this pod.

"Stop!"

Energy exploded from every pore in Naya's skin, leaving her body in a mad rush that sent out a massive shock wave. The ground shook with the force of it and sent bodies sprawling to the pavement. Ronan whipped around to look at her, shielding his eyes from the burst of bright golden light of Naya's magic. In the ensuing chaos and confusion she could hear nothing save the sound of music that rose to a crescendo in her ears.

"Naya . . . ! Naya . . . !"

Luz's screams were muted by the music of Naya's own magic. The rush of power as it funneled from her body left her weak and shaking. Her knees buckled and her vision blurred as Ronan changed course to rush to her side. The muscles of his arms bulged and cords of veins pressed to the surface of his skin as he yanked his wrists apart and snapped the gold chain that secured the cuffs together. He scooped Naya up in his arms and held her tight against his chest. "I've got you, love," he said close to her ear. "I've got you."

"No." She'd be okay. She just needed a minute to gather her focus. "Luz. Protect Luz and help her with Paul. Distraction, remember?" Ronan's brow furrowed with indecision and his jaw squared with his downturned mouth. "Don't think about it," she ordered. "Do it."

He set her down and took off toward Luz's 4Runner. They couldn't take their eyes off the prize when they were so close to getting some real answers. It was going to take a gallon of Ronan's blood—or a few hours of mind-blowing sex—to replenish Naya's stores and she wouldn't have an opportunity again tonight to run interference.

Thank the gods Naya and Luz had placed wards of protection on the city block that the pod occupied. Otherwise, there'd be a few of Crescent City's finest to add to the mess of the night. What happened on their block remained contained. Any sound, the shock wave created by Naya's magic, would be undetectable to anyone outside of their property. 'Cuz this was some fucked-up shit.

Joaquin and the others had begun to shake off their disorientation. They gathered en masse, their gazes fixated on Naya and all of them full of awe. And fear. She supposed the power she'd unleashed had been a little damned scary. Hell, she'd managed to shake herself up.

Over the murmur of voices, Luz's rang out. "On penalty of death, I, Luz Morales, apprentice *bruja* to the Crescent City pod, swear that the charm cast upon our chieftain, Paulo Alvarez, is sanctioned by the goddess, the mother of magic, the first of our ears. And the words hereby spoken from his mouth are truth." All eyes turned to Luz, including Naya's. She pushed herself up from the ground only to find Ronan by her side before she could stand up straight. He helped her to the 4Runner where Paul stood, immobile. "You wanna take it from here, Cuz?"

Naya's throat was raw, her voice a harsh rasp, as she asked, "Paulo Alvarez, did you willingly use foreign magic and allow it into your body?"

"Yes," Paul spat.

His malicious gaze slid over her, but Naya refused to be intimidated. "Have you created mapinguari from that same magic and unleashed them to do your bidding?"

His teeth audibly ground in his attempt to keep from answering. After a moment the word burst from his lips. "Yes!"

Murmured voices carried from the elders as they stopped dead in their tracks, stunned by their leader's admissions. Joaquin remained silent, his jaw hanging slack and his eyes wide as he looked from his father to Naya and back again.

"Are you in possession of a stolen vampire relic?"

Spittle dribbled down the chieftain's chin. "Y-yes."

Naya looked over at Ronan, took his hand in hers, and squeezed. "And have you taken captive a female dhampir?"

Paul's eyes narrowed with hate as he looked at Ronan. "Yes."

Ronan's body tensed beside her and Naya funneled every ounce of calm she could muster through their tether. She needed him to stay level, to let the pod handle this business, as was their right. He let out a rush of breath at the same moment she filled her lungs. "Where are the relic and dhampir? Tell me, now."

Paul's words were stilted as the magic forced them past his lips. "Beneath the ground. Fifteen miles from here. There's a cabin off of Humboldt Road, deep in the Elk Valley land trust." His eyes lit on Ronan's once again and his lip stretched in a sneer. "But the female isn't a dhampir. Not anymore."

"Does it offend your sense of originality to find out you're not the only one in the pod with a secret hideout?" Luz said to Naya as they sped down the Redwood Highway to the Elk Valley land trust. "Any guesses on what we're going to find there? I'm starting to think we should have brought an army just in case."

Ronan shifted in his seat, cracking his neck from side to side in an effort to relieve some of the tension that pulled his shoulders tight. He was inclined to agree with Luz. They had no idea who—or what—Paul might've set to guard his private sanctuary.

"He couldn't lie under the influence of the truth charm,

Luz." If only Ronan felt as confident as his mate sounded. "I asked him if anyone else was out there. He said no."

"Who's to say he couldn't have found a way around the truth?" Ronan suggested.

Naya cut him a look and her jaw screwed up in a lopsided set. "Are you saying you don't trust our *magia*?"

"Hell," Luz chimed in, "I don't know if *I* trust our *magia*. We've been through some shit tonight, Naya."

Sunrise was just over four hours away. Already Ronan could feel the brightening horizon as a prickle on his skin. What condition would they find Chelle in? And would they be able to get her—both of them—out of there before the sun crested the horizon?

"It'll be all right, Ronan."

Would it? "Chelle's a fighter. There's no doubt about that. But, Naya. I don't want you to sugarcoat anything. I know what we might find there. And I have to be prepared for what needs to be done."

There were no more reassurances to give. No conjecture to be made. The trio remained silent as they negotiated the back roads of the Elk Valley reserve, following Paul's instructions to the cabin that was tucked away in the forest, far from where anyone would find it.

Ronan took a deep breath and held it as the 4Runner came to a stop in front of a newer cabin that looked more like a large shed, isolated in the dense trees. Cold darkness rose up inside of him like the tide, and the thirst he'd managed to push to the back of his mind raged like an inferno in his throat. He wasn't worth a damn to anyone in this state, but he didn't have a choice. Chelle needed him.

"Ronan? Are you all right?" Naya's gaze searched his face, her brow furrowed with concern.

He swallowed against the dryness that coated his mouth as she tilted her head slightly to the right, revealing the delicate curve of her throat. *Starving.* Ronan was fucking starving. He wanted to open Naya's vein and glut himself.

"You're hurting me," Naya said in a calm, even tone. He looked down to find that he'd wrapped his hand around her wrist and squeezed it tight. With a shuddering breath he forced his fingers to uncurl, though they remained bent like stiff claws. Gods, if he didn't feed soon he was going to lose his damn mind. And why? He'd taken more than enough of Naya's blood to sustain him for weeks.

"I'm sorry." He wanted to smooth her skin, kiss her there, to soothe his careless rough touch, but Ronan didn't trust himself not to sink his fangs into her wrist. He didn't trust himself to stop at a sip or several swallows of her blood. His need was absolute and nothing short of drinking his mate to the point of death would satisfy him. "Gods, Naya." The words lodged in his throat, strained. "I'm *so* sorry."

"I think we should leave him here." Luz was the only one of them willing to make a decision that wasn't swayed by emotion. "He's volatile, Naya. I know you hear it."

"I'm fine." He wasn't. Not by a long shot. But he also wasn't going to sit here and wait in the car like a kid while his mate went on without him. His gaze focused on Naya and she returned his stare. She could hear the turmoil, the darkness, that swirled within him. He couldn't fool her if he tried. And yet he said the words, "I'm fine," once again hoping that she'd at least hear reassurance in his voice. He would never, *ever* hurt her or anyone she held dear.

"He's okay," she said without breaking eye contact. "Let's go get your sister."

The building couldn't have been more than five hundred square feet. Half of the space had been used for storage and the other half was furnished with a wood-stove, a futon couch, and a small kitchenette. At the south end of the structure Ronan found a trapdoor in the floor. Chelle had been held underground. Trapped in dank, cold darkness like the force that ate away at his soul. His hand shook with unrestrained rage as he lifted the latch and pulled open the door.

Naya's dagger scraped against the sheath as she stepped up beside him. Her hand came to rest on his shoulder, and for a quiet moment they remained still, each of them preparing for what they'd find below. One thing was certain: Whatever it was, they'd face it together, and Ronan had never been more in love with Naya than he was at this moment that she stood by his side.

"Ready?" she asked him.

Ronan gave a sharp nod of his head.

"Ready?" Naya glanced at Luz, who gave a nod as well.

The space below the house couldn't even be considered a basement. Concrete walls lent support to a dirt floor that stank with rot and mold. Luz coughed and drew the collar of her shirt over her nose. Fear and anxiety churned in Ronan's gut, damn near banishing his ever-present thirst.

"Chelle?"

His voice didn't echo in the open space. Instead, the sound died as it passed his lips, absorbed as though by a sponge.

"It's the magic," Naya whispered on a breath. Her eyes watered and she drew her breath in tight little gasps of air. "It's so thick in here that I almost can't breathe."

"Go back up." Ronan urged her toward the ladder. "I can take it from here. I don't need to breathe."

"No," Naya panted. "We do this together. Luz? You okay?"

"I can't catch my breath." The younger female's tone was much more frantic. "I feel like I'm suffocating, Naya."

"Go back up and wait for us," she said. "Take a look around the perimeter of the property; make sure we aren't met with any surprises."

"Got it." Luz climbed the ladder and disappeared up into the floor.

"Naya." Ronan didn't want her down here. Not when the magic clouding the air had such a damaging effect on her.

"Quiet, you." Her breath continued to race as Naya brought up her palm. A wan gold light glowed there, so dim in comparison to her display of magic earlier in the night. The magic leapt from her palm, bathing her body in glittering gold. Her breathing became easier and she urged him forward. "I can take care of myself. Don't worry about me."

Oh, but he did. He worried about anything, everything, in this world that threatened to take her from him. Most of all, he worried about himself. About the darkness inside of him and the thirst that burned his throat. Of all of the things in this world that could harm Naya, he worried the most about the threat he posed to her.

"Chelle?" Naya's voice projected better than Ronan's had. Her magic, perhaps? "Chelle, can you hear me? My name's Naya. I'm a friend. Ronan is here."

A low moan answered Naya, and Ronan's heart lodged in his throat. "Ro-nan?" Chelle's voice was weak, and in the thick of magic he couldn't discern a heartbeat. He rushed toward the sound of her voice and came to a skidding stop, the breath stalled in his chest at the sight of her.

"I'm here, Chelle. I'm here."

CHAPTER
35

That bastard had kept her in a cage like an animal. Rage welled hot and fresh in Ronan's throat. It was a good thing the pod's elders had taken Paul into their custody, because that son of a bitch would've been dead had Ronan known how he'd treated Chelle. The silver bars of her cage gleamed despite the darkness, and in the center of the space a dark shadow huddled.

"You're okay, Chelle." Ronan didn't know if his words of reassurance were for his sister's benefit or his. "I'm going to get you out of here."

In a violent streak of darkness Chelle threw her body against the cage. Her skin sizzled as she wrapped her palms around the bars and a feral hiss escaped between her . . . *Jesus* . . . dual sets of fangs. "Give her to me, Ronan!" Chelle rasped. As a mewling whine left her lips she reached through the bars toward Naya. "I'm starving. Starving! Let me drain her. Please." Chelle's eyes flashed brilliant silver in the darkness. "Please. Please. *Please!*"

Chelle had become a vampire. But *how*?

"I can smell her blood. It's so sweet! I'm dying, Ronan.

My throat." She clutched at her neck and her nails bit into the skin, drawing blood. "It's on fire."

Ronan stared, dumbstruck.

"Get me out of this cage, gods damn it!" Chelle's enraged shriek shook the house on its foundation, sending bits of dirt and debris raining down on their heads. She began to cry in earnest, sinking back to the floor of her cell, curled in a tight ball as she rocked back and forth.

"Naya, get out of here." The words were cinders in his throat. His fangs throbbed in his gums, anxious to sink into soft, yielding flesh. Ice chilled the blood in his veins and snaked over his skin. The mystery of his unquenchable thirst was beginning to make sense, but if Naya didn't get the hell away from him Ronan doubted he'd be able to stop himself from taking her life.

"No, Ronan. I'm not leaving you."

"Go!" he railed. He gripped on to the bars of Chelle's cage, letting the burn of silver clear his clouding mind. "Shut me in and don't open that door until you *hear* that I'm okay. Do you understand me?"

She took a tentative step back and then another. He sent a warning through their tether, willing her to feel the desperation that consumed Chelle. That consumed him. Love wouldn't stop him if he sank his fangs into Naya's delicate throat. Nothing would.

"Okay, Ronan." Naya continued to back away toward the ladder. "But please, be careful."

Ronan continued to grip the bars to keep him from turning and snatching her back. Her steps were barely audible as she climbed back up into the main building, and Ronan let out a shaking breath of relief as she shut the trapdoor behind her, leaving him in absolute darkness.

"I'm going to take care of you, Chelle." The need, the cold, harsh, undying thirst, was an echo of his twin's. Whatever that son of a bitch had done to them only served to further connect them past the bond they already shared as siblings. "I'm going to feed you."

He refused to care for her with the damned silver bars separating them, though. Silver blistered his palm as he grabbed the antique lock that secured the door. His fangs punctured his bottom lip as he locked his jaw down, and Chelle whimpered from her spot on the floor as his blood scented the air. Ronan let out a harsh shout as he gave the lock a final hard twist and it gave way. He ripped it free and pulled open the door. "I'm coming in, Chelle."

She twitched from her spot on the dirt floor as he took slow steps toward her. Inch by inch, Ronan lowered himself until he sat beside her. Chelle trembled like a delicate leaf in an autumn wind. Any mishandling and she'd crumple into dust.

For weeks she'd been kept in a state of sensory deprivation and starvation. Her transition had been a force of magic, not one of biology, if Ronan's assumptions were correct. And it had been violent. She'd endured the change without guidance. Without sustenance. Chelle had become as wild as any animal that roamed the forest.

Hell, as starved as she was, there was a good chance she'd drink him dry.

But she was his sister. His twin. They'd endured so much together already. He couldn't—wouldn't—let her suffer for another moment. Ronan gathered her up in his arms and rested her limp head against his shoulder. The sounds of her soft sobs speared his heart and he brought his wrist to her mouth. "Drink."

She struck out with ferocity, burying her fangs in Ronan's skin. Like a starved animal, she tore the flesh in her haste to feed. Blood welled hot and sticky, running down his arm in rivulets as she took pull after greedy pull. She grunted, moaned, her nails latching on to his arm as she bit him again and again, taking her fill of his blood.

His head lolled to one side and Ronan's thoughts grew fuzzy. As Chelle fed, so did the cold and darkness retreat from his center, leaving behind a pleasant glow of warmth that radiated throughout his body. His world tilted on its axis and Ronan fell to the dirt floor, Chelle still cradled in his arms. She continued to feed, without even registering the shift. She needed everything he could give her. It was worth the weakness, the light-headed disorientation.

"You're killing him! Stop!"

Panic laced Naya's tone and a few choice words came to Ronan's mind, though he couldn't lend them a voice. He'd told her to stay upstairs, damn it. To not come back until she *heard* that he was all right.

Chelle was pulled from his body and shoved to the far side of the cell. She didn't move. The only sound in the quiet space was that of her racing breath. Naya crouched by Ronan's side and brought her arm to his mouth. "Drink, you silly, stubborn vampire." He put his lips to her fragrant skin, but he couldn't muster the energy necessary to bite her. She smelled *so* good. "Damn it, Ronan." Her infuriated tone coaxed a lazy smile to his lips. The citrine glow of her dagger pierced the inky darkness as she laid the blade to her forearm. A ribbon of blood welled from the wound and she brought it back to his mouth. "Drink. Or I'll force it down your throat."

Gods, how he loved a forceful female.

Blood trickled over his lips, sweet and warm. He lapped at the wound with slow, languid passes of his tongue. Soon his strength was replenished enough for him to seal his mouth over the cut, and then his fangs pierced her flesh. Naya let out a slow, soft sigh that stirred his lusts as much as his thirst. Naya was brave, stubborn, strong, fierce, protective, and loyal. And he loved her so much that it hurt.

Ronan no longer felt the uncontrollable urge to drain

her. Instead, he took what he needed to replenish his strength and closed the wound, lapping gently at her skin as he closed the punctures and the cut she'd made with her dagger. Through the darkness, he spotted Chelle a couple of feet away. She watched them with wary eyes that were no longer wild silver but her natural clear green.

"When you got free, I hoped you'd come back." She still sounded weak, but Chelle was no longer manic. "Gods, Ronan. I had no idea. I knew the legends, but I didn't really believe."

"Chelle." *Fuck*. There were still too many missing pieces. "I don't remember any of it."

"I do," Chelle replied in a shuddering whisper. "I remember *everything*."

Luz had almost kept Naya from going back down the ladder. And had her bossy cousin succeeded, Ronan would have let his sister drain him. Gods, what had he been thinking? His own gallant foolishness had nearly gotten him killed. It was one of the reasons Naya loved him, but it also made her want to pull out her hair in frustration.

He spoke in hushed tones with his sister like they were two kids alone in their bedroom after lights-out. Naya listened as Ronan lounged against her chest and she stroked his hair, combing the silky strands through her fingertips.

"He'd shot you with some kind of dart. It was still sticking out of your neck when his monster threw you in this cage with me. I offered you my vein, but you refused, you stubborn ass." Well, that certainly sounded like the Ronan Naya knew. "He"—Chelle's voice hitched— "threw you in the chest first. To see what the magic would do to you. But you were already turned and when he opened the lid you were too crazed, too . . . strong for him to control."

Naya's hand reflexively went to her own neck. Someone had shot her with a dart and it had wiped her short-term memory. She'd need to bring that to the elders' attention. Magic like that needed to be regulated. Paul had obviously crafted the darts from the malicious magic Naya had inadvertently been collecting for him over the years.

"He put you inside of the chest," Ronan said. "Didn't he?"

"Yes," Chelle replied. "The transformation was . . ." A sob lodged itself in her throat. "I can't talk about it, Ronan."

Rage flared through the tether that bound him to Naya and she shared in his anger. What Paul had done was irresponsible, cruel, and sadistic. If the elders' council didn't bring swift retribution to their chieftain, Naya would.

"He didn't just put us in that chest. He took humans." Chelle sniffed back a fresh round of tears and Naya's heart broke for the female. "He turned them into monsters and set them loose. My gods, Ronan. I don't even know how many of them are out in the world. And then"—she let out a derisive snort—"the bastard climbed right in and shut the lid. When he emerged from the chest, he'd become . . . I don't even know what he was. That was yesterday and I haven't seen him since."

"The son of a bitch has been taken care of," Ronan bit out. "He's not going to hurt anyone ever again."

"She's one of them." Chelle's dark tone slithered over Naya's skin. "Like the male who took us. She has the same scent. What are you doing with one of them, Ronan?"

"She's not like him." Ronan reached up and cupped Naya's cheek. "She's my mate, Chelle."

"Your *mate*?" Chelle didn't sound too happy and a wave of anxiety crested over Naya. "She's no vampire, Brother."

"No," he said with a gentle laugh. "She's a witch. A beautiful, powerful, fierce, and furious witch. And I love her."

Any worry that she might have felt evaporated under Ronan's tender words. "And what do you say, witch?" Chelle was obviously protective of her brother, and Naya admired that. "How do you feel about being tethered to a vampire?"

Her gaze locked with his and Naya replied, "He's my mate. Our souls are bound. I love him and I dare *anyone* to try to come between us."

They'd made solemn vows to each other and, in the presence of his sister, declared their love. Naya knew of no other ceremony that would bind them together more completely. They were one. Now and for always.

"Luz?" Magic was still too heavy in the air for her to come down, and though Ronan's sister seemed to have calmed, Naya wasn't convinced of Chelle's stability yet. They needed to get out of here, though. And had more cargo than her cousin's 4Runner could haul.

"Glad to know you're not dead!" Luz's words were laced with sarcasm as she shouted through the trapdoor opening. "You're *loca,* Naya! Letting yourself be some kind of vampire snack pack down there!"

Ronan chuckled and nuzzled Naya's throat. "You're not funny. Listen, can you call Manny and see if he can meet us out here with a U-Haul? We need something big enough to transport a large coffin."

"*Dioses mio!*" Luz's exasperated shout brought a smile to Naya's face. "Vampires, coffins. You're fucking nuts, Naya! What's next?"

"Next?" Ronan said softly. "We break a blood troth."

One more obstacle. One more battle. And this was one fight that Naya was more than ready for. Whoever this female Siobhan was, she was going to know without a doubt to whom Ronan belonged. And Naya was more than ready to use any of the gifts at her disposal to drive her point home.

"Los Angeles?" She leaned in and planted a light kiss on his cheek. "I've never been. Should be an adventure."

"Oh, love." Ronan nipped at her ear and Naya's body was bathed in delicious chills. "We'll turn the town on its ear."

"Manny will be here in a half hour!" Luz shouted through the floor. "No U-Haul places open during vampire-appropriate hours, but he's bringing a truck that'll work for now. And can you two please stop? You're grossing me out with your flirty talk!"

"Whoever that female is, I like her," Chelle said weakly from her corner of the cell. "And I have to agree. You two are utterly disgusting."

"They're just jealous," Naya said to Ronan.

"Absolutely green," he agreed.

"Gag!" Luz's voice carried from the ground floor. "Hurry up and get your asses up here, guys. You're creeping me out with the way you're just hanging out in that cage!"

"Again, I'm going to agree with my new best friend," Chelle said. "I need to get the hell out of here."

Naya couldn't have agreed more. "As soon as Manny gets here, we'll load up the chest and take it back to my house until we can rent a U-Haul tomorrow. I don't want anyone else in the pod getting any ideas about what Paul had stashed out here."

"Good idea," Ronan said. "Until then, I'm taking you to bed and we're not leaving your house until the sun sets tomorrow night."

Naya could think of no better way to spend an entire day.

CHAPTER
36

What should have been a twelve-hour drive Ronan managed to accomplish in just under eleven. It was a damned good thing, too, because the sun nudged at the horizon by the time they made it to his penthouse apartment in the center of downtown. The sheer size of the city overwhelmed Naya, and it was so far from the places and people that were familiar to her she couldn't help the anxiety that twisted her stomach into a series of tight knots.

A hulking, broody vampire named Jenner met them at Ronan's building to take possession of the U-Haul and Chelle. "I'll meet you at sundown," Jenner said as he took the keys from Ronan. "And don't worry, I'll make sure she's taken care of."

"I have a feeling we have a lot to talk about," Ronan replied as he eyed the other male with concern.

Ronan was answered with a cranky grunt as Jenner hoisted himself up into the driver's seat and pulled onto the street with an angry squeal of tires.

"So, that was Jenner," Ronan said with a shrug.

"He seems . . . nice."

"Not at all," Ronan said with a laugh. "But he's as loyal as they come."

"Do you think Chelle is going to be okay?" Naya could only imagine what Ronan's sister had been through. According to him, her unique transformation kept her apart from the vampire collective memory and the interconnected energy that they shared. She was a creature created from magic and utterly alone. Naya's heart broke for Chelle, and she was going to do everything she could to help her. Naya had even offered her vein to Ronan's sister, but he'd refused to let Naya act as a donor while Chelle's thirst was still so volatile.

"She will be in time," Ronan said. "We'll all help her."

It would be a good while before their lives settled down. Naya agreed to return to Crescent City, as she was needed. With Paul in a secure facility managed by the Bororo tribe and the elders in the process of not only selecting a new chieftain but also dealing with a new—and very snarky—*bruja* in Luz, the transition was bound to be rocky. Ronan had his own issues to deal with. Since Chelle had fed, he no longer felt the effects of the dark magic, but it was going to take practice and a hell of a lot of research on Naya's part to help him master it. Ronan planned to bring Mikhail up to speed as soon as possible, and there was still the matter of Siobhan to deal with.

"Come on, love. Let's go inside."

Naya looked out over the vast cityscape, taking in the lights and distant sounds. The sun would be up soon and they'd be shut inside for the day. Until then, she let the warm autumn breeze waft over her. The air was thick here. It lacked the clean forest smell that she was used to. The city below her was so busy. Too alive. Would there ever be moments of stillness? Of quiet? There was too much concrete and not enough nature.

"We'll find a place outside of the city." Ronan came up

behind her on the terrace and wrapped his arms around
her waist. Naya relaxed into his embrace, allowing his
wide chest to support her. "On the beach, maybe. Whatever
makes you happy, Naya. Wherever you can be content."

"I'm happy," she assured him. "As long as I'm with
you, I can deal with anything else."

"You shouldn't have to *deal* with anything," Ronan replied. His mouth found the sensitive skin below her ear
and Naya shuddered. "I want you content. Happy. Every
minute of every day."

She turned in his embrace. His mouth found hers,
igniting not only her desire but also her magic. With every
passing day, Naya was learning better to control it, to give
it purpose, and it slid over Ronan's skin, permeating his
veins to form a protective barrier from the troth he'd given
to Siobhan. Perhaps, after tomorrow night, Naya wouldn't
have to protect him anymore.

He scooped her up in his arms and took her inside,
away from the light that steadily crested the horizon. Once
inside, he turned her again so that her back was flush with
his chest. His penthouse was enormous. Three times the
size of her house. Naya took in the lush furnishings, taste-
ful, high-end decorating, and wealth that surrounded
her. Ronan had once been nothing more than a slave. He'd
escaped from that life, become a powerful male who
lived like a king.

And he belonged to *her*.

Ronan cupped her throat gently in his massive palm.
The scrape of his fangs on her exposed throat sent a shiver
over Naya's skin as his opposite hand plunged down past
her belly. He unfastened her pants with deft haste and
plunged into her underwear, catching her sex in his heated
palm.

Her need for him was all-consuming.

Ronan's breath was hot in her ear as he stroked her

pussy, his fingers feathering over her slick flesh in search of her clit. Naya gasped at the contact, pleasure radiating through her body as a deep, hollow ache opened up inside of her. He licked the flesh at her throat, nipped without breaking the skin. Surely teasing himself as much as he was her, withholding what they both wanted until the last possible moment.

He circled her clit with achingly slow precision, holding her immobile with the palm that still clutched her throat. They'd spent the entire previous day in bed, and the drive from Crescent City had been torture. Not being able to touch him, taste him, take him deep inside of her the way she wanted to. Gods, at this rate, how would they ever live normal lives when they were so utterly starved for each other's bodies?

Naya reached around to grab his thigh. She wanted him out of his damned pants. Naked. His gorgeous body bare for her to enjoy. She shoved at her own pants, working them down to her ankles, and kicked them and her underwear off, sending them over the arm of an overstuffed chair. She reached back, tugging at Ronan's fly, and he broke their contact only as long as it took to shed his clothes. Naya stripped off her shirt and bra and Ronan tackled her, bending her over the same chair that was now decorated with their discarded garments.

Ronan urged one leg up on the arm and Naya obliged, resting her forearms in front of her. "Don't make me wait, Ronan. I want it hard. Gods, I need you to fuck me hard."

Desperation tightened Naya's chest. Her need for the male bent over her, mindless. He cupped her breast, plucking at the hardened peak of her nipple, and a ripple of sensation shot through Naya's body and settled in her pussy. Her clit throbbed with each delicious tug as Ronan continued to stoke her desire to a frenzied, mindless want that had her arching her back and thrusting her ass up toward him. If he didn't take her soon, she'd go out of her mind.

Ronan's tongue traced a path up Naya's spine, the wet heat causing her to shudder. His teeth grazed her shoulder and she tensed beneath him. Would he break the skin this time? He ventured to her other shoulder and Naya let out a frustrated whimper. "Ronan." Desperation accented her tone. "Please."

He knew exactly what to do to bring her to the height of pleasure without allowing her release. With a gentle flick of his fingers he reached between her thighs to brush her clit, and Naya cried out. She rocked back, desperate to increase the pressure, but he pulled away, allowing her not an ounce of control. He could keep her this way for hours. She was at his mercy. It was a dark, delicious torture that only made her want more. Naya was lost. Insatiable. Ronan drove her mad with want. And it only showed how powerful his hold on her was that she didn't want the sweet torture to end.

A savage need for the female in his arms overtook Ronan. She was so wet, so willing and responsive, and just as far gone for him as he was for her. The drive to L.A. had been infuriating. A race against daylight that allowed for no pit stops. Eleven hours next to his mate while her scent engulfed him, her mere presence aroused him. He couldn't wait to get her up to his penthouse so he could fuck her. He wanted it slow and steady. A build that took hours to sate. He wanted to take her with a fierceness that left them both breathless and shaking. He wanted to lap at her pussy until he'd had his fill. They had hours to kill until sundown, and Ronan intended to spend every one of them naked and in Naya's arms.

"Ronan, fuck me. I can't wait another second."

Right now his mate wanted him intensely. He was more than ready to oblige her. His cock pulsed hot and hard between his legs, brushing against her ass as he gave shallow thrusts of his hips. Her pussy dripped with her arousal, so slick and wet and hot that it drove him crazy. He spread the wetness over her mound, across her thighs, and up through the crease of her ass.

He couldn't wait another second to fuck her.

Ronan thrust hard and deep, a shout erupting from his throat as her tight heat accepted him. He lay over her, panting through the intense pleasure. Naya arched her shapely back and rocked against him. He pulled out, grabbing his cock in his hand as he slid the crown against the tight bud of Naya's clit. The sensation was intense for both of them and Naya's limbs trembled as he repeated the action. He guided his cock back to her entrance and thrust home, eliciting a cry of passion from his mate as he pulled out again, teasing them both with the contact, only to sheath himself in her welcoming warmth once again.

Naya fisted the cushion of the chair, grinding against him as little desperate mewls of sound burst from her lips. Ronan's pace increased, his own breath sawing in and out of his chest as he fucked her with all the desperation of a male about to get his final glimpse of life. His want for her would never slacken. He would never *not* be starved for her. She was his air, his sustenance, the very thing that kept him alive. His fingertips dug into Naya's soft hips as he fucked her, each punishing thrust a claim on her body. She reached back and clutched his thigh, her nails biting into the flesh, marking him as hers. Nothing—*no one*—would ever come between them.

A low moan built in Naya's throat as her sex clenched around Ronan's shaft. A tremor rippled through her body and she called out as she came, a string of words in that strange esoteric language that brought magic to life in her palm. Rose gold dust painted Naya's body as her pussy constricted around him, milking him and drawing him deep. Pressure built in his sac, working its way up the thick length of his cock, and Ronan bent over her. He buried his fangs in the juncture of her throat and shoulder and the skin gave way with a pop as his orgasm burst upon him, sending seismic waves of sensation through his body.

Another orgasm claimed Naya at the same time. "Ronan!" His name burst from her lips with all of the sanctity of a prayer as she came. For long moments they cleaved to each other and Ronan continued to move over her with slow, shallow thrusts that left them both shaking and panting for breath.

"This chair is officially christened," he teased low in her ear. He withdrew from her body as he closed the punctures at her throat.

Naya melted over the arm of the chair, her tiny form shuddering with each breath. "One piece of furniture down," she panted as she brought her head up to look around, "ten or twelve more pieces to go."

Ronan let out a soft chuckle as he rolled onto the chair and gathered Naya up in his lap. "I promise you, love, by sundown the entire place will be properly used. I don't plan to let you put a stitch of clothing on until it's absolutely necessary."

"Oh, really?" Her voice was a sensual purr that Ronan felt on every inch of his skin. "Even while we're cooking? Eating?"

Ronan nuzzled her throat as his hand came around to cup her full breast. Naya's breath left in a soft sigh that stirred his cock. "Who says we're going to stop for food? I have all of the sustenance I need right here."

He tugged at her nipple and Naya let out a sensual

moan. His opposite hand searched for the juncture of her thighs, sliding over the slick flesh of her still-swollen pussy. "Funny," she said as she flung a leg over the arm of the chair, opening her legs for him, "I was thinking the exact same thing."

Ah, gods. This was bound to be the best day of Ronan's existence.

CHAPTER
37

"I don't want you here. Let Jenner take you home."

Home. After a blissful twelve hours of daylight shut up with her mate, Ronan's penthouse had definitely begun to feel like home. Though he could have lived in a cave or a ramshackle old shed on the outskirts of town and it would have been home. Because wherever Ronan happened to be was Naya's home. And nothing would ever change that.

The building they stood before looked like it would be better off demolished. It seemed a strange place to meet the dhampir female whose reputation was far grander than the building she chose to live in. "I'm not going anywhere," Naya replied. She caressed the hilt of her dagger and shifted her weight to the balls of her feet. "We're a package deal now. Where you go, I go. Your fights are mine."

"Together, then," Ronan said.

He led the way into the building and up several flights of stairs. The place was certainly creepy. Their footsteps were amplified in the quiet, and every shadow that formed in the dusky gray of twilight caused Naya's senses to go on high alert. They'd ventured into enemy territory and Naya was about to publicly challenge a claim that another female made on her mate. Of course, she'd agreed to let Ronan take the lead and negotiate his freedom first. But if that didn't work, Naya was more than ready to kick a little ass.

They exited the stairwell on the tenth floor. Part of the floor had been gutted, forming a sort of common area that branched off to other rooms. At the far end of the space was an enormous bed decked out in luxurious black satin bedding. Apparently this fearsome dhampir was a bit of an exhibitionist as well. *This oughta be fun.*

The female in question lounged upon an ornate chair that had been elevated on a makeshift dais. From the way she lounged, one shapely leg slung over the arm, Naya had to assume that Siobhan had a flare for dramatics. Naya tried not to roll her eyes as she and Ronan strolled across the expanse of the room. She chanced a look around and noticed that parts of the ceiling had been torn out to expose the iron support beams above. Dhampirs dangled from their perches in the ceiling, lined the walls of the room, and lounged on the floor space. She thought herself a queen, this Siobhan, and she was currently holding court. This was a female who wouldn't let Ronan go without a fight. Good thing Naya came prepared for just that.

"Ronan."

His name rolled off of Siobhan's tongue in a dark, sensual purr that caused Naya's hackles to rise. Ronan gave her look for look, his expression an impassive mask that gave nothing away. "Siobhan." His own tone was cold, mechanical, as he said her name. Naya tried not to feel smug that his response lacked any heat. Because when Ronan spoke her name it nearly set Naya's skin aflame.

"I didn't give you permission to leave the city," Siobhan said. Her emerald green eyes narrowed into hateful slits as her gaze landed on Naya for the barest moment. "You realize I'll have to punish you for it."

Ronan snorted. "The last time I checked I was no longer a member of your coven, and I sure as hell don't need your permission to leave the city."

"I'd say that point is debatable." Her eyes slid to Naya again and her full mouth tilted in a seductive half smile. "But it appears you've brought me a peace offering? I can't say that I'm interested, but I'm sure she'll make a nice plaything for the members of my coven."

An appreciative murmur spread throughout the dhampirs present and Naya bristled. Ronan reached out and gave her hand a reassuring squeeze. "This female belongs to no creature save me, Siobhan. She's my mate."

Siobhan regarded Ronan as she flung her leg from the arm of her chair. The heel of her stiletto struck the floor with a crack as she leaned forward. "You lie."

"Do I?" His dark tone brought a pleasant chill to the surface of Naya's skin. "She's tethered me, Siobhan. You have no choice but to release me from my troth."

Anger boiled under the surface of the female's skin. The static charge of it brushed against Naya's senses. "I don't have to do *anything*!" Siobhan's shriek echoed throughout the building and faded into eerie silence. "I am not subject to vampire law. You sealed your troth with blood, Ronan. You. Are. Mine."

Naya took a step forward, more than ready to show Siobhan exactly what she thought of her claim on Ronan. He reached out with a staying hand and pulled Naya back, wrapping his arm protectively around her waist.

"What are you?" Siobhan asked Naya. Siobhan's eyes flashed with silver, her mouth forming a thin, hard line, as she studied Naya.

"She's *mine*," Ronan declared. "That's all you need to know."

"Carrig?" Siobhan ignored Ronan entirely. "What is this gutter rat that Ronan's brought into my coven?"

"A witch, Siobhan." A heavily muscled dhampir studied her from across the room, his head canted curiously. "Powerful too."

The male must have been a sensitive like Manny. Not that it mattered. Naya would have gladly supplied the information—along with a demonstration—had she been given the chance.

"The mighty vampire tethered by a lowly witch," Siobhan said with a sneer. "But powerful?" Her humorless laughter rippled through the air. "You're too generous in your compliments, Carrig."

The male seemed unfazed by her chiding. He simply continued to watch the scene unfold with morbid interest.

"You certainly enjoy adversity, don't you, Ronan? Gone for a little over three weeks and look at you: begging for your freedom when what you should have done was tend to your king's most recent fuckup." Ronan stiffened beside her and Naya sensed a coming storm. "Have you seen Jenner? What the transition has done to him? He hunts the members of my coven like a wolf, draining them of blood, fucking anything that walks past him. He's out of control. A fledgling with no one to mind him. From your own behavior, I can only surmise that being turned annihilates a male's common sense. You all can't help but let your dicks and your fangs make decisions for you. You are *not* released from your troth, Ronan. That female"—Siobhan stabbed a finger toward Naya—"will *never* know your body."

"Don't be so sure, Siobhan." Naya couldn't keep her mouth shut for another second. This female was out of her freaking mind if she thought she could talk to Ronan that way. "Like your Carrig said, I'm *very* powerful. I can see why you're reluctant to let him go, though. Ronan is quite the skilled lover, isn't he?"

Beside Naya, Ronan smirked. *Arrogant male.* A rush of delicious heat fanned out from her belly and spread between her thighs. The sooner they could get this situation resolved, the sooner they could return to his penthouse.

It was a wonder the female's head hadn't shot straight off of her shoulders from the rage that simmered under the surface of her calm façade. "Your bitch is obviously a good liar. I can't even smell the deceit on her."

"Make another disparaging remark about my *mate,* Siobhan, and it'll be the last words you ever speak."

She flounced back in her seat, clearly riled. Silver flickered in her eyes and Naya caught the slightest hint of fear in Siobhan's expression. She should've been afraid. Ronan was as deadly a male as she'd ever met.

"I didn't come here tonight to argue or play your games, Siobhan." It was clear from Ronan's tone that he wanted their business conducted as quickly as Naya did. "We have much to discuss, and I want our future dealings to be amicable. I'm not here to make demands. I'm here to make a deal."

"I already told you, I'm not interested in your *mate.*"

Good gods. Was everything about sex with this female?

"As if I'd share her," Ronan replied. "Come on, Siobhan. Stop being so damned stubborn and let's talk business. I promise I can make it worth your while."

"A trade?" she asked.

Ronan flashed a confident smile. "I can guarantee you, you're going to want to see what's behind door number one."

A long stretch of silence weighed down the air as Siobhan considered Ronan's offer. Her coven sat as still as statues, all eyes on her as they waited for her to make some grand proclamation. She certainly thought highly of herself, didn't she?

"Everyone out!" The command brought instant action as dhampirs dropped from the ceiling and scurried out from shadowed corners like mice. They emptied the common area in a matter of seconds, leaving Ronan and Naya alone with Siobhan. Finally, they were getting somewhere.

"As an act of goodwill, so that I know you're bargaining with me in good faith, I want you to tell me where you went and why."

Never one to give up the upper hand, Ronan indulged Siobhan, but only because filling her in would only help to seal their bargain. "I went to Crescent City to find Chelle. She found something there. Something *ancient*. A relic so powerful that a crazed shifter thought to take it from her and use it for his own gain."

Siobhan leaned forward in her seat. "Go on."

Siobhan frequently used Chelle to recover relics for her. Ronan knew that Siobhan would take anything that had to do with his sister very seriously. "I could offer this relic to you. *If* you release me from my troth."

A bark of disbelieving laughter escaped her mouth. "What relic would be worth sacrificing my favorite toy?" Her gaze slid to Naya, gauging her reaction. Ronan's mate remained calm. She simply met Siobhan look for look. Naya was far too powerful to cower in the dhampir's presence.

"You will," Ronan said with confidence. "When I tell you what it is."

"Well?" She flung her leg over the arm of the chair and settled back as though bored. "Are you going to tell me what it is or are you trying to kill me with suspense?"

"Chelle has found Set's chest."

"You lie." Siobhan's eyes grew large, her irises flashing silver.

"Do I?"

Siobhan beckoned him closer and Ronan grabbed Naya's hand and urged her forward. When they approached the female's makeshift throne, she shifted, her posture no longer relaxed but tense. Fear accented her fierce beauty, making her look almost softer. "Tell me everything," she said. "And don't leave out a single detail."

Naya hadn't spoken a word since they'd left Siobhan's. They were nearly to Mikhail's house, and Ronan didn't want to meet with his king if something weighed on Naya's mind. He didn't want to push her, but gods damn it, her silence was killing him. Her annoyance and discomfort pulled at their tether. Damn it, why wouldn't she talk to him?

Siobhan had been delighted to take Set's chest in exchange for releasing Ronan. Mikhail was going to blow a gasket when he found out, but in Ronan's opinion the relic was safer with Siobhan than anyone else. Her abhorrence for vampire-kind ensured that the chest would never be put to use. Chelle was proof that a vampire made from the magic contained in the chest was a volatile creature with insatiable thirst. Ronan knew that darkness. It lived inside of him now and probably always would. It was a weakness he would need to master, and he thanked the gods that he was given a mate who could help him shoulder the burden of that force that lived inside of him. He could only hope that his sister found a mate with equal strength.

Yes, the chest was best left in Siobhan's safekeeping. He didn't regret his decision to give it to her. But if her motives changed, if for one second Siobhan thought that the chest would give her an advantage in her efforts to depose Mikhail, Ronan's decision could mean his death. Until that time, however, he chose to give Siobhan his trust.

"I didn't like seeing her mouth on you." In order to break their troth, Ronan and Siobhan had been required to share blood again. For him, the act had been as erotic as taking a bite from an apple. Siobhan, however, had used the opportunity to push Naya's buttons. "It took all of the self-control I had not to rip her away from you."

Naya shouldn't have had to witness it. Ronan wanted her to leave, but if he'd asked her to it would have made Siobhan think that he lacked faith in the tether that bound him to Naya. And as painful as he knew it would be for her, it was important that Siobhan see them as a united front. "Believe me, love, I didn't like having it there. But now I'm free of her and that's all that matters."

"Drinking blood is sexual for you. She was aroused. She didn't even try to hide it."

True, Siobhan had taken his vein with all the subtlety of a feline in heat. "She didn't," Ronan agreed. "But it meant nothing to me. Taking her vein was a means to an end."

"I've never felt like that before, Ronan. I've never been jealous in my entire life. But tonight, watching her, I thought it would eat me alive. I'm still not even close to being level."

"Now you know how I felt the night Joaquin claimed you as his," Ronan replied with a smirk. "I wanted to rip his throat out for even thinking that you belonged to him. The tether is absolute, Naya. There is no halfway. I will want you, and only you, until the day I die. And that want is all-consuming."

"I know," Naya said on a breath. "The way I want you, it burns through me, Ronan. And the only thing that can quench that fire is you. I want all of you, Ronan. Your body. Your blood. Your heart and soul. And I won't *ever* want anyone else."

His foot eased off the gas and Ronan gripped the steering wheel in his fists. That all-consuming want prompted him to turn the hell around and race back to his apartment. Mikhail could wait until tomorrow night, couldn't he? Ronan sighed as he pressed down on the accelerator. He might have broken one troth tonight, but the one that he would never ignore was the one made to his king. There was a lot that Mikhail needed to be made aware of, and Ronan had a feeling he needed to be brought up to speed on a thing or two as well. Namely, Jenner.

"Just promise me that you won't ever let her put her mouth on you again and I can get past the urge to stab her with something sharp."

Ronan laughed. How he loved his fiery mate. "My sacred vow is yours, love. Never again. But what I got in exchange for a few moments with Siobhan tonight was well worth the sacrifice for me."

"What did you get?" Naya asked coyly.

Ronan pulled into Mikhail's driveway and cut the engine of his Vanquish. "I got you." He leaned in to kiss her. Slowly. "From this night forward, I'm free to love my mate however and whenever I wish."

Naya kissed him back and Ronan reveled in the petal softness of her lips. "I'm not kidding, Ronan. If she touches you again, I'm going to run my dagger through her chest," Naya said much too sweetly for her threatening words.

Ronan groaned into her mouth. They needed to wrap up this night so he could get her back home and into bed. "Gods, how I love a woman with a violent streak."

"Is that so?" Naya asked with the same innocent charm.

"I love you, Naya." He could no longer feel playful. His

want for her—his love—was too damned intense for levity. "Gods, how I love you."

Her dark eyes shimmered with emotion. "I love you, too. Forever."

A presence drew Ronan's attention and he looked over to see Mikhail standing in the open doorway of his house, watching them.

"You know, the faster we get done here, the faster we can go home," Naya said. She nibbled at his bottom lip and Ronan's cock jumped to attention, pressing against his fly.

"One last conversation for the night and I'm yours."

Naya pulled away and opened her door. "*Mine.* I like the sound of that. Now, let's get a move on. We haven't properly christened the bed yet."

Seven pieces of furniture down, five or so more to go. . . .

Read on for an excerpt from Kate Baxter's next book

THE DARK VAMPIRE

Coming soon from St. Martin's Paperbacks

From the corner of his eye, Jenner caught sight of Marissa, still watching them. Her longing gaze had obviously not gone unnoticed by Bria. The possessive edge to his mate's words caused Jenner's heart to beat wildly in his chest. The scent of her blood swirled in his head, as heady and intoxicating as the liquor in his glass. Her power astounded him. Her beauty stalled his breath. And her fire brought him to his damned knees. His secondary fangs throbbed in his gums, and he resisted the urge to seize her in his arms and nuzzle his face against her fragrant throat.

Jenner squeezed his eyes shut as he tried to get a grip on his control. Beside him, Bria shifted. His eyes flew open as he turned toward her. Bria had hopped up on the bar, putting her height level with his. She reached out to rake her nails through his hair, and chills broke out over his skin. Silver rimmed the amethyst depths of her irises. She leaned in close, and Jenner inhaled her delicious scent.

"What are you doing, Bria?" his voice rasped, and he swallowed against the fiery thirst burning in his throat.

Her response was a sensual caress in his ear as she lowered her mouth to his neck. "Taking my reward."

Jenner groaned as Bria's fangs broke the skin. She buried her face in the crook of his neck, sucking greedily as her hand dove back into his hair. He'd refused her his throat and for good reason. Mindless lust overtook him, a haze of need that clouded his mind and crippled any chances of coherent thought. He cast a sideways glance across the club, to where Marissa watched with narrowed eyes, her lips thinned. Bria sought to lay claim to what was hers and that knowledge only served to excite Jenner further.

Desperate need burned through him. He twisted in Bria's embrace to face her fully, urging her legs to part as he settled himself between them. With a guttural groan, Jenner wound his fist into the ponytail cascading from the top of her head and pressed her tighter against him. He wanted to experience the sting of her bite deep in his flesh, needed to feel her thirst and desperation in every deep pull of her mouth. For the second time tonight, he considered throwing caution to the wind and giving in to his desires.

Fuck. His cock ached in his jeans, pulsing in time with every wild beat of his heart. Bria was much too innocent for what he wanted to do to her. Too gentle for his pent-up and insatiable passions.

Jenner released his hold on her hair and slammed his palms against the wall behind her. Her nails bit into his scalp and he reveled in the pain. She fed from him with abandon, not as though she were ashamed. Bria was more in tune with her true nature than she thought. He wanted nothing more than to coax that wildness from her.

Her mouth at his vein had no equal. He'd fed others from his throat, his wrist. Mouths and lips had sealed over his flesh, he'd felt the sting of a dhampir's bite. Those experiences were gray in his memory compared to the vivid sensation that started as a tingle at the top of his scalp and trickled down his body to bathe him in warmth.

As she continued to feed from him, Jenner fought the urge to tear at her clothes, to slide his hand inside her pants and seek out the heat of Bria's pussy. Euphoric bliss fogged his brain and clouded his thoughts. Any common sense he might have possessed—any shred of control—evaporated under the gentle suction of Bria's mouth against his throat. How would she react if he popped the buttons of her blouse, jerked the cup of her bra aside and suckled her nipple to a stiff point? Would she push him away or would she cradle his head against her?

Viaton.

The reminder of her innocence should have cooled Jenner's jets, but all it did was heat him to the point of combustion. When he was through with her, she'd be anything but the wide-eyed *viaton*.

Bria's fangs disengaged from Jenner's throat and all he wanted to do was guide her back, to urge her to bite him again. Harder. Her tongue lapped at the punctures she'd made and Jenner shuddered. Another act of defiance after he'd continuously denied her the pleasure of it when she'd fed from his wrist. So full of fight, this female. His thirst for her mounted until Jenner feared if he didn't take her vein now, he'd surely tear her flesh in his haste to taste her.

His control hung by a single frayed thread. Jenner kept one palm firmly planted on the wall, and he gripped the back of her head with the other. In a forceful jerk, he pulled her head to the side and buried his fangs into her throat.

Her blood was ambrosia. The sweetest thing he'd ever tasted. Bria went liquid in his embrace, molding her chest to his. A low moan of pleasure vibrated against Jenner's ear, and he bit down harder, opening the wound to allow her blood to flow faster. His thirst for her raged. His desire pulled his muscles taut and hardened his cock to stone. He couldn't get enough.

He was lost to her.

Bria reveled in smug satisfaction. The dhampir who'd so obviously sought Jenner's attention glared her hatred as she watched him feed from her vein. He was lost to the thirst as he suckled her, his grunts and moans of pleasure vibrating through Bria's bones and settling as a deep thrum in her sex.

Taking his vein—and offering hers—in such a public display was a scandalous act. One that would have brought a heavy punishment from her uncle had she still been a member of the coven. Taboo. Forbidden. And feeling the eyes of onlookers on them only heightened Bria's pleasure. It was a slap in the face to every rule she'd ever been forced to follow.

Jenner bit down harder and Bria gasped. Did he realize the effect he had on her? That his aggressiveness sent a rush of want through her that slicked her thighs and stirred her desire? *I've never wanted anything as badly as I do this male.* A result of their tether? Or something else entirely?

Did it matter?

Jenner's tongue flicked out to seal the bites and Bria shivered. She wasn't ready for this moment to end. She needed to keep him on the edge, reckless. Before the bliss of feeding wore off and he regained the good sense to put her at arms' length yet again.

Bria wanted to teach Jenner a lesson tonight as well: She was more than the virginal image that had been painted of her. *So much more.*

He disengaged from her throat and Bria stilled. He rested his forehead against her shoulder, his breath coming in heavy gasps as though he fought off some deep, internal pain. Worry replaced any schemes she might have been devising, and she traced the tips of her fingers down his temple and across the rough stubble of his jaw. "Jenner?"

He pulled away with a tortured groan. A deep furrow marred his brow and his eyes were alight with brilliant silver. His full lips pulled away from his fangs with a snarl, and he wrapped his arms tightly around her as his mouth descended on hers in a violent and urgent kiss.

Oh . . . gods.

Bria let herself be swept away in the moment. She didn't give a second thought to the dhampir and her covetous gaze, to the other supernatural creatures that surrounded them, or the sizzle of magic in the air that sent a zing of anxiety through her bloodstream.

Jenner's lips were firm, yet demanding. His grip on her, possessive and commanding. The wet heat of his mouth seared her as his tongue lashed out at the seam of her lips, urging her to open up to him. The taste of his blood lingered and mingled with her own that still clung to his tongue. Exquisite. Heady, like an aged brandy that caused her thoughts to haze and her head to spin. *More.* She wanted more.

His mouth slanted across hers as his tongue thrust into her mouth. She released a pleasured moan at the silky glide and wound her fists into the fabric of his shirt, pulling him closer. Jenner gripped her hip in one strong hand and jerked her against him. The hard length of his erection brushed against her sex and Bria sighed into Jenner's mouth as delicious pressure built inside of her.

Jenner had brought her here tonight to teach her focus. To show her that danger was ever-present no matter her strength. To make sure that she knew the scope of what she was capable of as well as her limitations. None of that mattered when his mouth claimed hers. In his arms, the world melted away. Sensations and sounds, scents dissolved until there was only him. His taste on her lips. The rich musky scent of his arousal. The grip of his large hand on her hip and his fist in her hair. He drew her focus like no other thing in this world could. As for the danger . . . Bria realized as she further lost herself to his kisses, that the most dangerous thing in this world was the male in her arms and the way he made her feel.